MASTER OF THE GREATER PATH

Energy exploded from Milamber's hand. A bolt of blue flame, scintillating even in the sunlight, hurled downward, to strike the sand amid the Warlord's guards.

"Who dares this!" cried the Warlord.

"I dare!" Milamber shouted back.

The Warlord looked at Milamber with naked hatred on his face. He never took his eyes off the young magician's face.

"Destroy him!"

Milamber tensed, suffused with anger. Twice before in his life he had reached into a hidden reservoir of power and drawn upon it. Now he tore aside the last barriers between his conscious mind and those hidden reserves. They were no longer a mystery to him, but the wellspring from which all his powers stemmed.

For the first time in his experience, Milamber came to understand fully what he was, who he was: not a Black Robe, limited by the ancient teachings of one world, but an adept of the Greater Art, a master in full possession of all the energy provided by two worlds. . . .

Also by Raymond E. Feist

MAGICIAN: APPRENTICE
MAGICIAN: MASTER
SILVERTHORN
A DARKNESS AT SETHANON
FAERIE TALE
DAUGHTER OF THE EMPIRE

Magician: MASTER

Raymond E. Feist

BANTAM BOOKS

NEW YORK · TORONTO · LONDON · SYDNEY · AUCKLAND

*This edition contains the complete text
of the original hardcover edition.*
NOT ONE WORD HAS BEEN OMITTED.

MAGICIAN: MASTER

*A Bantam Spectra Book / published by arrangement with
Doubleday*

PRINTING HISTORY
Doubleday edition published November 1982
A Selection of the Science Fiction Book Club
Bantam edition / April 1986

ISBN 0-553-26761-2

Published simultaneously in the United States and Canada

---

*Bantam Books are published by Bantam Books, a division of Bantam
Doubleday Dell Publishing Group, Inc. Its trademark, consisting of the
words "Bantam Books" and the portrayal of a rooster, is Registered in
U.S. Patent and Trademark Office and in other countries. Marca Regis-
trada. Bantam Books, 666 Fifth Avenue, New York, New York 10103.*

PRINTED IN THE UNITED STATES OF AMERICA

O   21   20   19   18   17   16   15   14

This book is dedicated to the memory of my father,
Felix E. Feist,
in all ways, a magician

ACKNOWLEDGMENTS

Many people have provided me with incalculable aid in bringing this novel into existence. I would like to offer my heartfelt thanks to:

The Friday Nighters: April and Stephen Abrams; Steve Barrett; David Brin; Anita and Jon Everson; Dave Guinasso; Conan LaMotte; Tim LaSelle; Ethan Munson; Bob Potter; Rich Spahl; Alan Springer; and Lori and Jeff Velten, for their useful criticism, enthusiasm, support, belief, wise counsel, wonderful ideas, and, most of all, their friendship.

Billie and Russ Blake, and Lilian and Mike Fessier, for always being willing to help.

Harold Matson, my agent, for taking a chance on me.

Adrian Zackheim, my editor, for asking rather than demanding, and for working so hard to build a good book.

Kate Cronin, assistant to the editor, for having a sense of humor and for so gracefully putting up with all my nonsense.

Elaine Chubb, copy editor, for having such a gentle touch and for caring so much about the words.

And Barbara A. Feist, my mother, for all of the above and more.

RAYMOND E. FEIST
San Diego, California
July 1982

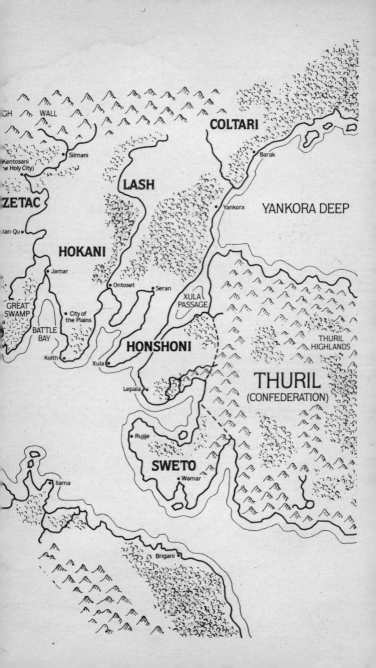

Our story so far . . .

Upon the world of Midkemia, the mighty Kingdom of the Isles rose, beside the vast Empire of Great Kesh to the south. The Kingdom was then nearing an era of greatness; the nation spanned a continent, from the Kingdom Sea to the Endless Sea.

In the twelfth year of the reign of Rodric IV, in the westernmost province of the Kingdom, the Duchy of Crydee, an orphan kitchen boy named Pug was made apprentice to the magician Kulgan. An indifferent student of magic, he rose to high station, for he saved the daughter of Duke Borric, Princess Carline, from a dire fate and became a squire of the Duke's court. Pug then found himself the object of Carline's girlish infatuation and, as a result, rival to young Squire Roland, a member of the court. With his best friend Tomas, Pug discovered the wreckage of an alien vessel and a dying man of unknown nationality. The Duke's priest, Father Tully, used his magic to learn the dying man was from another world, Kelewan, dominated by a mighty empire of warriors, the Tsurani. They had reached Midkemia by a magic gate, a rift in space, and might be preparing the way for invasion. Duke Borric took council with the Elf Queen, Aglaranna, who agreed some strange menace was approaching the Far Coast of the Kingdom; the elves had seen strange warriors mapping the west, men who vanished mysteriously.

Fearing this a prelude to invasion, Lord Borric and his younger son, Arutha, led a company of men to warn the King of the possible attack, leaving Crydee to the care of his elder son, Lyam, and Swordmaster Fannon. The company numbered among it Kulgan the magician, Pug, and Tomas, Sergeant Gardan and fifty soldiers of Crydee. In the forest called the Green Heart, the Duke's party was attacked by the dreaded moredhel, the dark elves known as the Brotherhood of the Dark Path. After a long bloody fight, the Duke and the other survivors were saved by Dolgan, a dwarven chief, and his companions.

Dolgan led them through the mines of Mac Mordain Cadal, where a wraith attacked, separating Tomas from the others in the company. Tomas fled deep into the ancient mine, while Dolgan led the others to safety.

Dolgan returned into the mine to find Tomas, discovering the boy had been given refuge by one of the last of the mighty golden dragons, ancient and near death. The dragon, Rhuragh, told of his life, his encounter with the strange sorceror Macros the Black and of other wonders. Rhuragh vanished in a wondrous final moment of glory, due to a gift of Macros, and left Tomas with a special gift, magic golden armor.

The Duke's company reached the city of Bordon, where they took ship for Krondor, capital of the Western Realm of the Kingdom. They were driven by a storm to Sorcerer's Isle, home of the legendary Macros. There Pug met a mysterious hermit, discovered later to be Macros. He warned of a time of terrible danger approaching, and promised to come when the need was greatest.

In Krondor, Prince Erland instructed the Duke to continue on to Rillanon, capital of the Kingdom, to see the King. While there, Pug met Princess Anita, Erland's only child, and learned she was expected to marry Prince Arutha when she grew up.

In Rillanon, Duke Borric discovered the King to be a man of vision, also a man of doubtful sanity, given to outbursts of temper and rambling discourse. Duke Caldric of Rillanon, Borric's uncle, warned that the burden of repelling the Tsurani would fall to the western lords should they come, for the King distrusted the Prince of Krondor, dreaming of plots against the crown, and refusing to allow the Armies of the East to leave the Eastern Realm. Then came the Tsurani invasion, and Borric was given command of the Armies of the West. He rushed westward as the Riftwar began.

During the early part of the war, a raid into Tsurani-held territory was mounted, and Pug was captured.

Tomas was, with Dolgan's force of dwarves, among the first to resist the invaders. Something alien had manifested itself in Tomas's armor, and while wearing it, he became a warrior of awesome power. Haunted by strange visions, he was slowly changing in appearance. In a frantic battle in the dwarven mines, the Tsurani forced Tomas and Dolgan's company to flee into the forests. Having no safe haven, the dwarves struck out for

Elvandar, seeking to ally themselves with the elves. Reaching the court of the Elf Queen they were made welcome. Something in Tomas's appearance caused the old elven Spellweavers to be fearful, though they would not speak of it.

Lyam left Crydee to join his father, and Swordmaster Fannon assumed command of the castle with Arutha his second-in-command. Carline grieved Pug's loss and turned to Roland for comfort. The Tsurani raided Crydee using a captured ship. During the battle, Arutha rescued Amos Trask, the ship's captain, a former pirate.

The Tsurani besieged Crydee, and were repulsed many times. During a battle, Swordmaster Fannon was wounded and Arutha assumed command. After a terrible underground battle between Arutha's men and Tsurani sappers, Arutha ordered the garrisons surrounding Crydee to coordinate for a final battle against the Tsurani. But before that battle could commence, the Tsurani commander, Kasumi of the Shinazawai, received orders to return home with his command.

But even with that unexpected turn of events, leaving Arutha the victor by default, the war continues indecisively, dragging on for four more years . . .

We were, fair queen,
Two lads that thought there was no more behind
But such a day to-morrow as to-day,
And to be boy eternal.
—SHAKESPEARE, *The Winter's Tale*,
Act I, Scene 2

ONE

SLAVE

The dying slave lay screaming.

The day was unmercifully hot. The other slaves went about their work, ignoring the sound as much as possible. Life in the work camp was cheap, and it did no good to dwell on the fate that awaited so many. The dying man had been bitten by a relli, a snakelike swamp creature. Its venom was slow-acting and painful; short of magic, there was no cure.

Suddenly there was silence. Pug looked over to see a Tsurani guard wipe off his sword. A hand fell on Pug's shoulder. Laurie's voice whispered in his ear, "Looks like our venerable overseer was disturbed by the sound of Toffston's dying."

Pug tied a coil of rope securely around his waist. "At least it ended quickly." He turned to the tall, blond singer from the Kingdom city of Tyr-Sog and said, "Keep a sharp eye out. This one's old and may be rotten." Without another word, Pug scampered up the bole of the ngaggi tree, a firlike swamp tree the Tsurani harvested for wood and resins. With few metals, the Tsurani had become clever in finding many substitutes. The wood of this tree could be worked like paper, then dried to an incredible hardness, useful in fashioning a hundred things. The resins were used to laminate woods and cure hides. Properly cured hides could produce a suit of leather armor as tough as Midkemian chain mail, and laminated wooden weapons were nearly the match of Midkemian steel.

Four years in the swamp camp had hardened Pug's body. His sinewy muscles strained as he climbed the tree. His skin had been tanned deeply by the harsh sun of the

Tsurani homeworld. His face was covered by a slave's beard.

Pug reached the first large branches and looked down at his friend. Laurie stood knee-deep in the murky water, absently swatting at the insects that plagued them while they worked. Pug liked Laurie. The troubadour had no business being here, but then he had had no business tagging along with a patrol in the hope of seeing Tsurani soldiers, either. He said he had wanted material for ballads that would make him famous throughout the Kingdom. He had seen more than he had hoped for. The patrol had ridden into a major Tsurani offensive and Laurie had been captured. He had come to this camp over four months ago, and he and Pug had quickly become friends.

Pug continued his climb, keeping one eye always searching for the dangerous tree dwellers of Kelewan. Reaching the most likely place for a topping, Pug froze as he caught a glimpse of movement. He relaxed when he saw it was only a needler, a creature whose protection was its resemblance to a clump of ngaggi needles. It scurried away from the presence of the human and made the short jump to the branch of a neighboring tree. Pug made another survey and started tying his ropes. His job was to cut away the tops of the huge trees, making the fall less dangerous to those below.

Pug took several cuts at the bark, then felt the edge of his wooden ax bite into the softer pulp beneath. A faint pungent odor greeted his careful sniffing. Swearing, he called down to Laurie, "This one's rotten. Tell the overseer."

He waited, looking out over the tops of trees. All around, strange insects and birdlike creatures flew. In the four years he had been a slave on this world, he had not grown used to the appearance of these life forms. They were not all that different from those on Midkemia, but it was the similarities as much as the differences that kept reminding him this was not his home. Bees should be yellow-and-black-striped, not bright red. Eagles shouldn't have yellow bands on their wings, nor hawks purple. These creatures were not bees, eagles, or hawks, but the resemblance was striking. Pug found it easier to accept the stranger creatures of Kelewan than these. The six-legged needra, the domesticated beast of burden that looked like some sort of bovine with two extra stumpy legs, or the choja, the insectoid creature who served the Tsurani and could speak their language: these he had come to find familiar. But each time he glimpsed a creature from the corner of his eye and turned, expecting it to be Midkemian only to find it was not, then the despair would strike.

Laurie's voice brought him from his reverie. "The overseer comes."

Pug swore. If the overseer had to get himself dirty by wading in the water, then he would be in a foul mood—which could mean beatings, or a reduction in the chronically meager food. He would already be angered by the delay in the cutting. A family of burrowers, beaverlike six-legged creatures, had made themselves at home in the roots of the great trees. They would gnaw the tender roots and the trees would sicken and die. The soft, pulpy wood would turn sour, then watery, and after a while the tree would collapse from within. Several burrower tunnels had been poisoned, but the damage had already been done to the trees.

A rough voice, swearing mightily while its owner splashed through the swamp, announced the arrival of the overseer, Nogamu. He himself was a slave, but he had attained the highest rank a slave could rise to, and while he could never hope to be free, he had many privileges and could order soldiers or freemen placed under his command. A young soldier came walking behind, a look of mild amusement on his face. He was clean-shaven in the manner of a Tsurani freeman, and as he looked up at Pug, the slave could get a good look at him. He had the high cheekbones and nearly black eyes that so many Tsurani possessed. His dark eyes caught sight of Pug, and he seemed to nod slightly. His blue armor was of a type unknown to Pug, but with the strange Tsurani military organization, that was not surprising. Every family, demesne, area, town, city, and province appeared to have its own army. How they all related one to another within the Empire was beyond Pug's understanding.

The overseer stood at the base of the tree, his short robe held above the water. He growled like the bear he resembled and shouted up at Pug, "What's this about another rotten tree?"

Pug spoke the Tsurani language better than any Midkemian in the camp, for he had been there longer than all but a few old Tsurani slaves. He shouted down, "It smells of rot. We should re-rig another and leave this one alone, Slave Master."

The overseer shook his fist. "You are all lazy. There is nothing wrong with this tree. It is fine. You only want to keep from working. Now cut it!"

Pug sighed. There was no arguing with the Bear, as all the Midkemian slaves called Nogamu. He was obviously upset about something, and the slaves would pay the price. Pug started hacking through the upper section, and it soon fell to the ground. The smell of rot was thick, and Pug removed the ropes quickly. Just as the last length was coiled around his waist, a splitting sound came from directly in front of him. "It falls!" he shouted down to the slaves standing in the water below. Without hesitation they all ran. The cry of "falls" was never ignored.

The bole of the tree was splitting down the middle now that the top had been cut away. While this was not common, if a tree was far enough gone for the pulp to have lost its strength, any flaw in the bark could cause it to split under its own weight. The tree's branches would pull the halves away from each other. Had Pug been tied to the bole, the ropes would have cut him in half before they snapped.

Pug gauged the direction of the fall, then as the half he stood upon started to move, he launched himself away from it. He hit the water flat, back first, trying to let the two feet of water break his fall as much as possible. The blow from the water was immediately followed by the harder impact with the ground. The bottom was mostly mud, so there was little damage done. The air in his lungs exploded from his mouth when he struck, and his senses reeled for a moment. He retained enough presence of mind to sit up and gasped a deep lungful of air.

Suddenly a heavy weight hit him across the stomach, knocking the wind from him and pushing his head back underwater. He struggled to move and found a large branch across his stomach. He could barely get his face out of the water to get air. His lungs burned and he breathed without control. Water came pouring down his windpipe, and he started to choke. Coughing and sputtering, he tried to keep calm but felt panic rise within him. He frantically pushed at the weight across him but couldn't move it.

Abruptly he found his head above water; Laurie said, "Spit, Pug! Get the muck out of your lungs, or you'll get lung fever."

Pug coughed and spit. With Laurie holding his head, he could catch his breath.

Laurie shouted, "Grab this branch. I'll pull him out from under."

Several slaves splashed over, sweat beading their bodies. They reached underwater and seized the branch. Heaving, they managed to move it slightly, but Laurie couldn't drag Pug out.

"Bring axes; we'll have to cut the branch from the tree."

Other slaves were starting to bring axes over when Nogamu shouted, "No. Leave him. We have no time for this. There are trees to cut."

Laurie nearly screamed at him, "We can't leave him! He'll drown!"

The overseer crossed over and struck Laurie across the face with a lash. It cut deep into the singer's cheek, but he didn't let go of his friend's head. "Back to work, slave. You'll be beaten tonight for speaking to me that way. There are others who can top. Now, let him go!" He struck Laurie again. Laurie winced, but held Pug's head above water.

Nogamu raised his lash for a third blow, but was halted by a voice from behind. "Cut the slave from under the branch." Laurie saw the speaker was the young soldier who had accompanied the slave master. The overseer whirled about, unaccustomed to having his orders questioned. When he saw who had spoken, he bit back the words that were on his lips. Bowing his head, he said, "My lord's will."

He signaled for the slaves with the axes to cut Pug loose, and in short order Pug was out from under the branch. Laurie carried him over to where the young soldier stood. Pug coughed the last water from out of his lungs and gasped, "I thank the master for my life."

The man said nothing, but when the overseer approached, directed his remarks to him. "The slave was right, and you were not. The tree was rotten. It is not proper for you to punish him for your bad judgment and ill-temper. I should have you beaten, but will not spare the time for it. The work goes slowly, and my father is displeased."

Nogamu bowed his head. "I lose much face in my lord's sight. May I have his permission to kill myself?"

"No. It is too much honor. Return to work."

The overseer's face grew red in silent shame and rage. Raising his lash, he pointed at Laurie and Pug. "You two, back to work."

Laurie stood, and Pug tried. His knees were wobbly from his near-drowning, but he managed to stand after a few attempts.

"These two shall be excused work the rest of the day," the young lord said. "This one"—he pointed to Pug—"is of little use. The other must dress those cuts you gave him, or festering will start." He turned to a guard. "Take them back to camp and see to their needs."

Pug was grateful, not so much for himself as for Laurie. With a little rest, Pug could have returned to work, but an open wound in the swamp was a death warrant as often as not. Infections came quickly in this hot, dirty place, and there were few ways of dealing with them.

They followed the guard. As they left, Pug could see the slave master watching them with naked hatred in his eyes.

There was a creaking of floorboards and Pug came instantly awake. His slave-bred wariness told him that the sound didn't belong in the hut during the dead of night. Through the gloom, footfalls could be heard coming closer, then they stopped at the foot of his pallet. From the next pallet, he could hear Laurie's sharp intake of breath, and he knew the minstrel was awake also. Probably half the slaves had been awakened by the intruder. The stranger hesitated over something, and Pug waited, tense with uncertainty. There was a grunt, and without hesitation, Pug rolled off his mat. A weight came crashing down, and Pug could hear a dull thud as a dagger struck where his chest had been only moments before. Suddenly the room exploded with activity. Slaves were shouting, and could be heard running for the door.

Pug felt hands reach for him in the dark, and a sharp pain exploded across his chest. He reached blindly for his assailant and grappled with him for the blade. Another slash, and his right hand was cut across the palm. Abruptly the attacker stopped moving, and Pug became aware that a third body was atop the would-be assassin.

Soldiers rushed into the hut, carrying lanterns, and Pug could see Laurie lying across the still body of Nogamu. The Bear was still breathing, but from the way the dagger protruded from his ribs, not for long.

The young soldier who had saved Pug's and Laurie's lives entered and the others made way for him. He stood over the three combatants and simply asked, "Is he dead?"

The overseer's eyes opened and in a faint whisper he said, "I live, lord. But I die by the blade." A weak but defiant smile showed on his sweat-drenched face.

The young soldier's expression betrayed no emotion, but his eyes looked as if ablaze. "I think not," he said softly. He turned to two of the soldiers in the room. "Take him outside at once and hang him. There will be no honors for his clan to sing. Leave the body there for the insects. It shall be a warning that I am not to be disobeyed. Go."

The dying man's face paled, and his lips quivered. "No, master. I pray, leave me to die by the blade. A few minutes longer." Bloody foam appeared at the corner of his mouth.

Two husky soldiers reached down for Nogamu and, with little thought for his pain, dragged him outside. He could be heard wailing the entire way. The amount of strength left in his voice was amazing, as if his fear of the rope had awakened some deep reserve.

They stood in frozen tableau until the sound was cut off in a strangled cry. The young officer then turned to Pug and Laurie. Pug sat, blood running from the long, shallow gash across his chest. He held his injured hand in the other. It was deeply cut, and his fingers wouldn't move.

"Bring your wounded friend," the young soldier commanded Laurie.

Laurie helped Pug to his feet and they followed the

officer out of the slave hut. He led them across the compound to his own quarters and ordered them to enter. Once inside, he instructed a guard to send for the camp physician. He had them stand in silence until the physician arrived. He was an old Tsurani, dressed in the robes of one of their gods, which one the Midkemians couldn't tell. He inspected Pug's wounds and judged the chest wound superficial. The hand, he said, would be another matter.

"The cut is deep, and the muscles and tendons have been cut. It will heal, but there will be a loss of movement and little strength for gripping. He most likely will be fit for only light duty."

The soldier nodded, a peculiar expression on his face: a mixture of disgust and impatience. "Very well. Dress the wounds, and leave us."

The physician set about cleaning the wounds. He took a score of stitches in the hand, bandaged it, admonished Pug to keep it clean, and left. Pug ignored the pain, easing his mind with an old mental exercise.

After the physician was gone, the soldier studied the two slaves before him. "By law, I should have you hung for killing the slave master."

They said nothing. They would remain silent until commanded to speak.

"But as I hung the slave master, I am free to keep you alive, should it suit my purpose. I can simply have you punished for wounding him." He paused. "Consider yourselves punished."

With a wave of his hand he said, "Leave me, but return here at daybreak. I have to decide what to do with you."

They left, feeling fortunate, for under most circumstances they would now be hanging next to the former slave master. As they crossed the compound, Laurie said, "I wonder what that was about?"

Pug responded, "I hurt too much to wonder why. I'm just thankful that we will see tomorrow."

Laurie said nothing until they reached the slave hut. "I think the young lord has something up his sleeve."

"Whatever. I have long since given up trying to understand our masters. That's why I've stayed alive so long, Laurie. I just do what I'm told to, and I endure." Pug pointed to the tree where the former overseer's body could be seen in the pale moonlight—only the small moon was out tonight. "It's much too easy to end up like that."

Laurie nodded. "Perhaps you're right. I still think about escape."

Pug laughed, a short, bitter sound. "Where, singer? Where could you run? Toward the rift and ten thousand Tsurani?"

Laurie said nothing. They returned to their pallets and tried to sleep in the humid heat.

The young officer sat upon a pile of cushions, Tsurani fashion. He sent the guard who had accompanied Pug and Laurie away, then motioned for the two slaves to sit. They did so hesitantly, for a slave was not usually permitted to sit in a master's presence.

"I am Hokanu, of the Shinzawai. My father owns this camp," he said without preamble. "He is deeply dissatisfied with the harvest this year. He has sent me to see what can be done. Now I have no overseer to manage the work, because a foolish man blamed you for his own stupidity. What am I to do?"

They said nothing, for they were not sure if the question was rhetorical. He asked, "You have been here, how long?"

Pug and Laurie answered in turn. He considered the answers, then said, "You"—pointing at Laurie—"are nothing unusual, save you speak our tongue better than most barbarians, all things considered. But you"—pointing at Pug—"have stayed alive longer than most of your stiff-necked countrymen and also speak our language well. You might even pass for a peasant from a remote province."

They sat still, unsure of what Hokanu was leading up to. Pug realized with a shock that he was probably older by a year or two than this young lord. He was young for such power. The ways of the Tsurani were very strange. In Crydee he would still be an apprentice, or if noble, continuing his education in statecraft.

"How do you speak so well?" he asked of Pug.

"Master, I was among the first captured and brought here. There were only seven of us among so many Tsurani slaves. We learned to survive. After some time, I was the

only one left. The others died of the burning fever or
festering wounds, or were killed by the guards. There were
none for me to talk with who spoke my own language. No
other countryman came to this camp for over a year."

The officer nodded, then to Laurie said, "And you?"

"Master, I am a singer, a minstrel in my own land. It is
our custom to travel broadly, and we must learn many
tongues. I have also a good ear for music. Your language is
what is called a tone language on my world; words with
the same sound save for the pitch with which they are
spoken have different meanings. We have several such
tongues to the south of our Kingdom. I learn quickly."

A glimmering appeared in the eyes of the soldier. "It is
good to know these things." He lapsed deep into thought.
After a moment he nodded to himself. "There are many
considerations that fashion a man's fortune, slaves." He
smiled, looking more like a boy than a man. "This camp is a
shambles. I am to prepare a report for my father, the Lord
of the Shinzawai. I think I know what the problems are."
He pointed at Pug. "I would have your thoughts on the
subject. You have been here longer than anyone."

Pug composed himself. It had been a long time since
anyone had asked him to venture an opinion on anything.
"Master, the first overseer, the one who was here when I
was captured, was a shrewd man, who understood that
men, even slaves, cannot be made to work well if they are
weak from hunger. We had better food and if injured were
given time for healing. Nogamu was an ill-tempered man
who took every setback as a personal affront. Should
burrowers ruin a grove, it was the fault of the slaves.
Should a slave die, it was a plot to discredit his oversight of
the work force. Each difficulty was rewarded by another
cut in food, or in longer work hours. Any good fortune was
regarded as his rightful due."

"I suspected as much. Nogamu was at one time a very
important man. He was the hadonra—demesne manager—
of his father's estates. His family was found to be guilty of
plotting against the Empire, and his own clan sold them all
into slavery, those that were not hung. He was never a
good slave. It was thought that giving him responsibility
for the camp might find some useful channel for his skills.
It proved not to be the case.

"Is there a good man among the slaves who could command ably?"

Laurie inclined his head, then said, "Master, Pug here . . ."

"I think not. I have plans for you both."

Pug was surprised, and wondered what he meant. He said, "Perhaps Chogana, master. He was a farmer, until his crops failed and he was sold into slavery for taxes. He has a level head."

The soldier clapped his hands once, and a guard was in the room in an instant. "Send for the slave Chogana."

The guard saluted and left. "It is good that he is Tsurani," said the soldier. "You barbarians do not know your place, and I hate to think what would happen should I leave one in charge. He would have my soldiers cutting the trees while the slaves stood guard."

There was a moment of silence, then Laurie laughed. It was a rich, deep sound. Hokanu smiled. Pug watched closely. The young man who had their lives in his hands seemed to be working hard at winning their trust. Laurie appeared to have taken a liking to him, but Pug held his feelings in check. He was further removed from the old Midkemian society, where war made noble and commoner comrades-in-arms, able to share meals and misery without regard for rank. One thing he had learned about the Tsurani early on was that they never for an instant forgot their station. Whatever was occurring in this hut was by this young soldier's design, not by chance. Hokanu seemed to feel Pug's eyes upon him and looked at him. Their eyes locked briefly before Pug dropped his as a slave is expected to do. For an instant a communication passed between them. It was as if the soldier had said: You do not believe that I am a friend. So be it, as long as you act your part.

With a wave of his hand, Hokanu said, "Return to your hut. Rest well, for we will leave after the noon meal."

They rose and bowed, then backed out of the hut. Pug walked in silence, but Laurie prattled. "I wonder where we are going?" When no answer came, he added, "In any event, it will have to be a better place than this."

Pug wondered if it would be.

* * *

A hand shook Pug's shoulder and he came awake. He had been dozing in the morning heat, taking advantage of the extra rest before he and Laurie left with the young noble after the noon meal. Chogana, the former farmer Pug had recommended, motioned for silence, pointing to where Laurie slept deeply.

Pug followed the old slave out of the hut, to sit in the shade of the building. Speaking slowly, as was his fashion, Chogana said, "My lord Hokanu tells me you were instrumental in my being selected slave master for the camp." His brown seamed face looked dignified as he bowed his head toward Pug. "I am in your debt."

Pug returned the bow, formal and unusual in this camp. "There is no debt. You will conduct yourself as an overseer should. You will care well for our brothers."

Chogana's old face split in a grin, revealing teeth stained brown by years of chewing tateen nuts. The mildly narcotic nut—easily found in the swamp—did not reduce efficiency but made the work seem less harsh. Pug had avoided the habit, for no reasons he could voice, as had most of the Midkemians. It seemed somehow to signify a final surrender of will.

Chogana stared at the camp, his eyes narrowed to slits by the harsh light. It stood empty, except for the young lord's bodyguard and the cook's crew. In the distance the sounds of the work crew echoed through the trees.

"When I was a boy, on my father's farm in Szetac," began Chogana, "it was discovered I had a talent. I was investigated, and found lacking." The meaning of that last statement was lost on Pug, but he didn't interrupt. "So I became a farmer like my father. But my talent was there. Sometimes I see things, Pug, things within men. As I grew, word of my talent spread and people, mostly poor people, would come and ask for my advice. As a young man I was arrogant and charged much, telling of what I saw. When I was older, I was humble and took whatever was offered, but still I told what I saw. Either way, people left angry. Do you know why?" he asked with a chuckle. Pug shook his head. "Because they didn't come to hear the truth, they came to hear what they wanted to hear."

Pug shared Chogana's laugh. "So I pretended the talent went away, and after a time people stopped coming to my farm. But the talent never went away, Pug, and I still can see things, sometimes. I have seen something in you, and I would tell you before you leave forever. I will die in this camp, but you have a different fate before you. Will you listen?" Pug said he would, and Chogana said, "Within you there is a trapped power. What it is and what it means, I do not know."

Knowing the strange Tsurani attitude toward magicians, Pug felt sudden panic at the possibility someone might have sensed his former calling. To most he was just another slave in the camp, and to a few, a former Squire.

Chogana continued, speaking with his eyes closed. "I dreamed about you, Pug. I saw you upon a tower and you faced a fearsome foe." He opened his eyes. "I do not know what the dream may mean, but this you must know. Before you mount that tower to face your foe, you must seek your wal; it is that secret center of your being, the perfect place of peace within. Once you reside there, you are safe from all harm. Your flesh may suffer, even die, but within your wal you will endure in peace. Seek hard, Pug, for few men find their wal."

Chogana stood. "You will leave soon. Come, we must wake Laurie."

As they walked to the hut entrance, Pug said, "Chogana, thank you. But one thing: you spoke of a foe upon the tower. Could you mark him?"

Chogana laughed, and bobbed his head up and down. "Oh, yes, I saw him." He continued to chuckle as he climbed the steps to the hut. "He is the foe to be feared most by any man." Narrow eyes regarded Pug. "He was you."

Pug and Laurie sat on the steps of the temple, with six Tsurani guards lounging around. The guards had been civil—barely—for the entire journey. The travel had been tiring, if not difficult. With no horses, nor anything to substitute for them, every Tsurani not riding in a needra cart moved by power of shanks' mare, their own or others. Nobles were carried up and down the wide boulevards on litters borne on the backs of puffing, sweating slaves.

Pug and Laurie had been given the short, plain grey robes of slaves. Their loincloths, adequate in the swamps,

were deemed unsightly for travel among Tsurani citizens.
Pug deduced that the Tsurani put store upon modesty—if
not so much as in the Kingdom.

They had come up the road along the coast of the great
body of water called Battle Bay. Pug had thought that if it
was a bay, it was larger than anything so named in
Midkemia, for even from the high cliffs overlooking it the
other side could not be seen. After several days' travel they
had entered cultivated pastureland, and soon after could
see the opposite shore closing in rapidly. Another few days
on the road, and they had come to the city of Jamar.

Pug and Laurie watched the passing traffic, while
Hokanu made an offering at the temple. The Tsurani
seemed mad for colors. Here even the lowliest worker was
likely to be dressed in a brightly colored short robe. Those
with wealth could be seen in more flamboyant dress,
covered with intricately executed designs. Only slaves
lacked colorful dress.

Everywhere around the city, people thronged:
farmers, traders, caravans, and travelers. Lines of needras
plodded by, pulling wagons filled with produce and goods.
The sheer numbers of people overwhelmed Pug and
Laurie, for the Tsurani seemed like ants scurrying about,
even in the unusual heat, as if the commerce of the Empire
could not wait upon the comfort of its citizens. Many who
passed stopped to stare at the Midkemians, whom they
regarded as giant barbarians. Their own height averaged
about five feet six inches, and even Pug was considered
tall, having come to his full growth at five feet eight. For
their part, the Midkemians had come to refer to the Tsurani
as runts.

Pug and Laurie looked about. They waited in the
center of the city, where the great temples were. Ten
pyramids, differing in size, but all richly appointed, sat
amid a series of parks. From where they were, the young
men could see three of the parks. Each was terraced, with
miniature watercourses winding through, complete with
tiny waterfalls. Dwarf trees, as well as large shade trees,
dotted the grass-covered grounds of the parks. Strolling
musicians played flutes and strange stringed instruments,
producing alien, polytonal music, entertaining those who
rested in the parks or passed by.

When Hokanu returned, they started off again. They made their way through the city, Pug still studying the people they passed. The press was incredible, and Pug wondered how they managed to stand it. Like farmers in a city for the first time, Pug and Laurie kept gawking at the wonders of Jamar. Even the supposedly worldly troubadour would exclaim about this sight or that. Soon the guards could be heard chuckling over the barbarians' obvious delight at the most mundane things.

Every building they passed was fashioned from wood and a translucent material, clothlike but rigid. A few, like the temples, were constructed with stone, but what was most remarkable was that every building they passed, from temple to worker's hut, was painted white, except for bordering beams and doorframes, which were polished deep brown. Every open surface was decorated with colorful paintings. Animals, landscapes, deities, and battle scenes abounded. Everywhere was a riot of color for the eyes to caress.

To the north of the temples, across from one of the parks and facing a wide boulevard, stood a single building, set apart by open lawns bordered with hedges. Two guards, dressed in armor and helm similar to those of their own guards, stood watch at the door. They saluted Hokanu when he approached.

Without a word, the other guards marched around the side of the house, leaving the slaves with the young officer. He signaled, and one of the door guards slid the large, cloth-covered door aside. They entered an open hallway leading back, with doors on each side. Hokanu marched them to a rear door, which a house slave opened for them.

Pug and Laurie then discovered the house was fashioned like a square, with a large garden in the center, accessible from all sides. Near a bubbling pool sat an older man, dressed in a plain but rich-looking dark blue robe. He was consulting a scroll. He looked up when the three entered, and rose to greet Hokanu.

The young man removed his helm and then came to attention. Pug and Laurie stood slightly behind and said nothing. The man nodded, and Hokanu approached. They embraced and the older man said, "My son, it is good to see you again. How were things at the camp?"

Hokanu made his report on the camp, briefly and to the point, leaving out nothing of importance. He then told of the actions taken to remedy the situation. "So the new overseer will see that the slaves have ample food and rest. He should increase production soon."

His father nodded. "I think you have acted wisely, my son. We shall have to send another in a few months' time to gauge progress, but things could not become any worse than they were. The Warlord demands higher production and we border on falling into his bad graces."

He seemed to notice the slaves for the first time. "These?" was all he said, pointing at Laurie and Pug.

"They are unusual. I was thinking of our talk on the night before my brother went to the north. They may prove valuable."

"Have you spoken of this to anyone?" His grey eyes were set in firm lines. Even though much shorter, he somehow reminded Pug of Lord Borric.

"No, my father. Only those who took council that night—"

The lord of the house cut him off with a wave of the hand. "Save your remarks for later. 'Trust no secrets to a city.' Inform Septiem. We close the house and leave for our estates in the morning."

Hokanu bowed slightly, then turned to leave. "Hokanu." His father's voice stopped him. "You have done well." Pride plainly showing on his face, the young man left the garden.

The lord of the house sat again upon a bench of carved stone, next to a small fountain, and regarded the two slaves. "What are you called?"

"Pug, master."

"Laurie, master."

He seemed to derive some sort of insight from these simple statements. "Through that door," he said, pointing to the left, "is the way to the cookhouse. My hadonra is called Septiem. He will see to your care. Go now."

They bowed and left the garden. As they made their way through the house, Pug nearly knocked over a young girl coming around a corner. She was dressed in a slave's robe and carried a large bundle of washing. It went flying across the hall.

"Oh!" she cried. "I've just now washed these. Now I'll have to do them over." Pug quickly bent to help her pick them up. She was tall for a Tsurani, nearly Pug's height, and well proportioned. Her brown hair was tied back, and her brown eyes were framed by long, dark lashes. Pug stopped gathering the clothing and stared at her in open admiration. She hesitated under his scrutiny, then quickly picked up the rest of the clothes and hurried off. Laurie watched her trim figure retreat, tan legs shown to good advantage by the short slave's robe.

Laurie slapped Pug's shoulder. "Ha! I told you things would be looking up."

They left the house and approached the cookhouse, where the smell of hot food set their appetites on edge. "I think you've made an impression on that girl, Pug."

Pug had never had much experience with women and felt his ears start to burn. At the slave camp much of the talk was about women, and this, more than anything else, had kept him feeling like a boy. He turned to see if Laurie was having sport with him, then saw the blond singer looking behind him. He followed Laurie's gaze and caught a glimpse of a shyly smiling face pull back from a window in the house.

The next day, the household of the Shinzawai family was in an uproar. Slaves and servants hurried every which way making ready for the journey to the north. Pug and Laurie were left to themselves, as there was no one among the household staff free enough to assign them tasks. They sat in the shade of a large, willowlike tree enjoying the novelty of free time as they observed the furor.

"These people are crazy, Pug. I've seen less preparation for caravans. It looks as if they plan on taking everything with them."

"Maybe they are. These people no longer surprise me." Pug stood, leaning against the bole. "I've seen things that defy logic."

"True enough. But when you've seen as many different lands as I have, you learn the more things look different, the more they are the same."

"What do you mean?"

Laurie rose and leaned on the other side of the tree. In

low tones he said, "I'm not sure, but something is afoot, and we play a part, be sure. If we keep sharp, we may be able to turn it to our advantage. Always remember that. Should a man want something from you, you can always make a bargain, no matter what the apparent differences in your stations."

"Of course. Give him what he wants and he'll let you live."

"You're too young to be so cynical," Laurie countered, with mirth sparkling in his eyes. "Tell you what. You leave the world-weary pose to old travelers such as myself, and I'll make sure that you don't miss a single opportunity."

Pug snorted. "What opportunity?"

"Well, for one thing," Laurie said, pointing behind Pug, "that little girl you nearly knocked over yesterday is appearing to have some difficulty in lifting those boxes." Pug, glancing back, saw the laundry girl struggling to stack several large crates ready to be loaded into wagons. "I think she might appreciate a little help, don't you think?"

Pug's confusion was evident on his face. "What . . . ?"

Laurie gave him a gentle push. "Off with you, dolt. A little help now, later . . . who knows?"

Pug stumbled away. "Later?"

"Gods!" laughed Laurie, fetching Pug a playful kick in the rump.

The troubadour's humor was infectious, and Pug was smiling as he approached the girl. She was trying to lift a large wooden crate atop another. Pug took it from her. "Here, I can do that."

She stepped away, uncertain. "It's not heavy. It's just too high for me." She looked everywhere but at Pug.

Pug lifted the crate easily and placed it on top of the others, favoring his tender hand only a little. "There you are," he said, trying to sound casual.

The girl brushed back a stray wisp of hair that had fallen into her eyes. "You're a barbarian, aren't you?" She spoke hesitantly.

Pug flinched. "You call us that. I like to think I'm as civilized as the next man."

She blushed. "I didn't mean any offense. My people are called barbarians also. Anyone who's not a Tsurani is called that. I meant you're from that other world."

Pug nodded. "What's your name?"

She said, "Katala," then in a rush, "What is your name?"

"Pug."

She smiled. "That's a strange name. Pug." She seemed to like the sound of it.

Just then the hadonra, Septiem, an old but erect man with the bearing of a retired general, came around the house. "You two!" he snapped. "There's work to do! Don't stand there."

Katala ran back into the house, and Pug was left hesitating before the yellow-robed estate manager. "You! What's your name?"

"Pug, sir."

"I see that you and your blond giant friend have been given nothing to do. I'll have to remedy that. Call him over."

Pug sighed. So much for their free time. He waved to Laurie to come over, and they were put to work loading wagons.

TWO

ESTATE

The weather had turned cooler during the last three weeks.

Still it hinted at the summer's heat. The winter season in this land, if a season it properly was, lasted a mere six weeks, with brief cold rains out of the north. The trees held most of their bluish green leaves, and there was nothing to mark the passing of fall. In the four years Pug had abided in Tsuranuanni there were none of the familiar signs that marked the passing seasons: no bird migrations, frost in the mornings, rains that froze, snow, or blooming of wild flowers. This land seemed eternally set in the soft amber of summer.

The Shinzawai caravan was approaching the boundaries of the family's northern estates. Pug and Laurie had little to do along the way except occasional chores: dumping the cook pots, cleaning up needra droppings, loading and unloading supplies. Now they were riding on the back of a wagon, feet dangling over the rear. Laurie bit into a ripe jomach fruit, something like a large green pomegranate. Spitting out seeds, he said, "How's the hand?"

Pug studied his right hand, examining the red puckered scar that ran across the palm. "It's still stiff. I expect it's as healed as it will ever be."

Laurie took a look. "Don't think you'll ever carry a sword again." He grinned.

Pug laughed. "I doubt you will either. I somehow don't think they'll be finding a place for you in the Imperial Horse Lance."

Laurie spat a burst of seeds, bouncing them off the nose of the needra who pulled the wagon behind them. The six-legged beast snorted, and the driver waved his steering stick angrily at them. "Except for the fact that the Emperor doesn't have any lancers, due to the fact that he also doesn't have any horses, I can't think of a finer choice."

Pug laughed derisively.

"I'll have you know, fella-me-lad," said Laurie in aristocratic tones, "that we troubadours are often beset by a less savory sort of customer, brigands and cutthroats seeking our hard-earned wages—scant though they may be. If one doesn't develop the ability to defend oneself, one doesn't stay in business, if you catch my meaning."

Pug smiled. He knew that a troubadour was nearly sacrosanct in a town, for should he be harmed or robbed, word would spread and no other would ever come there again. But on the road it was a different matter. He had no doubt of Laurie's ability to take care of himself, but wasn't about to let him use that pompous tone and sit without a rejoinder. As he was about to speak, though, he was cut off by shouts coming from the front of the caravan. Guards came rushing forward, and Laurie turned to his shorter companion. "What do you suppose that is all about?"

Not waiting for an answer, he jumped down and ran forward. Pug followed. As they reached the head of the caravan, behind the Lord of the Shinzawai's litter, they could see shapes advancing up the road toward them. Laurie grabbed Pug's sleeve. "Riders!"

Pug could scarcely believe his eyes, for indeed it appeared that riders were approaching along the road from the Shinzawai manor. As they got closer, he could see that, rather than riders, there was one horseman and three cho-ja, all three a rich dark blue color.

The rider, a young, brown-haired Tsurani, taller than most, dismounted. His movement was clumsy and Laurie observed, "They will never pose any military threat if that's the best seat they can keep. Look, there is no saddle, nor bridle, only a rude hackamore fashioned from leather straps. And the poor horse looks like it hasn't been properly groomed for a month."

The curtain of the litter was pulled back as the rider approached. The slaves put it down and the Lord of the Shinzawai got out. Hokanu had reached his father's side, from his place among the guards at the rear of the caravan, and was embracing the rider, exchanging greetings. The rider then embraced the Lord of the Shinzawai. Pug and Laurie could hear the rider say, "Father! It is good to see you."

The Shinzawai lord said, "Kasumi! It is good to see my firstborn son. When did you return?"

"Less than a week ago. I would have come to Jamar, but I heard that you were due here, so I waited."

"I am glad. Who are these with you?" He indicated the creatures.

"This," he said, pointing to the foremost, "is Strike Leader X'calak, back from fighting the short ones under the mountains on Midkemia."

The creature stepped forward and raised his right hand—very humanlike—in salute, and in a high, piping voice said, "Hail, Kamatsu, Lord of the Shinzawai. Honors to your house."

The Lord of the Shinzawai bowed slightly from the waist. "Greetings, X'calak. Honors to your hive. The cho-ja are always welcome guests."

The creature stepped back and waited. The lord turned to look at the horse. "What is this upon which you sit, my son?"

"A horse, Father. A creature the barbarians ride into battle. I've told you of them before. It is a truly marvelous creature. On its back I can run faster than the swiftest cho-ja runner."

"How do you stay on?"

The older Shinzawai son laughed. "With great difficulty, I'm afraid. The barbarians have tricks to it I have yet to learn."

Hokanu smiled. "Perhaps we can arrange for lessons."

Kasumi slapped him playfully on the back. "I have asked several barbarians, but unfortunately they were all dead."

"I have two here who are not."

Kasumi looked past his brother and saw Laurie, standing a full head taller than the other slaves who had gathered around. "So I see. Well, we must ask him. Father, with your permission, I will ride back to the house and have all made ready for your homecoming."

Kamatsu embraced his son, and agreed. The older son remounted and with a wave rode off.

Pug and Laurie quickly returned to their places on the wagon. Laurie asked, "Have you seen the like of those things before?"

Pug nodded. "Yes. The Tsurani call them the cho-ja. They live in large hive mounds, like ants. The Tsurani slaves I spoke with in the camp tell me they have been around as long as can be remembered. They are loyal to the Empire, though I seem to remember someone saying that each hive has its own queen."

Laurie peered around the front of the wagon, hanging on with one hand. "I wouldn't like to face one on foot. Look at the way they run."

Pug said nothing. The older Shinzawai son's remark about the short ones under the mountain brought back old memories. If Tomas is alive, he thought, he is a man now. If he is alive.

The Shinzawai manor was huge. It was easily the biggest single building—short of temples and palaces—that Pug had seen. It sat atop a hill, commanding a view of the countryside for miles. The house was square, like the one in Jamar, but several times the size. The town house could easily have fit inside this one's central garden. Behind it were the outbuildings, cookhouse, and slave quarters.

 or Pug craned his neck to take in the garden, for they were walking quickly through and there was little time to absorb all of it. The hadonra, Septiem, scolded him. "Don't tarry."

Pug quickened his step and fell in beside Laurie. Still, on a brief viewing, the garden was impressive. Several shade trees had been planted beside three pools that sat in the midst of miniature trees and flowering plants. Stone benches had been placed for contemplative rest, and paths of gravel wandered throughout. Around this tiny park the building rose, three stories tall. The top two stories had balconies, and several staircases rose to connect them. Servants could be seen hurrying along the upper levels, but there appeared to be no one else in the garden, or at least that portion they had crossed.

They reached a sliding door and Septiem turned to face them. In stern tones he said, "You two barbarians will watch your manners before the lords of this house, or by the gods, I'll have every inch of skin off your backs. Now make sure you do all that I've told you, or you'll wish that Master Hokanu had left you to rot in the swamps."

He slid the door to one side and announced the slaves. The command for them to enter was given and Septiem shooed them inside. They found themselves in a warmly lit room, the light coming through the large, translucent door. On the walls hung carvings, tapestries, and paintings, all done in fine style, small and delicate. The floor was covered, in Tsurani fashion, with a thick pile of furs and cushions. Upon a large cushion Kamatsu, Lord of the Shinzawai, sat; across from him were his two sons. All were dressed in the short robes of expensive fabric and cut they used when off duty. Pug and Laurie stood with their eyes downcast until they were spoken to.

Hokanu spoke first. "The blond giant is called Loh-'re, and the more normal-sized one is Poog."

Laurie started to open his mouth, but a quick elbow from Pug silenced him before he could speak.

The older son noticed the exchange, and said, "You would speak?"

Laurie looked up, then quickly down again. The instructions had been clear: not to speak until commanded to. Laurie wasn't sure the question was a command.

The lord of the house said, "Speak."

Laurie looked at Kasumi. "I am Laurie, master. Lor-ee. And my friend is Pug, not Poog."

Hokanu looked taken aback at being corrected, but the older brother nodded and pronounced the names several times over, until he spoke them correctly. He then said, "Have you ridden horses?"

Both slaves nodded. Kasumi said, "Good. Then you can show me the best way."

Pug's gaze wandered as much as was possible with his head down, but something caught his eye. Next to the Lord of the Shinzawai sat a game board and what looked like familiar figures. Kamatsu noticed and said, "You know this game?" He reached over and brought the board forward, so that it lay before him.

Pug said, "Master, I know the game. We call it chess."

Hokanu looked at his brother, who leaned forward. "As several have said, Father, there has been contact with the barbarians before."

His father waved away the comment. "It is a theory." To Pug he said, "Sit here and show me how the pieces move."

Pug sat and tried to remember what Kulgan had taught him. He had been an indifferent student of the game, but knew a few basic openings. He moved a pawn forward and said, "This piece may only move forward one space, except when it is first moved, master. Then it may move two." The lord of the house nodded, motioning that he should continue. "This piece is a knight, and moves like so," said Pug.

After he had demonstrated the moves of the various pieces, the Lord of the Shinzawai said, "We call this game shāh. The pieces are called by different names, but it is the same. Come, we will play."

Kamatsu gave the white pieces to Pug. He opened with a conventional king's pawn move, and Kamatsu countered. Pug played badly and was quickly beaten. The others watched the entire game without a sound. When it was over, the lord said, "Do you play well, among your people?"

"No, master. I play poorly."

He smiled, his eyes wrinkling at the edges. "Then I

would guess that your people are not as barbarous as is commonly held. We will play again soon."

He nodded to his older son, and Kasumi rose. Bowing to his father, he said to Pug and Laurie, "Come."

They bowed to the lord of the house and followed Kasumi out of the room. He led them through the house, to a smaller room with sleeping pallets and cushions. "You will sleep here. My room is next door. I would have you at hand at all times."

Laurie spoke up boldly. "What does the master want of us?"

Kasumi regarded him for a moment. "You barbarians will never make good slaves. You forget your place too often."

Laurie started to stammer an apology but was cut off. "It is of little matter. You are to teach me things, Laurie. You will teach me to ride, and how to speak your language. Both of you. I would learn what those"—he paused, then made a flat, nasal *wa-wa-wa* sound—"noises mean when you speak to each other."

Further conversation was cut off by the sound of a single chime that reverberated throughout the house. Kasumi said, "A Great One comes. Stay in your rooms. I must go to welcome him with my father." He hurried off, leaving the two Midkemians to sit in their new quarters wondering at this newest twist in their lives.

Twice during the following two days, Pug and Laurie glimpsed the Shinzawai's important visitor. He was much like the Shinzawai lord in appearance, but thinner, and he wore the black robe of a Tsurani Great One. Pug asked a few questions of the house staff and gained a little information. Pug and Laurie had seen nothing that compared with the awe the Great Ones were held in by the Tsurani. They seemed a power apart, and with what little understanding of Tsurani social reality Pug had, he couldn't exactly comprehend how they fit into the scheme of things. At first he had thought they were some social stigma, for all he was ever told was that the Great Ones were "outside the law." He then was made to understand, by an exasperated Tsurani slave who couldn't believe his ignorance of important matters, that the Great Ones had little or no social constraints in exchange for some nameless service to the Empire.

Pug had made a discovery during this time which lightened the alien feeling of his captivity somewhat. Behind the needra pens he had found a kennel full of yapping, tail-wagging dogs. They were the only Midkemianike animals he had seen on Kelewan, and he felt an unexplained joy at their presence. He had rushed back to their room to fetch Laurie and had brought him to the kennel. Now they sat in one of the runs, amid a group of playful canines.

Laurie laughed at their boisterous play. They were unlike the duke's hunting hounds, being longer of leg, and more gaunt. Their ears were pointed, and perked at every sound.

"I've seen their like, before, in Gulbi. It's a town in the Great Northern Trade Route of Kesh. They are called greyhounds and are used to run down the fast cats and antelope of the grasslands near the Valley of the Sun."

The kennel master, a thin, droopy-eyelidded slave named Rachmad, came over and watched them suspiciously. "What are you doing here?"

Laurie regarded the dour man and playfully pulled the muzzle of a rambunctious puppy. "We haven't seen dogs since we left our homeland, Rachmad. Our master is busy with the Great One, so we thought we would visit your fine kennel."

At mention of his "fine kennel" the gloomy countenance brightened considerably. "I try and keep the dogs healthy. We must keep them locked up, for they try and harry the cho-ja, who like them not at all." For a moment Pug thought perhaps they had been taken from Midkemia as the horse had been. When he asked where they had come from, Rachmad looked at him as if he were crazy. "You speak like you have been too long in the sun. There have always been dogs." With that final pronouncement on the matter, he judged the conversation closed and left.

Later that night, Pug awoke to find Laurie entering their room. "Where have you been?"

"Shh! You want to wake the whole household? Go back to sleep."

"Where did you go?" Pug asked in hushed tones.

Laurie could be seen grinning in the dim light. "I paid a visit to a certain cook's assistant, for . . . a chat."

"Oh. Almorella?"

"Yes," came the cheerful reply. "She's quite a girl." The young slave who served in the kitchen had been making big eyes at Laurie ever since the caravan had arrived four days ago.

After a moment of silence, Laurie said, "You should cultivate a few friends yourself. Gives a whole new look to things."

"I'll bet," Pug said, disapproval mixed with more than a little envy. Almorella was a bright and cheerful girl, near Pug's age, with merry dark eyes.

"That little Katala, now. She has her eye on you, I'm thinking."

Cheeks burning, Pug threw a cushion at his friend. "Oh, shut up and go to sleep."

Laurie stifled a laugh. He retired to his pallet and left Pug alone in thought.

There was the faint promise of rain on the wind, and Pug welcomed the coolness he felt in its touch. Laurie was sitting astride Kasumi's horse, and the young officer stood by and watched. Laurie had directed Tsurani craftsmen as they fashioned a saddle and bridle for the mount, and was now demonstrating their use.

"This horse is combat-trained," Laurie shouted. "He can be neck-reined"—he demonstrated by laying the reins on one side of the horse's neck, then the other—"or he can be turned by using your knees." He raised his hands and showed the older son of the house how this was done.

For three weeks they had been instructing the young noble in riding and he had showed natural ability. Laurie jumped from the horse and Kasumi took his place. The Tsurani rode roughly at first, the saddle feeling strange under him, but soon smoothed out with the horse and had the animal running over the fields.

Laurie pulled up a long stem of grass from the ground and put it between his teeth. He hunkered down and scratched the ear of a bitch who lay at his feet, as much to distract the dog from running after the horse as to play with her. She rolled over on her back and playfully bit his hand.

Laurie turned his attention to Pug. "I wonder what game our young friend is playing at?"

Pug shrugged. "What do you mean?"

"Remember when we first arrived? I heard Kasumi was about to head out with his cho-ja companions. Well, those three cho-ja soldiers left this morning—which is why Bethel here is out of her pen—and I heard some gossip that the orders of the older son of the Shinzawai were suddenly changed. Put that together with these riding and language lessons and what do you have?"

Pug stretched. "I don't know."

"I don't know either." Laurie sounded disgusted. "But these matters are of high import." He looked across the plain and said lightly, "All I ever wanted to do was to travel and tell my stories, sing my songs, and someday find a widow who owned an inn."

Pug laughed. "I think you would find tavern keeping dull business after all this fine adventure."

"Some fine adventuring. I'm riding along with a bunch of provincial militia and run right smack into the entire Tsurani army. Since then I've been beaten several times, spent four months mucking about in the swamps, walked over half this world—"

"Ridden in a wagon, as I remember."

"Well, traveled over half this world, and now I'm giving riding lessons to Kasumi Shinzawai, older son of a lord of Tsuranuanni. Not the stuff great ballads are made of."

Pug smiled ruefully. "It could have been four years in the swamps. Consider yourself lucky. At least you can count on being here tomorrow. At least as long as Septiem doesn't catch you creeping around the kitchen late at night."

Laurie studied Pug closely. "I know you're joking, about Septiem, I mean. It has occurred to me several times to ask you, Pug. Why do you never speak of your life before you were captured?"

Pug looked away absently. "I guess it's a habit I picked up in the swamp camp. It doesn't pay to remind yourself of what you used to be. I've seen brave men die because they couldn't forget they were born free."

Laurie pulled at the dog's ear. "But things are different here."

"Are they? Remember what you said back in Jamar about a man wanting something from you. I think the more comfortable you become here, the easier it is for them to get whatever it is they want from you. This Shinzawai lord is no one's fool." Seemingly shifting topics, he said, "Is it better to train a dog or horse with a whip or with kindness?"

Laurie looked up. "What? Why, with kindness, but you have to use discipline also."

Pug nodded. "We are being shown the same consideration as Bethel and her kind, I think. But we still are slaves. Never forget that."

Laurie looked out over the field for a long time and said nothing.

The pair were rousted from their thoughts by the shouts of the older son of the house as he rode back into view. He pulled the horse up before them and jumped down. "He flies," he said, in his broken King's Tongue. Kasumi was an apt student and was picking up the language quickly. He supplemented his language lessons with a constant stream of questions about the lands and people of Midkemia. There was not a single aspect of life in the Kingdom that he seemed uninterested in. He had asked for examples of the most mundane things, such as the manner in which one bargains with tradespeople, and the proper forms of address when speaking to people of different ranks.

Kasumi led the horse back to the shed that had been built for him, and Pug watched for any sign of foot-soreness. They had fashioned shoes for him from wood treated with resin, by trial and error, but these seemed to be holding up well enough. As he walked, Kasumi said, "I have been thinking about a thing. I don't understand how your King rules, with all you have said about this Congress of Lords. Please explain this thing."

Laurie looked at Pug with an eyebrow raised. While no more an authority on Kingdom politics than Laurie, he seemed better able to explain what he knew. Pug said, "The congress elects the King, though it is mostly a matter of form."

"Form?"

"A tradition. The heir to the throne is always elected, except when there is no clear successor. It is considered the best way to stem civil war, for the ruling of the congress is final." He explained how the Prince of Krondor had deferred to his nephew, and how the congress had acquiesced to his wishes. "How is it with the Empire?"

Kasumi thought, then said, "Perhaps not so different. Each Emperor is the elect of the gods, but from what you have told me he is unlike your King. He rules in the Holy City, but his leadership is spiritual. He protects us from the wrath of the gods."

Laurie asked, "Who then rules?"

They reached the shed and Kasumi took the saddle and bridle off the horse and began rubbing him down. "Here it is different from your land." He seemed to have difficulty with the language and shifted into Tsurani. "Each family belongs to a clan. Within that clan, each lord of a family holds certain powers. The Shinzawai belong to the Kanazawai Clan. We are the second most powerful family in that clan next to the Keda. My father in his youth was commander of the clan armies, a warchief, what you would call a general. The position of families shifts from generation to generation, so that it is unlikely I will reach so exalted a position.

"The leading lord of each clan sits in the High Council. This advises the Warlord. He rules in the name of the Emperor, though the Emperor could overrule him."

"Does the Emperor in fact ever overrule the Warlord?" asked Laurie.

"Never."

"How is the Warlord chosen?" asked Pug.

"It is difficult to explain. When the old Warlord dies, the clans meet. It is a large gathering of lords, for not only the council comes, but also the heads of every family. They meet and plot, and sometimes blood feuds develop, but in the end a new Warlord is elected."

Pug brushed back the hair from his eyes. "Then what is to keep the Warlord's clan from claiming the office, if they are the most powerful?"

Kasumi looked troubled. "It is not an easy thing to explain. You would have to be Tsurani to understand.

There are laws, but more important, there are customs. No matter how powerful a clan becomes, or a family within it, only the lord of one of five families may be elected Warlord. They are the Keda, Tonmargu, Minwanabi, Oaxatucan, and the Xacatecas. So there are only five lords who may be considered. This Warlord is a Oaxatucan, so the light of the Kanazawai clan burns dimly. His clan, the Omechan, is in ascension now. That is the way of it."

Laurie shook his head. "This family and clan business makes our own politics seem simple."

Kasumi laughed. "That is not politics. Politics is the province of the parties."

"Parties?" asked Laurie, obviously getting lost in the conversation.

"There are many parties. The Blue Wheel, the Golden Flower, the Jade Eye, the Party for Progress, the War Party, and others. Families may belong to different parties, each trying to further their own needs. Sometimes families from the same clan will belong to different parties. Sometimes they switch alliances to suit their needs for the moment. Other times they may support two parties at once, or none."

"It seems a most unstable government," remarked Laurie.

Kasumi laughed. "It has lasted for over two thousand years. We have an old saying: 'In the High Council, there is no brother.' Remember that and you may understand."

Pug weighed his next question carefully. "Master, in all this you have not mentioned the Great Ones. Why is that?"

Kasumi stopped rubbing down the horse and looked at Pug for a moment, then resumed his ministrations. "They have nothing to do with politics. They are outside the law, and have no clan." He paused again. "Why do you ask?"

"It is only that they seem to command a great amount of respect, and since one has called here so recently, I thought you could enlighten me."

"They are given respect because the fate of the Empire is at all times in their hands. It is a grave responsibility. They renounce all their ties, and few have personal lives. Those with families live apart, and their children are sent to live with their former families when they come of age. It is a difficult thing. They make many sacrifices."

Pug watched Kasumi closely. He seemed somehow troubled by what he was saying. "The Great One who came to see my father was, when a boy, a member of this family. He was my uncle. It is difficult for us now, for he must observe the formalities, and cannot claim kinship. It would be better if he stayed away, I think." The last was spoken softly.

"Why is that, master?" Laurie asked, in hushed tones.

"Because it is hard for Hokanu. Before he became my brother, he was that Great One's son."

They finished caring for the horse and left the shack. Bethel ran ahead, for she knew it was close to feeding time. As they passed the kennel, Rachmad called her over and she joined the other dogs.

The entire way, there was no conversation, and Kasumi entered his room with no further remark for either of the Midkemians. Pug sat on his pallet, waiting for the call for dinner, and thought about what he had learned. For all their strange ways, the Tsurani were much like other men. He found this somehow both comforting and troublesome.

Two weeks later, Pug was faced with another problem to mull over. Lately Katala had been making it obvious she was less than pleased with Pug's lack of attention. In little ways at first, then with more blatant signs, she had tried to spark his interest. Finally things came to a head when he had run into her behind the cook shed one afternoon.

Laurie and Kasumi were trying to build a small lute, with the aid of a Shinzawai woodcrafter. Kasumi had expressed interest in the music of the troubadour and, the last few days, had watched closely while Laurie argued with the artisan over the selection of proper grains, the way to cut the wood, and the manner of fashioning the instrument. He was perplexed about whether or not needra gut would make suitable strings, and a thousand other details. Pug had found all this less than engrossing, and after a few days had found every excuse to wander off. The smell of curing wood reminded him too much of cutting trees in the swamp for him to enjoy being around the resin pots in the woodcarver's shed.

He had been lying in the shade of the cook shed when

Katala came around the corner. He had felt his stomach constrict. He thought her very attractive, but each time he wanted to speak to her, he found he couldn't think of anything to say. He would simply make a few inane remarks, become embarrassed, then hurry off. Lately he had taken to saying nothing. He had smiled, noncommittally, and she had started to walk past. Suddenly she had turned and looked as if near to tears.

"What is the matter with me? Am I so ugly that you can't stand the sight of me?"

Pug had sat speechless, his mouth open. She had stood for a moment, then kicked him in the leg. "Stupid barbarian," she had sniffed, then run off.

Now he sat in his room, feeling confused and uneasy over that afternoon's encounter. Laurie was carving pegs for his lute. Finally he put knife and wood aside and said, "What's troubling you, Pug? You look as if they're promoting you to slave master and sending you back to the swamp."

Pug lay back on his pallet, staring at the ceiling. "It's Katala."

"Oh," Laurie said.

"What do you mean, 'Oh'?"

"Nothing, except that Almorella tells me the girl has been impossible for the last two weeks, and you look about as bright as a poleaxed steer these days. What's the matter?"

"I don't know. She's just . . . she's just . . . She kicked me today."

Laurie threw back his head and laughed. "Why in the name of heaven did she do that?"

"I don't know. She just kicked me."

"What did you do?"

"I didn't do anything."

"Ha!" Laurie exploded with mirth. "That's the trouble, Pug. There is only one thing I know of that a woman hates more than a man she doesn't like paying her too much attention—and that's lack of attention from a man she does like."

Pug looked despondent. "I thought it was something like that."

Surprise registered on Laurie's face. "What is it? Don't you like her?"

Leaning forward, his elbows on his knees, Pug said, "It's not that. I like her. She's very pretty and seems nice enough. It's just that . . ."

"What?"

Pug glanced sharply over at his friend, to see if he was being mocked. Laurie was smiling, but in a friendly, reassuring way. Pug continued, "It's just . . . there's someone else."

Laurie's mouth fell open, then popped shut. "Who? Except for Almorella, Katala's the prettiest wench I've seen on this gods-forsaken world." He sighed. "In honesty, she's prettier than Almorella, though only a little. Besides, I've not seen you ever speak to another woman, and I'd have noticed you skulking off with anyone."

Pug shook his head and looked down. "No, Laurie. I mean back home."

Laurie's mouth popped open again, then he fell over backward and groaned. "Back home! What am I to do with this child? He's bereft of all wit!" He pulled himself up on an elbow and said, "Can this be Pug speaking? The lad who counsels me to put the past behind? The one who insists that dwelling on how things were at home leads only to a quick death?"

Pug ignored the sting of the questions. "This is different."

"How is it different? By Ruthia—who in her more tender moments protects fools, drunks, and minstrels—how can you tell me this is different? Do you imagine for a moment you have one hope in ten times ten thousand of ever seeing this girl again, whoever she is?"

"I know, but thinking of Carline has kept me from losing my mind more times . . ." He sighed loudly. "We all need one dream, Laurie."

Laurie studied his young friend for a quiet moment. "Yes, Pug, we all need one dream. Still," he added brightly, "a dream is one thing, a living, breathing, warm woman is another." Seeing Pug become irritated at the remark, he switched topics. "Who is Carline, Pug?"

"My lord Borric's daughter."

Laurie's eyes grew round. "Princess Carline?" Pug nodded. Laurie's voice showed amusement. "The most eligible noble daughter in the Western Realm after the daughter of the Prince of Krondor? There are sides to you I never would have thought possible! Tell me about her."

Pug began to speak slowly at first, telling of his boyhood infatuation for her, then of how their relationship developed. Laurie remained silent, putting aside questions, letting Pug relieve himself of the pent-up emotions of years. Finally Pug said, "Perhaps that's what bothers me so much about Katala. In certain ways she's like Carline. She's got a strong will and makes her moods known. She sparks, does Katala."

Laurie nodded, not saying anything. Pug lapsed into silence, then after a moment said, "When I was at Crydee, I thought for a time I was in love with Carline. But I don't know. Is that strange?"

Laurie shook his head. "No, Pug. There are many ways to love someone. Sometimes we want love so much we're not too choosy about who we love. Other times we make love such a pure and noble thing no poor human can ever meet our vision. But for the most part, love is a recognition, an opportunity to say, 'There is something about you I cherish.' It doesn't entail marriage, or even physical love. There's love of parents, love of city or nation, love of life, and love of people. All different, all love. But tell me, do you find your feelings for Katala much as they were for Carline?"

Pug shrugged and smiled. "No, they're not, not quite the same. With Carline, I felt as if I had to keep her away, you know, at arm's length. Sort of keeping control of what went on, I think."

Laurie probed lightly, "And Katala?"

Pug shrugged again. "I don't know. It's different. I don't feel as if I have to keep her under control. It's more as if there are things I want to tell her, but I don't know how. Like the way I got all jammed up inside when she smiled at me the first time. I could talk to Carline, when she kept quiet and let me. Katala keeps quiet, but I don't know what to say." He paused a moment, then made a sound half sigh, half groan. "Just thinking about her makes me hurt, Laurie."

Laurie lay back, a friendly chuckle escaping his lips. "Aye, it's well I've known that ache. And I must admit your taste runs to interesting women. From what I can see, Katala's a prize. And the Princess Carline . . ."

A little snappishly, Pug said, "I'll make a point of introducing you when we get back."

Laurie ignored the tone. "I'll hold you to that, Pug. Look, all I mean is it seems you've developed an excellent knack for finding worthwhile women." A little sadly, he said, "I wish I could claim as much. My life has been mostly caught up with tavern wenches, farmers' daughters, and common street whores. I don't know what to tell you."

"Laurie," said Pug. Laurie sat up and looked at his friend. "I don't know . . . I don't know what to do."

Laurie studied Pug a moment, then comprehension dawned and he threw back his head, laughing. He could see Pug's anger rising, and put his hands up in supplication. "I'm sorry, Pug. I didn't mean to embarrass you. It was just not what I expected to hear."

Somewhat placated, Pug said, "I was young when I was captured, less than sixteen years of age. I was never of a size like the other boys, so the girls didn't pay much attention to me, until Carline, I mean, and after I became a Squire, they were afraid to talk to me. After that . . . Damn it all, Laurie. I've been in the swamps for four years. What chance have I had to know a woman?"

Laurie sat quietly for a moment and the tension left the room. "Pug, I never would have imagined, but as you said, when have you had the time?"

"Laurie, what am I to do?"

"I think you should just go to the girl, and make your feelings known."

"Just talk to her?"

"Of course. Love is like a lot of things, it is always best done with the head. Save mindless efforts for mindless things. Now go."

"Now?" Pug looked panic-stricken.

"You can't start any sooner, right?"

Pug nodded and without a word left. He walked down the dark and quiet corridors, outside to the slave quarters, and found his way to her door. He raised his hand to knock on the doorframe, then stopped. He stood quietly for a moment trying to make up his mind what to do, when the door slid open. Almorella stood in the doorway, clutching her robe about her, her hair disheveled. "Oh," she whispered, "I thought it was Laurie. Wait a moment." She disappeared into the room, then shortly reappeared with a bundle of things in her arms. She patted Pug's arm and set off in the direction of his and Laurie's room.

Pug stood at the door, then slowly entered. He could see Katala lying under a blanket on her pallet. He stepped over to where she lay, and squatted next to her. He touched her shoulder and softly spoke her name. She came awake and sat up suddenly, gathered her blanket around her, and said, "What are you doing here?"

"I . . . I wanted to talk to you." Once started, the words came out in a tumbling rush. "I am sorry if I've done anything to make you angry with me. Or haven't done anything. I mean, Laurie said that if you don't do something when someone expects you to, that's as bad as paying too much attention. I'm not sure, you see." She covered her mouth to hide a giggle, for she could see his distress in spite of the gloom. "What I mean . . . what I mean is I'm sorry. Sorry for what I've done. Or didn't do . . ."

She silenced him by placing her fingertips across his mouth. Her arm snaked out and around his neck, pulling his head downward. She kissed him slowly, then said, "Silly. Go close the door."

They lay together, Katala's arm across Pug's chest, while he stared at the ceiling. She made sleepy sounds, and he ran his hands through her thick hair and across her soft shoulder.

"What?" she asked sleepily.

"I was just thinking that I haven't been happier since I was made a member of the Duke's court."

"'Sgood." She came a bit more awake. "What's a duke?"

Pug thought for a moment. "It's like a lord here, only different. My Duke was cousin to the King, and the third most powerful man in the Kingdom."

She snuggled closer to him. "You must have been important to be part of the court of such a man."

"Not really; I did him a service and was rewarded for it." He didn't think he wanted to bring up Carline's name here. Somehow his boyish fantasies about the Princess seemed childish in light of this night.

Katala rolled over onto her stomach. She raised her head and rested it on a hand, forming a triangle with her arm. "I wish things could be different."

"How so, love?"

"My father was a farmer in Thuril. We are among the last free people in Kelewan. If we could go there, you could take a position with the Coaldra, the Council of Warriors. They always have need for resourceful men. Then we could be together."

"We're together here, aren't we?"

Katala kissed him lightly. "Yes, dear Pug, we are. But we both remember what it was to be free, don't we?"

Pug sat up. "I try and put that sort of thing out of my mind."

She placed her arms around him, holding him as she would a child. "It must have been terrible in the swamps. We hear stories, but no one knows," she said softly.

"It is well that you don't."

She kissed him and soon they returned to that timeless, safe place shared by two, all thoughts of things terrible and alien forgotten. For the rest of the night they took pleasure in each other, discovering a depth of feeling new to each. Pug couldn't tell if she had known other men before, and didn't ask. It wasn't important to him. The only important thing was being there, with her, now. He was awash in a sea of new delights and emotions. He didn't understand his feelings entirely, but there was little doubt what he felt for Katala was more real, more compelling, than the worshipful, confused longings he had known when with Carline.

Weeks passed, and Pug found his life falling into a reassuring routine. He spent occasional evenings with the Lord of the Shinzawai playing chess—or shāh, as it was called here—and their conversations gave Pug insights into the nature of Tsurani life. He could no longer think of these people as aliens, for he saw their daily life as similar to what he had known as a boy. There were surprising differences, such as the strict adherence to an honor code, but the similarities far outnumbered the differences.

Katala became the centerpiece of his existence. They came together whenever they found time, sharing meals, a quick exchange of words, and every night that they could steal together. Pug was sure the other slaves in the household knew of their nighttime assignations, but the proximity of people in Tsurani life had bred a certain blindness to the personal habits of others, and no one cared a great deal about the comings and goings of two slaves.

Several weeks after his first night with Katala, Pug found himself alone with Kasumi, as Laurie was embroiled in another shouting match with the woodcrafter who was finishing his lute. The man considered Laurie somewhat unreasonable in objecting to the instrument's being finished in bright yellow paint with purple trim. And he saw absolutely no merit in leaving the natural wood tones exposed. Pug and Kasumi left the singer explaining to the woodcrafter the requirements of wood for proper resonance, seemingly intent on convincing by volume as much as by logic.

They walked toward the stable area. Several more captured horses had been purchased by agents of the Lord of the Shinzawai and had been sent to his estate, at what Pug took to be a great deal of expense and some political maneuvering. Whenever alone with the slaves, Kasumi spoke the King's Tongue and insisted they call him by name. He showed a quickness in learning the language that matched his quickness in learning to ride.

"Friend Laurie," said the older son of the house, "will never make a proper slave from a Tsurani point of view. He has no appreciation of our arts."

Pug listened to the argument that still could be heard coming from the woodcarver's building. "I think it more the case of his being concerned over the proper appreciation of his art."

They reached the corral and watched as a spirited grey stallion reared and whinnied at their approach. The horse had been brought in a week ago, securely tied by several leads to a wagon, and had repeatedly tried to attack anyone who came close.

"Why do you think this one is so troublesome, Pug?"

Pug watched the magnificent animal run around the corral, herding the other horses away from the men. When the mares and another, less dominant, stallion were safely away, the grey turned and watched the two men warily.

"I'm not sure. Either he's simply a badly tempered animal, perhaps from mishandling, or he's a specially trained war-horse. Most of our war mounts are trained not to shy in battle, to remain silent when held, to respond to their rider's command in times of stress. A few, mostly ridden by lords, are specially trained to obey only their master, and they are weapons as much as transport, being schooled to attack. He may be one of these."

Kasumi watched him closely as he pawed the ground and tossed his head. "I shall ride him someday," he said. "In any event, he will sire a strong line. We now number five mares, and Father has secured another five. They will arrive in a few weeks, and we are scouring every estate in the Empire to find more." Kasumi got a far-off look and mused, "When I was first upon your world, Pug, I hated the sight of horses. They rode down upon us and our soldiers died. But then I came to see what magnificent creatures they are. There were other prisoners, when I was still upon your world, who said you have noble families who are known for nothing so much as the fine stock of horses they breed. Someday the finest horses in the Empire shall be Shinzawai horses."

"By the look of these, you have a good start, though from what little I know, I think you need a larger stock for breeding."

"We shall have as many as it takes."

"Kasumi, how can your leaders spare these captured animals from the war effort? You must surely see the need to quickly build mounted units if you are going to advance your conquest."

Kasumi's face took on a rueful expression. "Our leaders, for the most part, are tradition-bound, Pug. They refuse to see any wisdom in training cavalry. They are fools. Your horsemen ride over our warriors and yet they pretend we cannot learn anything, calling your people barbarians. I once sieged a castle in your homeland, and those who defended taught me much about warcraft. Many would brand me traitor for saying such, but we have held our own only by force of numbers. For the most part, your generals have more skill. Trying to keep one's soldiers alive, rather than sending them to their death, teaches a certain craftiness.

"No, the truth of the matter is we are led by men who—" he stopped, realizing he was speaking dangerously. "The truth is," he said at last, "we are as stiff-necked a people as you."

He studied Pug's face for a moment, then smiled. "We raided for horses during the first year, so that the Warlord's Great Ones could study the beasts, to see if they were intelligent allies, like our cho-ja, or merely animals. It was a fairly comical scene. The Warlord insisted he be the first to try to ride a horse. I suspect he chose one much like this big grey, for no sooner did he approach the animal than the horse attacked, nearly killing him. His honor won't permit any other to ride when he failed. And I think he was fearful of trying again with another animal. Our Warlord, Almecho, is a man of considerable pride and temper, even for a Tsurani."

Pug said, "Then how can your father continue to purchase captured horses? And how can you ride in defiance of his order?"

Kasumi's smile broadened. "My father is a man of considerable influence in the council. Our politics is strangely twisted, and there are ways to bend any command, even from the Warlord or High Council, and any order, save one from the Light of Heaven himself. But most of all it is because these horses are here and the Warlord is not."

Since coming to the estate of the Shinzawai, Pug had been troubled by whatever Kasumi and his father were plotting. That they were embroiled in some Tsurani political intrigue he doubted not, but what it might prove to be he had no idea. A powerful lord like Kamatsu would not spend this much effort upon satisfying a whim of even a son as favored as Kasumi. Still, Pug knew better than to involve himself any more than he was involved by circumstance. He changed the topic of conversation. "Kasumi, I was wondering something."

"Yes?"

"What is the law regarding the marriage of slaves?"

Kasumi seemed unsurprised by the question. "Slaves may marry with their master's permission. But permission is rarely given. Once married, a man and wife may not be separated, nor can children be sold away so long as the parents live. That is the law. Should a married couple live a long time, an estate could become burdened with three or four generations of slaves, many more than they could economically support. But occasionally permission is granted. Why, do you wish Katala for your wife?"

Pug looked surprised. "You know?"

Without arrogance, Kasumi said, "Nothing occurs upon my father's estate which he is ignorant of, and he confides in me. It is a great honor."

Pug nodded thoughtfully. "I don't know yet. I feel much for her, but something holds me back. It's as if . . ." He shrugged, at a loss for words.

Kasumi regarded him closely for a time, then said, "It is by my father's whim you live and by his whim how you live." Kasumi stopped for a minute, and Pug became painfully aware of how large a gulf still stood between the two men, one the son of a powerful lord and the other the lowest of his father's property, a slave. The false veneer of friendship was ripped away, and Pug again knew what he had learned in the swamp: here life was cheap, and only this man's pleasure, or his father's, stood between Pug and destruction.

As if reading Pug's mind, Kasumi said, "Remember, Pug, the law is strict. A slave may never be freed. Still, there is the swamp, and there is here. And to us of Tsuranuanni, you of the Kingdom are very impatient."

Pug knew Kasumi was trying to tell him something, something perhaps important. For all his openness at times, Kasumi could easily revert to a Tsurani manner Pug could only call cryptic. There was an unvoiced tension behind Kasami's words, and Pug thought it best not to press. Changing the topic of conversation again, he asked, "How goes the war, Kasumi?"

Kasumi sighed. "Badly for both sides." He watched the grey stallion. "We fight along stable lines, unchanged in the last three years. Our last two offensives were blunted, but your army also could make no gains. Now weeks pass without fighting. Then your countrymen raid one of our enclaves, and we return the compliment. Little is accomplished except the spilling of blood. It is all very senseless and there is little honor to be won."

Pug was surprised. Everything he had seen of the

Tsurani reinforced Meecham's observation of years ago, that the Tsurani were a very warlike race. Everywhere he had looked when traveling to this estate, he had seen soldiers. Both sons of the house were soldiers, as had been their father in his youth. Hokanu was commander of the household guard—and a soldier by courtesy only—but he would someday command as his older brother did. His dealing with the slave master at the swamp camp showed a ruthless efficiency in Hokanu, and Pug knew it to be no quirk. He was Tsurani, and the Tsurani code was taught at a very early age, and fiercely followed.

Kasumi sensed he was being studied, and said, "I fear I am becoming softened by your outlandish ways, Pug."

Suddenly Pug spoke up. "Kasumi, I do wish to ask your father's permission to marry Katala."

Kasumi sighed. "Listen well, Pug. I tried to instruct you, but you did not seem to catch my meaning. Now I will put it plainly. You may ask, but it will be refused."

Pug began to object, but Kasumi cut him off. "I have said, you are impatient people. More I cannot say, but there are reasons, Pug."

Anger flared in Pug's eyes, and Kasumi said, in the King's Tongue, "Say a word in anger within earshot of any soldier of this house, and you are a dead slave." He indicated soldiers walking toward them.

Stiffly, Pug said, "Your will, master."

Witnessing the bitterness of Pug's expression, Kasumi softly repeated, "There are reasons, Pug." For a moment he was trying to be other than a Tsurani master, a friend trying to ease pain. He locked gaze with Pug, then a veil dropped over Kasumi's eyes and once more they were slave and master.

Pug lowered his eyes as was expected of a slave and Kasumi said, "See to the horses." He strode away, leaving Pug alone.

Pug never spoke of his request to Katala. She sensed that something troubled him deeply, something that seemed to add a bitter note to their otherwise joyful time together. He learned the depth of his love for her, and began to explore her complex nature. Besides being strong-willed, she was quick-minded. He only had to explain something to her once, and she understood. He learned to love her dry wit, a quality native to her people, the Thuril, and sharpened to a razor's edge by her captivity. She was an observant student of everything around her and commented unmercifully upon the foibles of everyone in the household, to their detriment and Pug's amusement. She insisted upon learning some of Pug's language, so he began teaching her the King's Tongue. She proved an apt student.

Two months went by uneventfully; then one night Pug and Laurie were called to the dining room of the master of the house. Laurie had completed work upon his lute and, though dissatisfied in a hundred little ways, judged it passable for playing. Tonight he was to play for the Lord of the Shinzawai.

They entered the room and saw that the lord was entertaining a guest, a black-robed man, the Great One whom they had glimpsed months ago. Pug stood by the door while Laurie took a place at the foot of the low dining table. Adjusting the cushion he sat upon, he began to play.

As the first notes hung in the air, he started singing: an old tune that Pug knew well. It sang of the joys of harvest and the riches of the land, and was a favorite in farm villages throughout the Kingdom. Besides Pug, only Kasumi understood the words, though his father could pick out a few that he had learned during his chess matches with Pug.

Pug had never heard Laurie sing before, and he was genuinely impressed. For all the troubadour's braggadocio, he was better than any Pug had heard. His voice was a clear, true instrument, expressive in both words and music of what he sang. When he was finished, the diners politely struck the table with eating knives, in what Pug assumed was the Tsurani equivalent of applause.

Laurie began another tune, a merry air played at festivals throughout the Kingdom. Pug remembered when he had last heard it, at the Festival of Banapis the year before he had left Crydee for Rillanon. He could almost see once more the familiar sights of home. For the first time in years, Pug felt a deep sadness and longing that nearly overwhelmed him.

Pug swallowed hard, easing the tightness in his

throat. Homesickness and hopeless frustration warred within him, and he could feel his hard-learned self-control slipping away. He quickly invoked one of the calming exercises he had been taught by Kulgan. A sense of well-being swept over him, and he relaxed. While Laurie performed, Pug used all his concentration to fend off the haunting memories of home. All his skills created an aura of calm he could stand within, a refuge from useless rage, the only legacy of reminiscence.

Several times during the performance, Pug felt the gaze of the Great One upon him. The man seemed to study him with some question in his eyes. When Laurie was finished, the magician leaned over and spoke to his host.

The Lord of the Shinzawai beckoned Pug to the table. When he was seated, the Great One spoke. "I must ask you something." His voice was clear and strong, and his tone reminded Pug of Kulgan when he was preparing Pug for lessons. "Who are you?"

The direct, simple question caught everyone at the table by surprise. The lord of the house seemed uncertain as to the magician's question and started to reply, "He is a slave—"

He was interrupted by the Great One's upraised hand. Pug said, "I am called Pug, master."

Again the man's dark eyes studied him. "Who are you?"

Pug felt flustered. He had never liked being the center of attention, and this time it was focused on him as never before in his life.

"I am Pug, once of the Duke of Crydee's court."

"Who are you, to stand here radiating the power?" At this all three men of the Shinzawai household started, and Laurie looked at Pug in confusion.

"I am a slave, master."

"Give me your hand."

Pug reached out and his hand was taken by the Great One. The man's lips moved and his eyes clouded over. Pug felt a warmth flow through his hand and over him. The room seemed to glow with a soft white haze. Soon all he could see was the magician's eyes. His mind fogged over, and time was suspended. He felt a pressure inside his head as if something was trying to intrude. He fought against it, and the pressure withdrew.

His vision cleared and the two dark eyes seemed to withdraw from his face, until he could see the entire room again. The magician let go of his hand. "Who are you?" A brief flicker in his eyes was the only sign of his deep concern.

"I am Pug, apprentice to the magician Kulgan."

At this the Lord of the Shinzawai blanched, confusion registering on his face. "How . . ."

The black-robed Great One rose and announced, "This slave is no longer property of this house. He is now the province of the Assembly."

The room fell silent. Pug couldn't understand what was happening and felt afraid.

The magician drew forth a device from his robe. Pug remembered that he had seen one before, during the raid on the Tsurani camp, and his fear mounted. The magician activated it, and it buzzed as the other one had. He placed his hand on Pug's shoulder, and the room disappeared in a grey haze.

THREE

Changeling

The Elf Prince sat quietly.

Calin awaited his mother. There was much on his mind, and he needed to speak with her this night. There had been little chance for that of late, for as the war had grown in scope he found less time to abide in the bowers of Elvandar. As Warleader of the elves, he had been in the field nearly every day since the last time the outworlders had tried to forge across the river.

Since the siege of Castle Crydee three years before, the outworlders had come each spring, swarming across the river like ants, a dozen for each elf. Each year elven magic had defeated them. Hundreds would enter the sleeping glades to fall into the endless sleep, their bodies being consumed by the soil, to nourish the magic trees. Others would answer the dryads' call, following the enchanted sprites' songs, until in their passion for the elemental beings they would die of thirst while still in their inhuman lovers' embrace, feeding the dryads with their lives. Others would fall to the creatures of the forests, the giant wolves, bears, and lions who answered the call of the elven war horns. The very branches and roots of the trees of the elven forests would resist the invaders until they turned and fled.

But this year, for the first time, the Black Robes had come. Much of the elven magic had been blunted. The elves had prevailed, but Calin wondered how they would fare when the outworlders returned.

This year the dwarves of the Grey Towers had again aided the elves. With the moredhel gone from the Green Heart, the dwarves had made swift passage from their wintering in the mountains, adding their numbers to the defense of Elvandar. For the third year since the siege at Crydee, the dwarves had proved the difference in holding the outworlders across the river. And again with the dwarves came the man called Tomas.

Calin looked up, then rose as his mother approached. Queen Aglaranna seated herself upon her throne and said, "My son, it is good to see you again."

"Mother, it is good to see you also." He sat at her feet and waited for the words he needed to come. His mother sat patiently, sensing his dark mood.

Finally he spoke. "I am troubled by Tomas."

"As am I," said the Queen, her expression clouded and pensive.

"Is that why you absent yourself when he comes to court?"

"For that . . . and other reasons."

"How can it be the Old Ones' magic still holds so strong after all these ages?"

A voice came from behind the throne. "So that's it, then?"

They turned, surprised, and Dolgan stepped from the gloom, lighting his pipe. Aglaranna looked incensed. "Are the dwarves of the Grey Towers known for eavesdropping, Dolgan?"

The dwarven chief ignored the bite of the question. "Usually not, my lady. But I was out for a walk—those little tree rooms fill with smoke right quickly—and I happened to overhear. I did not wish to interrupt."

Calin said, "You can move with stealth when you choose, friend Dolgan."

Dolgan shrugged and blew a cloud of smoke. "Elvenfolk are not the only ones with the knack of treading lightly. But we were speaking of the lad. If what you say is true, then it is a serious matter indeed. Had I known, I would never have allowed him to take the gift."

The Queen smiled at him. "It is not your fault, Dolgan. You could not have known. I have feared this since Tomas came among us in the mantle of the Old Ones. At first I thought the magic of the Valheru would not work for him, being a mortal, but now I can see he is less mortal each year.

"It was an unfortunate series of events brought this to pass. Our Spellweavers would have discovered that treasure ages ago, but for the dragon's magic. We spent centuries seeking out and destroying such relics, preventing their use by the moredhel. Now it is too late, for Tomas would never willingly let the armor be destroyed."

Dolgan puffed at his pipe. "Each winter he broods in the long halls, awaiting the coming of spring, and the coming of battle. There is little else for him. He sits and drinks, or stands at the door staring out into the snow, seeing what no other can see. He keeps the armor locked away in his room during such times, and when campaigning he never removes it, even to sleep. He has changed and it is not a natural changing. No, he would never willingly give up the armor."

"We could try to force him," said the Queen, "but that could prove unwise. There is something coming into being in him, something that may save my people, and I would risk much for them."

Dolgan said, "I do not understand, my lady."

"I am not sure I do either, Dolgan, but I am Queen of a people at war. A terrible foe savages our lands and each year grows bolder. The outworld magic is strong, perhaps stronger than any since the Old Ones vanished. It may be the magic in the dragon's gift will save my people."

Dolgan shook his head. "It seems strange such power could still reside in metal armor."

Aglaranna smiled at the dwarf. "Does it? What of the Hammer of Tholin you carry? Is it not vested with powers from ages past? Powers that mark you once more heir to the throne of the dwarves of the West?"

Dolgan looked hard at the Queen. "You know much of our ways, lady. I must never forget your girlish countenance masks ages of knowledge." He then brushed away her comment. "We have been done with kings for many years in the West, since Tholin vanished in the Mac Mordain Cadal. We do as well as those who obey old King Halfdan in Dorgin. But should my people wish the throne restored, we shall meet in moot, though not until this war is over. Now, what of the lad?"

Aglaranna looked troubled. "He is becoming what he is becoming. We can aid that transformation. Our Spellweavers work to this end already. Should the full power of the Valheru rise up in Tomas untempered, he would be able to brush aside our protective magic much as you would a bothersome twig barring your way upon the trail. But he is not an Old One born. His nature is as alien to the Valheru as their nature was to all others. Aided by our Spellweavers, his human ability to love, to know compassion, to understand, may temper the unchecked power of the Valheru. If so, he may . . . he may prove a boon to us all." Dolgan was visited by the certainty the Queen had been about to say something else, but remained silent as she continued. "Should that Valheru power become coupled with a human's capacity for blind hatred, savagery, and cruelty, then he would become something to fear. Only time will tell us what such a blending will produce."

"The Dragon Lords . . ." said Dolgan. "We have some mention of the Valheru in our lore, but only scraps here and there. I would understand more, if you'll permit."

The Queen looked off into the distance. "Our lore, eldest of all in the world today, tells of the Valheru, Dolgan. There is much of which I am forbidden to speak, names of power, fearful to invoke, things terrible to recall, but I may tell you this much. Long before man or dwarf came to this world, the Valheru ruled. They were part of this world, fashioned from the very fabric of its creation, nearly godlike in power and unfathomable in purpose. Their nature was chaotic and unpredictable. They were more powerful than any others. Upon the backs of the great dragons they flew, no place in the universe beyond their reach. To other worlds they roamed, bringing back that which pleased them, treasure and knowledge plundered from other beings. They were subject to no law but their own will and whim. They fought among themselves as often as not, and only death resolved conflicts. This world was their dominion. And we were their creatures.

"We and the moredhel were of one race then, and the Valheru bred us as you would cattle. Some were taken, from both races, for . . . personal pets, bred for beauty . . . and other qualities. Others were bred to tend the forests and fields. Those who lived in the wild became the forerunners of the elves, while those who remained with the Valheru were the forerunners of the moredhel.

"But then came a time of changing. Our masters ceased their internecine struggles and banded together. Why they did so is forgotten, though some among the moredhel may still know, for they were closer to our masters than we elves. We may have known their reasons then, but this was the time of the Chaos Wars and much was lost. Only this we know: all the servants of the Valheru were given freedom, and the Old Ones were never again seen by elf or moredhel. When the Chaos Wars raged, great rifts in time and space were opened, and it was through these that goblins, men, and dwarves came to this world. Few of our people or of the moredhel survived, but those that did rebuilt our homes. The moredhel longed to inherit the might of their lost masters, rather than seek their own destiny as the elves did, and used their cunning to find tokens of the Valheru, taking to the Dark Path. It is the reason we are so unalike, who once were brothers.

"The old magic is still powerful. In strength and bravery Tomas matches any. He took the magic unwittingly, and that may prove the difference. The old magic changed the moredhel into the Brotherhood of the Dark Path because they sought the power out of dark longings. Tomas was a boy of good and noble heart, with no taint of evil in his soul. Perchance he will grow to master the dark side of the magic."

Dolgan scratched his head. "'Tis a grave risk, then, from what you say. I was concerned for the lad, true, and gave little thought to the larger scheme of things. You know the way of it better than I, but I hope we'll not live to regret letting him keep the armor."

The Queen stepped down from her throne. "I also hope there will be no regrets, Dolgan. Here in Elvandar the old magic is softened, and Tomas is of lighter heart. Perhaps that is a sign we do the right thing, tempering the change rather than opposing it."

Dolgan made a courtly bow. "I yield to your wisdom, my lady. And I pray you are right."

The Queen bade them good night and left. Calin said, "I also pray my Mother-Queen speaks from wisdom, and not from some other feeling."

"I don't take your meaning, Elf Prince."

Calin looked down upon the short figure. "Don't play the fool with me, Dolgan. Your wisdom is widely known and rightly respected. You see it as well as I. Between my mother and Tomas there is something growing."

Dolgan sighed, the freshening breeze carrying away his pipe's smoke. "Aye, Calin, I've seen it as well. A look, little more, but enough."

"She looks upon Tomas as she once looked upon my Father-King, though she still denies it within herself."

"And there is something within Tomas," said the dwarf, watching the Elf Prince closely, "though it is less tender than what your lady feels. Still, he holds it well in check."

"Look to your friend, Dolgan. Should he try to press his suit for the Queen, there will be trouble."

"So much do you dislike him, Calin?"

Calin looked thoughtfully at Dolgan. "No, Dolgan. I do not dislike Tomas. I fear him. That is enough." Calin was silent for a while, then said, "We will never again bend knee before another master, we who live in Elvandar. Should my mother's hopes of how Tomas will change prove false, we shall have a reckoning."

Dolgan shook his head slowly. "That would prove a sorry day, Calin."

"That it would, Dolgan." Calin walked from the council ring, past his mother's throne, and left the dwarf alone. Dolgan looked out at the fairy lights of Elvandar, praying the Elf Queen's hopes would not prove unfounded.

Winds howled across the plains. Ashen-Shugar sat astride the broad shoulders of Shuruga. The great golden dragon's thoughts reached his master. *Do we hunt?* There was hunger in the dragon's mind.

"No. We wait."

A roar from above sounded as another great dragon came spiraling down, a magnificent black bellowing challenge. Shuruga raised his head and trumpeted his reply. To his master he said, *Do we fight?*

"No."

Ashen-Shugar sensed disappointment in his mount, but chose to ignore it. He watched as the other dragon settled gracefully to the ground a short distance away, folding its mighty wings across its back. Black scales reflected the hazy sunlight like polished ebony. The dragon's rider raised his hand in salute.

Ashen-Shugar returned the greeting and the other's dragon approached cautiously. Shuruga hissed, and Ashen-Shugar absently struck the beast with his fist. Shuruga lapsed into silence.

"Has the Ruler of the Eagles' Reaches finally come to join us?" asked the newcomer, Draken-Korin, the Lord of Tigers. His black-and-orange-striped armor sparkled as he dismounted from his dragon.

Out of courtesy, Ashen-Shugar dismounted as well. His hand never strayed far from his white-hilted sword of gold, for though times were changing, trust was unknown among the Valheru. In times past they would have fought as likely as not, but now the need for information was more pressing. Ashen-Shugar said, "No. I simply watch."

Draken-Korin regarded the Ruler of the Eagles' Reaches, his pale blue eyes revealing no emotion. "You alone have not agreed, Ashen-Shugar."

"Joining to plunder across the cosmos is one thing, Draken-Korin. This . . . this plan of yours is madness."

"What is this madness? I know not of what you speak. We are. We do. What more is there?"

"This is not our way."

"It is not our way to let others stand against our will. These new beings, they contest with us."

Ashen-Shugar raised his eyes skyward. "Yes, that is so. But they are not like others. They also are formed from the very stuff of this world, as are we."

"What does that matter? How many of our kin have you killed? How much blood has passed your lips? Whoever stands against you must be killed, or kill you. That is all."

"What of those left behind, the moredhel and the elves?"

"What of them? They are nothing."

"They are ours."

"You have grown strange under your mountains, Ashen-Shugar. They are our servants. It is not as if they possessed true power. They exist for our pleasure, nothing more. What concerns you?"

"I do not know. There is something. . . ."

"Tomas."

For an instant Tomas existed in two places. He shook his head and the visions vanished. He turned his head and saw Galain lying in the brush next to him. A force of elves and dwarves waited some distance behind. The young cousin of Prince Calin pointed toward the Tsurani camp across the river. Tomas followed his companion's gesture and saw the outworld soldiers sitting near their campfires, and smiled. "They hug their camps," he whispered.

Galain nodded. "We have stung them enough that they seek the warmth of their campfires."

The late spring evening mist shrouded the area, mantling the Tsurani camp in haze. Even the campfires seemed to burn less brightly. Tomas again studied the camp. "I mark thirty, with thirty more in each camp east and west."

Galain said nothing, waiting for Tomas's next command. Though Calin was Warleader of Elvandar, Tomas had assumed command of the forces of elves and dwarves. It was never clear when captaincy had passed to him, but slowly, as he had grown in stature, he had grown in leadership. In battle he would simply shout for something to be done, and elves and dwarves would rush to obey. At first it had been because the commands were logical and obvious. But the pattern had become accepted, and now they obeyed because it was Tomas who commanded.

Tomas motioned for Galin to follow and moved away from the riverbank, until they were safely out of sight of the Tsurani camp, among those who waited deep within the trees. Dolgan looked at the young man who once had been the boy he saved from the mines of Mac Mordain Cadal.

Tomas stood six inches past six feet in height, as tall as any elf. He walked with a powerful self-assurance, a warrior born. In the six years he had been with the dwarves he had become a man . . . and more. Dolgan watched him, as Tomas surveyed the warriors gathered before him, and knew Tomas could now walk the dark mines of the Grey Towers without fear or danger.

"Have the other scouts returned?"

Dolgan nodded, signaling for them to come forward. Three elves and three dwarves approached. "Any signs of the Black Robes?"

When the scouts indicated no, the man in white and gold frowned. "We would do well to capture one of them, and carry him to Elvandar. Their last attack was the deepest yet. I would give much to know the limits of their power."

Dolgan took out his pipe, gauging they were far enough from the river for it not to be seen. As he lit it, he said, "The Tsurani guard the Black Robes like a dragon guards its treasure."

Tomas laughed at that, and Dolgan caught a glimpse of the boy he had known. "Aye, and it's a brave dwarf who loots a dragon's lair."

Galain said, "If they follow the pattern of the last three years, they most likely are done with us for the season. It is possible we shall not see another Black Robe until next spring."

Tomas looked thoughtful, his pale eyes seemingly aglow with a light of their own. "Their pattern . . . their pattern is to take, to hold, then to take more. We have been willing to let them do as they wish, so long as they do not cross the river. It is time to change that pattern. And if we trouble them enough, we may have the opportunity to seize one of these Black Robes."

Dolgan shook his head at the risk implicit in what Tomas proposed. Then, with a smile, Tomas added, "Besides, if we can't loosen their hold along the river for a time, the dwarves and I will be forced to winter here, for the outworlders are now deep into the Green Heart."

Galain looked at his tall friend. Tomas grew more elf-like each year, and Galain could appreciate the obscure humor that often marked his words. He knew Tomas would welcome staying near the Queen. But in spite of his worries over Tomas's magic, he had come to like the man. "How?"

"Send bowmen to the camps on the right and the left and beyond. When I call with the honk of a greylag, have them volley across the river, but from beyond those positions as if the main attack were coming from east and west." He smiled and there was no humor in his expression. "That should isolate this camp long enough to do some bloody work."

Galain nodded, and sent ten bowmen to each camp. The others made ready for the attack, and after sufficient time, Tomas raised his hands to his mouth. Cupping them, he made the sound of a wild goose. A moment later he could hear shouting coming from east and west of the position across the river. The soldiers in the Tsurani camp stood and looked both ways, with several coming to the edge of the water, peering into the dark forest. Tomas raised his hand and dropped it with a chopping motion.

Suddenly it was raining elven arrows on the camp across the river and Tsurani soldiers were diving for their shields. Before they could fully recover, Tomas was leading a charge of dwarves across the shallow sandbar ford. Another flight of arrows passed overhead, then the elves shouldered bows, drew swords, and charged after the dwarves, all save a dozen who would stay to offer covering fire should it be needed.

Tomas was first ashore and struck down a Tsurani guard who met him at the river's edge. Quickly he was among them, wreaking mayhem. Tsurani blood exploded off his golden blade, and the screams of wounded and dying men filled the damp night.

Dolgan slew a guard and found none to stand against him. He turned and saw Galain standing over another dead Tsurani, but staring at something beyond. The dwarf followed his gaze to where Tomas was standing over a wounded Tsurani soldier who lay with blood running down his face from a scalp wound, an arm upraised in a plea for mercy. Over him stood Tomas, his face an alien mask of rage. With a strange and terrible cry, in a voice cruel and harsh, he brought down his golden sword and ended the Tsurani's life. He turned quickly, seeking more foes. When none presented themselves, he seemed to go blank for a moment, then his eyes refocused.

Galain heard a dwarf call, "They come." Shouts came from the other Tsurani camps as they discovered the ruse and quickly approached the true battle site.

Without a word, Tomas's party hurried across the water. They reached the other side as Tsurani bowmen fired upon them, to be answered by elves on the opposite shore. The attacking group quickly fell back deeply into the trees, until they were a safe distance away.

When they stopped, the elves and dwarves sat down, to catch their wind, and to rest from the battle surge still in their blood. Galain looked to Tomas and said, "We did well. No one lost, and only a few slightly wounded, and thirty outworlders slain."

Tomas didn't smile, but looked thoughtful for a moment, as if hearing something. He turned to look at Galain, as if the elf's words were finally registering. "Aye, we did well, but we must strike again, tomorrow and the next day and the next, until they act."

Night after night they crossed the river. They would attack a camp, and the next night strike miles away. A night would pass without attack, then the same camp would be raided three nights running. Sometimes a single arrow would take a guard from the opposite shore, then nothing, while his companions stood waiting for an attack that never came. Once they struck through the lines at dawn, after the defenders had decided that no attack was coming. They overran a camp, ranging miles into the south forest, and took a baggage train, even slaughtering the strange six-legged beasts who pulled the wagons. Five separate fights were fought as they returned from that raid, and two dwarves and three elves were lost.

Now Tomas and his band, numbering over three

hundred elves and dwarves, sat awaiting word from other camps. They were eating a stew of venison, seasoned with mosses, roots, and tubers.

A runner came up to Tomas and Galain. "Word from the King's army." Behind him a figure in grey approached the campfire.

Tomas and Galain stood. "Hail, Long Leon of Natal," said the elf.

"Hail, Galain," answered the tall, black-skinned ranger.

An elf brought over bread and a bowl of steaming stew to the two newcomers and as they sat, Tomas said, "What news from the Duke?"

Between mouthfuls of food, the ranger said, "Lord Borric sends greetings. Things stand poorly. Like moss on a tree, the Tsurani slowly advance in the east. They take a few yards, then sit. They seem to be in no hurry. The Duke's best guess is they seek to reach the coast by next year, isolating the Free Cities from the north. Then perhaps an attack toward Zūn or LaMut. Who can say?"

Tomas asked, "Any news from Crydee?"

"Pigeons arrived just before I left. Prince Arutha holds fast against the Tsurani. They have luck as poor there as here. But they move southward through the Green Heart." He surveyed the dwarves and Tomas. "I am surprised that you could reach Elvandar."

Dolgan puffed his pipe. "It was a long trek. We had to move swiftly and with stealth. It is unlikely we will be able to return to the mountains now the invaders are aroused. Once in place, they are loath to yield what they have gained."

Tomas paced before the fire. "How did you elude their sentries?"

"Your raids are causing much confusion in their ranks. Men who faced the Armies of the West were pulled out of the line to rush to the river. I simply followed one such group. They never thought to look behind. I had only to slip past their lines when they withdrew and then again across the river."

Calin said, "How many do they bring against us?"

Leon shrugged. "I saw six companies, there must be others." They had estimated a Tsurani company at twenty squads each of thirty men.

Tomas slapped his gloved hand together. "They would bring three thousand men back only if they were planning another crossing. They must seek to drive us deep into the forest again, to keep us from harrying their positions." He crossed to stand over the ranger. "Do any of the black-robed ones come?"

"From time to time I saw one with the company I followed."

Tomas again slapped his hands. "This time they come in force. Send word to the other camps. In two days' time all the host of Elvandar is to meet at the Queen's court, save scouts and runners who will watch the outworlders."

Silently runners sprang up from the fire and hurried off to carry word to the other elven bands strung out along the banks of the river Crydee.

Ashen-Shugar sat upon his throne, oblivious to the dancers. The moredhel females had been chosen for their beauty and grace, but he saw them not. His mind's eye was far away, seeking the coming battle. Inside, a strangeness, a hollow feeling without name, came into being.

It is called sadness, said the voice within.

Ashen-Shugar thought: Who are you to visit me in my solitude?

I am you. I am what you will become. I am what you were. I am Tomas.

A shout from below brought Tomas from his reverie. He rose and left his small room, crossing a tree-branch bridge to the level of the Queen's court. At a rail, he could make out the dim figures of hundreds of dwarves camped below the heights of Elvandar. He stood for a time watching the campfires below. Each hour, hundreds more elven and dwarven warriors made their way to join this army he marshaled. Tomorrow he would sit in council with Calin, Tathar, Dolgan, and others and make known his plan to meet the coming assault.

Six years of fighting had given Tomas a strange counterpoint to the dreams that still troubled his sleep. When the battle rage took him, he existed in another's dreams. When he was away from the elven forest, the call to enter those dreams became ever more difficult to stem.

He felt no fear of these visitations, as he had at first. He was more than human because of some long-dead being's dreams. There were powers within him, powers that he could use, and they were now part of him, as they had been part of the wearer of the white and gold. He knew that he would never be Tomas of Crydee again, but what was he becoming . . . ?

The slightest hint of a footfall sounded behind him. Without turning, he said, "Good eve, my lady."

The Elf Queen came to stand next to him, a studied expression on her face. "Your senses are elven now," she said in her own language.

"So it seems, Shining Moon," he answered in the same language, using the ancient translation of her name.

He turned to face her and saw wonder in her eyes. She reached out and gently touched his face. "Is this the boy who stood so flustered in the Duke's council chamber at the thought of speaking before the Elf Queen, who now speaks the true tongue as if born to it?"

He pushed away her hand, gently. "I am what I am, what you see." His voice was firm, commanding.

She studied his face, holding back a shudder as she recognized something fearful within his countenance. "But what do I see, Tomas?"

Ignoring her question, he said, "Why do you avoid me, lady?"

Gently she spoke. "There is this thing growing between us that may not be. It sprang into existence the moment you first came to us, Tomas."

Almost with a note of amusement, Tomas said, "Before that, lady, from the first I gazed upon you." He stood tall over her. "And why may this thing not be? Who better to sit at your side?"

She moved away from him, her control lost for a brief moment. In that instant he saw what few had ever seen: the Elf Queen confused and unsure, doubting her own ancient wisdom. "Whatever else, you are man. Despite what powers are granted you, it is a man's span alloted to you. I will reign until my spirit travels to the Blessed Isles to be with my lord who has already made the journey. Then Calin rules, as son of a king, as King. Thus it is with my people."

Tomas reached for her and turned her to face him. "It
was not always so."

Her eyes showed a spark of fear. "No, we were not
always a free people."

She sensed impatience within him, but she also saw
him struggle with it as he forced his voice to calmness. "Do
you then feel nothing?"

She took a step away. "I would lie if I said not. But it is
a strange pulling, and something that fills me with uncertainty and with no small dread. If you become more the
Valheru, more than the man can master, then we should
not welcome you here. We would not allow the return of
the Old Ones."

Tomas laughed, with a strange mixture of humor and
bitterness. "As a boy I beheld you, and was filled with a
boy's longing. Now I am a man and behold you with a
man's longing. Is the power which makes me bold enough
to seek you out, the power which gives me the means to do
so, that which will also keep us apart?"

Aglaranna put her hand to her cheek. "I know not. It
has never been with the royal family to be other than what
we are. Others may seek alliance with humans. I would not
have that sadness when you are old and grey and I am still
as you see me."

Tomas's eyes flashed, and his voice gained a harsh
edge. "That will never happen, lady. I shall live a thousand
years in this glade. Of that I have no doubt. But I shall
trouble you no more . . . until other matters are settled.
This thing is willed by fate to be, Aglaranna. You will come
to know that."

She stood with her hand raised to her mouth, and her
eyes moist with emotion. He walked away, leaving her
alone in her court to consider what he had said. For the first
time since her Lord-King had passed over, Aglaranna knew
two conflicting emotions: fear and longing.

Tomas turned at a shout from the edge of the clearing.
An elf was walking from the trees followed by a simply
dressed man. He stopped his conversation with Calin and
Dolgan and the three hurried to follow the stranger as he
was guided up to the Queen's court. Aglaranna sat on her
throne, her elders arranged on benches to either side.
Tathar stood next to the Queen.

The stranger approached the throne and made a slight bow. Tathar threw a quick glance at the sentry who had escorted the man, but the elf looked bemused. The man in brown said, "Greetings, lady," in perfect Elvish.

Aglaranna answered in the King's Tongue. "You come boldly among us, stranger."

The man smiled, leaning on his staff. "Still, I did seek a guide, for I would not enter Elvandar unbidden."

Tathar said, "I think yon guide had little choice."

The man said, "There is always a choice, though it is not always apparent."

Tomas stepped forward. "What is your purpose here?"

Turning at the voice, the man smiled. "Ah! The wearer of the dragon's gift. Well met, Tomas of Crydee."

Tomas stepped back. The man's eyes radiated power and his easy manner veiled strength that Tomas could feel. "Who are you?"

The man said, "I have many names, but here I am called Macros the Black." He pointed with his staff and swept it around the gathered watchers. "I have come, for you have embarked upon a bold plan." At the last, he pointed his staff at Tomas. He dropped the tip and leaned on the staff again. "But the plan to capture a Black Robe will bring naught but destruction to Elvandar should you not have my aid." He smiled slightly. "A Black Robe you shall have in time, but not yet."

Aglaranna arose. Her shoulders were back and her eyes looked straight into his. "You know much."

Macros inclined his head slightly. "Aye, I know much, more than is sometimes comforting." He stepped past her and placed a hand upon Tomas's shoulder. Guiding Tomas to a seat near where the Queen stood, Macros forced him to sit with a gentle pressure on his shoulder. He took a seat next to him and laid the staff against the crook of his neck. Looking at the Queen, he said, "The Tsurani come at first light, and they will drive straight through to Elvandar."

Tathar stepped before Macros and said, "How do you know this?"

Macros smiled again. "Do you not remember me in council with your father?"

Tathar stepped back, his eyes widening. "You . . ."

"I am he, though I am no longer called as I was then."

Tathar looked troubled. "So long ago. I would not have thought it possible."

Macros said, "Much is possible." He looked pointedly from the Queen to Tomas.

Aglaranna slowly sat down, masking her discomfort. "Are you the sorcerer?"

Macros nodded. "So I am called, though there is more in the tale than can be told now. Will you heed me?"

Tathar nodded to the Queen. "Long ago, this one came to our aid. I do not understand how it can be the same man, but he was then a true friend to your father and mine. He can be trusted."

"What, then, is your counsel?" asked the Queen.

"The Tsurani magicians have marked your sentries, knowing where they hide. At first light they will come, breaking across the river in two waves, like the horns of a bull. As you meet them, a wave of the creatures called cho-ja will come through the center, where your strength is weak. They have not thrown them against you yet, but the dwarves can tell you of their skill in warfare."

Dolgan stepped forward. "Aye, lady. They are fearsome creatures and fight in the dark as well as do my people. I had thought them confined to the mines."

Macros said, "And so they were, until the raids. They have brought up a host of them, which ready themselves across the river, beyond the sight of your scouts. They will come in numbers. The Tsurani tire of your raids and would put an end to the warring across the river. Their magicians have worked hard to learn the secrets of Elvandar, and now they know that should the sacred heart of the elven forests fall, the elves will be a force no longer."

Tomas said, "Then we shall hold back, and defend against the center."

Macros sat quietly for a moment, as if remembering something. "That is a start, but they bring their magicians with them, anxious as they are for an ending. Their magic will let their warriors pass through your forests unchecked by the power of your Spellweavers, and here they will come."

Aglaranna said, "Then we shall meet them here, and stand until the end."

Macros nodded. "Bravely said, lady, but you will need my aid."

Dolgan studied the sorcerer. "What can one man do?"

Macros stood. "Much. Upon the morrow, you shall see. Fear not, dwarf, the battle will be harsh and many will travel to the Blessed Isles, but with firm resolve, we shall prevail."

Tomas said, "You speak like one who has already seen these things happen."

Macros smiled, and his eyes said a thousand things, and nothing. "I do, Tomas of Crydee, do I not?" He turned to the others and with a sweep of his staff said, "Ready yourselves. I shall be with you." To the Queen he said, "I would rest; if you have a place for me?"

The Queen turned to the elf who had brought Macros to the council. "Take him to a room, bring him whatever he requires."

The sorcerer bowed and followed the guide. The others stood in silence, until Tomas said, "Let us make ready."

The night was soon to give way to dawn and the Queen stood alone near her throne. In all the years of her rule, she had never known a time like this. Her thoughts ran with hundreds of images, from times as long ago as her youth, and as recently as two nights ago.

"Seeking answers in the past, lady?"

She turned to see the sorcerer standing behind her, leaning on his staff. He approached and stood next to her.

"Can you read my mind, sorcerer?"

With a smile and a wave of his hand, Macros said, "No, my lady. But there is much I do know and can see. Your heart is heavy, and your mind burdened."

"Do you understand why?"

Macros laughed softly. "Without question. Still, I would speak to you of these things."

"Why, sorcerer? What part do you play?"

Macros looked out over the lights of Elvandar. "A part, much as any man plays."

"But you know yours well."

"True. It is given to some to understand what is obscure to others. Such is my fate."

"Why have you come?"

"Because there is need. Without me, Elvandar may

fall, and that must not be. It is so ordained, and I can only do my part."

"Will you stay if the battle is won?"

"No. I have other tasks. But I will come once more, when the need is again great."

"When?"

"That I may not tell you."

"Will it be soon?"

"Soon enough, though not soon enough."

"You speak in riddles."

Macros smiled, a crooked, sad smile. "Life is a riddle. It is in the hands of the gods. Their will shall prevail, and many mortals will find their lives changed."

"Tomas?" Aglaranna looked deep into the sorcerer's dark eyes.

"He most visibly, but all who live through these times."

"What is he?"

"What would you have him be?"

The Elf Queen found herself unable to answer. Macros placed his hand lightly on her shoulder. She felt calm flow from his fingers and heard herself say, "I would wish nothing of trouble upon my people, but the sight of him fills me with longing. I long for a man . . . a man with his . . . might. Tomas is more like my lost lord than he will ever know. And I fear him, for once I make the pledge, once I place him above me, I lose the power to rule. Do you think the elders would allow this? My people would never willingly place the yoke of the Valheru upon their necks again."

The sorcerer was silent for a time, then said, "For all my arts, there are things hidden from me, but understand this: there is a magic here fey beyond imagining. I cannot explain save to say it reaches across time, more than is apparent. For while the Valheru is present within Tomas now, so is Tomas present within the Valheru in ages past.

"Tomas wears the garb of Ashen-Shugar, last of the Dragon Lords. When the Chaos Wars raged, he alone remained upon this world, for he felt things alien to his kind."

"Tomas?"

Macros smiled. "Think not upon this overly long, lady.

These sorts of paradox can send the mind reeling. What Ashen-Shugar felt was an obligation to protect this world."

Aglaranna studied Macros's face in the twinkling lights of Elvandar. "You know more of the ancient lore than any other man, sorcerer."

"I have been . . . given much, lady." He looked over the elven forests and spoke more to himself than to the Queen: "Soon will come a time of testing for Tomas. I cannot be sure what will occur, but this much I do know. Somehow the boy from Crydee, in his love for you and yours, in his simple human caring, has so far withstood the most powerful member of the most powerful mortal race ever to have lived upon this world. And he is well served in withstanding the terrible pain of that conflict of two natures by the soft arts of your Spellweavers."

She looked hard at Macros. "You know of this?"

He laughed with genuine amusement. "Lady, I am not without some vanity. Little magic in this world escapes my notice. What you have done is wise, and may tip the balance in Tomas's favor."

"That is the thought I plead to myself," said Aglaranna quietly, "when I see in Tomas a lord to match the King of my youth, the husband taken too soon from my side. Can it be true?"

"Should he survive the time of testing, yes. It may be the conflict will prove the end of both Tomas and Ashen-Shugar. But should Tomas survive, he may become what you most secretly long for.

"Now I shall tell you something only the gods and I know. I can judge many things yet to come, but much is still unknown to me. One thing I know is this: at your side, Tomas may grow to rule wisely and well and, as his youth is replaced by wisdom, grow to be the lord of your wishes, if his power can be somehow tempered by his human heart. Should he be sent away, a terrible fate may await both the Kingdom and the free peoples of the West."

Her eyes asked the question and he continued, "I cannot see into that dark future, lady; I can only surmise. Should he come into his powers with the dark side in preeminence, he will be a terrible force, one that must be destroyed. Those who see the battle madness come upon him see but a shadow of the true darkness bound up within him. Even if a balance is struck and Tomas's humanity survives, but still you send him away, then humanity's capacity for anger, pain, and hate may come forth. I ask you: should Tomas be driven away and someday raise the dragon standard in the north, what would occur?"

The Queen became frightened, and openly showed it, her mask of control lost completely. "The moredhel would gather."

"Aye, my lady. Not as bands of troublesome bandits, but as a host. Twenty thousand Dark Brothers, and with them a hundred thousand goblins, and companies of men whose dark nature would seek profit in the destruction and savagery to follow. A mighty army under the steel glove of a warrior born, a general whom even your own people follow without question."

"Do you advise me to keep him here?"

"I can only point out the alternatives. You must decide."

The Elf Queen threw back her head, her red-gold locks flying and her eyes moist, looking out over Elvandar. The first light of day was breaking. Rosy light lanced through the trees, casting shadows of deep blue. The morning songs of birds could be heard around the glades. She turned to Macros, wishing to thank him for his counsel, and found him gone.

The Tsurani advanced as Macros had foretold. The cho-ja attacked across the river, after the two human waves had carried the flanks. Tomas had set skirmishers, lines of bowmen with a few shield guards, who retreated and fired into the advancing army, giving the impression of resistance.

Tomas stood before the assembled army of Elvandar and the dwarves of the Grey Towers, only fifteen hundred arrayed against the six thousand invaders and their magicians. In silence they waited. As the enemy approached, the shouts of Tsurani warriors and the cries of those who fell to elvish arrows could be heard through the forest. Tomas looked up at the Queen, standing on a balcony overlooking the scene of the coming battle, next to the sorcerer.

Suddenly elves were running toward them, and the first flashes of brightly colored Tsurani armor could be seen through the trees. When the skirmishers had rejoined the main force, Tomas raised his sword.

"Wait," a voice cried out from above and the sorcerer pointed across the open clearing, where the first elements of the Tsurani forces were running into the clearing. Confronted by the waiting elven army, the vanguard halted and waited as their comrades joined them. Their officers ordered ranks formed, for here was fighting they could understand, two armies meeting on an open plain, and the advantage was theirs.

The cho-ja also stood in ordered ranks, heeding the officers' shouted commands. Tomas was fascinated, for he still knew little of these creatures and counted them animals as much as intelligent allies of the Tsurani.

Macros shouted, "Wait!" again and waved his staff above his head, inscribing broad circles in the air. A stillness descended upon the glade.

Suddenly an owl flew past Tomas's head, straight for the Tsurani lines. It circled above the aliens for a moment, then swooped and struck a soldier in the face. The man screamed in pain as its talons clawed his eyes.

A hawk sped past and duplicated the owl's attack. Then a large black rook descended from the sky. A flight of sparrows erupted from the trees behind the Tsurani and pecked at faces and unprotected arms. Birds came flying from every part of the forest and attacked the invaders. Soon the air was filled with the sound of flapping wings as every manner of bird in the forest descended upon the Tsurani. Thousands of them, from the smallest hummingbird to the mighty eagle, attacked the outworld host. Men cried out, and broke formation and ran, trying to avoid the wicked beaks and talons that tried to scratch at eyes, pull at cloaks, and tear flesh. The cho-ja reared, for though their armored hide was immune to the pecking and clawing, their large, jewellike eyes were easy targets for the feathered attackers.

A shout went up from the elves as the Tsurani lines dissolved in disorder. Tomas gave the order, and elven bowmen added feathered arrows to the fray. Tsurani soldiers were struck and fell before they could come to

grips with the enemy. Their own bowmen could not return
the fire, for they were harried by a hundred tiny foes.

The elves watched as the Tsurani tried to hold position, while the birds continued their bloody work in their
midst. The Tsurani fought back as best they could, striking
down many birds in mid-flight, but for each one killed,
three took its place.

Suddenly a hissing, tearing sound cut through the din.
There was an instant of silence as everything on the
Tsurani side of the clearing seemed to pause. Then the
birds exploded upward, accompanied by a sizzling crackle
of energy, as if thrown back by some unseen force. As the
birds cleared the area, Tomas could see the black robes of
the Tsurani magicians as they moved through their forces,
restoring order. Hundreds of wounded Tsurani lay upon
the ground, but the battle-tempered aliens quickly re-
formed their lines, ignoring the injured.

The enormous flight of birds gathered again above the
invaders and started to dive. Instantly a glowing red shield
of energy formed around the Tsurani. As the birds struck,
they stiffened and fell, their feathers smoldering and filling
the air with a pungent burning stench. Elven arrows that
struck the barrier were halted in mid-flight and burst into
flame, falling harmlessly to the ground.

Tomas gave the order to stop the bow fire and turned
to look at Macros. Again the sorcerer shouted, "Wait!"

Macros waved his staff and the birds dispersed,
hearing his silent command. The staff extended toward the
Tsurani, as Macros aimed it at the red barrier. A golden bolt
of energy shot forth. It sped across the clearing and pierced
the red barrier, to strike a black-robed magician in the
chest. The magician crumpled to the ground, and a shout
of horror and outrage went up from the assembled Tsurani.
The other magicians turned their attention to the platform
above the elven army, and blue globes of fire shot toward
Macros. Tomas shouted, "Aglaranna!" in rage as the tiny
blue stars struck the platform, obliterating all sight of her in
a blinding display of exploding light. Then he could see
again.

The sorcerer stood upon the platform unharmed, as
did the Queen. Tathar pulled her away, and Macros
pointed with his staff again. Another black-robed magician

fell. The four remaining magicians looked upon Macros's survival and counterattack with expressions of mixed awe and anger, clearly seen across the glade. They redoubled their assault upon the sorcerer, wave after wave of blue light and fire striking Macros's protective barrier. All upon the ground were forced to turn away from the sight, lest they become blinded by the terrible energies being unleashed. After this magical onslaught was ended, Tomas looked upward, and again the sorcerer was unharmed.

One magician gave out a cry of pure anguish and pulled a device from his robe. Activating it, he vanished from the clearing, followed moments later by his three companions. Macros looked down at Tomas, pointed his staff at the Tsurani host, and called, "Now!"

Tomas raised his sword and gave the signal to attack. A hail of arrows passed overhead as he led the charge across the clearing. The Tsurani were demoralized, their attack blunted by the birds and the sight of their magicians being driven away. Yet they stood their ground and took the charge. Hundreds had died from the claws and beaks of the birds, and more from the flights of arrows, but still they numbered three to one of the elves and dwarves.

The battle was joined and Tomas was caught up in a red haze that washed away any thought but to kill. Hacking right and left, he carved a path through the Tsurani, confounding their every attempt to strike him down. Tsurani and cho-ja both fell to his blade, as he delivered death with an even hand to all who stood before him.

Back and forth across the clearing the battle moved, as men and cho-ja, elf and dwarf fell. The sun moved higher in the sky, and there was no respite from the fray. The sounds of death filled the air, and high overhead the kites and vultures gathered.

Slowly the Tsurani press forced the elves and dwarves back. Slowly they moved toward the heart of Elvandar. There was a brief pause, as if both sides had struck a balance, when the adversaries moved away from each other leaving an open space between. Tomas heard the voice of the sorcerer ringing clear above the sounds of battle. "Back!" it cried, and to a man, the forces of Elvandar retreated.

The Tsurani paused a moment, then, sensing the hesitation of the elves and dwarves, started to press forward. Abruptly there came a rumbling sound and the earth trembled. All stopped moving and the Tsurani looked fearful, for dread premonitions filled them.

Tomas could see the trees shake, more and more violently, as the trembling increased. Suddenly there came a crescendo of noise, as if the grandfather of all thunder-claps pealed overhead. With the booming sound, a huge piece of earth erupted upward, as if heaved by some invisible giant's hand. The Tsurani who were standing on it shot upward, to fall hard to the ground, and those nearby were knocked aside.

Another piece of the ground erupted, then a third. Suddenly the air was full of giant pieces of earth that flew upward, then fell upon the Tsurani. Screams of terror filled the air, and the Tsurani turned and fled. There was no order to their retreat, for they flew from a place where the very earth attacked them. Tomas watched as the clearing was emptied of all but the dead and dying.

In a matter of minutes, the clearing was quiet, as the earth subsided and the shocked onlookers stood mute. The sounds of the Tsurani army retreating through the woods could be heard. Their cries told of other horrors being visited upon them as they fled.

Tomas felt weak and weary, and looked down to find his arms covered with blood. His tabard and shield and his golden sword were clean as they always were, but for the first time he could feel human life splattered upon himself. In Elvandar the battle madness did not stay with him, and he felt sick to his inner being.

He turned and said softly, "It is over." There was a faint cheer from the elves and dwarves, but it was halfhearted, for none felt like victors. They had seen a mighty host felled by primeval forces, elemental powers that defied description.

Tomas walked slowly past Calin and Dolgan and mounted the stairs. The Elf Prince sent soldiers to follow the retreating invaders, to care for the wounded, and to give the dying Tsurani quick mercy.

Tomas made his way to the small room where he abided, and pulled aside the curtain. He sat heavily upon his pallet, tossing aside his sword and shield. A dull throbbing in his head caused him to close his eyes. Memories came flooding in.

The heavens were torn with mad vortices of energy crashing from horizon to horizon. Ashen-Shugar sat upon mighty Shuruga's back, watching the very fabric of time and space rent.

A clarion rang, the heralding note heard by dint of his magic. The moment he awaited had come. Urging Shuruga upward, Ashen-Shugar's eyes searched the heavens, seeking what must come against the mad display in the skies. A sudden stiffening of Shuruga under him coincided with his sighting of his prey. The figure of Draken-Korin grew recognizable as he reined in his black dragon. There was a strangeness in his eyes, and for the first time in his long memory Ashen-Shugar began to understand the meaning of horror. He could not put a name to it, could not describe it, but in the tortured eyes of Draken-Korin he saw it.

Ashen-Shugar spurred Shuruga forward. The mighty golden dragon roared his challenge, answered by Draken-Korin's equally mighty black. The two clashed in the sky, and their riders worked their arts upon each other.

Ashen-Shugar's golden blade arched overhead and struck, cleaving the black shield with the grinning tiger's head in twain. It was almost too easy, as Ashen-Shugar had known it would be. Draken-Korin had given up too much of his essence to that which was forming. Before the might of the last Valheru, he was little more than a mortal. Once, twice, three times more Ashen-Shugar struck and the last of his brothers fell from the back of his black dragon. Downward he tumbled to strike the ground. By force of will, Ashen-Shugar left Shuruga's back and floated to stand beside the helpless body of Draken-Korin, leaving Shuruga to finish his contest with the near-dead black dragon.

A spark of life still persisted within the broken form, life ages past remembering. A pleading look entered Draken-Korin's eyes as Ashen-Shugar approached. He whispered, "Why?"

Pointing heavenward with his golden blade, Ashen-Shugar said, "This obscenity should never have been allowed. You bring an end to all we knew."

Draken-Korin looked skyward to where Ashen-Shugar pointed. He watched the tumbling, raging display of energies, twisted, screaming rainbows of light jagged across the vault of the sky. He witnessed the new horror being formed from the twisted life force of his brothers and sisters, a raging, mindless thing of hate and anger.

In a croaking voice, Draken-Korin said, "They were so strong. We could never have dreamed." His face contorted in terror and hate as Ashen-Shugar raised his golden blade. "But I had the right!" he screamed.

Ashen-Shugar brought down his blade, cleanly severing the head of Draken-Korin from his body. At once both head and body were engulfed with a glimmering light, and the air hissed around Ashen-Shugar. Then the fallen Valheru vanished without trace, his essence returning to that mindless monster raging against the new gods. With bitterness Ashen-Shugar said, "There is no right. There is only power."

Is that how it was?

"Yes, that is how I slew the last of my brethren."

The others?

"They are now part of that." He indicated the terrible sky.

Together, never apart, they watched the madness above as the Chaos Wars raged. After a time, Ashen-Shugar said, "Come, this is an ending. Let us be done with it."

They began to walk toward the waiting Shuruga. Then a voice came.

"You are quiet."

Tomas opened his eyes. Before him knelt Aglaranna, a basin of herb-sweetened water and a cloth in her hand. She began washing the blood from his face and arms, saying nothing as he watched her.

When he was clean, she took a dry cloth to his face and said, "You look tired, my lord."

"I see many things, Aglaranna, things not meant for a man to see. I bear the weight of ages upon my soul and I am tired."

"Is there no comfort to be sought?"

He looked at her, their eyes locking. The commanding

gaze was tempered by a hint of gentleness, but still she was
forced to drop her eyes.

"Do you mock me, lady?"

She shook her head. "No, Tomas. I . . . came to
comfort you, if you have need."

He reached out and took her hand, and drew her
toward him, hunger in his eyes. When she was encircled
by his embrace, feeling the rising passion in his body, she
heard him say, "My need is great, lady."

Looking into his pale eyes, she dropped the final
barriers between them. "As is mine, my lord."

FOUR

TRAINING

He arose in the darkness.

He donned a simple white robe, a mark of his station,
and left his cell. He waited outside the small and simple
room, containing a sleeping mat, a single candle, and a
shelf for scrolls: all that was deemed necessary for his
education. Down the corridor he could see the others, all
years younger than himself, standing quietly before the
doors of their cells. The first black-clad master came along
the corridor and stopped before one of the others. Without
a word the man nodded, the other fell in behind him, and
they marched away into the gloom. The dawn sent soft
grey light through the high narrow windows in the
hallway. He, like the others, extinguished the torch on the
wall opposite his door, at the first hint of day. Another man
in black came down the corridor and another waiting youth
left behind him. Soon a third. Then a fourth. After a time
he found himself alone. The hallway was silent.

A figure emerged from the darkness, his robes con-
spiring to mask his coming until the last few feet. He stood
before the young man in white and nodded, pointing

down the corridor. The youth fell in behind his black-robed
guide, and they made their way down a series of torchlit
passages, into the heart of the great building that had been
the young man's home as long as he could remember. Soon
they were traveling through a series of low tunnels, rank
with the smell of age, and wet, as if deep below the lake
that surrounded the building on all sides.

The man in black paused at a wooden door, slid a bolt
aside, and opened it. The younger man entered behind the
other, and came to stand before a series of wooden
troughs. Each was half the length of a man's height, and
half that wide. One stood on the floor, and the others were
arrayed above it, suspended by wooden supports in steps,
one above the next, until the highest stood near the height
of a man's head. All of those above had single holes in the
end that overhung the trough below. In the bottom trough,
water could be heard sloshing, as it responded to the
vibrations of their footfalls on the stone floor.

The man in black pointed to a bucket and turned and
left the young man in white alone.

The young man picked up the bucket and set about his
task. All commands to those in white were given without
words and, as he had quickly learned when he had first
become aware, those in white were not allowed to speak.
He knew he could speak, for he understood the concept
and had quietly tried to form a few words while lying on
his mat in the dark. As with so many other things, he
understood the fact, without being aware of how he
understood. He knew that he existed before his first
awakening in his cell, but was not in the least alarmed by
his lack of memory. It seemed somehow proper.

He started his task. Like so many other things he was
commanded to do, it seemed an impossible undertaking.
He took the bucket and filled the topmost trough from the
bottom one. As it had on days before, the water spilled
from the top down into each successive trough, until the
contents of the bucket rested again at the bottom. Dog-
gedly he pursued his work, letting his mind go vacant,
while his body undertook the mindless task.

As it did so many other times when left to its own
devices, his mind danced from image to image, bright
flashes of shapes and colors that eluded his grasp as he

sought to close mental fingers around them. First came a brief glimpse of a beach, with crashing waves on rocks, black and weathered. Fighting. A strange-looking cold white substance lying on the ground—a word, *snow*, that fled as quickly as it came. A muddy camp. A great kitchen with boys hurrying about many tasks. A room in a high tower. Each passed with blinding quickness, leaving only an afterimage in its passing.

Daily, a voice would sound in his head, and his mind's voice would respond with an answer, while he labored at his endless task. The voice would ask a simple question, and his mind's voice would answer. Should the answer be incorrect, the question would be repeated. If several wrong answers were made, the voice would cease its questioning, sometimes returning later in the day, sometimes not.

The white-clad worker felt the familiar pressure against the fabric of his thoughts.

—*What is the law?*—the voice asked.

—*The law is the structure that surrounds our lives, and gives them meaning*—he answered.

—*What is the highest embodiment of the law?*—

—*The Empire is the highest embodiment of the law*—

—*What are you?*—came the next question.

—*I am a servant of the Empire*—

The thought contact flickered for a moment, then returned, as if the other was considering the following question carefully.

—*In what manner are you allowed to serve?*—

The question had been asked several times before, and always his answer had been met with the blank inner silence that told him he had answered incorrectly. This time he carefully considered, eliminating all the answers he had made previously, as well as those that were combinations or extrapolations of the previously incorrect ones.

Finally he answered, —*As I see fit*—

There was a surge of feeling from without, a feeling of approval. Quickly another question followed.

—*Where is your allotted place?*—

He thought about this, knowing that the obvious answer was likely to be the incorrect one, but still one that needed to be tested. He answered.

—*My place is here*—

The mind contact was broken, as he suspected it
would be. He knew that he was being trained, though the
purpose of the training was masked from his mind. Now
he could ponder the last question in light of his previous
answers and perhaps ascertain the correct response.

His consideration of the last question he had been
asked was interrupted when the door behind him opened,
and his guide motioned for him to follow. They moved
through long passages, winding their way up to the level
where they would eat the scant morning meal.

When they entered the hall, the guide took a place by
the door, while others in black robes similarly escorted the
white-clad ones into the hall. This was the day that the
young man's guide would stand and watch the boys in
white, who, along with the young man, were bound to eat
in silence. Each day a different wearer of the black robe
filled this function.

The young man ate and considered the last question of
the morning. He weighed each possible answer, seeking
out possible flaws, and as they were discovered, discarding
them. Abruptly one answer came unbidden to his mind, an
intuitive leap, as his subconscious provided him with a
solution to the question. Several times in the past, when
particularly knotty problems had stopped his progress, this
had occurred, which accounted for his rapid advancement
in his lessons. He weighed the possible flaws in this
answer, and when he was certain he was correct, he stood.
Other eyes regarded him furtively, for this was a violation
of the rules.

He went over to stand before his guide, who regarded
his approach with a controlled expression, his only sign of
curiosity being a slight arching of his brows.

Without preamble the young man in white said, "This
is no longer my place."

The man in black showed no emotion, but placed a
hand on the young man's shoulder, and nodded slightly.
He reached inside his robe and removed a small bell, which
he rang once. Another black-robed individual appeared
moments later. Without word, the newcomer took the
place at the door, as the guide motioned for the young man
to follow him.

They walked in silence as they had done many times

before, until they came to a room. The man in black turned to the young man and said, "Open the door."

The young man started to reach for the door, then with a flash of insight pulled his hand away. Knitting his brow in concentration, he opened the door by the power of his mind. Slowly it swung inward. The man in black turned and smiled. "Good," he said, in a soft, pleasant voice.

They entered a room with many white, grey, and black robes hanging upon hooks. The man in black said, "Change to a grey robe."

The young man did so quickly and faced the other man. The man in black studied the new wearer of the grey. "You are no longer bound to silence. Any question you may have will be answered, as well as is possible, though there are still things that will be waited upon, until you don the black. Then you will fully understand. Come."

The young man in grey followed his guide to another room, where cushions surrounded a low table, upon which rested a pot of hot chocha, a pungent, bitter-sweet drink. The man in black poured two cups and handed one to the young man, indicating he should sit. They both sat, and the young man said, "Who am I?"

The man in black shrugged. "You will have to decide that, for only you can glean your true name. It is a name that must never be spoken to others, lest they gain power over you. Henceforward you will be called Milamber."

The newly named Milamber thought for a moment, then said, "It will serve. What are you called?"

"I am called Shimone."

"Who are you?"

"Your guide, your teacher. Now you will have others, but it was given to me to be responsible for the first part of your training, the longest part."

"How long have I been here?"

"Nearly four years."

Milamber was surprised by this, for his memory stretched back only a little, several months at best. "When will my memories be returned to me?"

Shimone smiled, for he was pleased that Milamber had not asked if they would be returned, and said as much. "Your mind will call up your past life as you progress in the balance of your training, slowly at first, with more rapidity later. There is a reason for this. You must be able to withstand the lure of former ties, of family and nations, of friends and home. In your case that is particularly vital."

"Why is that?"

"When your past returns to you, you will understand," was all Shimone said, a smile on his face. His hawkish features and dark eyes were set in an expression that communicated the feeling this was the end of that topic.

Milamber thought of several questions, quickly discarding them as of less immediate consequence. Finally he asked, "What would have happened if I had opened the door by hand?"

"You would have died." Shimone said this flatly, without emotion.

Milamber was not surprised or shocked, he simply accepted it. "To what end?"

Shimone was a little surprised by the question and showed it. "We cannot rule each other, all we can do is ensure that each new magician is able to discharge the responsibility attendant upon his actions. You made the judgment that your place was no longer with those who wore the white, the novices. If that was not your place, then you would have to demonstrate your ability to deal with the responsibilities of this change. The bright but foolish ones often die at this stage."

Milamber considered this, and acknowledged the propriety of such a test. "How long will my training continue?"

Shimone made a noncommittal gesture. "As long as it takes. You rise rapidly, however, so I think it will not be too much longer in your case. You have certain natural gifts, and—you will understand this when your memory returns—a certain advantage over the other, younger, students who started with you."

Milamber studied the contents of his cup. In the thin, dark fluid he seemed to glimpse a single word, as if seen from the corner of the eye, that vanished when he tried to focus upon it. He couldn't hang on to it, but it had been a short name, a simple name.

He spent weeks in the company of Shimone and a few others. He knew more of his life, though only a fragment of what was missing. He had been a slave, and he had been discovered to have the power. He remembered a woman, and felt a faint tugging at the thought of her vaguely remembered image.

He was quick to learn. Each lesson was accomplished in a single day, or at most two. He would quickly dissect each problem given, and when it was time to discuss it with his teachers, his questions were to the point, well thought out, and proper.

One day he arose, in a newer but still simple cell, and emerged to find Shimone waiting for him. The black-robed magician said, "From this point on, you may not speak until you have finished the task set for you."

Milamber nodded his understanding and followed his guide down the hall. The older magician led him through a series of long tunnels to a place in the building he had never been before. They mounted a long staircase, rising many stories above where they had started. Upward they climbed, until Shimone opened a door for him. Milamber preceded Shimone through the door and found himself upon an open flat roof, atop a high tower. From the center of the roof a single spire of stone rose. Skyward it shot, a needle of fashioned rock. Winding upward around it was a narrow series of steps, carved into the side of the needle. Milamber's eyes followed it until the top was lost in the clouds. He found the sight fascinating, for it seemed to violate several canons of physical law that he had studied. Still, it stood before him, and what was more, his guide was indicating that he should mount the steps.

He started upward. As he completed his first circum-navigation, he noted that Shimone had disappeared through the wooden door. Relieved of his presence, Milamber turned his gaze outward from the roof, drinking in the vista around him.

He was atop the highest tower of an immense city of towers. Everywhere he looked, hundreds of stone fingers pointed upward, strong structures with windows turning blind eyes outward. Some were open to the sky, as this one was; others were roofed in stone, or in shimmering lights. But of them all, this one alone was topped by a thin spire. Below the hundreds of towers, bridges arched through the sky, connecting them, and farther down could be seen the bulk of the single, incredible building that supported all he saw. It was a monster of construction. Sprawling below him, it stretched away for miles in every direction. He had known it would be a large place, from his travels within, but this knowledge did nothing to lessen his awe at the sight.

Still farther down, in the dim extreme of his vision, he could see the faint green of grass, a thin border edging the dark bulk of the building. On all sides he saw water, the once glimpsed lake. In the distance he could make out the hazy suggestion of mountains, but unless he strained to see them, it was as if the entire world were arrayed below.

Plodding upward, he turned around the spire as he climbed. Each circle brought him a new detail of the vista. A single bird wheeled high above all else, ignorant of the affairs of men, its scarlet wings spread to catch the air as it watched with keen eye the lake below. Seeing a telltale flicker on the water, it folded back its wings and stooped, hitting the surface for the briefest moment before it climbed aloft once more, a flopping prize clutched in its talons. With a cry of victory it circled once, then sped westward.

A turn. A play of winds. Each carried suggestions of far and alien lands. From the south a gust with a hint of hot jungles where slaves toiled to reclaim farmlands from deadly, water-shrouded marshes. From the east a breeze carried the victory chant of a dozen warriors of the Thuril Confederation, after defeating an equal number of Empire soldiers in a border clash. In counterpoint there was a faint echo of a dying Tsurani soldier, crying for his family. From the north came the smell of ice and the sound of the hooves of thousands of Thūn pounding over the frozen tundra, heading south for warmer lands. From the west, the laughter of the young wife of a powerful noble teasing a half-horrified, half-aroused household guard into betraying her husband, away conducting business with a merchant in Tusan to the south. From the east, the smell of spices as merchants haggled in the market square in far Yankora. Again south, and the smell of salt from the Sea of Blood. North, and windswept ice fields that had never known the tread of human feet, but over which beings old and wise in ways unknown to men walked, seeking a sign in the heavens—one that never came. Each breeze brought a note and tone, a color and hue, a taste and fragrance. The texture of the world blew by and he breathed deeply, savoring it.

A turn. From the steps below came a pulsing as the world beat with a life of its own. Upward through the island, through the building, through the tower, the spire, and his very body came the urgent yet eternal beating of the planet's heart. He cast his eyes downward and saw deep caverns, the upper ones worked by slaves who harvested the few rare metals to be found, along with coal for heat and stone for building. Below these were other caverns, some natural, others the remnants of a lost city, overblown by dust that became soil as the ages passed. Here once dwelled creatures beyond his ability to imagine. Deeper still his vision plunged him, to a region of heat and light, where primeval forces contested. Liquid rock, inflamed and glowing, pushed against its solid cousin, seeking a passage upward, mindlessly driven by forces as basic as nature. Deeper still, to a world of pure force, where lines of energy ran through the heart of the world.

A turn, and he stepped upon a small platform atop the spire. It was less than his own height in size on each side, an impossibly precarious perch. He stepped to the middle, overcoming a vertigo that tried to send him screaming over the edge. He employed every part of his ability and training to stand there, for he understood without being told that to fail here was to die.

He cleared his mind of fear and looked around at the scene before him, awed by the expanse of emptiness. Never before had he felt so truly isolated, so truly alone. Here he stood with nothing between him and whatever fate was allotted to him.

Below him stretched the world and above him an empty sky. The wind held a hint of moisture, and he saw dark clouds racing up from the south. The tower, or the needle upon it, swayed slightly and he unconsciously shifted his weight to compensate.

Lightning flashed as the storm clouds rushed toward him, and thunder broke around his head. The very sound was enough to dislodge him from the small platform, and he was forced to delve deeper into his inner well of power, into that silent place known only as wal, and there he found the strength to resist the onslaught of the storm.

Winds buffeted him, slamming him toward the platform's edge. He reeled and recovered, the darkling abyss below beckoning to him, inviting his fall. With a surge of will, he brushed aside the vertigo once again and set his mind to the task ahead.

In his mind a voice cried,—*Now is the time of testing. Upon this tower you must stand, and should your will falter, from it you will fall—*

There was a momentary pause, then the voice cried once more, —*Behold! Witness and understand how it was—*

Blackness swept upward and he was consumed.

For a time he floats, nameless and lost. A pinpoint of flickering consciousness, an unknown swimmer through a black and empty sea. Then a single note invades the void. It reverberates, a soundless sound, a sense-lacking intruder on the senses. —*Without senses, how is there perception?*—his mind asks. His mind!—*I am!*—he cries, and a million philosophies cry out in wonder. —*If I am, then what is not me?*—he wonders.

An echo replies,—*You are that which you are, and not that which you are not—*

—*An unsatisfactory answer*—he muses.

—*Good*—replies the echo.

—*What is that note?*—he asks.

—*It is an alarm to wake you—*

He floats. Around him swim a billion billion stars. Great clusters drift by, ablaze with energy. In riots of color they spin, giant reds and blues, the smaller oranges and yellows, and the tiny reds and whites. The colorless and angry black ones drink in the storm of light around them, and a few twist the fabric of space and time, sending his vision swimming as he tries to fathom their passing. From each to each a line of force stretches, binding them all in a net of power. Back and forth along the strands of this web energy flows, pulsing with a life that is not life. The stars know as they fly by. They are aware of his presence, but acknowledge it not. He is too small for them to be concerned with. Around him stretches away the whole of the universe.

At various points in the web, creatures of power rest

or work, each different from the others, but all somehow the same. Some he can see are gods, for they are familiar to him, and others are less or more. Each plays a role. Some regard him, for his passing is not without notice; some are beyond him, too great to comprehend him, and so being, are less than he. Others study him closely, weighing his power and abilities against their own. He studies them in return. All speak not.

He speeds among the stars and the beings of power, until he espies a star, one among the multitude, but one that calls to him. From the star, twenty lines of energy lead away, and near each is a being of power. Without knowing why, he understands that here are the ancient gods of Kelewan. Each plays on the nearest line of power influencing the structure of space and time nearby. Some contest among themselves, others work oblivious to the strife, and still others do nothing that is discernible.

He moves closer. A single planet swings about the star, a blue and green sphere shrouded in white clouds. Kelewan.

Down the lines of force he plunges, until he is on the surface. Here he sees a world untouched by the footprint of man. He stands on a cliff looking down upon a great plain of grass separated from the sea by a small beach. A shimmering in the air begins, and the sea beyond the plain is distorted. Like the agitation of the air by the heat of the day, the scene ripples. Scintillating colors appear in the air. Then, as if by two giant hands, the very fabric of space and time is torn, an ever widening gap through which he can see. Beyond this fracture in the air, a vision of chaos is revealed, a mad display of energy, as if all the lines of power in that universe are torn asunder. Bolts of energy sufficient to destroy suns explode in displays of color beyond the ability of mortal eyes to describe, leaving them dazzled with lesser lights. From deep within this giant rift a wide bridge of golden light extends downward, until it touches the grass of the plain. Upon the bridge thousands of figures are moving, escaping the madness beyond the rift to the serenity of the plain.

Downward they hurry, some carrying all they own on their backs, others with animals pulling wagons and sleds heaped with valuables. All press forward, fleeing a nameless horror behind.

He studies the figures, and though much is alien, he can see much that is also familiar. Many wear short robes of plain fashion, and he knows he is looking upon the seeds of the Tsurani race. Their faces are more basic, showing less of the blending with others that would take place in years to come. Most were fair with brown or blond hair. At their feet run barking dogs, sleek and swift greyhounds.

Next to them stride proud warriors, with slanted eyes and bronze skin. These are fighting men, but not organized soldiers, for they wear robes of different cut and color one from the other. Each steps down off the bridge, some showing wounds, all hiding terror behind implacable expressions. Over their shoulders they carry long swords of fine steel, fashioned with great care. The tops of their heads are shaved, with the hair around pulled back into a knot. These bear the proud look of men unsure if they are better off for having survived the battle. Mixed among them are others, all strangers.

A race of short people carry nets that proclaim them fishers, though of what sea only they know. All have dark hair, sallow skins, and grey-green eyes. Men, women, and children all wear simple fur trousers, leaving upper bodies bare.

Behind them come a nation of tall, noble, black-skinned people. Their robes are richly fashioned of soft and subtle colors. Many have gems adorning their foreheads, and gold bands on their arms. All are weeping for a homeland never to be seen again.

Then come riders upon impossible beasts that look like flying serpents with feathered birds' heads. Upon their faces are mask of animals and birds, brightly painted and plumed. They are covered in paint alone, for their home-world was a hot place. They wear their nakedness like a cloak, for there is beauty in their form, as if each had been fashioned by a master sculptor, and they bear weapons of black glass. Women and children ride behind the men unmasked, revealing expressions made harsh by the cruel world they flee. The Serpent Riders turn their creatures eastward and fly away. The great flying snakes will die out in the cold highlands of the east, but will remain forever in the legends of the proud Thuril.

Thousands more come, all walking down the golden

ramp to set foot upon Kelewan. When they reach the plain, some move off, traveling to other parts of the planet, but many stay and watch as thousands more come across the bridge. Time passes, night follows day, then gives way to day once more, while the hosts enter from the insane storm of chaos.

With them come twenty beings of power, also fleeing the utter destruction of a universe. The multitudes upon the plain see them not, but he watches. He knows they will become the twenty gods of Kelewan, the Ten Higher and Ten Lower Beings. They fly upward, to wrest the lines of power from the ancient, feeble beings who hold station around this world. There is no struggle as the new gods take their stations, for the old beings of power know a new order is coming into the world.

After days of watching, he sees that the stream of humanity is thinning. Hundreds of men and women pull huge boats made from some metal, shining in the sun, mounted on wheels of a black substance. They reach the plain and see the ocean beyond the narrow beach. They give a shout and pull their boats to the water and launch them. Fifty boats raise sail and set out across the ocean, heading southward, for the land that will become Tsubar, the lost nation.

The last group is composed of thousands of men in robes of many designs and colors. He knows that these are the priests and magicians of many nations. Together they stand, holding back the raging madness beyond. As he watches, many fall, their lives burning out like spent candles. At some prearranged signal, many of them, but less than one for each hundred standing at the top of the golden bridge, turn and flee downward. All are holding books, scrolls, and other tomes of knowledge. When they reach the bottom of the bridge, they turn and watch the unfolding drama at the top.

Those above, looking not at those who have fled but at what they hold back, give forth a shout, incanting a mighty spell, wielding magic of enormous power. Those below echo their cries, and all who can hear them quail in dread at the sound. The bridge begins to dissolve, from the ground up. A flood of terror and hate comes pouring through the rift, and those who stand atop the bridge begin to crumple before its onslaught. As the bridge and the opening above disappear from sight, a single blast of fury comes through that stuns many who stand upon the plain below, felling them as if with a blow.

For some time those who escaped the nameless terror behind the rift stand mute. Then slowly they start to disperse. Groups break away and move off. He knows that, in years to come, these ragged refugees will conquer this world, for they are the seeds of the nations that populate Kelewan.

He knows he has seen the beginning of the nations, and their flight from the Enemy, the nameless terror that destroyed the homes of the races of mankind, dispersing them to other universes.

Again the cloak of time is drawn over him, creating darkness.

Followed by light.

On the plain that had been empty, a great city stands. Its white towers ascend to the skies. Its people are industrious and the city prospers. Caravans of trade goods come overland, and great ships call from across the sea. Years speed by, bringing war and famine, peace and bounty.

One day a ship pulls into the harbor, as scarred and ill as its crew. A great battle has been fought and this ship is one of the few to survive. Those across the water will come soon, and the City of the Plains will fall if help is not forthcoming. Runners are sent north to the cities along the great river, for should the white city fall, nothing will prevent the invaders from striking northward. Runners return, carrying the news. The armies of the other cities will come. He watches as they gather and meet the invaders near the sea. The invaders are repulsed, but the cost is great, for the battle rages twelve days. A hundred thousand men die, and the sands are red for months. A thousand ships burn, and the sky is filled with black smoke, and for days it falls upon the land, covering miles about with a fine, powdery ash. The city of white becomes the city of grey. The sea is called Blood from that day forward, and the great bay is called Battle. But out of the battle an alliance is formed, and the seeds of the great

Empire are planted, the world-spanning Empire of Tsuranuanni.

In the east, the sky darkens as night approaches.

As the sun rises, he stands near a magician who has
worked the night through. The man grows alarmed at
what his calculations have shown, and he incants a spell
that takes him to another place. The watcher follows. In a
small hall, several more magicians react with expressions
of dread to the news the first magician brings. A messenger
is dispatched to the Warlord, ruler of the Empire in the
Emperor's name. The Warlord summons the magicians.
The watcher follows. The magicians explain the news. The
signs in the stars, along with ancient writings, herald
the coming of a great disaster. A star, a wanderer in the
heavens sighted where none has been seen before, stands
motionless but grows brighter. It will bring destruction to
the nations. The Warlord is skeptical, but of late more and
more nobles have come to heed the words of magicians.
There have always been legends of magicians saving the
nations from the Enemy, but few think them likely. Still,
there is now this new convocation of magicians, who have
formed something called the Assembly, toward what ends
only the magicians know. So, with the changing times in
mind, the Warlord agrees to take the news to the Emperor.
After a time, an order is sent to the Assembly by the
Emperor. His demand: bring proof. The magicians shake
their heads and return to their modest halls.

Decades pass, and the magicians conduct a campaign
of propaganda, seeking to influence any noble of the
Empire who will listen. The day arrives when the news is
proclaimed that the Emperor is dead and his son now
reigns. The magicians gather with all who can travel to the
Holy City for the coronation of the new Emperor.

Thousands of people line the streets, while slaves bear
the nobles of the land in litters to the great temples. The
new Emperor rides the ancient golden throne, born by a
hundred husky slaves. He is crowned, while the symbolic
slaying of a slave is performed deep within the halls of the
temple of the death god, Turakamu, as a petition to the
gods to allow the old Emperor's soul to rest in heaven.
The crowd cheers, for Sudkahanchoza, thirty-four

times Emperor, is well loved and this will be the last time they will ever look upon him. He will now retire to the Holy Palace, where his soul will stand forever vigilant on behalf of his subjects, while the Warlord and the High Council conduct the business of governing the Empire. The new Emperor will live a contemplative life, reading, painting, studying the great books of the temples, seeking to purify his soul for this arduous life.

This Emperor is unlike his father and, after hearing the grave news from the Assembly, orders the building of a great castle upon an island in the center of the giant lake in the midst of the mountains of Ambolina.

Time . . .

. . . passes.

Hundreds of black-clad magicians stand atop towers that rise from the city of the island, not yet the magnificent single entity of the future. Two hundred years have passed and now two suns burn in the sky, one warm and yellow-green, the other small, white, and angry. The watcher sees the men work their magic, the greatest spell cast in the history of the nations. Even the legendary bridge from the outside, the beginning of time, was not so great a feat, for then they had only moved between worlds, now they would move a star. Below he can feel the presence of hundreds of other magicians, adding their power to those above. The spell has been wrought over the last few years, each step taken with the greatest care, as the Stranger approaches. Though powerful beyond compare, this enchantment is also delicate in the extreme. Any misstep and its work will be undone. He looks up and sees the Stranger, its course marked toward the path of this world. It will not strike Kelewan, but there is little doubt that its heat added to Kelewan's already hot star will render the planet lifeless. Kelewan will hang for over a year between its own primary and the Stranger, in constant daylight, and all magicians agree that only a few might survive in deep caves, to emerge to a burned-out planet. Now they must act, before it is too late to try again should the enchantment fail.

Now they do act, all in concert, incanting the last piece of the great arcane work. The world seems to stand still for a moment, reverberating with the final word of the spell.

Slowly that reverberation grows louder, picking up resonance, developing new harmonies, new overtones, a
character of its own. Soon it is loud enough to deafen those
in the towers, who cover their ears. Below, those on the
ground stand in mute wonder, looking to the sky where a
blaze of color begins to form. Ragged bolts of energy flash
and the light from the two stars is dimmed in momentarily
blinding displays that will leave some who viewed them
sightless for the rest of their lives. He is not affected by the
sound or light, as if some agency has taken care to protect
him from their effects. A great rift appears in the sky, much
like the one the golden bridge came through ages ago. He
watches without emotion, his strongest feeling being
detached fascination. It grows in the sky, between the
Stranger and Kelewan, and begins to move away from the
planet, toward the invading star.

But something else occurs. From the heart of the rift,
more violent than at the time of the golden bridge, an
unprecedented display of erupting energies comes forth.
The chaotic scene is matched with an overwhelming wave
of hatred. The Enemy, the evil power that drove the
nations to Kelewan, still abides in the other universe, and it
has not forgotten those who escaped it ages ago. It cannot
pierce the barrier of the rift, for it needs more time to move
between universes than the life-span of the rift, but it
reaches forth and warps it, sending it away from the
Stranger. The rift grows larger, and those on the ground
see it is going to engulf Kelewan, bringing the planet back
into the dominion of the Enemy.

The watcher looks on impassively, unlike those around
him, for he knows that this is not the end of the world. The
rift rushes toward the planet, and one magician comes
forth.

He is somehow familiar to the one who watches. The
man, unlike those around him, wears a brown robe,
fastened round with a whipcord belt, and holds a staff of
wood. He raises the staff above his head and incants. The
rift changes, from colors impossible to describe to inky
black, and it strikes the planet.

The heavens explode for a moment, then all around is
black. When the darkness lifts, the sun, Kelewan's own, is
dropping below the horizon. The magicians who are not

dead or mad stare upward in horror. Above them the sky is
a void, without stars.

Blackness . . .

. . . heralds the passing of time again. He is standing
in the halls of the Assembly. Magicians are appearing
regularly, using the pattern on the floor as a focal point for
their transit. Each remembers the pattern like an address,
and wills himself there. The question at hand is what is to
be done to return Kelewan to its own universe. A message
arrives from the Emperor. He begs the Assembly to solve
the problem, promising them whatever aid they require.

The watcher moves forward through generations to
find the magicians again upon the towers. Now, instead of
the invading Stranger, they regard a starless sky. Another
spell, years in the fashioning, is being incanted. When it is
finished, the earth reverberates with violent energies.
Suddenly the sky is ablaze with stars and Kelewan is again
in its normal place.

The Emperor sends a command that the full Assembly
should come to the Holy City at once. By ones and twos
they use the patterns to travel to Kentosani. The watcher
follows. There they are taken to the inner chamber of the
Emperor's palace, something unheard of in the history of
the Empire.

Of the seven thousand magicians who gathered a
century before to thwart the Stranger only two hundred
survived. Even now that number has increased but slightly,
so that not even one magician for each twenty who stood
upon towers against the Stranger answers the Emperor's
call. They advance to stand before Tukamaco, forty times
Emperor, descendant of Sudkahanchoza, and Light of
Heaven. The Emperor asks if the Assembly will accept the
charge to stand ever vigilant over the Empire, protecting it
until the end of time. The magicians confer, and agree. The
Emperor then leaves his throne and abases himself before
the assembled magicians, something never done before.
He sits back and, still on his knees before them, throws
wide his arms and proclaims that from this day forth the
magicians are the Great Ones, free from all obligations,
save the charge just accepted. They are outside the law and
none may command them, including the Warlord, who

stands to one side, a frown upon his face. Whatever they desire is theirs to ask, for their words will be as law.

Darkness . . .

. . . and time passes.

The watcher stands before the Warlord's throne. A delegation of magicians stand before the Warlord. They present him with proof of what they have claimed. A controllable rift, free from the Enemy's influence, has been opened, and another world has been found. This is unsuitable for life—but a second has been discovered, a rich, ripe world. They show him a lifetime's worth of wealth in metals, all found lying about, discarded. He who watches smiles to himself over the Warlord's eagerness at the sight of a broken breastplate, a rusted sword, and a handful of bent nails. To further prove this is an alien world they present him with a strange but beautiful flower. The Warlord smells it and is pleased with its rich fragrance. The watcher nods, for he, too, knows the richness of the Midkemian rose.

The black wing of passing time covers him again.

Once more he stood upon the platform. He looked around and saw that the full fury of the storm was breaking around him. Only by his unconscious will had he been able to stand upon this platform, whil his conscious mind was occupied by the unfolding history of Kelewan. He now understood the nature of the test, for he found himself exhausted from the energy he had expended during the ordeal. While being instilled with the final instruction in his place in this society, he had been tested with the raw fury of nature.

He took a last look around, finding the grim view of the storm-tossed lake and the shuttered windows of the towers somehow satisfying. He strove to capture this image, as if to ensure that he would forever remember the moment he came to his full awakening as a Great One, for there were no more blocks on his memory, or his emotions. He exulted in his power: no longer Pug the keep boy, but now a magician of power to dwarf the imagination of his former master, Kulgan. And never again will either of these worlds, Midkemia or Kelewan, seem the same to him.

By force of will he descended to the roof, floating gently through the raging wind. The door opened in anticipation of his coming. He entered, and it closed behind him. Shimone was waiting for him, a smile upon his face. As they moved down the long halls of the Assembly building-city, the skies outside exploded with clashes of thunder, as if heralding his arrival.

Hochopepa sat upon his mat, awaiting the arrival of his guest. The heavy, bald magician was interested in gauging the mettle of the newest member of the Assembly, come into his estate as a wearer of the black robe the previous day.

A chime sounded, announcing his guest's arrival. Hochopepa stood and crossed his richly furnished apartment. He pulled aside the sliding door. "Welcome, Milamber. I am pleased you saw fit to accept my invitation."

"I am honored," was all Milamber said as he entered and regarded the room. Of all the quarters in the Assembly building he had seen, this was by far the most opulent. The hangings on the walls were rich cloth, enhanced with the finest threadwork, and there were several valuable metal objects adorning various shelves.

Milamber made a study of his host as well. The heavy-set magician showed Milamber to a cushion before a low table and then poured cups of chocha. His plump hands moved with controlled ease, precisely and efficiently. His dark, nearly black, eyes shone from under the thick brows that accented an otherwise deceptively bland face. He was the stockiest magician Milamber had seen yet, as most who wore the black robe tended to be thin and ascetic-looking. Milamber sensed this was largely by design, as if someone occupied with the pleasures of the flesh couldn't be too concerned with matters of deep thought.

After the first sip of chocha had been taken, Hochopepa said, "You pose something of a problem for me, Milamber."

When Milamber made no comment, Hochopepa said, "You make no remark." Milamber inclined his head in agreement. "Perhaps your background accounts for a bit more native wariness than is the rule here."

Milamber said, "A slave become magician is something to ponder."

Hochopepa waved his hand. "It is a rarity for a slave to don the black robe, but not unheard of. Occasionally the power is not recognized until adulthood. But that is not for this discussion. Your particular situation, the one that makes you somewhat of a problem for me, is that you are a barbarian—excuse me, were a barbarian."

Milamber smiled again. He had left the Tower of Testing with all his memories of his life, though much about his training was still sketchy. He understood the processes that had been used to bring him into control of his magic. They had singled him out as one among a hundred thousand, a Great One. Of the two hundred million people of the Empire, he was one of two thousand magicians of the black robe. His slave-bred wariness, as Hochopepa pointed out, combined with his own native intelligence to keep him silent. Hochopepa was trying to make a point and Milamber would wait to hear what it was, no matter how roundabout the stout magician insisted on being.

When Milamber said nothing, Hochopepa continued. "Your position is strange for several reasons. The obvious one is that you are the first to wear the black who is not of this world. The second is that you were the apprentice of a Lesser Magician."

Milamber raised an eyebrow. "Kulgan? You know of my training?"

Hochopepa laughed, a genuine belly laugh, which made Milamber relax his guard a little and regard the other man with a little less distrust. "Of course. There was not one aspect of your background that was not closely examined, for you provided a wealth of information about your world." Hochopepa looked closely at his guest. "The Warlord might choose to launch an invasion into a world we know little about—over the objections of his magician advisers, I might add—but we of the Assembly prefer to study our adversaries. We were most relieved to learn magic is restricted to the province of priests and followers of the Lesser Path on your world."

"Again you mention a Lesser Magic. What is your meaning?"

It was Hochopepa's turn to look slightly surprised. "I assumed you knew." Milamber shook his head. "The Path of Lesser Magic is walked by some who can operate certain forces by power of will, though of a different order than we of the black robe."

"Then you know of my previous failure."

Hochopepa laughed again. "Yes. Had you been less suited to the Greater Path, you might have learned his ways. As it is, you had too much ability to have succeeded as a Lesser Path magician. It is a talent rather than an art, the Lesser Path. The Greater Path is for scholars."

Milamber nodded. Each time Hochopepa explained a concept, it was as if Milamber had known it all his life. He remarked on this.

"It is easy enough to understand. During your training, many facts and concepts were taught you. The basic concepts of magic were taught early, your responsibility to the Empire later. Part of the process of bringing all your abilities to maturity requires that all these facts be there when you need them. But much of what you were taught was also masked, to be revealed when you needed it, when you could fully understand what was in your mind. There will be a period when thoughts will come unbidden from time to time. As you frame a question, the answer will appear in your mind. And sometimes an answer will come as you read it or hear it, as if you had already known it. It serves to keep you from reeling under the impact of years of learning coming upon you in an instant."

Milamber said, "Again, I would hear of your problem."

Hochopepa adjusted his robe, smoothing the creases. "Indulge me a moment longer for a brief digression. It all has bearing on why I asked you here." Milamber signified that Hochopepa should continue.

"Little is known of our peoples before the Escape. We know that the nations came from many different worlds. There is also some speculation that others fled the Enemy to different worlds, your former homeworld among them perhaps. There are a few shreds of evidence to support that hypothesis, but it is only conjecture at this point." Milamber thought about the games of shāh he had played with the Lord of the Shinzawai and considered the possibility.

"We came as refugees. Of millions, only thousands survived to plant seeds here. We found this world old and used up. Great civilizations once flourished here, and all

that is left of them is one, smooth stones where once cities
stood. Who these creatures were, no one knows. This
world has few metals, and what was brought with us in the
Escape wore away over the ages. Our animals, like your
horses and cattle, died out, all save dogs. We had to adjust
to our new homeworld, and to each other.

"We fought many wars between the time of the Escape
and the advent of the Stranger. We were little more than
city-states until the Battle of a Thousand Ships. Then the
humblest of the races, the Tsurani, rose to conquer all
others, uniting most of this world in a single Empire.

"We of the Assembly support the Empire because on
this world it is the single most powerful force for order—
not because it is noble, or fair, or beautiful, or just. But
because of it the majority of humanity can live and work
without war in their homelands, can live without famine,
plagues, and the other disasters of older times. And with
this order around us, we of the Assembly can work
unhindered.

"It was the attempt to dispel the Stranger that first
made it apparent that we must be able to work unhindered
by anyone, including the Emperor, with whatever resources are necessary. We were robbed of precious time for
action by the Emperor's lack of cooperation when we first
learned of the Stranger. Had we been given support at
once, we might have been able to deal with the Enemy
when it acted to warp the rift. That is why we accepted the
charge to defend and serve the Empire, in exchange for
total freedom."

Milamber said, "This is all apparent as you speak of it.
I am still waiting to hear of your problem regarding me."

Hochopepa sighed. "In good time, my friend. I must
finish one last comment. You must understand why the
Assembly functions as it does to have any hope of surviving more than a few weeks."

Milamber looked openly surprised at this remark.
"Survive?"

"Yes, Milamber, survive, for there are many here who
would have seen you at the bottom of the lake during your
training."

"Why?"

"We work to restore the Greater Art. When we fled the
Enemy, at the dawn of history, only one magician in a

thousand who battled the Enemy survived. They, for the most part, were the lesser magicians and apprentices. They banded together in small groups to protect the knowledge they brought with them from their homeworlds. At first, countrymen would seek out countrymen, then, later, larger associations grew, as desire grew to restore the lost arts. After centuries had passed, the Assembly was founded, and magicians from all parts of the world came, until today all who walk the Greater Path are members of the Assembly. Most of those who practice the Lesser Art serve here as well, though they are afforded a different level of respect and freedom. They tend to be better at building devices and understanding the forces of nature than we of the black robes. While not outside the law, they are protected from interference from others by the Assembly. All magicians are the province of the Assembly."

Milamber said, "So we gain freedom to act as we see fit, as long as we act in the best interest of the Empire."

Hochopepa nodded. "It does not matter what we do, or even that two magicians may find themselves at odds over some action or another, as long as both are working in what they believe is the best interest of the Empire."

"From my somewhat 'barbaric' point of view, a strange law."

"Not a law, but a tradition. On this world, my barbaric friend, tradition and custom can be a much stronger constraint than law. Laws are changed, but tradition endures."

"I think I see what your problem is, my civilized friend. You are not sure if I will act in the best interest of the Empire, being an outlander."

Hochopepa nodded. "Were we certain that you were capable of acting against the Empire, you would have been killed. As it is, we are uncertain, though we tend to believe it unlikely you are capable of such action."

For the first time, Milamber was completely unsure of what he was hearing. "I was under the assumption that you had ways of ensuring that all who are trained are loyal to the Empire, as the first duty."

"Normally, yes. In your case we faced problems new to us. As far as we can tell, you are submerged in the underlying cause of the brotherhood of magicians, the order of the Empire. Usually we are certain. We simply read the apprentice's mind. With you we couldn't. We had to rely on truth drugs, long interrogations, and training drills designed to show any duplicity."

"Why?"

"Not for any reason we understand. The spells of thought masking are known. It was nothing of that sort. It was as if your mind held some property we had never encountered before. Perhaps a natural talent unknown to us, but common to your world, or the result of some training at the hands of your Lesser Path master protected you against our mind-reading arts.

"In any event, it created something of a stir in these halls, you may be sure. Several times during your training, the question of your continuing was raised, and each time our inability to read your mind was given as reason for your termination. Each time, more were willing to see you continue than not. On the whole you present a possible wealth of new knowledge and, as such, deserve every benefit of the doubt—to ensure we do not lose such a valuable addition to our storehouse of talents, of course."

"Of course," Milamber said dryly.

"Yesterday the question of your continuation became critical. When the time came for your final acceptance into the Assembly, the issue was put to the vote and ended in a tie. There was one abstention, myself. As long as I remain unallied with one side or the other, the question of your survival is moot. You are free to act as a full member of the Assembly until I recast my vote to ratify your selection into the Assembly, or not. Our tradition does not allow a change of vote, once cast, except abstentions. As no one absent during the voting may add their vote later, I am the only one who can break the tie. So the result of the voting, no matter how long delayed, is mine to decide."

Milamber looked long and hard at the older magician. "I see."

Hochopepa shook his head slowly. "I wonder if you do. To put it in its simplest form, the question of the moment is, what am I to do with you? Without meaning to, I find your life in my hands. What I have to decide is whether or not you should be killed. That is why I wished to see you, to see if I might have erred in judgment."

Suddenly Milamber threw back his head and laughed, long and hard. In a moment, tears were running down his cheeks. When he quieted, Hochopepa said, "I fail to see the humor."

Milamber raised his hand in a placating gesture. "No offense was intended, my civilized friend. But surely you must see the irony of the situation. I was a slave, my life subject to the whim of others. For all my training, and advancement in station, I find that this fact has not been altered." He paused for a moment, and his smile was friendly. "Still, I would rather have you hold my life in your hands than my former overseer. That is what I find so funny."

Hochopepa was startled by the answer, then he, too, started to laugh. "Many of our brothers pay little heed to the ancient teachings, but if you are familiar with our older philosophers you will understand my meaning. You seem to be a man who has found his wal. I think we have an understanding, my barbaric friend. I think we have started well."

Milamber studied Hochopepa. Without knowing the unconscious process whereby he reached the conclusion, he judged he had found an ally, and perhaps a friend. "I think so, as well. And I think you also a man who has found his wal."

Feigning modesty, Hochopepa said, "I am but a simple man, too much a slave to pleasures of the flesh to have reached such a state of perfect centering." With a sigh, he leaned forward and began to speak intently. "Listen to me well, Milamber. For all the reasons enumerated before, you are as much a weapon to be feared as a possible source of knowledge. Many of our brothers are little more than superstitious peasants, distrusting that which is alien and unknown. From this day forward, you must bend yourself to one task. Stay peacefully hidden within your wal, and become Tsurani. To all outward appearances, you must become more Tsurani than anyone else in the Assembly. Is that understood?"

"It is," Milamber said simply.

Hochopepa poured another cup of hot chocha each. "Be especially wary of the Warlord's pets. Their master rankles at the progress of the war upon your former homeworld and is suspicious of the Assembly. Now that two of our brothers died in the last major campaign, fewer of our brothers are willing to lend further aid to that undertaking. The few magicians left within his faction are overtaxed, and it is rumored he will be unable to subdue any more of your world without a miracle. It would take a united High Council—which should happen when the Thūn raiders become agriculturalists and poets, and not before—or a large number of Black Robes agreeing to do his bidding. The latter should occur about a year after the former, so you can see he is in a somewhat poor political situation. Warlords who fail in conducting war tend to fall from grace quickly." With a smile he added, "Of course, we of the Assembly are far above matters political." His tone turned serious once more. "You must face one thing: he may view you as a potential threat, either influencing others not to aid him, or openly opposing him from some deep-rooted sympathy for your former homeland. You are protected from his direct actions, but you still might run afoul of his pets. Some still blindly follow his lead."

"'The path of power is a path of turns within turns,'" Milamber quoted.

Hochopepa nodded, a satisfied expression upon his face. His eyes seemed to glint. "That is Tsurani. You learn quickly."

In the following weeks, Milamber grew into the fullness of his new position, learning the responsibilities of his office. It was remarked on more than once, and occasionally with distrust, that there had been few who had demonstrated so much ability so soon after donning the black robe.

For all the changes in his existence, Milamber discovered many things were unchanged. With practice, he discovered he still had untapped wells of power within, which could be called up only in times of stress. He studied to bring this wild augmentation of power under control, but with little success. He also discovered he was able to put aside the mental conditions placed upon him during training. He chose not to reveal this fact to anyone, not even Hochopepa. His reordering of these mental conditionings also regained him something else, a nearly overwhelming desire to be with Katala once again. He put aside that desire, to go to her at once and demand her release from the Lord of the Shinzawai, well within his ability now he was a Great One. He hesitated for fear of the reaction of the other magicians, and for fear her feelings might have changed toward him. Instead he plunged into his studies.

His time in the Assembly brought forth his true identity, as he had been told it would. This identity proved the key to his unusual mastery of the Greater Path. He was a being of both worlds, worlds bound together by the great rift. And for as long as those worlds stayed bound together he drew power from both, twice the power available to others of the black robe. This knowledge revealed his true name, that name which could not be spoken lest it let another gain power over him. In the ancient Tsurani language, unused since the time of the Escape, it meant, "One who stands between worlds."

FIVE

VOYAGE

Sea breezes swept the walls.

Arutha looked out at the town of Crydee and the sea beyond, his brown hair ruffled by the wind. Patches of light and dark flashed across the landscape as high, fluffy clouds raced overhead. Arutha watched the distant horizon, taking in the vista of the Endless Sea whipped to a froth of whitecaps, as the noise of workmen restoring another building in the town blew by on the wind.

Another autumn visited Crydee, the eighth since the start of the war. Arutha considered it fortunate another spring and summer had passed without a major Tsurani offensive; still, he felt little cause for comfort. He was no longer a boy fresh to command, but a seasoned soldier. At twenty-seven years he had seen more conflict, and had made more decisions, than most men of the Kingdom knew in their lives. In his best judgment, he knew the Tsurani were slowly winning the war.

He let his mind drift a little, then shook himself out of his brooding. While no longer a moody boy, he still tended to let introspection overtake him. He found it best to keep busy and avoid such wasteful pastimes.

"It is a short autumn."

Arutha looked to his left and found Roland standing nearby. The Squire had caught the Prince lost in thought and had made his approach without detection. Arutha found himself irritated. He shrugged it off and said, "And a short winter will follow, Roland. And in the spring . . ."

"What news of Longbow?"

Arutha balled a gloved fist and gently struck the stones of the wall, the slow, controlled gesture a clear sign of his frustration. "I've regretted the need for his going a hundred times. Of the three, only Garret shows any sense of caution. That Charles is a Tsurani madman, consumed by honor, and Longbow is . . ."

"Longbow," finished Roland.

"I've never met a man who reveals so little of himself, Roland. If I live as long as an elf, I don't think I'll ever understand what makes him the way he is."

Roland leaned against the cool stones of the wall and said, "Do you think they're safe?"

Arutha returned his attention to the sea. "If any man in Crydee can crest the mountains into the Tsurani-held valley and get back, it is Martin. Still, I worry."

Roland found the admission surprising. Like Martin, Arutha was not a man to reveal what he felt. Sensing the Prince's deep trouble, Roland changed the topic. "I've a message from my father, Arutha."

"I was told there was a personal message among the dispatches from Tulan."

"Then you know Father's calling me home."

"Yes. I'm sorry about the broken leg."

"Father was never much of a rider. It's the second time he's fallen from his horse and broken something. Last time, when I was little, it was his arm."

"It's been a long time since you were home."

Roland shrugged. "With the war, I felt little need to

return. Most of the fighting's been around here. And," he added with a grin, "there are other reasons to stay."

Sharing the smile, Arutha said, "Have you told Carline yet?"

Roland lost his grin. "Not yet. I thought I'd wait until I'd arranged for a ship south." With the Brotherhood's abandonment of the Green Heart, travel by land to the south was nearly impossible, for the Tsurani had cut off the roads to Carse and Tulan.

A shout from the tower caused them to turn. "Trackers approaching!"

Arutha squinted against the glare reflecting off the distant sea and could make out three figures trotting easily along the road. When they were close enough to be seen clearly, Arutha said, "Longbow." There was a note of relief in his voice.

Leaving the wall, Arutha descended the steps to the courtyard to wait for the Huntmaster and his men. Roland stood by his side as the three dusty men entered the gates of the castle. Both Garret and Charles remained silent as Martin said, "Greetings, Highness."

"Greetings, Martin. What news?" asked the Prince.

Martin began to recount the facts unearthed at the Tsurani camp, and after a moment, Arutha cut him off. "Better save your wind for the council, Martin. Roland, go gather Father Tully, Swordmaster Fannon, and Amos Trask, and bring them to the council hall."

Roland hurried off and Arutha said, "Charles and Garret are to come as well, Martin."

Garret glanced at the former Tsurani slave, who shrugged. Both knew the long-anticipated hot meal would have to wait a little longer upon the Prince's convenience.

Martin took the seat next to Amos Trask, while Charles and Garret remained standing. The former sea captain nodded a greeting to Martin, as Arutha pulled out his own chair, as was his habit, ignoring most formalities when with his councillors. Amos had become an unofficial member of Arutha's staff since the siege of the castle; he was an enterprising man of many unexpected skills.

Arutha said, "Martin has just returned from a mission of special importance. Martin, tell us what you've seen."

Martin said, "We climbed the Grey Towers and entered the valley where the Tsurani have their headquarters."

Fannon and Tully looked at the Huntmaster with surprise, while Amos Trask guffawed. "You toss aside a small saga in one sentence," said the seaman.

Martin ignored the comment and said, "I think it best to let Charles tell you what we saw."

The former Tsurani slave's voice held a note of concern. "Ill news, Highness. From all signs, the Warlord will launch another major offensive next spring."

All in the room sat speechless, save Fannon. "How can you be sure? Are there new armies in his camp?"

Charles shook his head. "No, the new soldiers will not arrive until just before the first spring thaw. My former countrymen have little liking for your cold climate. They will stage during the winter months outside the City of the Plains on Kelewan, at ease in milder weather. They'll move through the rift just before the offensive."

Even after five years, Fannon still had lingering doubts about Charles's loyalty, though Longbow held none. "How, then," said the Swordmaster, "can you be certain there is to be an offensive? We've had none since the assault on Elvandar three years ago."

"There are new banners in the Warlord's camp. They are the banners of the clans of the Blue Wheel Party, absent since the siege of Crydee. It can only mean another shift in the politics of the High Council. It tells us the Alliance for War is again formed."

Of all in the room, only Tully seemed to grasp what Charles was saying. He made a study of the Tsurani, learning all he could from the captured slaves. He said, "You had better explain, Charles."

Charles took a moment to organize his remarks and said, "You must understand one thing of my former homeland. Above everything except honor and obedience to the Emperor, there is the High Council. To gain in the High Council is worth much, even the risk of life itself. More than one family has been destroyed by plots and intrigues within the Council. We of the Empire refer to this as the 'Game of the Council.'

"My family was well placed within the Hunzan Clan,

neither great enough to warrant notice by our clan's rivals, nor small enough to be relegated to only minor roles. We had the benefit of knowing much of the matters before the High Council without having to worry overly much about what decisions were made. Our clan was active in the Party for Progress, for we numbered many scholars, teachers, healers, priests, and artists in our families.

"Then for a time the Hunzan Clan left the Party for Progress, for reasons not clear to any but the highest family leaders, reasons I can only speculate on. My clan joined with the clans of the Blue Wheel Party, one of the oldest in the High Council. While not so powerful as the Warlord's War Party, or the traditionalists of the Imperial Party, it still has much honor and influence.

"Six years ago, when I first came here, the Blue Wheel Party had joined with the War Party to form the Alliance for War. Those of us in the lesser families were not told why such a radical change in alignment had come about, but there was little doubt it was a matter of the Game of the Council.

"My personal fall from grace and my enslavement was certainly necessary to ensure that those of my clan would stay above suspicion until the time was right for whatever move was being planned. It is now clear what that move was.

"Since the siege of this castle, I have seen no sign of any soldier who's a member of the Blue Wheel families. I took it to mean the Alliance for War had been ended."

Fannon interrupted. "Are you then saying the conduct of this war is but an aspect of some political game in this High Council?"

Charles said, "Swordmaster, I know it is difficult for a man as steadfast in his loyalty to his nation as you are to understand such a thing. But that is exactly what I am saying.

"There are reasons, Tsurani reasons, for such a war. Your world is rich in metals, metals we treasure on Kelewan. Also, ours is a bloody history, and all who are not of Tsuranuanni are to be feared and subjugated. If we could find your world, then might not you someday find ours?

"But more, it is a way for the Warlord to gain great influence in the High Council. For centuries we have

fought the Thuril Confederation, and when we at last were
forced to the treaty table, the War Party lost a great deal of
power within the council. This war is a way for that lost
power to be regained. The Emperor rarely commands,
leaving the Warlord supreme, but the Warlord is still the
Lord of a family, the Warchief of a clan, and as such is
constantly seeking to gain advantage for his own people in
the Game of the Council."

Tully looked fascinated. "So the Blue Wheel Party
joining with the Warlord's party, then suddenly withdraw-
ing, was but a ploy in this political game, a maneuver to
gain some advantage?"

Charles smiled. "It is very Tsurani, good father. The
Warlord planned his first campaign with great care, then
three years into it finds himself with only half an army. He
is overextended, unable to bring news of smashing victories to the High Council and the Emperor. He loses
position and prestige in the game."

Fannon said, "Unbelievable! Hundreds of men dying
for such a thing."

"As I have said, Swordmaster, it is very Tsurani. Any
who had no direct stake in the game would applaud the
move as a masterstroke. Many families hovering near the
edge of the War Party would be drawn to the Blue Wheel
and their allies for delivering such a blow."

Arutha said, "But the important fact for us is that this
Blue Wheel is once more allied with the Warlord, and their
soldiers will be rejoining the war come spring."

Charles looked at those in the council hall. "I cannot
begin to guess why there has once again been a realign-
ment in the council. I am too removed from the game. But
as His Highness has said, what is important for those of us
here in Crydee to know is that as many as ten thousand
fresh soldiers may come against one of the fronts in the
spring."

Amos scowled. "That's a backbreaker, for certain."

Arutha unfolded a half-dozen parchments. "Over the
last few months, most of you have read these messages."
He looked at Tully and Fannon. "You've seen the pattern
begin to emerge." He picked up one parchment. "From
Father: 'Constant Tsurani sorties and raids keep our men in
a state of unease. Our inability to close with the enemy has

lent a dark aspect to all we do. I fear we shall never see an
end to this business. . . .' From Baron Bellamy: '. . . increased Tsurani activity near the Jonril garrison. I deem it
advisable to increase our commitment there this winter,
while the Tsurani are normally inactive, lest we lose that
position next spring.' Squire Roland will be supervising a
joint reinforcement from Carse and Tulan at Jonril this
winter."

Several in the room glanced at Roland, who stood near
Arutha's shoulder. The Prince continued. "From Lord
Dulanic, Knight-Marshal of Krondor: 'While His Highness
shares your concern, there is little to indicate the need for
alarm. Unless some intelligence can be produced to give
credence to your fears of possible future Tsurani offensives,
I have advised the Prince of Krondor to refuse your request
for elements of the Krondorian garrison to be sent to the
Far Coast. . . .'" Arutha looked around the room. "Now
the pattern is clear."

Setting aside the parchments, Arutha pointed at the
map affixed to the tabletop. "We have committed every
available soldier. We dare not pull men from the south for
fear of the Tsurani moving against Jonril. With the garrison
strengthened, we will have a stable situation down there
for a while. Should the enemy attack the garrison, it can be
reinforced from Carse and Tulan. Should the enemy move
against either castle, they leave Jonril at their back. But all
that will fail should we strip those garrisons.

"And Father is committed to a long front and has no
men to spare." He looked at Charles. "Where would you
expect the attack to come?"

The former Tsurani slave looked over the map, then
shrugged. "It's difficult to say, Highness. Should the
situation be decided solely upon military merits, the
Warlord should attack against the weaker front, either
toward the elves or here. But little done in the Empire is
free of political considerations." He studied troop disposi-
tions on the map, then said, "Were I the Warlord, in need
of a simple victory to bolster my position in the High
Council, I would attack Crydee once more. But were I the
Warlord and my position in the High Council precarious, in
need of a bold stroke to regain lost prestige, I might risk an
all-out offensive against the main force of the Kingdom,

those armies under Duke Borric's command. To crush the main strength of the Kingdom would give him dominance within the council for years to come."

Fannon leaned back in his chair and sighed. "Then we are faced with the possibility of another assault upon Crydee this spring without recourse to reinforcements for fear of attack elsewhere." He indicated the map with a sweep of his hand. "Now we face the same problem as the Duke. All our forces are committed along the Tsurani front. The only men we have available are those in the towns on leave, only a small part of the whole.

"We can't maintain the army in the field indefinitely; even Lords Borric and Brucal winter in LaMut with the Earl, leaving small companies to guard the Tsurani." Waving his hand in the air, he said, "I digress. What is important is to notify your father at once, Arutha, of the possibility of attack. Then should the Tsurani hit his lines, he'll be back from LaMut early, in position and ready. Even should the Tsurani bring ten thousand fresh troops, he can call up more soldiers from the outlying garrisons in Yabon, fully another two thousand."

Amos said, "Two thousand against ten thousand sounds poor odds, Swordmaster."

Fannon was inclined to agree. "We do all we can. There are no guarantees it will be enough."

Charles said, "At least they will be horse soldiers, Swordmaster. My former comrades still have little liking for horses."

Fannon nodded agreement. "But even so, it is a bleak picture."

"There is one thing," said Arutha, holding up a parchment. "The message from Lord Dulanic stated the need for intelligence to give credence to our request for aid. We now have enough intelligence to satisfy him, I think."

Fannon said, "Even a small portion of the Krondorian garrison here would give us the strength to resist an offensive. Still, it is late in the season and a message would have to be dispatched at once."

"That's the gods' truth," said Amos. "If you left this afternoon, you'd barely clear the Straits of Darkness before winter shuts them off. In another two weeks it'd be a close thing."

Arutha said, "I have given the matter some thought. I think there is enough need to risk my going to Krondor."

Fannon sat up straight in his chair. "But you're the commander of the Duchy's army, Arutha. You can't abandon that responsibility."

Arutha smiled. "I can and I will. I know you have no wish to resume command here once more, but resume command you will. If we are to win support from Erland, I must convince him myself. When Father first carried word of the Tsurani to Erland and the King, I learned the advantage of speaking in person. Erland's a cautious man. I will need every persuasion I can bring to bear."

Amos snorted. "And how do you plan on reaching Krondor, begging Your Highness's pardon? There's the better part of three Tsurani armies bewteen here and the Free Cities should you go overland. And there are only a few luggers fit for coasting in the harbor, and you'd need a deep-water ship for a sea journey."

"There's one deep-water ship, Amos. The *Wind of Dawn* is still in port."

Amos's mouth dropped open. "The *Wind of Dawn*?" he cried in disbelief. "Beside the fact she's little better than a lugger herself, she's laid up for the winter. I heard her captain crying over her broken keelson when the muddleheaded fool came limping into harbor a month ago. She needs to be hauled out, have the keel inspected and the keelson replaced. Without repair her keel's too weak to take the pounding she'll get from the winter storms. You might as well stick your head in a rain barrel, begging Your Highness's pardon. You'd still drown, but you'd save a lot of other people a great deal of trouble."

Fannon looked incensed at the seaman's remarks, but Tully, Martin, Roland, and Arutha only looked amused. "When I sent Martin out," said Arutha, "I considered the possibility I might need a ship for Krondor. I ordered her repaired two weeks ago. There's a swarm of shipwrights aboard her now." He fixed Amos with a questioning look. "Of course I've been told it won't be as good a job as if they'd hauled her out, but it will serve."

"Aye, for potting up and down the coast in the light winds of spring, perhaps. But you're talking about winter storms, and you're talking about running the Straits of Darkness."

Arutha said, "Well, she will have to do. I'm leaving in a few days' time. Someone must convince Erland we need aid, and I have to be the one."

Amos refused to let the subject drop. "And has Oscar Danteen agreed to captain his ship through the straits for you?"

Arutha said, "I've not told him our destination as yet."

Amos shook his head. "As I thought. That man's got the heart of a shark, which is to say none, and the courage of a jellyfish, which is also to say none. Soon as you give the order, he'll cut your throat, drop you over the side, winter with the pirates of the Sunset Islands, then head straight for the Free Cities come spring. He'll then have some Natalese scribe pen a most grieving and flowery message to your father, describing your valor just before you were lost overboard in high seas while fighting pirates. Then he'll spend a year drinking up the gold you gave him for passage."

Arutha said, "But I purchased his ship. I'm ship's master now."

Amos said, "Owner or not, Prince or not, aboard ship there is but one master, the captain. He is King and High Priest, and no man tells him what to do, save when a pilot's aboard and then only with respect. No, Highness, you'll not survive this journey with Oscar Danteen on the quarterdeck."

Faint lines of mirth began to crinkle at the corners of Arutha's eyes. "Have you another suggestion, *Captain*?"

Amos sighed as he sank back into his chair. "I've been hooked; I might as well be gutted and cleaned. Send word to Danteen to clear out the captain's cabin and discharge the crew. I'll see to getting a replacement crew for that band of cutthroats, though there's mostly drunkards and boys left in port this time of year. And for the love of the gods, don't mention to anyone where we're bound. If so much as one of those drink-besotted scoundrels learns you mean to risk the Straits of Darkness this late in the season, you'll have to turn out the garrison to comb the woods for deserters."

Arutha said, "Very well. I'll leave all preparations to you. We depart as soon as you judge the ship ready." He said to Longbow, "I'll want you to come as well, Huntmaster."

Longbow looked a little surprised. "Me, Highness?"

"I'll want an eyewitness for Lord Dulanic and the Prince."

Martin frowned, but after a moment said, "I've never been to Krondor, Highness." He smiled his crooked smile. "I may never have the chance again."

Amos Trask's voice cut through the shriek of the wind. Gusts from the sea carried his words to a confused-looking lad aloft. "No, you warped-brained landlubber, don't pull the sheets so damn tight. They'll be humming like a lute string. They don't pull the ship, the mast does. The lines help when the wind changes quarter." He watched as the boy adjusted the sheets. "Yes, that's it; no, that's too loose." He swore loudly. "Now; there you have it!"

He looked disgusted as Arutha came up the gangway. "Fishing boys who want to be sailors. And drunkards. And a few of Danteen's rogues I had to rehire. This is some crew, Highness."

"Will they serve?"

"They bloody well better, or they'll answer to me." He watched with a critical eye as the sailors crawled over the spars aloft, checking every knot and splice, every line and sheet. "We need thirty good men. I can count on eight. The rest? I mean to put into Carse as well as Tulan on the way down. Maybe then we can replace the boys and less dependable men with experienced seamen."

"What of the delay clearing the straits?"

"If we were there today, we would manage. By the time we get there a dependable crew will prove more important than arriving a week earlier. The season will be full upon us." He studied Arutha. "Do you know why the passage is called the Straits of Darkness?"

Arutha shrugged. Amos said, "It's no simple sailor's superstition. It's a description of what you find there." He got a far-off look as he said, "Now, I can tell you about the different currents from the Endless Sea and Bitter Sea that come together there, or about the changing, crazy tides of winter when the moons are all in the worst possible aspect in the heavens, or how winds come sweeping down from the north, blowing snow so thick you can't see the decks from the yards. But then . . . There are no words to describe the straits in winter. It is one, two, three days traveling blind. And if the prevailing wind's not blowing you back into the Endless Sea, then it's blowing you to the southern rocks. Or there's no wind, and fog blots out everything as the currents turn you around."

"You paint a bleak picture, Captain," said Arutha with a grim smile.

"Only the truth. You're a young man of uncommonly practical wits and cold nerve, Highness. I've seen you stand when many men of greater experience would have broken and run. I'm not trying to put any scare upon you. I simply wish you to understand what you propose to do. If any can clear the straits in winter in this bucket, it is Amos Trask, and that's no idle boast. I've cut the season so fine before, there's little to tell between autumn and winter, winter and spring. But I would also tell you this: before leaving Crydee, say tender good-byes to your sister, write your father and brother, and leave any testaments and legacies in order."

Without changing expression, Arutha said, "The letters and legacies are written, and Carline and I dine alone tonight."

Amos nodded. "We'll leave on the morning tide. This ship's a slab-sided, wattle-bottomed, water-rotted coaster, Highness, but she'll make it through if I have to pick her up and carry her."

Arutha took his leave, and when he was out of sight, Amos turned his attention heavenward. "Astalon," he invoked the god of justice, "I'm a sinner, it's true. But if you had to measure out justice, did it have to be this?" Now at peace with his fate, Amos returned to the business of seeing everything in order.

Carline walked in the garden, the withering blooms reflecting her own sad mood. Roland watched her from a short way off, trying to find words of comfort. Finally he said, "I will be Baron of Tulan someday. It is over nine years since I've been home. I must go down the coast with Arutha."

Softly she said, "I know."

He saw the resignation on her face and crossed to hold her. "You will be Baroness there someday, also."

She hugged him tightly, then stepped away, forcing herself to a lighter mood. "Still, you'd think after all these years your father would have learned to do without you."

He smiled. "He was to have wintered in Jonril with Baron Bellamy, overseeing the enlargement of the garrison. I will go in his stead. My brothers are all too young. With the Tsurani dug in for the winter, it is our only chance to expand the fort."

With forced gaiety, she said, "At least I won't have to worry about your breaking the hearts of the ladies of your father's court."

He laughed. "Little chance of that. Supplies and men are already assembling and the barges ready to travel up the river Wyndermeer. After Amos puts me ashore in Tulan, I'll spend one or two days at home, no more, then off I go. It will be a long winter in Jonril with no one for company but soldiers and a few farmers in that gods-forsaken fort."

Carline covered her mouth as she giggled. "I hope your father doesn't discover you've gambled away his barony to the soldiers come spring."

Roland smiled at her. "I'll miss you."

Carline took his hands in hers. "And I you."

They stood in frozen tableau for a time, then suddenly Carline's façade of bravery cracked and she was in his arms. "Don't let anything happen. I couldn't bear losing you."

"I know," he said gently. "But you must continue to put on a brave face for others. Fannon will need your help in conducting court, and you will have the responsibility for the entire household. You are mistress of Crydee, and many people will depend upon your guidance."

They watched the banners on the walls snapping in the late afternoon wind. The air was harsh and he drew his cloak about them. Trembling, she said, "Come back to me, Roland."

Softly he said, "I'll come back, Carline." He tried to shake a cold, icy feeling that had risen within, but could not.

They stood on the dock, in the darkness of morning before the sunrise. Arutha and Roland waited by the gangway. Arutha said, "Take care of everything, Swordmaster."

Fannon stood with his hand upon his sword, still proud and erect despite advancing years. "I will, Highness."

With a slight smile, Arutha said, "And when Gardan and Algon return from patrol, instruct them to take care of you."

Fannon's eyes blazed as he shot back. "Insolent pup! I can best any man of the castle, save your father. Step down from the gangway and draw your sword and I'll show you why I still wear the badge of Swordmaster."

Arutha held his hands up in mock supplication. "Fannon, it is good to see such sparks again. Crydee is well protected by her Swordmaster."

Fannon stepped forward and placed his hand upon Arutha's shoulder. "Take care, Arutha. You were always my best student. I should hate to lose you."

Arutha smiled fondly at his old teacher. "My thanks, Fannon." Then his manner turned wry. "I would hate to lose me, also. I'll be back— And I'll have Erland's soldiers with me."

Arutha and Roland sprang up the gangway, while those on the dock waved good-bye. Martin Longbow waited at the rail, watching as the gangway was removed and the men upon the quay cast off lines. Amos Trask shouted orders and sails were lowered. Slowly the ship moved away from the quayside into the harbor. Arutha watched silently, with Roland and Martin beside, as the docks fell behind.

Roland said, "I was glad the Princess chose not to come. One more good-bye would be more than I could manage."

"I understand," said Arutha. "She cares for you greatly, Squire, though I can't see why." Roland looked to see if the Prince was joking, and found Arutha smiling faintly. "I've not spoken of it," the Prince continued. "But since we may not see each other for some time after you leave us in Tulan, you should know when the opportunity comes for you to speak to Father, you'll have my word on your behalf."

"Thank you, Arutha."

The town slipped by in darkness, replaced by the causeway to the lighthouse. The false dawn pierced the gloom slightly, casting everything into greys and blacks. Then after some time the large upthrust form of the Guardian Rocks appeared off the starboard quarter.

Amos ordered the helm put over and they turned southwestward, more sails set to bring them full before the wind. The ship picked up speed and Arutha could hear gulls crying overhead. Suddenly he was struck with the knowledge they were now out of Crydee. He felt chilled and gathered his cloak tightly around him.

Arutha stood on the quarterdeck, sword held ready, Martin to one side notching an arrow to his bowstring. Amos Trask and his first mate, Vasco, also had weapons drawn. Six angry-looking seamen were assembled upon the deck below, while the rest of the crew watched the confrontation.

One sailor shouted from the deck, "You've lied to us, Captain. You've not put back north for Crydee as you said in Tulan. Unless you mean for us to sail on to Keshian Elarial, there's nothing south save the straits. Do you mean to pass the Straits of Darkness?"

Amos roared, "Damn you, man. Do you question my orders?"

"Aye, Captain. Tradition holds there's no valid compact between captain and crew to sail the straits in winter, save by agreement. You lied to us and we're not obliged to sail with you."

Arutha heard Amos mutter, "A bloody sea lawyer." To the sailor he said, "Very well," and handed his cutlass to Vasco. Descending the ladder to the main deck, he approached the seaman with a friendly smile upon his face.

"Look, lads," he began as he reached the six recalcitrant sailors, all holding belaying pins or marlinespikes. "I'll be honest with you. The Prince must reach Krondor, or there'll be hell to pay come spring. The Tsurani gather a large force which may come against Crydee." He placed his hand upon the shoulder of the sailors' spokesman and said, "So what it comes down to is this: we must sail to Krondor." With a sudden motion, Amos had his arm around the man's neck. He ran to the side of the ship and heaved the helpless sailor over. "If you don't wish to come along," he shouted, "you can swim back to Tulan!"

Another sailor started to move toward Amos when an arrow struck the deck at his feet. He looked up and saw Martin taking a bead upon him. The Huntmaster said, "I wouldn't."

The man dropped his marlinespike and stepped back. Amos turned to face the sailors. "By the time I reach the quarterdeck, you had better be in the rigging—or over the side, it makes no difference to me. Any man not working will be hung for the mutinous dog he is."

The faint cries for help of the man in the water could be heard as Amos returned to the quarterdeck. To Vasco he said, "Toss that fool a rope, and if he doesn't relent, pitch him overboard again." Amos shouted, "Set sail for the Straits of Darkness."

Arutha blinked seawater out of his eyes and held on to the guide rope with all the strength he possessed. The entire ship had been rigged with safety lines, for in the rough sea it was impossible to keep a footing without something to hang on to.

Arutha pulled himself up the ladder to the quarterdeck and stumbled as much as walked to Amos Trask. The captain waited beside the helmsman, lending his weight to the large tiller when needed. He stood as if rooted to the wood of the deck, feet wide apart, weight shifting with each move of the ship, his eyes peering into the gloom above. He watched, listened, each sense tuned to the ship's rhythm. Arutha knew he had not slept for two days and a night, and most of this night as well.

"How much longer?" Arutha shouted.

"One, two days, who can say?" A snap from above sounded like cracking spring ice upon the river Crydee. "Hard aport!" Amos shouted, leaning heavily into the tiller. When the ship heeled, he shouted to Arutha, "Another day of these gods-cursed winds buffeting this ship and we'll be lucky if we can turn and run back to Tulan."

"Weather break!" came the shout from above.

"Where away?" cried Amos.

"Dead starboard!"

"Come about!" ordered Amos, and the helmsman leaned against the tiller.

Arutha strained his eyes against the stinging salt spray and saw a faint glow seem to swing about until it stood off the bow. Then it grew larger as they drove for the thinning weather. As if walking out of a dark room, they moved from gloom to light. The heavens seemed to open above them and they could see grey skies. The waves still ran high, but Arutha sensed the weather had turned at last. He looked over his shoulder and saw the black mass of the storm as it moved away from them.

Moment by moment the combers subsided, and after the raging clamor of the storm the sea seemed suddenly silent. The sky was quickly brightening and Amos said, "It's morning. I must have lost track of time. I thought it still night."

Arutha watched the receding storm and could see it clearly outlined, a churning mass of darkness against the lighter grey of the sky above. The grey quickly turned to slate, then blue grey as the morning sun broke through the storm. For the better part of an hour Arutha watched the spectacle, while Amos ordered his men about their tasks, sending the night watch below and the day watch above.

The storm raced eastward, leaving a choppy but otherwise tranquil sea behind. Time seemed to pass without record as Arutha stood in awe of the scene on the horizon. A portion of the storm seemed to have stopped, between distant fingers of land. Great spouts of water danced between the boundaries of the narrow passage in the distance. It looked as if a mass of dark, boiling clouds had been trapped within that area by some supernatural force.

"The Straits of Darkness," said Amos Trask at his shoulder.

"When do we put through them?" Arutha asked quietly.

"Now," answered Amos. The captain turned and shouted, "Day watch aloft! Mid-watch turn to and stand ready! Helmsman, set course due east!"

Men scrambled into the rigging, while others came from below, still haggard and showing little benefit from the few hours' sleep since they last stood watch. Arutha pulled back the hood of his cloak and felt the cold sting of the wind against his wet hair. Amos gripped him by the arm and said, "We could wait for weeks and not have the wind favorable again. That storm was a blessing in disguise, for it will give us a bold start through."

Arutha watched in fascination as they headed for the straits. Some freak of weather and current had created the conditions that held the straits in water-shrouded gloom all winter. In fair weather the straits were a difficult passage, for though they appeared wide at most points, dangerous rocks were hidden just below the water in many critical places. In foul weather they were considered impossible for most captains to negotiate. Sheets of water or flurries of snow blown down from the Grey Towers tried to fall, only to be caught by blasts of wind and tossed back upward again, to try to fall once more. Waterspouts suddenly erupted upward to spin madly for minutes, then dissolve into blinding cascades. Ragged bolts of lightning cracked and were followed by booming thunder as all the fury of colliding weather fronts was unleashed. Currents from two seas met and swirled about, creating sudden shifts and eddies that could turn a ship unexpectedly.

"The sea's running high," yelled Amos. "That's good. We'll have more room to clear the rocks and we'll be through or dashed to pieces in short order. If the wind holds we'll be through before the day is done."

"What if the winds change?"

"That is not something to dwell on!"

They raced forward, attacking the edge of the swirling weather inside the straits. The ship shuddered as if reluctant once again to face foul weather. Arutha gripped the rail tightly as the ship began to buck and lurch. Amos picked his way along, avoiding the sudden wayward gusts, keeping the ship in the westerly trail of the passed storm.

All light disappeared. The ship was illuminated only by the dancing light of the storm lanterns, casting flickering yellow darts into murk. The distant booming of waves upon rocks reverberated from all quarters, confusing the senses. Hours passed in cacophonous fury, while Amos commanded his crew to answer every challenge of wind and tide. Occasionally the darkness was punctuated by a blinding flash of lightning, bringing every detail into sharp focus, leaving dazzling afterimages in the darkness.

In a sudden lurch, the ship seemed to slip sideways, and Arutha felt his feet go out from under him as the ship heeled over. He held to the rail with all his strength, his ears deafened by a monstrous grinding. The ship righted itself, and Arutha pulled himself around to see, in the flickering glow of the storm lanterns, the tiller swinging wildly back and forth and the helmsman slumped down upon the deck, his face darkened by blood flowing from his open mouth. Amos was desperately scrambling upright, reaching for the lashing tiller. Risking broken ribs as he seized it, he fought desperately to hang on and bring the ship back under control.

Arutha half stumbled to the tiller and threw his weight against it. A long, low grinding sound came from the starboard side and the ship shuddered.

"Turn, you motherless bitch!" cried Amos as he heaved against the tiller, marshaling what strength he had left. Arutha felt his muscles protesting in pain as he strained against the seemingly immobile tiller. Slowly it moved, first an inch, then another. The grinding rose in volume, until Arutha's ears rang from the sound of it.

Suddenly the tiller swung free once more. Arutha overbalanced and went flying across the desk. He struck the hard wood and slid along the wet surface until he crashed into the bulwark, gasping as wind exploded from his lungs. A wave drenched him and he spluttered, spitting out a lungful of seawater. Groggily he pulled himself up and staggered back to the tiller.

In the faint light, Amos's face was white from exertion, but it was set in a wide-eyed, manic expression as he laughed. "Thought you'd gone over the side for a moment."

Arutha leaned into the tiller, and together they forced it to move once more. Amos's mad laughter rang out, and Arutha said, "What's so damn funny?"

"Look!"

Panting, Arutha looked where Amos indicated. In the darkness he saw huge forms rearing up alongside the ship, blacker shapes against the blackness. Amos yelled, "We're clearing the Great South Rocks. Pull, Prince of Crydee! Pull if you wish to ever see dry land again!"

Arutha hauled upon the tiller, forcing the balky ship away from the terrible stone embrace mere yards away. Again they felt the ship shudder as another low grinding sound came from below. Amos whooped. "If this barge has a bottom when we're through, I'll be amazed."

Arutha entered a new state of awareness. Seconds, minutes, hours lost all meaning. He struggled, with Amos, to keep the ship under control, but his senses recorded everything around him in minute detail. He could feel the grain of the wood through the wet leather of his gloves. The fabric of his stockings was gathered between his toes in his water-soaked boots. The wind smelled of salt and pitch, wet wool caps, and rain-drenched canvas. Every groan of timber, smack of rope against wood, and shout of men above could be clearly heard. Upon his face he felt the wind and cold touch of melting snow and seawater, and he laughed. Never had he felt so close to death, and never had he felt more alive. Muscles bunched and he pitted himself against forces primeval and formidable. On and on they plunged, deeper and deeper into the madness of the Straits of Darkness.

Arutha heard Amos as he shouted orders, orchestrating every man's move by the second. He played his ship as a master musician played a lute, sensing each vibration and sound, striving for that harmony of motion which kept the *Wind of Dawn* moving safely through perilous seas. The crew answered his every demand instantly, risking death in the treacherous rigging, for they knew their safe passage rested solely upon his skill.

Then it was over. One moment they were fighting with mad strength to clear the rocks and pass through the fury of the straits, the next they were running before a stiff breeze with the darkness behind.

Ahead the sky was overcast, but the storm that had held them for days was a distant gloom upon the eastern horizon. Arutha looked at his hands, as if at things apart, and willed them to release their hold upon the tiller.

Sailors caught him as he collapsed, and lowered him to the deck. For a time his senses reeled, then he saw Amos sitting a short way off as Vasco took the tiller. Amos's face was still mirthful as he said, "We did it, boy. We're in the Bitter Sea."

Arutha looked about. "Why is it still so dark?"

Amos laughed. "It's nearly sundown. We were on that tiller for hours."

Arutha began to laugh too. Never had he felt such triumph. He laughed until tears of exhaustion ran down his face, until his sides hurt. Amos half crawled to his side. "You know what it is to laugh at death, Arutha. You'll never be the same man again."

Arutha caught his breath. "I thought you mad there for a time."

Amos took a wineskin a sailor handed him and drew a deep drink. He passed it to Arutha and said, "Aye, as you were. It is something only a few know in their lives. It is a vision of something so clear, so true, it can only be a madness. You see what life is worth, and you know what death means."

Arutha looked up at the sailor standing by them, and saw it was the man Amos had pitched over the rail to head off the mutiny. Vasco threw the man a frown as he watched, but the man didn't move. Amos looked up at him and the seaman said, "Captain, I just wanted to say . . . I was wrong. Thirteen years a sailor, and I'd have wagered my soul to Lims-Kragma no master could pilot a ship such as this through the straits." Lowering his eyes, he said, "I'd willingly stand for flogging for what I done, Captain. But after, I'd sail to the Seven Lower Hells with you, and so would any man here."

Arutha looked about and saw other sailors gathering upon the quarterdeck or looking down from the rigging. Shouts of "Aye, Captain," and "He has the truth of it" could be heard.

Amos pulled himself up, gripping the rail of the ship, his legs wobbling a little. He surveyed the men gathered around, then shouted, "Night watch above! Mid-watch and day watch stand down." He turned to Vasco. "Check below for damage to the hull, then open the galley. Set course for Krondor."

Arutha came awake in his cabin. Martin Longbow was sitting by his side. "Here." The Huntmaster held out a steaming mug of broth.

Arutha levered himself up on his elbow, his bruised

and tired body protesting. He sipped at the hot broth. "How long was I asleep?"

"You fell asleep on deck last night, just after sundown. Or passed out, if you want the truth. It's three hours after sunrise."

"The weather?"

"Fair, or at least not storming. Amos is back on deck. He thinks it might hold most of the way. The damage below is not too bad; we'll be all right if we don't have to withstand another gale. Even so, Amos says there are a few fair anchorages to be found along the Keshian coast should the need arise."

Arutha pulled himself out of his bunk, put on his cloak, and went up on deck, Martin following. Amos stood by the tiller, his eyes studying the way the sail held the wind. He lowered his gaze to watch as Arutha and Martin climbed the ladder to the quarterdeck. For a moment he studied the pair, as if struck by some thought or another, then smiled as Arutha asked, "How do we fare?"

Amos said, "We've a broad reach to the winds; had it since we cleared the straits. If it holds from the northwest, we should reach Krondor quickly enough. But winds rarely do hold, so we may take a bit longer."

The rest of the day passed uneventfully and Arutha enjoyed a sense of respite after the dangers of the last few days. The night brought a clear display of stars; he spent several hours on deck studying the bright array in the heavens. Martin came on deck and found him looking upward. Arutha heard the arrival of the Huntmaster and said, "Kulgan and Tully say the stars are suns much like our own, made small by vast distances."

Martin said, "An incredible thought, but I think they are right."

"Have you wondered if one of those is where the Tsurani homeworld lies?"

Martin leaned upon the rail. "Many times, Highness. In the hills you can see the stars like this, after the campfires are out. Undimmed by lights from town or keep, they blaze across the sky. I also have wondered if one of them might be where our enemies live. Charles has told me their sun is brighter than ours, and their world hotter."

"It seems impossible. To make war across such a void defies all logic."

They stood quietly together watching the glory of the night, ignoring the bite of the crisp wind that carried them to Krondor. Footfalls behind caused them to turn as one, and Amos Trask appeared. He hesitated a moment, studying the two faces before him, then joined them at the rail. "Stargazing, is it?"

The others said nothing, and Trask watched the wake of the ship, then the sky. "There is no place like the sea, gentlemen. Those who live on land all their lives can never truly understand. The sea is basic, sometimes cruel, sometimes gentle, and never predictable. But it is nights like this that make me thankful the gods allowed me to be a sailor."

Arutha said, "And something of a philosopher as well."

Amos chuckled. "Take any deep-water sailor who's faced death at sea as many times as I have, and scratch him lightly. Underneath you'll find a philosopher, Highness. No fancy words, I'll warrant you, but a deep abiding sense of his place in the world."

Martin spoke quietly, almost to himself. "When I was a boy, among the great trees, I knew such feelings. To stand by a bole so ancient it is older than the oldest living memory of man gives such a sense of place in the world."

Arutha stretched. "It is late. I shall bid you both a good night." As he started to leave, he seemed taken by some thought. "I am not given to your philosophies, but . . . I am pleased to have shared this voyage with you both."

After he was gone, Martin watched the stars for a time, then became aware Amos was studying him. He faced the seaman and said, "You seem taken by some thought, Amos."

"Aye, Master Longbow." Leaning against the rail, he said, "Nearly seven full years have passed since I came to Crydee. Something has tickled my mind since first meeting you."

"What is that, Amos?"

"You're a man of mysteries, Martin. There're many things in my own life I'd not wish recounted now, but with you it's something else."

Martin appeared indifferent to the course of conversation, but his eyes narrowed slightly. "There's little about me not well known in Crydee."

"True, but it is that little which troubles me."

"Put your mind at ease, Amos. I am the Duke's Huntmaster, nothing more."

Quietly Amos said, "I think more, Martin. In my travels through the town, overseeing the rebuilding, I've met a lot of people, and in seven years I've heard a lot of gossip about you. Some time back I put the pieces together and came up with an answer. It explains why I see your manner change—only a little, but enough to notice—when you're around Arutha, and especially when you're around the Princess."

Martin laughed. "You spin an old and tired bard's tale, Amos. You think I am the poor hunter desperate for love of a young Princess? You think me in love with Carline?"

Amos said, "No, though I have no doubt you love her. As much as any brother loves his sister."

Martin had his belt knife half out when Amos's hand caught his wrist. The thickset seaman held the hunter's wrist in a viselike grip and Martin could not move his arm. "Stay your anger, Martin. I'd not like to have to pitch you over the side to cool you off."

Martin ceased his struggling against Amos and released his knife, letting it slide back into its sheath. Amos held the hunter's wrist a moment longer, then let go. After a moment Martin said, "She has no knowledge, nor do her brothers. Until this time I thought only the Duke and one or two others might know. How did you learn of it?"

Amos said, "It was not hard. People most often don't see what is right before them." Amos turned and watched the sails above, absently checking each detail of the ship's crew as he spoke. "I've seen the Duke's likeness in the great hall. Should you grow a beard like his, the resemblance would shout for the world to see. All in the castle remark how Arutha grows to resemble his mother less and father more each passing year, and I've been nagged since we first met why no one else noticed he resembles you as well. I expect they don't notice because they choose not to. It explains so much: why you were granted special favor by the Duke in placing you with the old Huntmaster, and why you were chosen Huntmaster when a new one was needed. For some time now I've suspected, but tonight I was certain. When I came up from the lower deck and you

both turned in the darkness, for a moment I couldn't tell
which of you was which."

Martin spoke with no emotion, just a statement of fact.
"It's your life should you breathe a word of it to anyone."

Amos settled himself against the rail. "I'm a bad man
to threaten, Martin Longbow."

"It is a matter of honor."

Amos crossed his arms over his chest. "Lord Borric is
not the first noble to father a bastard, nor will he be the last.
Many are even given offices and rank. How is the Duke of
Crydee's honor endangered?"

Martin gripped the rail, standing like a statue in the
night. His words seemed to come from a great distance.
"Not his honor, Captain. Mine." He faced Amos, and in
the night his eyes seemed alive with inner light as they
reflected the lantern hung behind the seaman. "The Duke
knows of my birth, and for his own reasons chose to bring
me to Crydee when I was still little more than a boy. I am
sure Father Tully has been told, for he stands highest in the
Duke's trust, and possibly Kulgan as well. But none of
them suspect I know. They think me ignorant of my
heritage."

Amos stroked his beard. "A knotty problem, Martin.
Secrets within secrets, and such. Well, you have my
word—from friendship, not from threat—I'll not speak to
anyone of this, save by your leave. Still, if I judge Arutha
aright, he would sooner know as not."

"That is for me to decide, Amos, no one else. Someday
perhaps I'll tell him, or I may not."

Amos pushed himself from the rail. "I've much to do
before I turn in, Martin, but I'll say one more thing. You've
plotted a lonely course. I do not envy you your journey
upon it. Good night."

"Good night." After Amos had returned to the quarterdeck, Martin watched the familiar stars in the sky. All
the companions of his solitary travels through the hills of
Crydee looked down upon him. The great and lesser
constellations shone in the night, the Beasthunter and the
Beasthound, the Dragon, the Kraken, and the Five Jewels.
He turned his attention to the sea, staring down into the
blackness, lost in thoughts he had once imagined buried
forever.

* * *

"Land ho!" shouted the lookout.

"Where away?" answered Amos.

"Dead ahead, Captain."

Arutha, Martin, and Amos left the quarterdeck and quickly made their way to the bow. As they stood waiting for land to heave into sight, Amos said, "Can you feel that trembling each time we breast a trough? It's that keelson, if I know how a ship's made, and I do. We'll need to put in at a shipyard for refitting in Krondor."

Arutha watched as the thin strip of land in the distance grew clearer in the afternoon light. While not bright, the day was relatively fair, only slightly overcast. "We should have time. I'll want to return to Crydee as soon as Erland's convinced of the risk, but even if he agrees at once, it will take some time to gather the men and ships."

Martin said, dryly, "And I for one would not care to pass the Straits of Darkness again until the weather is a bit more agreeable."

Amos said, "Man of faint heart. You've already done it the hard way. Going to the Far Coast in the dead of winter is only slightly suicidal."

Arutha waited in silence as the distant landfall began to resolve in detail. In less than an hour they could clearly make out the sights of Krondor's towers rising into the air, and ships at anchor in the harbor.

"Well," said Amos, "if you wish a state welcome, I'd better have your banner broken out and run up the mast."

Arutha held him back, saying, "Wait, Amos. Do you mark that ship by the harbor's mouth?"

As they closed upon the harbor, Amos studied the ship in question. "She's a beastly bitch. Look at the size of her. The Prince's building them a damn sight bigger than when I was last in Krondor. Three-masted, and rigged for thirty or better sail from flying jib to spanker. From the lines of her hull, she's a greyhound, no doubt. I'd not want to run up against her with less than three Quegan galleys. You'd need the rowers, for those oversized crossbows she mounts fore and aft would quickly make a hash of your rigging."

"Mark the banner at her masthead, Amos," said Arutha.

Entering the harbor, they passed near the ship. On her bow was painted her name, *Royal Griffin*. Amos said, "A Kingdom warship, no doubt, but I've never seen one under any banner but Krondor's." Atop the ship's highest mast a black banner emblazoned with a golden eagle snapped in the breeze. "I thought I knew every banner seen on the Bitter Sea, but that one is new to me."

"The same banner flies above the docks, Arutha," said Martin, pointing toward the distant city.

Quietly Arutha said, "That banner has never been seen on the Bitter Sea before." His expression turned grim as he said, "Unless I say otherwise, we are Natalese traders, nothing more."

"Whose banner is that?" asked Amos.

Gripping the rail, Arutha replied, "It is the banner of the second-oldest house in the Kingdom. It announces that my distant cousin, Guy, the Duke of Bas-Tyra, is in Krondor."

SIX

KRONDOR

The inn was crowded.

Amos led Arutha and Martin through the common room to an empty table near the fireplace. Snatches of conversation reached Arutha's ears as they took their seats. On close inspection the mood in the room was more restrained than it had first appeared.

Arutha's thoughts raced. His plans for securing Erland's help had been crushed within minutes of reaching the harbor. Everywhere in the city were signs that Guy du Bas-Tyra was not simply guesting in Krondor, but was now fully in control. Men of the city watch followed officers wearing the black and gold of Bas-Tyra, and Guy's banner flew over every tower in the city.

When a dowdy serving wench came, Amos ordered three mugs of ale, and the men waited in silence until they were brought. When the serving-woman was gone Amos said, "We'll have to pick our way carefully now."

Arutha's expression remained fixed. "How long before we can sail?"

"Weeks, at least three. We've got to get the hull repaired, and the keelson replaced correctly. How long will depend on the shipwrights. Winter's a bad time: the fair-weather traders haul out their ships, so they'll be fit come spring. I'll begin inquiries first thing tomorrow."

"That may take too long. If needs be, buy another."

Amos raised an eyebrow. "You've funds?"

"In my chest aboard ship." With a grim smile, he said, "The Tsurani aren't the only ones who play politics with war. To many of the nobles in Krondor and the East, the war is a distant thing, hardly imaginable. It has gone on for nearly nine years, and all they ever see is dispatches.

"And our loyal Kingdom merchants don't donate supplies and ships out of love for King Rodric. My gold is a hedge against underwriting the cost of bringing Krondorian soldiers to Crydee, both in expenses and bribes."

"Well then," said Amos, "even so it will be a week or two. You don't usually stroll into a ship's brokerage and pay gold for the first ship offered, not if you wish to avoid notice. And most of the ships sold are fairly worthless. It will take time."

"And," put in Martin, "there's the straits."

"That's true," agreed Amos, "though we could take a leisurely turn up the coast to Sarth and wait to time our run through the Straits."

"No," said Arutha. "Sarth is still in the Principality. If Guy's in control of Krondor, he'll have agents and soldiers there. We won't be safe until we're out of the Bitter Sea. We'll attract less attention in Krondor than in Sarth: strangers are not uncommon here."

Amos looked long at Arutha, then said, "Now, I don't claim to know you as well as some men I've met, but I don't think you're as concerned for your own skin as something else."

Arutha glanced about the room. "We better find a less public place to talk."

With a sound between a sigh and a groan, Amos
heaved himself out of his chair. "The Sailor's Ease is not
where I'd prefer to stay, but for our purposes it will serve."
He made his way to the long bar and spoke at length to the
innkeeper. The heavyset owner of the inn pointed up the
stairs and Amos nodded. He signed for his companions to
accompany him and led them through the press of the
common room, up the stairs, and down a long hall to the
last door. Pushing it aside, he motioned for them to enter.

Inside they found a room with little to recommend
itself by way of comforts. Four straw-stuffed pallets rested
on the floor. A large box in the corner served as a common
closet. A crude lamp, a simple wick floating in a bowl of oil,
sat upon a rude table; it burned with a pungent odor when
Longbow struck a spark to it.

Amos closed the door as Arutha said, "I can see what
you meant about choices in rooms."

"I've slept in far worse," answered Amos, settling
down on one of the pallets. "If we're to keep our liberty,
we'd best establish believable identities. For the time
being, we'll call you Arthur. It's close enough to your own
to afford a passable explanation should someone call out
your real name and cause you to turn or answer. Also, it
will be easy to remember."

Arutha and Martin sat down, and Amos continued.
"Arthur—get used to that name—of navigating cities you
know less than a thimbleful, which is twice as much as
Martin knows. You'll do well to play the role of some minor
noble's son, from some out-of-the-way place. Martin, you
are a hunter from the hills of Natal."

"I can speak the language passing well."

Arutha gave a half-smile. "Get him a grey cloak and
he'd make a fair ranger. I don't speak the language of
Natal, or the Keshian tongue, so I'll be the son of a minor
eastern noble, visiting for recreation. Few in Krondor could
know half the barons of the East."

"Just so long as it's not too close to Bas-Tyra. With all
those black tabards about, it would be a pretty thing to run
into a supposed cousin among Guy's officers."

Arutha's expression turned dark. "You were correct
about my concerns, Amos. I'll not leave Krondor until I've
discovered exactly what Guy is doing here and what it
means for the war."

"Even should I find us a ship tomorrow," said Amos, "which is unlikely, you should have plenty of time to snoop about. Probably find out more than you'll want to know. The city's a lousy place for secrets. The rumormongers will be plying their trade in the market, and every commoner in the city will know enough to give you a fair picture of what's taken place. Just remember to keep your mouth shut and ears open. Rumormongers'll sell you what you want to know, then turn around and sell news of your asking to the city guard so fast it'd make you spin to watch." Amos stretched, then said, "It's still early, but I think we should have a hot meal, then to bed. We've a lot of prowling about to accomplish." With that he rose and opened the door, and the three men returned to the common room.

Arutha munched upon a nearly cold meat pie. Lowering his head, he forced himself to continue consuming the pieman's greasy ware. He refused to consider what was contained within the soggy crust in addition to the beef and pork the seller claimed.

Casting a sidelong glance across the busy square, Arutha studied the gates to Prince Erland's palace. Finishing the pie, he quickly crossed to an ale stand and ordered a large mug to wash away the aftertaste. For the last hour he had moved, seemingly without purpose, from seller's cart to seller's cart, purchasing this and that, posing as a minor noble's son. And in that hour he had learned a great deal.

Martin and Amos came into sight, nearly an hour before the appointed time. Both wore grim expressions and kept glancing nervously about. Without comment, Amos motioned for Arutha to follow as they walked by. They pushed through the midday throng and passed quickly away from the great-square district. Reaching a less hospitable-looking though no less busy area, they continued until Amos indicated they should enter a particular building.

Once through the door, Amos was met by a hot, steamy atmosphere as an attendant came to greet them. "A bathhouse?" said Arutha.

Without humor, Amos said, "You need to get rid of

some road dirt, Arthur." To the attendant he said, "A steam for us all."

The man led them to a changing room and handed each a rough towel and a canvas bag for belongings. Arutha stood quietly as first Amos, then Martin stripped down, then followed suit. They wrapped the towels about them and carried their clothing and weapons in the bags into the steam room.

The large room was completely tiled, though the walls and floors were stained and showed patches of green. The air was close and fetid. A small half-naked boy squatted in the center of the room, before the bed of rocks that supplied the steam. He alternately fed wood to the huge brazier below the stones and poured water upon them, generating giant clouds of steam.

When they were seated upon a bench, in the farthest corner of the room, Arutha said, "Why a bathhouse?"

Amos whispered, "A great deal of business is conducted in places such as these, so three men whispering in the corner won't draw undue attention." He shouted to the boy, "You, lad, run and fetch some chilled wine." Amos tossed a silver coin at the boy, who caught it in midair. When he didn't move, Amos tossed him another and the boy scampered off. With a sigh, Amos said, "The price of chilled wine has doubled since I was last here. He'll be gone for a while, but not too long."

"What is this?" asked Arutha, not taking pains to hide his ill humor. The towel itched and the room stank, and he doubted if he'd be any cleaner for the time spent here than if he'd stayed in the square.

"Martin and I both have troublesome news."

"As do I. I already know Guy is Viceroy in Krondor. What else have you learned?"

Martin said, "I overheard some conversation which makes me believe Guy has imprisoned Erland and his family in the palace."

Arutha's eyes narrowed and his voice was low and angry. "Even Guy wouldn't dare harm the Prince of Krondor."

Martin said, "He would should the King give his leave. I know little of this trouble between the King and the Prince, but it is clear that Guy is now the power in Krondor, and acts with the King's permission, if not his blessing. You told me of Caldric's warning when you were last in Rillanon. Perhaps the King's sickness has grown worse."

"Madness, if you mean to speak clearly," snapped Arutha.

"To further cloud things in Krondor," said Amos, "it seems we are at war with Great Kesh."

"What!" said Arutha.

"A rumor, nothing more." Amos spoke quietly and quickly. "Before finding Martin, I was nosing around a local joy house, not too far from the garrison barracks. I overheard some soldiers at their ease saying they were to leave at first light for a campaign. When the object of one soldier's momentary ardor asked when she would see him again, he said, 'As long as it takes to march to the vale and back, should luck be with us,' at which point he invoked Ruthia's name, so that the Lady of Luck would not view his discussion of her province disfavorably."

"The vale?" said Arutha. "That can only mean a campaign down into the Vale of Dreams. Kesh must have hit the garrison at Shamata with an expeditionary force of dog soldiers. Guy's no fool. He'll know the only answer's a quick, unhesitating strike from Krondor, to show Great Kesh's Empress we can still defend our borders. Once the dog soldiers have been driven south of the vale, we'll have another round of useless treaty talks over who has the right to it. That means even should Guy wish to aid Crydee, which I doubt, he could not. There's no time to deal with Kesh, return, and reach Crydee by spring, or even early summer." Arutha swore. "This is bitter news, Amos."

"There is still more. Earlier today, I took the trouble to visit the ship, just to ensure Vasco had everything in hand, and that the men weren't chafing too much at being kept aboard. Our ship is being watched."

"Are you sure?"

"Certain. There's a couple of boys who stand around, playing at net mending, but they do no real work. They watched closely as I rowed out and back."

"Who do you think they are?"

"I can't begin to guess. They could be Guy's men, or men still loyal to Erland. They could be agents of Great Kesh, smugglers, even Mockers."

"Mockers?" asked Martin.

"The Guild of Thieves," said Arutha. "Little goes on in Krondor without notice by their leader, the Upright Man."

Amos said, "That mysterious personage runs the Mockers with tighter control than a captain has over his crew. There are places in the city where even the Prince cannot reach, but no place in Krondor is beyond the Upright Man. If he's taken an interest in us, for whatever reason, we have much to fear."

The conversation was interrupted by the serving boy's return. He set down a chilled pewter pitcher of wine and three cups. Amos said, "Fetch yourself to the nearest incense vendor, boy. This place stinks. Buy something sweet to toss upon the fire."

The boy regarded them a little warily, then shrugged as Amos tossed him another coin. He ran from the room, and Amos said, "He'll be back soon, and I've run out of reasons to send him away. In any event this place will soon be thick with merchants taking an afternoon steam.

"When the boy comes back, sip some wine, try to relax, and don't leave too soon. Now, in all this bleak mess, there is one small glimmer of light."

"Then I would hear what it is," said Arutha.

"Guy will soon be gone from the city."

Arutha's eyes narrowed. "Still, his men will be left in charge. But what you say does have some aspect of comfort. There are a few in Krondor likely to mark me by sight, for it's nearly nine years since I was last here, and most of those have likely disappeared with the Prince. Also, there is a plan I've been considering. With Guy out of Krondor, I would have an even better chance of success."

"What plan?" asked Amos.

Quietly and quickly, Arutha said, "I noticed two things this morning: Erland's personal guards still patrol the palace grounds, so there must be limits to Guy's control. Second, several of Erland's courtiers entered and left freely enough, so some large portion of the daily business of governing the Western Realm must remain unchanged."

Amos stroked his chin, thinking. "That would seem logical. Guy brought his army with him, not his administrators. They're still back running Bas-Tyra."

"Which means Lord Dulanic and others not entirely

sympathetic to Guy might still be able to aid us. If Dulanic will help, I can still succeed with my mission."

"How?" asked Amos.

"As Erland's Knight-Marshal, Dulanic has control of vassal garrisons to Krondor. Upon his signature alone he could call up the garrisons at Durrony's Vale and Malac's Cross. If he ordered them to march to Sarth, they could join the garrison there and take ship for Crydee. It would be a hard march, but we could still bring them to Crydee by spring."

"And no hardship to your father, either. I was going to tell you: I have heard Guy has sent soldiers the Krondorian garrison to your father."

Arutha said, "That seems strange. I can't imagine Guy wishing to aid Father."

Amos shook his head. "Not so strange. To your father it will seem as if Guy has only been sent by the King to aid Erland, for I suspect the rumors of Erland's being a prisoner in his own palace are not as yet widespread. Also, it is a fine pretext to rid the city of officers and men loyal to the Prince.

"Still, it is no small boon to your father. From all accounts nearly four thousand men have left or are leaving for the north. That might be enough to deal with the Tsurani should they come against the Duke."

Martin said, "But should they come against Crydee?"

"For that we must seek aid. We must get inside the palace and find Dulanic."

"How?" Amos asked.

"It was my hope you might have a suggestion."

Amos looked down, then said, "Is there anyone in the palace you know to be trustworthy?"

"Before, I could have named a dozen, but this business makes me doubt everyone. Who stands with the Viceroy and who with the Prince I can't begin to guess."

"Then we'll have to nose about some more. And we'll have to listen for news of likely ships for transport. Once we've hired a few, we'll slip them out of Krondor one or two at a time, every few days. We'll need at least a score to carry the men of three garrisons. Assuming you get Dulanic's support, which brings us back to gaining entrance to the palace." Amos swore softly. "Are you sure you wouldn't care to chuck this business and become a privateer?" Arutha's expression clearly showed he was unamused. Amos sighed. "I thought not."

Arutha said, "You seem to know the underside of the city well, Amos. Use your experience to find us a way into the palace, even if through the sewer. I'll keep my eyes open for any of Erland's men who might wander through the great square. Martin, you'll have to simply keep your ears open."

With a long sigh of resignation, Amos said, "Getting into the palace is a risky plan, and I don't mind telling you I don't care for the odds. I may even bounce into Ruthia's temple and ask the Lady of Luck to smile upon us."

Arutha dug a gold coin from his belongings and tossed it to Amos. "Say a prayer to the Lady for me as well."

The boy returned and tossed a small bundle of incense upon the fire, cutting off conversation. Arutha settled back and drank the chilled wine, rapidly warming in the heat of the steam room. He closed his eyes, but was not relaxing, as he considered the situation. After a while he began to feel his plan might work if he could reach Dulanic. Running out of patience, he was the first to rise, rinse off, dress, and leave.

The night's silence was ruptured by trumpets calling men to arms. Arutha was the first to the window, thrusting aside the wooden shutters and peering through. With most of the city asleep, there were few lights to mask the glow in the east. Amos reached Arutha's side, Martin a step behind.

Martin said, "Campfires, hundreds of them." The Huntmaster glanced heavenward, marking the stars' positions in the clear sky, and said, "Two hours to dawn."

"Guy's readying his army for the march," said Arutha quietly.

Amos leaned far out the window. By craning his neck, he could catch a glimpse of the harbor. In the distance men were calling aboard ships. "Sounds like they're readying ships as well."

Arutha leaned with both hands upon the table by the window. "Guy will send his foot soldiers by ship down the coast, into the Sea of Dreams, to Shamata, while his cavalry rides to the south. His foot will reach the city fresh enough to help bolster the defense, and when his horses arrive, they aren't sick from traveling by ship. And they'll arrive within days of one another."

As if to prove his words, from the east came the sounds of marching men. Then a few minutes later the first company of Bas-Tyra's foot soldiers came into view. Arutha and his companions watched them march past the open gate of the inn's courtyard. Lanterns gave the soldiers a strange, otherworld appearance as they marched in columns down the street. They stepped in cadence, their golden eagle banners snapping above their heads. Martin said, "They are well-schooled troops."

Arutha said, "Guy is many things, most of them unpleasant, but one thing cannot be argued: he is the finest general in the Kingdom. Even Father is forced to admit that, though he'll say nothing else good about the man. Were I the King, I would send the Armies of the East under his command to fight the Tsurani. Three times Guy has marched against Kesh, and three times he has thrashed them. If the Keshians do not know he's come west, the very sight of his banner in the field may drive them to the peace table, for they fear and respect him." Arutha's voice became thoughtful in tone. "There is one thing. When Guy first came to be Duke of Bas-Tyra, he suffered some sort of personal dishonor—Father never told what that shame was—and took to wearing only black as a badge of sorts, earning him the name Black Guy. That type of thing takes a strange brand of personal courage. Whatever else can be said of Black Guy du Bas-Tyra, none will call him craven."

While the soldiers continued to pass below, Arutha and his companions watched in silence. Then, with the sun rising in the east, the last soldiers disappeared along the streets to the harbor.

The morning after Guy's army had marched, it was announced the city was sealed, the gates closed to all travelers and the harbor blockaded. Arutha judged it a normal practice, to prevent Keshian agents from leaving the city by fast sloop or fast horse to carry word of Guy's march. Amos used a visit to the *Wind of Dawn* to view the harbor blockade and discovered it was a light one, for Guy had ordered most of the fleet to stand off the coast at sea ambush, watching for any Keshian flotillas should Kesh learn the city was stripped of her garrison. The city was now policed by city guards in Guy's livery, as the last Krondorian soldiers departed for the north. Rumor had it Guy would also send the garrison at Shamata to the front once the fighting with Kesh had been settled, leaving every garrison in the Principality manned by soldiers loyal to Bas-Tyra.

Arutha spent most of his time in taverns, places of business, and the open markets most likely to be frequented by those from the palace. Amos prowled near the docks or in the city's seedier sections, especially the infamous Poor Quarter, and began making discreet inquiries about the availability of ships. Martin used his guise as a simple woodsman to blunder into any place that looked promising.

Nearly a week went by this way, with little new information being unearthed. Then, late the sixth day after Guy had quit the city, Arutha found himself being hailed in the middle of the busy square by Martin.

"Arthur!" shouted the hunter as he ran up to Arutha. "Best come quickly." He set off toward the waterfront and the Sailor's Ease.

Back at the inn they found Amos already in the room, resting upon his pallet before his nightly sojourn into the Poor Quarter. Once the door was closed, Martin said, "I think they may know Arutha's in Krondor."

Amos bolted upright as Arutha said, "What? How . . . ?"

"I wandered into a tavern near the barracks, just before the midday meal. With the army gone from the city, there was little business. One man did enter, just as I was readying to leave. A scribe with the city's Quartermaster, he was fit to burst with a rumor and in need of someone to tell it to. So, with the aid of some wine, I obliged him by playing the simple woodsy, and by showing respect for so important a personage.

"Three things this man told me. Lord Dulanic has disappeared from Krondor, gone the night Guy left. There's some business of his having retired to nameless estates to the north, now that Guy's Viceroy, but the scribe thought that unlikely. The second thing was news of Lord Barry's death."

Arutha's face showed shock. "The Prince's Lord Admiral dead?"

"This man told me Barry had died under mysterious circumstances, though there's no official announcement planned. Some eastern lord, Jessup, has been given command of the Krondorian fleet."

"Jessup is Guy's man," said Arutha. "He commanded the Bas-Tyra squadrons of the King's fleet."

"And lastly, the man made a display of knowing some secret concerning a search for someone he only called 'the Viceroy's royal cousin.'"

Amos swore. "I don't know how, but someone's marked you. With Erland and his family virtual captives in the palace, there's hardly a chance another royal cousin's come wandering into Krondor in the last few days, unless you've a few out and about you've not told us of."

Arutha ignored Amos's feeble humor. In the span of time it took for Longbow to tell his tale, all his plans for aiding Crydee were dashed. The city was firmly in control of those either loyal to Guy or indifferent to who ruled in the King's name. There was no one in the city he could turn to for help, and his failure in bringing aid home was a bitter thing. Quietly he said, "Then there's no other course but to return to Crydee as soon as possible."

"That may not be so easy," said Amos. "There's more strange things occurring. I've been in places where a man can usually make contact with those needed for a dishonest task or two, but everywhere I've made inquiries—discreet, have no doubt—I came up against only hard silence. If I didn't know better, I'd swear the Upright Man's closed up shop and all the Mockers are now serving in Guy's army. I've never seen such a collection of dumb barmen, ignorant whores, uninformed beggars, and tongueless gamblers. You don't need to be a genius to see the word's gone out. No one is to talk to strangers, no matter how promising a transaction's being offered. So we can look for no aid in getting free of the city, and if Guy's agents know you're in Krondor, there'll be no lifting of the blockade or opening of the gates until you've been found, no matter how loudly the merchants scream."

"We're deep in the snare," agreed Martin.

Amos slowly shook his head. "A bollixed mission this, and through no fault of yours, Arutha." He sighed. "Still, we can't be startled into panic. Friend Martin may have misunderstood the scribe's last remark, or the man may have been speaking simply to hear himself talk. We'll have to be cautious, but we can't bolt and run. Should you vanish from sight completely, someone might take notice. Best if you stay close to the inn, but act as you have been, for the time being. I'll continue to make attempts at reaching someone who may have ways to get us clear of the city—smugglers, if not the Mockers."

Arutha rose from the pallet and said, "I've no appetite, but we've eaten together in the common room every night. I expect we best go down for supper soon."

Amos waved him back to his bed. "Stay awhile longer. I'm going to run down to the docks and visit the ship. If Martin's scribe was not just breaking wind, they'll certainly search the ships in the harbor. I'd better warn Vasco and the crew to be ready to go over the side if necessary, and find some place to store your chest. We aren't due to be hauled out for refitting for another week, so we must act with care. I've run blockades before. I wouldn't want to risk it in a hulk as leaky as the *Wind of Dawn*, but if I can't find another ship . . ." At the door he turned back to face Arutha and Martin. "It's a black storm, boys, but we've weathered worse."

Arutha and Martin sat quietly as Amos entered the common room. The seaman pulled out a chair and called for ale and a meal. Once he was served, he said, "All is taken care of. Your chest is safe as long as the ship is left moored."

"Where did you hide it?"

"It's snugly wrapped in oilcloth and tied securely to the anchor."

Arutha looked impressed. "Underwater?"

"You can buy new clothes, and gold and gems don't rust."

Martin said, "How are the men?"

"Grumbling over being in port another week and still aboard ship, but they're good lads."

The door to the inn opened and six men entered. Five took chairs near the door while one stood surveying the room. Amos hissed, "See that rat-faced fellow who just sat down? He's one of the boys who've been watching the docks for the last week. Look's like I've been followed."

The man who remained standing spotted Amos and approached the table. He was a plain-looking man, of open countenance. His reddish blond hair was flyaway around his head, and he wore a common sailor's clothing. He clutched a wool cap in hand as he smiled at them.

Amos nodded, and the man said, "If you're the master of the *Wind of Dawn*, I'd have words with you."

Amos raised an eyebrow, but said nothing. He indicated the free chair and the man sat. "Name's Radburn. I'm looking for a berth, Captain."

Amos looked about, seeing Radburn's companions were pretending not to notice what was transpiring at the table. "Why my ship?"

"I've tried others. They're all full up. Just thought I'd ask you."

"Who was your last master and why did you leave his service?"

Radburn laughed, a friendly sound. "Well, I last sailed with a company of barge ferrymen, taking cargo from ship to shore in the harbor. Been stuck doing that for a year." He fell silent as the serving wench approached. Amos ordered another round of ale, and when one was set before Radburn, he said, "Thank you, Captain." He took a long pull and wiped his mouth with the back of his hand. "Before I came to be beached, I sailed with Captain John Avery, aboard the *Bantamina*."

"I know the Little Rooster, and John Avery, though I haven't seen him since I was last in Durbin, five or six years back."

"Well, I got a little drunk, and the captain told me he'd have none who drank aboard his ship. I drink no more than the next man, Captain, but you know Master Avery's reputation, being an abstentious follower of Sung the White."

Amos looked at Martin and Arutha, but said nothing. Radburn said, "These your officers, Captain?"

"No, business partners." When it was clear Amos was

going to say nothing more, Radburn let the topic of
identities drop. Amos finally said, "We've been in the city
little more than a week, and I've been busy with personal
matters. What news?"

"Since the Viceroy's come," said Radburn quietly,
"things haven't been the same in Krondor. An honest man
isn't safe on the streets anymore, what with Durbin slavers
running about and the press gangs almost as bad. That's
why I need a ship, Captain."

"Press gangs!" Amos exploded. "There hasn't been a
press gang in a Kingdom city in thirty years."

"Once was, but now things have changed again. You
get a little drunk and don't find a safe berth for the night,
the press gang comes along and slaps you into the
dungeon. It just isn't right, no sir. Just because a man's
between ships doesn't give anyone the right to ship him
out with Lord Jessup's fleet for seven years. Seven years of
chasing pirates and fighting Quegan war galleys!"

"Well, Radburn, I can always use a good man who's
sailed with John Avery. I'll tell you what. I've one more trip
to the ship to make tonight, and there're some personal
belongings in my room I'll want aboard. Come along and
carry them."

Amos rose and, giving the man no time to object,
gripped him by the arm and propelled him toward the
stairs. Arutha shot a glance at the group who entered with
Radburn. They seemed unaware for the moment of what
was transpiring across the crowded common room as
Amos took Radburn up the stairs, Arutha and Martin
following behind.

Amos hustled Radburn down the hall and, once
through the door to their room, spun and delivered a
staggering blow to Radburn's stomach, doubling him over.
A brutal knee to the face, and Radburn lay stunned upon
the floor.

"What is this all about?" said Arutha.

"That man's a liar. John Avery's a marked man in Kesh.
He betrayed the Durbin Captains to a Quegan raiding fleet
twenty years ago. Yet Radburn didn't bat an eye when I
said I saw Avery in Durbin six years ago. And he's too free
in showing disrespect to the Viceroy. His story stinks like a
week-dead fish. We go out the door with him, and inside of
two blocks a dozen men or more will be upon us."

"What shall we do?" said Arutha.

"We leave. His friends will be up those stairs in a minute." He pointed to the window. Martin stood by the door as Arutha ripped aside a dirty canvas shade and pushed open the wooden shutters. Amos said, "Now you see why I chose this room." Less than a yard below the window's ledge was the roof of the stable.

Arutha stepped out, Amos and Martin following. They hurried carefully down the steeply sloping roof until they reached the edge. Arutha leaped down, landing quietly, followed a moment later by Martin. Amos landed more heavily, but suffered only a minor bruise to his dignity.

They heard a cough and an oath, and looked up to see a bloodied face at the window. Radburn shouted, "They're in the courtyard!" as the three fugitives started for the gate.

Amos swore. "I should have cut his throat."

They ran to the gate, and as they entered the street, Amos grabbed at Arutha. A group of men were running down the street toward them. Arutha and his companions fled the opposite way, ducking into a dark alley.

Hurrying along between the blank walls of two buildings, they cut across a busy street, overturning several pushcarts, and ducked into another alley, the cart owners' curses following. They continued to run, the sounds of pursuit never far behind, following a twisting maze of back alleys and side streets through darkened Krondor.

Turning a corner, they found themselves intersecting a long narrow street, little more than an alley, flanked on both sides by tall buildings. Amos rounded the corner first and motioned for Arutha and Martin to halt. In low tones, he said, "Martin, hurry down to the corner and take a look around. Arutha, go the other way." He pointed toward a spot where dim light could be seen. "I'll stand watch here. If we become separated, make for the ship."

Arutha and Martin ran down the street in opposite directions and Amos stood watch behind. Abruptly shouts came down the narrow street and Arutha looked back. At the other end of the street he could see the dim figure of Martin struggling with several men. He started back, but Amos shouted, "Go on. I'll help him. Get away!"

Arutha hesitated, then resumed his run toward the

distant light. He was panting when he reached the corner and nearly skidded to a halt as he entered a well-traveled, brightly lit avenue. From carts decorated with lanterns hawkers sold their wares to passing citizens out for a stroll after supper. The weather was mild—there looked to be little chance of snow this winter—and large numbers of people were about. From the condition of the buildings and the fashions of those in the area, Arutha knew he was in a more prosperous section of the city.

Arutha stepped into the street and walked at a forced leisurely pace. He turned and made a display of examining a garment seller's wares as several men appeared from the street he had just fled. He tugged a garish red cloak from among the goods and swirled it about his shoulder, pulling the hood over his head. "Here now, what do you think you're doing?" asked a dried-faced old man in a reedy whisper.

Affecting a nasal voice, Arutha said, "My good man, you don't expect me to purchase a garment without seeing if it fits?"

Suddenly confronted by a buyer, the man became unctuously friendly. "Oh no, certainly, sir." Looking at Arutha in the ill-tailored cloak, he said, "It's a perfect fit, sir, and the color suits you well, if I may say."

Arutha chanced a glance at his pursuers. The man called Radburn stood at the corner, blood dried upon his face and his nose swollen, but still able to direct his men's search. Arutha adjusted the cloak, a great, cumbersome thing that hung nearly to the ground. In a display of fussiness, he said, "You think so? I wouldn't care to appear at court looking like a vagabond."

"Oh, court is it, sir? Well, it's just the thing, mark me. It adds a certain elegance to your appearance."

"How much is it?" Arutha saw Radburn's men walking through the busy crowd, some looking into each tavern and storefront as they passed, others hurrying on to other destinations. More followed from the smaller street, and Radburn spoke quickly to them. He set some to watching those in the street, then turned and led the rest back the way they had come.

"It's the finest cloth made in Ran, sir," said the seller. "It was brought at great expense from the shore of the

Kingdom Sea. I couldn't let it go for less than twenty golden sovereigns."

Arutha blanched, and for a moment was so struck by the outrageous price he nearly forgot himself. "Twenty!" He lowered his voice as a passing member of Radburn's company threw him a quick glance. "My dear man," he said, returning to character, "I seek to purchase a cloak, not establish an annuity for your grandchildren." Radburn's man turned away, and disappeared into the press of the crowd. "It is rather a plain wrap, after all. I should think two sovereigns more than sufficient."

The man looked stricken. "Sir, you seek to beggar me. I couldn't think of parting with it for a sum of less than eighteen sovereigns."

They haggled for another ten minutes, and Arutha finally departed with the cloak for the price of eight sovereigns and two silver royals. It was double the price he should have paid, but the searchers had ignored a man haggling with a street seller, and escaping detection was worth the price a hundred times over.

Arutha kept alert for signs he was being watched as he made his way along the street. Unfortunately he knew little of Krondor and had no idea where he was after the flight. He kept to the busier part of the street, staying close to larger groups, seeking to blend in.

Arutha saw a man standing at the corner, seemingly idling the night away, but clearly watching those who passed. Arutha looked around and saw a tavern on the other side of the street, marked by a brightly painted sign of a white dove. He quickly crossed the street, keeping his face turned away from the man at the corner, and approached the doorway of the tavern. As he reached for the door, a hand gripped his cloak, and Arutha spun, his sword halfway out of its scabbard. A boy of about thirteen stood there, wearing a simple, oft-patched tunic and men's trousers cut off at the knees. He had dark hair and eyes and his smudged face was set in a grin. "Not there, sir," he said with a merry note in his voice.

Arutha slipped his sword back into the scabbard and fell into character. "Begone, boy. I've no time for beggars or panderers, even those of limited stature."

The boy's grin broadened. "If you insist, but there are two of them in there."

Arutha dropped his nasal accent. "Who?"

"The men who chased you from the side street."

Arutha glanced about. The boy appeared alone. He looked into the boy's eyes and said, "What are you talking about?"

"I saw how you acted. Quick on your feet, sir. But they've blanketed the area and you'll not be slipping them by yourself."

Arutha leaned forward. "Who are you, boy?"

With a toss of his ragged hair he said, "Name's Jimmy. I work hereabouts. I can get you out. For a fee, of course."

"And what makes you think I wish to get out?"

"Don't play the fool with me, like you did with the merchant, sir. You need to get clear of somebody who's likely to pay me to show him where you are. I've run afoul of Radburn and his men before, so you have more of my sympathy than he's likely to get. As long as you can bid more for your freedom than he will for your capture."

"You know Radburn?"

Jimmy grinned. "Not so as I'd care to admit, but yes, we've had dealings before."

Arutha was struck by the boy's cool manner, not what he would have expected from the boys he knew back home. Here stood an old hand at negotiating the treacherous byways of the city. "How much?"

"Radburn will pay me twenty-five gold to find you, fifty if he especially wants your skin."

Arutha took out his coin pouch and handed it to the boy. "Over a hundred sovereigns in there, boy. Get me out of here and to the docks and I'll double it."

The boy's eyes flickered wide a moment, but he never lost his grin. "You must have offended someone with a lot of influence. Come along."

He darted away so quickly, Arutha almost lost him in the heavy crowd. The boy moved with the ease of experience through the press, while Arutha had to struggle to keep from jostling people in the street.

Jimmy led him into an alley, several blocks away. When they were a short way down the alley, Jimmy stopped. "Better toss that cloak. Red's not my favorite color for looking inconspicuous." When Arutha had pitched the cloak into an empty barrel, Jimmy said, "You'll be pointed at the docks in a moment. If someone tumbles on to us, you're on your own. But for that other hundred gold, I'll try to see you all the way."

They worked their way to the end of the alley, apparently seldom used from the heavy accumulation of trash and discarded objects, packing crates, broken furniture, and nameless goods against the walls around them. Jimmy pulled aside a crate, revealing a hole. "This should put us outside Radburn's net, at least I hope so," said Jimmy.

Arutha found he had to crouch to follow the boy through the small passage. From the rank odor in the tunnel, it was clear something had crawled in here to die fairly recently. As if reading his mind, Jimmy said, "We toss a dead cat in here every few days. Keeps others from sticking their noses too far in."

"We?" said Arutha.

Jimmy ignored the question and kept moving. Soon they exited into another alley overburdened with trash. At the mouth of the alley, Jimmy motioned for Arutha to stop and wait. He hurried along the dark street, then returned at a run. "Radburn's men. They must have known you'd head for the harbor."

"Can we slip past them?"

"No chance. They're as thick as lice on a beggar." The boy took off in the opposite direction down the street they had entered from the alley. Arutha followed as Jimmy turned up another small byway. Arutha hoped he hadn't bargained wrongly in trusting the street boy. After a few minutes of traveling, Jimmy stopped. "I know a place you can hold up awhile, until I can find some others to help get you to your ship. But it'll cost you more than a hundred."

"Get me to my ship before dawn and I'll give you whatever you ask."

Jimmy grinned. "I can ask a lot." He regarded Arutha for a moment longer, then with a curt nod of his head led off. Arutha followed and they wound their way deeper into the city. The sounds of people in the streets fell off, and Arutha judged they were moving into an area less well traveled at night. The buildings around them showed they were heading into another poor area of the city, though not close to the docks as far as Arutha could tell.

Several sharp turns through dark, narrow alleys, and Arutha was completely lost. Abruptly Jimmy turned and said, "We're there." He pulled open a door in an otherwise blank wall and stepped through. Arutha climbed a long flight of stairs after him.

Jimmy led him down a long hall at the top of the stairs, to a door. The boy opened it and indicated Arutha should enter. Arutha took a single step, then halted as he discovered three sword points leveled at his stomach.

SEVEN

ESCAPE

A man motioned for Arutha to enter.

He sat behind a small table facing the door. Leaning forward into the light of the small lamp on the table, he said, "Please come in." The light revealed his face was covered with pockmarks and he possessed a large hooked nose. His eyes never strayed from Arutha as the three swordsmen stepped back, allowing the Prince entrance. Arutha hesitated as he saw the bound and unconscious forms of Amos and Martin slumped against the wall. Amos groaned and stirred, but Martin remained motionless.

Arutha measured the distance between himself and the three swordsmen, his hand hovering near the hilt of his rapier. Any notion of leaping back and drawing his sword vanished when he felt a dagger point pressed against the small of his back. A hand snaked around from behind and relieved him of his sword.

Jimmy then stepped around the Prince, examining the rapier as he carefully hid his dagger in the folds of his loose tunic. He grinned broadly. "I've seen a few of these about. It's light enough I could use it."

Dryly Arutha said, "Under the circumstances, it might

not be inappropriate to make it my legacy to you. Use it in good health."

The pock-faced man said, "You keep your wits about you," as Arutha was ushered into the room by a swordsman. Another put away his weapon and tied Arutha's arms behind him. He was then roughly thrust into a chair, opposite the man who had spoken, who continued. "My name is Aaron Cook, and you've already met Jimmy the Hand." He indicated the boy. "These others prefer to remain anonymous at present."

Arutha looked at the boy. "Jimmy the Hand?"

The boy executed a fair imitation of a courtly bow, and Cook said, "The finest pickpocket in Krondor and well on his way to becoming the finest thief as well, should you be inclined to believe his self-appraisal.

"Now, to matters of business. Who are you?"

Arutha related the story of being Amos's business partner, calling himself Arthur, and Cook studied him stoically. With a sigh, he nodded and one of the silent men stepped forward and struck Arutha across the mouth. Arutha's head snapped back from the force of the blow and his eyes watered. "Friend Arthur," said Aaron Cook, shaking his head, "we can go about this interview two ways. I'd advise you not to make the choice of the difficult way. It will prove most unpleasant and we shall know what we want in the end in any event. So please consider your answer carefully." He stood and came around the table. "Who are you?"

Arutha began to repeat his story and the man who struck him stepped forward again, ending his answer with another ringing blow. The man called Cook leaned down so his face was level with Arutha's. Arutha blinked to clear the tears from his eyes, and Cook said, "Friend, tell us what we ask. Now, so as not to waste time"—he pointed at Amos—"that he is the captain of your ship we concede, but you his business partner . . . I think not. That other fellow played the part of a hunter from the mountains in several taverns about town, and I think it no mummery; he has the look of one who knows mountains better than city streets, a look hard to forge." He studied Arutha. "But you . . . you are a soldier at least, and your rich boots and fine sword mark you a gentleman. But I think there is more." Looking into Arutha's eyes, he said, "Now, why is Jocko Radburn so intent upon finding you?"

Arutha looked Aaron Cook squarely in the eyes. "I don't know."

The man who had struck Arutha began to step forward again, but Cook held up his hand. "That may be true. You've been something of a fool, the way you've been popping up here and there, hanging around the gates of the palace, playing the innocent. You are either poor spies, or poor fools, but there is no doubt you've aroused the interest of the Viceroy's men, and therefore ours."

"Who are you?"

Cook ignored the question. "Jocko Radburn's the senior officer in the Viceroy's secret police. Despite that open, honest face on him, Radburn's one of the most steel-nerved, unmovable bastards the gods ever graced this world with. He'd happily cut his grandmother's heart out if he thought the old girl was making free with state secrets. The fact he put in a personal appearance shows he, at the very least, judges you potentially important.

"We first learned three men were nosing about town a day or two after you arrived, and when our people heard some of Radburn's men were keeping an eye upon you, we decided to do likewise. When they began offering small bribes for information about you three, we became especially interested. We were content to simply keep watching you, waiting until you showed your hand. ·

"But when Jocko and his men showed at the Sailor's Ease, we were forced to act. We snatched those two from under Jocko's nose, but Jocko and his bully boys came down the alley between you and us, so we hurried them away. Jimmy's finding you was a bit of luck, for he didn't know we were ready to bring you in." He nodded approval to the boy. "You did right bringing him here."

Jimmy laughed. "I was on the rooftops, watching the whole thing. I knew you wanted him in as soon as you grabbed the other two."

One of the men swore. "You'd better not have been trying for a boost without writ from the Nightmaster, boy."

Cook raised his hand, and the man fell silent. "It will not hurt for you to know that some here are Mockers, others are not, but we are all united in an undertaking of great importance. Mark me well, Arthur. Your only hope of leaving here alive rests upon our being satisfied you do not endanger that undertaking I spoke of. It may be Radburn's interest in you is only coincidental to his interest in other matters. Or there may be a weaving of threads here, some pattern as yet unseen. In any event, we shall have the truth, and when we are satisfied with what you have told us, we shall set you free—perhaps even aid you and your companions—or we shall kill you. Now start at the beginning. Why did you come to Krondor?"

Arutha considered. There was little but pain to be gained by lying, yet he was not willing to tell the entire truth. That these men were not working with Guy's men wasn't proved. This could be a ploy, with Radburn in the next room listening to every word. He decided what part of the truth to tell. "I'm an agent for Crydee. I came to speak to Prince Erland and Lord Dulanic in person, to ask for aid against a coming Tsurani offensive. When we learned Guy du Bas-Tyra was in possession of the city, we decided to gauge the temper of things before committing ourselves to a course of action."

Cook listened closely, then said, "Why should an emissary of Crydee slip into the city? Why not come in with banners flying and receive a state welcome?"

"Because Black Guy'd just as soon toss him into a cell as not, you stupid bastard."

Cook's head snapped around: Amos was sitting up against the wall, groggily shaking his head. "I think you busted my skull, Cook."

Aaron Cook looked hard at Amos. "You know me?"

"Aye, you wooden-headed sea rat, I know you. I know you well enough to know we're not speaking another word until you go fetch Trevor Hull."

Aaron Cook rose from the table, an uncertain expression on his face. He motioned to one of the men by the door, who also looked discomforted by Amos's words. The man nodded to Cook and left the room. Minutes later he returned, followed by another man, tall, with a shock of grey hair, but still powerful-looking. A ragged scar ran from his forehead through his right eye, which was milky white, and down his cheek. He took a long look at Amos, then laughed aloud and pointed at the captives. "Untie them."

Amos was lifted by two men, then untied. As his ropes were loosened, he said, "I thought they'd hung you years ago, Trevor."

The man clapped Amos on the back. "And I you, Amos."

Cook looked questioningly at the new arrival, while Arutha was untied and Martin revived with a cup of water. The man called Trevor Hull looked at Cook and said, "Have your wits fled, man? He's grown a beard and cut his famous flowing locks—lost some on top and put on a few pounds as well—but he's still Amos Trask."

Cook studied Amos a moment longer, then his eyes widened. "Captain Trenchard?"

Amos nodded and Arutha looked on in astonishment. Even in far Crydee they had heard of Trenchard the Pirate, the Dagger of the Sea. It was reputed even Quegan war galleys had turned and fled at sight of Trenchard's fleet, and not a town along the coasts of the Bitter Sea did not fear his marauders.

Aaron Cook extended his hand. "Sorry, Captain. It's been so many years since we last met. We couldn't be certain you weren't part of some plot of Radburn's to locate us."

"Who are you?" asked Arutha.

"All in good time," answered Hull. "Come."

One of the men helped the still-groggy Martin to his feet, and Cook and Hull led them to a more comfortable room, with chairs enough for all. When all were sitting, Amos said, "This old rogue is Trevor Hull, Captain White-eye, master of the *Red Raven.*"

Hull shook his head sadly. "No longer, Amos. Burned off of Elarial she was, three years ago, by imperial Keshian cutters. My mate Cook here and a few of my boys got to shore with me, but most of the crew went down with the *Red Raven.* We made our way back to Durbin, but things are changing, what with the wars and all. Came to Krondor a year ago, and have been working here since."

"Working? You, Trevor?"

The man smiled, his scar wrinkling, as he said, "Smuggling, in fact. That's what brought us together with the Mockers. Not much can happen in Krondor along those lines without the Upright Man's permission.

"When the Viceroy first came to Krondor, we started running up against Jocko Radburn and his secret police. He's been a thorn in our side from the first. This business of guards sneaking about dressed as common folk, there's just no honor in it."

Amos muttered, "I knew I should have cut his throat when I had the chance. Next time I won't be so damned civilized."

"Slowing down a bit, Amos? Well, a week ago we got word from the Upright Man he had a precious cargo to leave the city. We've had to bide our time until the right ship was ready. Radburn's very anxious to find that cargo before it leaves Krondor. So, you see, it's a most delicate situation, for we can't ship it until the blockade's lifted, or we find a blockade captain we can bribe. When we first caught wind you three were asking questions, we thought it might be some grand plot of Jocko's to find that cargo. Now we've cleared the air, I'd like to hear the answer to Cook's question explained. Why should an emissary from Crydee fear discovery by the Viceroy's men?"

"Listening in, were you?" Amos turned to Arutha, who nodded. "This is no simple emissary, Trevor. Our young friend is Prince Arutha, son of Duke Borric."

Aaron Cook's eyes went wide and the man who struck Arutha paled. Trevor Hull nodded understanding. "The Viceroy'd pay handsomely to get his hands upon the son of his old enemy, especially when it came time to press his claim in the Congress of Lords."

"What claim?" said Arutha.

Hull leaned forward, resting his elbows on his knees. "You'd not know, of course. We only heard the news a few days ago ourselves, and it's not common knowledge. Still, I'm not free to speak plainly without permission."

He rose and left the room. Arutha and Amos exchanged questioning glances, then Arutha looked toward Martin. "Are you all right?"

Martin carefully touched his head. "I'll recover, though they must have hit me with a tree."

One of the men grinned in a friendly, almost apologetic way. Patting a wooden billy in his belt sash, he said, "He's a hard one to bring down, that's for certain."

Hull returned to the room, followed by another. The

men in the room rose, and Arutha, Amos, and Martin
slowly followed suit. Behind Hull came a young girl no
more than sixteen years of age. Arutha was instantly struck
by the promise of beauty in her features: large sea-green
eyes, straight and delicate nose, and slightly full mouth. A
faint hint of freckles dusted her otherwise fair skin. She
was tall and slender and walked with poise. She came
across the room to Arutha, rose up on tiptoes, and kissed
him lightly upon the cheek. Arutha looked surprised at this
gesture and watched as she stepped back with a smile
upon her lips. She wore a simple dress of dark blue, and
her red-brown hair hung loosely to her shoulders. After a
second she said, "Of course, how silly I am. You'd not
know me. I saw you when you were last in Krondor, but
we never met. I'm your cousin Anita, Erland's daughter."

Arutha stood thunderstruck. Besides the girl's dis-
quieting effect upon his composure, with her winning
smile and clear gaze, he was doubly surprised to find her in
this company of brigands. He sat down slowly and she
took a chair. So used to the informality of his father's court,
he was somewhat surprised when she gave the others permission to sit.

"How . . . ?" Arutha began.

Amos interrupted. "The Upright Man's precious cargo?"

Hull nodded and the Princess spoke. Her pretty face
clouded with emotion. "When the Duke of Bas-Trya came
with orders from the King, Father greeted him warmly and
offered no resistance. At first Father did all he could to aid
him in taking command of the army, but when he heard of
the things Guy was doing with his secret police and press
gangs, Father protested. Then when Lord Barry died and
Guy put Lord Jessup in command of the fleet over Father's
objections, and Lord Dulanic disappeared so mysteriously,
Father sent a letter to the King, demanding Guy's recall.
Guy intercepted the message and ordered us kept under
guard in a wing of the palace. Then Guy came to my room
one night."

She shuddered. Arutha nearly spat when he said,
"You don't have to speak of such things." The sudden rage
startled the girl.

"No," she said, "it was nothing like that. He was very

proper, nearly formal. He simply informed me we were to be wed, and that King Rodric was to name him heir to the throne of Krondor. If anything, he seemed irritated by the bother of having to take such a course."

Arutha slammed his fist against the wall behind. "That tears it! Guy means to have Erland's crown and Rodric's after. He means to be King."

Anita looked at Arutha shyly. "So it seems. Father's not well and couldn't resist, though he refused to sign the proclamation of betrothal. Guy had him taken to the dungeon until he would sign." Her eyes teared as she said, "Father cannot live long in such cold and damp quarters. I fear he will die before agreeing to Guy's wishes." She continued to speak, her face a mask of control, though tears ran down her cheeks as she talked of her mother and father's imprisonment. "Then one of my ladies told me a maid knew some people in the city who might be willing to help."

Trevor Hull said, "With your permission, Highness. One of the girls in the palace is sister to a Mocker. With everything up in the wind, the Upright Man decided it might be to his advantage to take a hand. He arranged to smuggle the Princess out of the palace the night of Guy's departure and she's been here since."

Amos said, "Then the rumor we overheard before we fled the Sailor's Ease about there being a hunt on for a 'royal cousin' was about Anita, not Arutha."

Hull pointed at the Prince. "It may be Radburn and his boys still have no idea who you are. Most likely, they jumped on you in the hope you'd turn out to be party to the Princess's escape. We're almost certain the Viceroy has no idea she's gone from the palace, for she fled after he rode out. I expect Radburn is desperate to get her back before his master returns from the war with Kesh."

Arutha studied the Princess, feeling a strong desire to do something on her behalf, a desire beyond the consideration of foiling Guy. He shunted aside the strange tug of emotions. He asked Trevor Hull, "Why does the Upright Man wish to contend with Guy? Why isn't he turning her in for a reward?"

Trevor Hull looked to Jimmy the Hand, who answered with a grin. "My master, a most perceptive man, saw at once his own interests were best served by aiding the Princess. Since Erland has been Prince of Krondor, the business of the city runs smoothly, an environment conducive to the success of my master's many undertakings. Stability profits us all, you see. With Guy here, we've his secret police about, upsetting the normal commerce of our guild. And whatever else, we are most loyal subjects of His Highness the Prince of Krondor. If he does not wish his daughter to marry the Viceroy, we do not wish it as well." With a laugh, Jimmy added, "Besides, the Princess has agreed to pay twenty-five thousand gold sovereigns to our master should the guild get her free of Krondor, to be delivered when her father returns to power, or some other fate places her upon the throne."

Arutha took Anita's hand and said, "Well, cousin, there is nothing else to be done. We must take you to Crydee at the first chance."

Anita smiled and Arutha found himself smiling back. Trevor Hull said, "As I said before, we were waiting for the right opportunity to smuggle her from the city." He turned to Amos. "You're the man for this, Amos. There's no better blockade runner on the Bitter Sea—excepting myself, of course, but I've other matters to take care of here."

Trask said, "We can't leave for a few weeks yet. Even if the blockade was lifted, my ship's in desperate need of refitting. And if we left now we'd have to sail about until the weather in the straits breaks. With Jessup's fleet at sea ambush, that would be risky. I'd rather hide here awhile, then a quick run west, through the straits, and up the Far Coast with no delay."

Hull slapped him on the shoulder. "Good, that will give us time. I've heard of your ship; the boys tell me it's little better than a barge. We'll find you another. I'll send word to your men when the time is right. Radburn'll most likely leave your crew alone, hoping you'll turn up. We'll slip them aboard the new ship a few at a time at night and replace them with my own boys, so Radburn's men won't notice anything unusual aboard."

He turned to Arutha. "You'll be safe enough here, Highness. This building is one of many owned by the Mockers, and none will get close without our having ample warning. When the time is right, we'll get you all free of the city. Now we'll take you to your room, so you may rest."

Arutha, Martin, and Amos were shown to a room down the hall from the one where they had met Anita, while the Princess returned to her own quarters. The room they entered was a simple affair, but clean. All three men were tired. Martin fell heavily on one pallet and was quickly asleep. Amos lowered himself slowly, and Arutha watched him for a moment. With a slight smile he said, "When you first came to Crydee, I thought you a pirate."

Struggling to remove a boot, Amos said, "In truth, I tried to leave that behind me, Highness." He laughed. "Perhaps it was the gods working their revenge upon me, but you know, for fifteen years I was a corsair, then when I try my hand at honest trading for the first time, my ship is captured and burned, my crew slaughtered, and I find myself beached as far from the heart of the Kingdom as you can get and still be in it."

Arutha lay down upon his pallet. "You've been a good counselor, Amos Trask, and a brave companion. Your help over the years has earned you a good deal of forgiveness for past wrongdoings, but"—he shook his head—"Trenchard the Pirate! Gods, man, there's so much to forgive."

Amos yawned and stretched. "When we return to Crydee, you can hang me, Arutha, but for now please have the good grace to keep silent and put out the light. I am getting too old for this foolishness. I need some sleep."

Anita clapped appreciatively as Arutha turned aside the point of Jimmy's sword. The boy thief blushed at his awkwardness, but Arutha said, "That was better."

He and Jimmy were practicing basic swordwork, Jimmy with a rapier purchased with some of the gold Arutha had given him. For a month they had passed the time this way and Anita had taken to watching. Whenever the Princess was around, the usually brash Jimmy the Hand became subdued, and he blushed furiously whenever she spoke to him. Arutha was now certain the boy thief was afflicted by the worst sort of infatuation for the Princess, only three years older than himself. Arutha appreciated Jimmy's distress, for he also found the girl's presence a distraction. Still in the first years of womanhood, she nevertheless carried herself with court-bred grace, had wit and education and showed the promise of mature beauty. Arutha found it easier to turn his thoughts to other topics than the Princess.

The door opened and Amos walked in with Martin and Trevor Hull. Amos said, "The worse damn luck— begging the Princess's pardon. Arutha, the worst has occurred."

Arutha wiped the perspiration off his brow with a towel and said, "Don't stand there waiting for me to guess. What?"

"News came this morning," said Hull. "Guy is returning to Krondor."

"Why?" asked Anita.

Amos said, "It seems our Lord of Bas-Tyra rode into Shamata and ran his banner up above the walls. The Keshian commander had the good grace to mount one more attack, for the sake of form, then nearly gave himself a ruptured gut racing back home. He left a handful of minor nobles haggling with Guy's lieutenants over the conditions of armistice until a formal treaty can be drawn up between the King and the Keshian Empress. There's only one reason Guy can be hurrying back here."

Quietly Anita said, "He knows I've escaped."

Trevor Hull said, "Yes, Highness. This Black Guy's a wily one. He must have a spy in Radburn's company. It appears he doesn't even trust his own secret police overmuch. Luckily we still have people inside the palace loyal to your father, or we would never have learned of this turn."

Arutha sat down near the Princess. "Well, then we must soon be gone. It's either sail for home or toward Ylith to reach Father."

Amos said, "Looking at the choices, it seems there is little to recommend one course over the other. Both have dangers and advantages."

Martin looked at the girl, then said, "Though I don't think the Duke's war camp any place for a young woman."

Amos sat down by Arutha. "Your presence in Crydee is not vital, at least not for now. Fannon and Gardan are able men, and should the need arise, I think your sister would prove no mean commander. They should be able to keep things under control as well as you."

Martin said, "But you must ask yourself this: what will your father do when he learns Guy does not simply rule in Krondor as Erland's aide but holds the city completely in his power, that he's sending no aid to the Far Coast, and that he means to have the throne?"

Arutha nodded vigorously. "You are right, Martin. You know Father well. It will mean civil war." There was sorrow on his face. "He'll withdraw half the Armies of the West and march down the coast to Krondor and not stop until Guy's head is on a pole before the city's gates. Then the course will be set. He'll have to turn east and march against Rodric. He'd never wish the crown for himself, but once begun, he cannot stop short of total victory or defeat. But we'd lose the West to the Tsurani in time. Brucal couldn't hold them long with only half an army."

Jimmy said, "This civil war sounds a nasty sort of business."

Arutha sat forward. Wiping his forehead, he looked up from under damp locks. "We've not had one in two hundred fifty years, since the first Borric slew his half brother, Jon the Pretender. Compared to what this would be, with all the East marshaled against the West, that was only a skirmish."

Amos looked at Arutha with concern upon his face. "History's not my strong suit, but it seems to me you'd do best by your father keeping him in ignorance of this turn of events until the Tsurani spring offensive is finished."

Arutha exhaled a long, low breath. "There's nothing else for it. We know no aid will be forthcoming for Crydee. I can best decide what to do when I return. Perhaps in council with Fannon and the others we can work out some defense for when the Tsurani come." His tone was one of near-resignation. "Father will learn of Guy's plotting in due time. This sort of news is too hard to keep. The best we can hope for is he'll not hear of it until after the Tsurani offensive. Perhaps by then the situation will have changed." It was obvious from his tone he didn't think that likely.

Martin said, "It may be the Tsurani will choose to march against Elvandar, or carry the battle to your father. Who can say?"

Arutha leaned back and became aware of Anita's hand

resting gently upon his arm. "What a choice we have," he said quietly. "To face the possible loss of Crydee and the Far Coast to the Tsurani or to plunge the Kingdom into civil war. Truly the gods must hate the Kingdom."

Amos stood. "Trevor tells me he has a ship. We can sail in a few days. With luck, the straits will be clearing when we arrive."

Lost in the gloom of his own personal defeat, Arutha barely heard him. He had come to Krondor in such confidence. He would win Erland's support for his cause, and Crydee would be rescued from the Tsurani. Now he faced an even more desperate situation than had he stayed home. Those around left him alone, save for Anita, who spent silent minutes just sitting at his side.

Dark figures moved quietly toward the waterfront. Trevor Hull led a dozen men with Arutha and his companions down the silent street. They hugged the walls of the buildings, and every few yards, Arutha would cast a backwards glance to see how Anita fared. She returned his concern with brave smiles, faintly perceived in the predawn darkness.

Arutha knew over a hundred men moved down adjacent streets, sweeping the area of the city watch and Radburn's agents. The Mockers had turned out in force so Arutha and the others could safely quit the city. Hull had carried word the night before that for a considerable cost the Upright Man had arranged for one of the blockade ships to "drift" off station. Since learning the true situation, including Guy's plan to become Prince of Krondor, the Upright Man had given over his not inconsiderable resources to aid the Princess's and Arutha's escape. Arutha wondered if anyone outside the Guild of Thieves would ever learn the mysterious leader's true identity. From what chance remarks Arutha had overheard, it seemed only a few within the Mockers knew who he was.

With Guy on his way back to the city, Jocko Radburn's men had increased their searching to a near-frenzied pitch. Curfew had been instituted and homes randomly entered and searched in the middle of the night. Every known informant in the city, and many of the beggars and rumormongers as well, had been dragged off to the dungeons and questioned, but whatever else Radburn's men accomplished, they did not learn where the Princess was hidden. No matter how much the denizens of the street feared Radburn, they feared the Upright Man more.

Arutha heard Hull speaking quietly to Amos. "She's a blockade runner, called the *Sea Swift,* and she's well named. There's no faster ship left in the harbor, with all the big warships out with Jessup's fleet. You should make good time westward. The prevailing winds are northerly, so you'll have a broad reach most of the way."

Amos said, "Trevor, I've sailed the Bitter Sea a bit. I know how the winds blow this time of year as well as any man."

Hull snorted. "Well then, as you say. Your men and the Prince's gold are all safely aboard, and Radburn's watch-dogs don't seem to have a notion. They still watch the *Wind of Dawn* like a mouser a rathole, but the *Sea Swift* is left alone. We've arranged for false papers to be posted with a broker, announcing she's for sale, so even if there was no blockade, they'd not imagine she'd be leaving harbor for some time."

They reached the docks and hurried along to a waiting longboat. There were muffled noises, and Arutha knew the Mockers and Trevor's smugglers were disposing of Radburn's watchmen.

Then to the rear, shouts erupted. The clamor of steel broke the still of the morning and Arutha heard Hull shout, "To the boat!"

The pounding of boots upon the wood of the docks set up a racket as Mockers came swarming out of nearby streets, intercepting whoever sought to cut off the escape.

They reached the end of the dock and hurried down the ladder to the longboat. Arutha waited at the top of the ladder until Anita was safely down, then turned. As he stepped upon the top rung, he heard the sound of hoofbeats approaching and saw horses crashing through the press of Mockers, who fell before the onslaught. Riders in the black and gold of Bas-Tyra hacked down with swords, to break free of those seeking to slow them.

Martin shouted from the boat, and Arutha hurried down the ladder. As he reached the boat, a voice from above shouted, "Farewell!"

Arutha looked up and saw Jimmy the Hand hanging over the edge of the dock, a nervous grin on his face. How the boy had managed to join them when all thought him safely back at the hiding place, Arutha couldn't guess. Seeing the unarmed boy gave the Prince a momentary start. He unbuckled his rapier and tossed it high. "Here, use it in good health!" As quick as a striking serpent, Jimmy caught the scabbard, then vanished.

Sailors pulled hard against the oars and the boat sped away from the docks. Lanterns appeared upon the wharves as the sound of battle became louder. Even in the predawn hour, many cries of "What passes?" and "Who goes there?" came from those set to guard ships and cargo in the harbor. Arutha watched over his shoulder, trying to see what was occurring behind. More lanterns were being brought and a fire erupted on the docks. Large bales of something, stored under canvas, exploded into flames.

Those in the boat could now clearly see the fight. Many of the thieves were escaping down city streets, or leaping into the icy water of the harbor. Arutha couldn't see the grey-haired figure of Trevor Hull anywhere, or the small one of Jimmy the Hand. Then clearly he saw Jocko Radburn, dressed in a simple tunic, as before. Radburn came to the edge of the dock and watched the retreating boat. He pointed at the fleeing longboat with his sword and shouted something lost in the clamor.

Arutha turned and saw Anita sitting opposite him, her cloak thrown back, her face clearly visible in the blaze of light from the wharf. Her gaze was caught by the spectacle on shore and she seemed unaware of her discovery. Arutha quickly pulled her cloak hood about her face, snapping her from her glamour, but he knew the damage was done. He looked back again and saw Radburn ordering his men after the fleeing Mockers, retreating down the docks. He stood there alone, then turned away, vanishing in the gloom by the time the longboat reached the *Sea Swift*.

As soon as all were aboard, Amos's crew cast mooring lines and scrambled aloft to set sails. The *Sea Swift* began to move from the harbor.

The promised gap in the harbor blockade appeared and Amos set course for it. He was through before any attempt to cut them off could materialize, and suddenly they were outside the harbor, in the open sea.

Arutha felt a strange elation as it struck him they were free of Krondor. Then he heard Amos swear. "Look!"

In the faint light of the false dawn, Arutha saw the dim shape where Amos pointed. The *Royal Griffin*, the three-masted warship they had seen when coming into the harbor, was at anchor beyond the breakwater, hidden from the view of any in the city. Amos said, "I thought her out with Jessup's fleet. Damn that Radburn for a crafty swine. She'll be on our wake as soon as he can get aboard." He shouted for all sails to be set and then watched the retreating ship behind. "I'd say a prayer to Ruthia, Highness. If we can steal enough time before she gets under way, we still may be free. But we'll need all the good fortune the Lady of Luck can spare."

The morning was clear and cold. Amos and Vasco watched the crew work with approval. The less experienced men had been replaced by men hand-picked by Trevor Hull. They did their work quickly and well, and the *Sea Swift* raced westward.

Anita had been shown to a cabin below and Arutha and Martin stood on deck with Amos. The lookout reported the horizon clear.

Amos said, "It's a close thing, Highness. If they've gotten that brute of a ship underway as quickly as possible, we've only stole an hour or two on them. Their captain may guess wrong and choose the wrong course, but seeing as we're trying to stay free of Jessup's sea ambush, they're a good bet to follow close to the Keshian coast, and risk running into a Keshian warship, rather than losing us. I'll not feel comfortable until we're two days free of pursuit.

"But even if they started at once, they'll only make up a small distance each hour. So until we know for certain they have us in sight, we'd all do with a bit of rest. Go below, and I'll call you should anything occur."

Arutha nodded and left, Martin following. He bid Martin a good rest, and watched as the Huntmaster entered the cabin he shared with Vasco. Arutha entered his own cabin and stopped when he saw Anita sitting on his bunk. Slowly he closed the door and said, "I thought you asleep in your own cabin."

She shook her head slightly, then suddenly she was

across the short space separating them, her head buried against his chest. Sobs shook her as she said, "I've tried to be brave, Arutha, but I've been so frightened."

He stood there awkwardly for a moment, then gently placed his arms around her. The self-reliant pose had crumbled, and Arutha now realized how young she was. Her court training and manners had served her well in maintaining poise among the rough company of the Mockers over the month, but her mask could no longer withstand the pressure. He stroked her hair and said, "You'll be fine."

He made other reassuring sounds, not aware of what he was saying, finding her closeness disturbing. She was young enough to make him judge her still a girl, but old enough to make him doubt that judgment. He had never been able to banter lightly with the young women of the court like Roland, preferring a straightforward conversation, which seemed to leave the ladies cold. And he had never commanded their attention the way Lyam had, with his blond good looks and his laughing, easy manner. On the whole women made him uncomfortable, and this woman—or girl, he couldn't decide which—more than usual.

When the tears subsided, he ushered her to the single chair in the cramped cabin and sat upon the bunk. She sniffed once, then said, "I'm sorry, this is so unseemly."

Suddenly Arutha laughed. "What a girl you are!" he said with genuine affection. "Were I in your place, smuggling myself from the palace, hiding amid cutthroats and thieves, dodging Radburn's weasels and all, I'd have fallen apart long since."

She drew a small handkerchief from her sleeve and delicately wiped her nose. Then she smiled at him. "Thank you for saying that, but I think you'd have done better. Martin has told me a lot about you over the last few weeks and you are a rather brave man by his accounts."

Arutha felt embarrassed by the attention. "The Huntmaster has a tendency to overboast," he said, knowing it to be untrue, and changed the subject. "Amos tells me if we don't sight that ship for two days, we'll have won free."

She lowered her eyes. "That's good."

He leaned forward and brushed a tear from her cheek,

then, feeling self-conscious, pulled his hand away. "You will be safe with us in Crydee, free from Guy's plottings. My sister will make you a welcome guest in our house."

She smiled faintly. "Still, I am worried about Father and Mother."

Arutha tried his best to lay her fears to rest. "With you safely gone from Krondor, Guy cannot gain by causing your parents harm. He may still force a consent to marry from your father, but Erland could do no harm by giving it now. With you out of reach, it's a hollow betrothal. Before this is all done, we shall have an accounting with dear cousin Guy."

She sighed and her smile broadened. "Thank you, Arutha. You've made me feel better."

He rose and said, "Try to sleep. I'll use your cabin for the time being." She smiled as she went to his bunk. He closed the door behind him. All at once he felt little need for rest and returned to the deck. Amos stood by the helmsman, eyes fixed behind. Arutha came to stand at his side. Amos said, "There, on the horizon, can you see it?"

Arutha squinted and made out a faint white speck against the blue of the sky. "Radburn?"

Amos spat over the transom. "My guess. Whatever start we've had is being slowly eaten away. But a stern chase is a long chase, as the saying goes. If we can keep far enough ahead for the rest of the day, we might slip them at night— If there's enough cloud cover so the moons don't mark our passage."

Arutha said nothing, watching the faint speck in the distance.

Throughout the day they had watched the pursuing ship grow slowly in size. At first the tiny speck grew with maddening slowness, but now with alarming rapidity. Arutha could see the sails clearly defined, no longer a simple blur of white, and he could see a hint of a black speck at the masthead, undoubtedly Guy's banner.

Amos regarded the setting sun, directly ahead of the fleeing *Sea Swift*, then watched the following ship. He shouted to the watch aloft, "Can you mark her?"

The lookout cried down, "Three-masted warship, Captain."

Amos looked at Arutha. "It's the *Royal Griffin*. She'll overtake us at sundown. If we had but ten more minutes, or some weather to hide in, or she was just a trifle slower . . ."

"What can you do?"

"Little. In a broad reach she's faster, fast enough that we can't shake her with any sort of fancy sailing. If I tried to turn to a beam reach just as she came near, I could put a bit of space between us, for we'd both lose speed, but she'd fall off faster for a time. Then as soon as they trimmed sails, they'd overhaul us. But that'd send us southward, and there're some fairly nasty shoals and reefs along this stretch of coast, not far from here. It'd be chancy. No, she'll come in somewhat to the windward. When she's alongside, her taller masts will cut our wind and we'll slow enough for them to board without so much as a by-your-leave."

Arutha watched the closing ship for another half hour. Martin came on deck and watched as the distance between the two ships shrank by a few feet each minute. Amos held the ship tight to the wind, driving her to the limit of her speed, but still the other closed.

"Damn!" said Amos, nearly spitting from frustration. "If we were running east, we'd lose them in the dark, but westward we'll be outlined against the evening sky for some time after the sun sets. They'll still be able to see us when we'll be blind to them."

The sun sank and the chase continued. As the sun neared the horizon, an angry red ball above the black-green sea, the warship followed by less than a thousand yards.

Amos said, "They might try to foul the rigging or sweep the decks clear with those oversized crossbows, but with the girl aboard, Radburn might not risk it for fear of injuring her."

Nine hundred, eight hundred yards, the *Royal Griffin* came on, rolling inexorably toward them. Arutha could see figures, small specks in the rigging, black against sails turned blood-red by the setting sun.

When the pursuing ship was five hundred yards behind, the lookout shouted, "Fog!"

Amos looked up. "Where away?"

"South by west. A mile or more."

Amos sped for the bow and Arutha followed. In the distance they could see the sun setting, while off to the left a hazy white band stretched across the top of the black sea. "Gods!" shouted Amos. "We have a chance."

Amos shouted for the helmsman to come to a south-west heading, then sprinted for the stern, Arutha behind him by a step. When they reached the stern, they saw the turn had halved the distance between the ships. Amos said, "Martin, can you mark their helmsman?"

Martin squinted, then said, "It's a bit gloomy, but he's no difficult mark."

Amos said, "See if you can take his mind off holding course."

Martin uncovered his ever-present bow and strung it. He drew out a cloth-yard shaft and sighted on the pursuing ship. He waited, shifting weight to compensate for the rolling of the ship, then let fly. Like an angry bird, the arrow arched over the water and struck in the transom, quivering mere inches from the helmsman's head.

From the *Sea Swift* they could see the *Royal Griffin's* helmsman dive for the deck, releasing the tiller. The warship swung over and began to fall away. Martin said, "A little gusty for fine shooting," and sent another arrow to strike within inches of the first, keeping the tiller unmanned.

Slowly the distance between the ships began to widen, and Amos turned to his crew. "Pass the word. When I give the order for silence, any man who drops so much as a whisper is fishbait."

The warship wobbled behind a minute, then swung back on course. Martin said, "Looks like they'll keep a little less broad to us, Amos. I can't shoot through sails."

"No, but if you'd oblige me by keeping those lads in the bow away from their ballista, I'd be thankful. I think you irritated Radburn."

Martin and Arutha saw the ballista crew readying their weapons. The Huntmaster sent a flurry of arrows at the pursuing ship's bow, one arrow following the last before it was halfway to the target. The first struck a man in the leg, felling him, and the other men dove for cover.

"Fog dead ahead, Captain!" came the shout from above.

Amos turned to the helmsman. "Hard to port."

The *Sea Swift* angled to the south. The *Royal Griffin* came hard after, now less than four hundred yards behind.

Abruptly they entered a wall of grey, murky fog, quickly becoming black as the sun sank over the horizon. As soon as the warship vanished from sight, Amos said, "Reef sails!"

The crew hauled in sails, quickly slowing the ship. Then Amos said, "Hard to starboard, and pass the word for silence."

Suddenly the ship became graveyard quiet. Amos truned to Arutha and whispered, "The wind's fallen off to less than a bilious fart. There's currents here running to the west. We'll let them carry us away from here and hope Radburn's captain is a Kingdom Sea man.

"Tiller to midships," he whispered to the helmsman.

Suddenly Arutha became aware of the quiet. After the clamor of the chase, with the fresh north wind blowing, the ropes and sheets singing in the yards, the canvas snapping constantly, this muffled fogbank was unnaturally silent. Fear dragged the minutes out in the seemingly endless vigil.

Then, like an alarm ringing out, they heard voices and the sounds of a ship. Arutha couldn't see anything for minutes, until a faint glow pierced through the murk to the rear, passing from northeast to southwest, lanterns from the pursuing *Royal Griffin*. Every man aboard the *Sea Swift*, on deck and above, stayed at his station, afraid to move for the noise that would carry over the water like a clarion. In the distance they could hear a shout from the other ship, "Quiet, damn it! We can't hear them for our own noise!" Then it was suddenly still, save for the rippling of canvas and ropes from the *Royal Griffin*.

Time passed without measure as they waited in the blackness. Then came a hideous grinding sound, ringing like a thunder peal, a tearing, cracking shriek of wood being crushed. Instantly the cries of men could be heard, shouts of panic.

Amos turned to the others, half seen in the darkness. "They've shoaled out. From the sound, they've torn the hull right out from under. They're dead men." He ordered the helm put over to the northwest, away from the shoals and reefs, as sailors hurriedly set sail.

"A bad way to die," said Arutha.

Martin shrugged, half lit by the lanterns being brought up on deck. "Is there a good way? I've seen worse."

Arutha left the quarterdeck, the faint, pitiful cries of the drowning men still carrying across the water, a grisly counterpoint to Vasco's more mundane shout to open the galley. He closed the door to the companionway and shut out those unhappy sounds. He quietly opened the door to his cabin and saw Anita lying asleep in the faint light of a shuttered candle. Her red-brown hair looked nearly black as it lay spread about her head. He started to close the door, when he heard her say, "Arutha?"

He stepped in, finding her watching him in the dim light. He sat on the edge of the berth. "Are you well?" he asked.

She stretched and nodded. "I've been sleeping hard." Her eyes widened. "Is everything all right?" She sat up, bringing her face close to his.

He reached out and put his arms around her, holding her close. "Everything is fine. We're safe now."

She sighed as she rested her head on his shoulder. "Thank you for everything, Arutha."

He said nothing, suddenly caught up in strong emotion, a protective feeling, a need to keep Anita from harm's way, to care for her. For long moments they sat this way, then Arutha regained control over his surging feelings. Pulling away a little, he said, "You'd be hungry, I'd think."

She laughed, an honestly merry sound. "Why yes, as a matter of fact I'm famished."

He said, "I'll have something sent down, though it will be plain fare, I'm afraid, even compared to what you were given by the Mockers."

"Anything."

He went on deck and ordered a seaman to the galley to fetch something for the Princess, then returned to find her combing her hair. "I must look a mess," she said.

Arutha suddenly found himself fighting the urge to grin. He didn't know why, but he was inexplicably happy. "Not at all," he said. "You look quite nice, actually."

She stopped her combing, and Arutha marveled at how she looked so young one minute, so womanly the next. She smiled at him. "I remember sneaking a peek at you during Father's court dinner, when you were last in Krondor."

"At me? What in heaven's name for?"

She seemed to ignore the question. "I thought you looked nice then as well, though a bit stern. There was a boy there who held me up to see. He was with your father's party. I've forgotten his name, but he said he was apprentice to a magician."

Arutha's smile faded. "That was Pug."

"What ever happened to him?"

"He was lost in the first year of the war."

She put aside her comb. "I'm sorry. He was kind to a bothersome child."

"He was a kind lad, given to doing brave things, and he was very special to my sister. She grieved for a long time when he was lost." Fighting back a gloomy mood, he said, "Now, why did a Princess of Krondor want to sneak a look at a distant and rural cousin?"

Anita watched Arutha for a long moment, then said, "I wanted to see you because our fathers thought it likely we would marry."

Arutha was stunned. It took all his control to retain his composure. He pulled over the single chair and sat. Anita said, "Didn't your father ever mention it to you?"

For want of anything clever to say, Arutha merely shook his head.

Anita nodded. "I know, the war and all. Things did get quite frantic soon after you left for Rillanon."

Arutha swallowed hard, finding his mouth suddenly dry. "Now, what is this about our fathers' plans for . . . our marriage?"

Anita looked at Arutha, her green eyes flickering with reflected candlelight, and something else. "Matters of state, I'm afraid. Father wanted my claim to the throne bolstered, and Lyam's too dangerous a match, being the older. You'd be ideal, for the King would not likely object . . . or wouldn't have then, I guess. Now, with Guy set upon having me, I suppose the King is in agreement."

Arutha became suddenly irritated, though he wasn't certain why. "And I suppose we're not to be consulted in the matter!" His voice rose.

"Please, it's not my doing."

"I'm sorry. I didn't mean to alarm you. It's only I'd never give much thought to marriage, and certainly not for reasons of state." The wry grin reappeared. "That is usually the province of eldest sons. We second-born as a rule are left to get by as best we can, an old widowed countess, or a rich merchant's daughter." He tried to make light of it. "A rich merchant's beautiful daughter, if we're lucky, which we usually are not." He couldn't manage a light tone and sat back. Finally he said, "Anita, you will stay at Crydee as long as need be. It may prove dangerous because of the Tsurani for a time, but we'll see that through, somehow. Send you down to Carse, perhaps. When this war is over, you'll go home in safety; I promise you. And never, never shall anyone force you to do anything against your will."

The conversation was interrupted by a knock on the door and a seaman entered with a steaming bowl of chowder, with hard bread and salted pork on a platter. As he placed the food on the table and poured a cup of wine, Anita watched Arutha. When the sailor was gone, Anita began to eat.

Arutha spoke of little things with Anita, finding himself once more captivated by the girl's open, appealing manner. When he finally bade her good night and closed the door, he was abruptly aware the idea of a state marriage was causing him only a little discomfort. He went up on deck; the fog had lifted and once more they were running before a light breeze. He watched the stars above and, for the first time in years, whistled a happy air.

Near the helm, Martin and Amos shared a wineskin and spoke low. "The Prince seems unusually cheerful tonight," said Amos.

Martin blew a puff of smoke from a pipe, which was quickly carried away on the wind. "And it's a good bet he's not even aware why he feels so cheerful. Anita's young, but not so young he'll be able to ignore her attentions for very long. If she's made up her mind, and I think she has, she'll have him snared within the year. And he'll be glad to be caught."

Amos laughed. "Though it will be some time before he owns up to it. I'm willing to wager young Roland is hauled up before the altar sooner than Arutha."

Martin shook his head. "That's no wager. Roland's
been caught for years. Anita has some work to do yet."

"You've never been in love, then, Martin?"

Martin said, "No, Amos, foresters, like sailors, make
poor husbands. Never at home long, and spending days,
even weeks, alone. Tends to make them a brooding,
solitary lot. You?"

"Not so you'd notice." Amos sighed. "The older I get,
the more I wonder what I've missed."

"But would you change anything?"

With a chuckle, Amos said, "Probably not, Martin,
probably not."

As the ship put in at the quayside, Fannon and Gardan
dismounted. Arutha led Anita down the gangway and
introduced her to the Swordmaster of Crydee.

"We've no carriages in Crydee, Highness," Fannon
said to her, "but I'll have a cart sent for at once. It's a long
walk to the castle."

Anita smiled. "I can ride, Mister Fannon. Any horse
that's not too spirited will do."

Fannon ordered two of his men to ride to the stable
and bring one of Carline's palfreys with a proper sidesad-
dle. Arutha said, "What news?"

Fannon led the Prince off a short distance and said, "A
late thaw in the mountains, Highness, so there has been no
major Tsurani movement as yet. A few of the smaller
garrisons have been raided, but there is nothing to indicate
a spring offensive here. Perhaps they'll move against your
father."

"I hope you're right, for Father's received most of the
Krondorian garrison." He quickly outlined what had occurred in Krondor, and Fannon listened closely.

"You did well not sailing for your father's camp. I think
you judged things correctly. Nothing could prove more
disastrous than a major Tsurani offensive against Duke
Borric's position as he was marshaling to march against
Guy. Let us keep this to ourselves for a time. Your father
will learn what has occurred soon enough, but the more
time it takes for him to discover Guy's treachery, the more
chance we have of keeping the Tsurani at bay another
year."

Arutha looked troubled. "This cannot continue much

longer, Fannon. We must soon see an end to this war." He turned for a moment and saw townspeople begin to gawk at the Princess. "Still, we at least have a little time to come up with something to counter the Tsurani, if we can but think of it."

Fannon fell quiet, and started to speak, then stopped. His expression became grim, almost painful. Arutha said, "What is it, Swordmaster?"

"I have grave and sorry news to greet you with, Highness. Squire Roland is dead."

Arutha was rocked by the news. For a brief moment he wondered if Fannon made some tasteless joke, for his mind would not accept what he had heard. Finally he said, "What . . . how?"

"News came three days ago from Baron Tolburt, who is most sorely grieved. The Squire was killed in a Tsurani raid."

Arutha looked at the castle upon the hill. "Carline?"

"As you would expect. She weeps, but she also bears up well."

Arutha fought back a choking sensation. His face was a grim mask as he moved back to Anita, Amos, and Martin. Word had spread that the Princess of Krondor was upon the wharf. The soldiers who had ridden with Fannon and Gardan formed a quiet ring around her, keeping the towns-folk at a respectful distance, while Arutha shared the sad news with Amos and Martin.

Soon the horses arrived and they were in the saddle, riding toward the castle. Arutha spurred his horse on and was dismounted before the others had entered the court-yard. Most of the household staff awaited him, and with little ceremony he shouted to Housecarl Samuel, "The Princess of Krondor is guesting with us. See rooms are made ready. Escort her to the great hall and tell her I will join her shortly."

He hurried through the entrance of the keep, past guards who snapped to attention as their Prince strode by. He reached Carline's suite and knocked upon the door.

"Who is it?" came the soft voice from within.

"Arutha."

The door flew open and Carline rushed into her brother's arms, holding him tightly. "Oh, I'm so glad you are back. You don't know how glad." She stepped back and looked at him. "I'm sorry. I was going to ride down to meet you, but I just couldn't seem to gather myself together."

"Fannon just told me. I'm so very sorry."

She regarded him calmly, her face set in an expression of acceptance. She took him by the hand and led him to her chambers. Sitting upon a divan, she said, "I always knew it might happen. It was the silliest thing, you know. Baron Tolburt wrote a very long letter, the poor man. He saw so little of his son and was stricken." Tears began to come, and she swallowed hard, looking away from Arutha. "Roland died . . ."

"You don't have to tell me."

She shook her head. "It's all right. It hurts . . ." Again tears came, but she spoke through them. "Oh, it hurts, but I'll get over the pain. Roland taught me that, Arutha. He knew there were going to be risks and should he die I'd have to keep living my own life. He taught me well. I think because I finally learned how much I loved him, and told him so, I gained the strength to cope with this loss.

"Roland died trying to save some farmer's cows." Through the tears, she smiled. "Isn't that like him? He spent the entire winter building up the fort, and then the first time there's trouble it's some hungry Tsurani trying to steal some skinny cows. Roland went riding out with his men to chase them away, but got shot by an arrow. He was the only one hurt, and he died before they could get him back to the fort." She sighed long. "He was such a jester at times, I almost think he did it on purpose."

She began to weep and Arutha watched in silence. Quickly she gained control over herself and said, "No good comes from this, you know." She rose and looked out a window and quietly said, "Damn this stupid war."

Arutha came over to her, holding her tightly for a moment. "Damn all wars," he said.

For a few minutes they were quiet, then she said, "Now tell me, what news from Krondor?"

Arutha gave her a brief account of his experiences in Krondor, half his attention on her. She seemed much more accepting of Roland's loss than she had when grieving for Pug. Arutha shared her pain, but also felt certain she would be all right. He was pleased to discover just how much Carline had matured over the last few years. When he finished telling of Anita's rescue, Carline interrupted. "Anita, the Princess of Krondor, is here?"

Arutha nodded and Carline said, "I must look a fright, and you bring the Princess of Krondor here. Arutha, you are a monster." She rushed to a polished metal mirror and fussed with her face, daubing at it with a damp cloth.

Arutha smiled. Under the mantle of mourning his sister still showed a spark of her natural spirit.

Combing her hair out, Carline turned to face her brother. "Is she pretty, Arutha?"

Arutha's wry smile was replaced by a grin. "Yes, I'd say she is pretty."

Carline studied Arutha's face. "I can see I'll have to get to know her well." She put down her comb and straightened her gown. Extending her hand to him, she said, "Come, we can't keep your young lady waiting."

Hand in hand they left the room and walked down the stairs to the main hallway, to welcome Anita to Crydee.

EIGHT

GREAT ONE

An abandoned house overlooked the city.

The site upon which the house had been constructed had once seen the lights of a great family manse. On top of the highest of many rolling hills surrounding the city of Ontoset, it was considered the choicest view of the city and the sea beyond. The family had come to low estate, the result of being on the losing side in one of the Empire's many subtle but lethal political struggles. The house had fallen into disrepair and the property been ignored, for while it was as fine a building site as any found in the area, the association of ill fortune with the property was too real for the superstitious Tsurani.

Now a new and strange house stood atop the hill. It was the source of both some speculation and a little envy. The speculation was about its owner, the strange Great One. The envy was over its design and construction, something of a revolution in Tsurani architecture. Gone was the traditional three-story, open-center building. In its place was a long, single-story building, with several smaller ones attached to it by covered walkways. It was a rambling affair, with many small gardens and waterways winding between the structures. Its construction was as much a sensation as its design, for it consisted mainly of stone, with fired brick tiles upon the roof. It was speculated that it offered cool protection during the heat of the summer.

Two other facts added to the fascination evidenced over the house and its owner. First was the manner in which the project had been commissioned. The magician had first appeared in Ontoset one day, at the home of Tumacel, the richest moneylender in the city. He appropriated over thirty thousand imperials in funds, and left the moneylender stricken over his loss of liquidity. This was Milamber's method of dealing with the Tsurani passion for bureaucracy. Any merchant or tradesman commanded to render service to a Great One was forced to petition the imperial treasury for repayment. This resulted in slow delivery of ordered materials, less than enthusiastic service, and resentment. Milamber simply paid in advance, and left it to the moneylender—who was better able to account for his losses than most other merchants, by nature of his bookkeeping—to recover from the treasury. The second fact was the style of decoration. Instead of the garishly bold wall paintings, the building was left mostly unpainted, except for an occasional landscape in muted, natural colors. Many fine young artists were employed on this project, and when it was done, the demand for their services was phenomenal. Within a month, a new wave in Tsurani art was in progress.

Fifty slaves now worked in the outlying fields, all free to come and go as they wished, dressed in the garb of their homeworld, Midkemia. All had been taken from the slave market one day, without payment, by the Great One.

Many travelers to Ontoset would make an afternoon of climbing the hills nearby to see the house. From a respectable distance, of course.

"The belief that the current great rift to Midkemia is controllable is only partially correct." Milamber paused, allowing his scribe to complete copying the dictation. "It can be stated that rifts may be established without the release of destructive energies associated with their accidental creation, either through poorly effected magic spells or by the proximity of too many unstable magic devices."

Milamber's research into the special aspects of rift energies would be added to the Assembly's archives when completed. Like other projects he had read of in the archives, research into rifts had showed what Milamber took to be a grievous flaw in most of his brother magicians' work. In general, projects were not carried through to completion, showing a lack of thoroughness. Once the procedure to establish rifts safely had been developed, further research into their nature had been halted.

Continuing, he dictated: "What is lacking in the concent of control is the ability to select the terminus of contact, the ability to 'target' the rift. It has been shown by the appearance of the ship carrying Fanatha on the shores of Crydee, on the world of Midkemia, that a certain affinity between a newly forming rift and an existing one is probable. However, as shown by further testing, this affinity is limited, such limits being as yet not fully understood. While there is increased probability of a second rift appearing within a regional proximity to the first, it is by no means a certainty."

Milamber's narration was interrupted by the sound of the gong announcing the arrival of someone from the Assembly. He dismissed his scribe and made his way to the pattern room. As he walked he mused on the real reason for his submersion in research over the last two months. He was avoiding the decision he must soon make, whether or not to return to the Shinzawai estate for Katala.

Milamber knew there was a chance she had become the wife of another, for their separation had been nearly five years, and she would have no reason to think he'd ever be returning. But time and training had done nothing to dull his feelings toward her. As he reached the transporting room with its tiled pattern, he made his decision: tomorrow he would go to see her.

As he entered the room, he saw Hochopepa step off the pattern in the tile floor. "Ah," said the plump magician, "there you are. Since it has been two weeks since I last saw you, I decided to pay a visit."

"I am glad to see you. I have been deeply involved in study and could do with a short respite."

They walked from the room into one of the several gardens nearby. Milamber clapped his hands and a servant arrived with a platter of refreshments. The servant, Netoha, at one time had been hadonra for the family that resided there previously. Milamber had found him while securing someone to plant the varieties of vegetation he wanted in his gardens. The man was bold enough to approach, something that singled him out from the common Tsurani. Unable to find the work he was trained for since the demise of his employer's estate, Netoha had scratched out a meager living over the years. Milamber had taken him on as much out of sympathy as out of any real need. He had quickly made himself useful in a hundred ways the young magician had never dreamed of, and the relationship was mutually satisfactory.

Hochopepa took the offered sweets and drink. "I have come to tell you some news. There is to be an Imperial Festival in two months' time, with games. Will you come?"

Milamber found his curiosity piqued. With a wave he dismissed Netoha. "And what makes this festival so special? I can't remember having seen you so animated before."

"This festival is being given by the Warlord in honor of his nephew, the Emperor. He has plans for a new major offensive the week before the games, and it is hoped he will announce the success of the campaign." He lowered his voice. "It is no secret to those with access to court gossip he is under a great deal of pressure to justify his conduct of the war before the High Council. Rumor has it he has been forced to offer major concessions to the Blue Wheel Party to regain their support in the war.

"But what will make the games unusual is that the Light of Heaven will leave his Palace of Contemplation, breaking with ancient tradition. It would be a proper occasion for you to make some sort of entrance into court society."

"I'm sorry, Hocho," Milamber said, "I have little desire to attend any festivals. I have been to one earlier this month, in Ontoset, as part of my studies. The dances are boring, the food tends toward the awful, and the wine is as flat as the speeches. The games are of less interest still. If this is the court society you speak of, then I'll be fine without it."

"Milamber, there are many holes left in your education. Gaining the black robe did not mean instant mastery of our craft. There is quite a bit more involved in protecting the Empire than sitting about dreaming up new ways of tossing energy around, or creating economic chaos with the local merchants." He took another sweet, and returned to his chiding. "There are several reasons you must come with me to the festivities, Milamber. First, you are something of a celebrity to the nobles of the realm, for news of your wondrous house has spread from one corner of the Empire to the other, mostly by aid of those young bandits you paid so well to execute the delicate paintings you love so much. It is now considered the mark of some distinction to have the same sort of work done.

"And this place"—his hand inscribed an arc before them, mock wonder upon his face—"anyone who could be so clever to design such an edifice must surely be worthy of attention." His mocking tone vanished as he added, "By the way, this entire bit of nonsense has not been diminished one whit by your mysterious isolation here in the hinterlands. If anything, it has added to your reputation.

"Now to more important reasons than social ones. As you no doubt know, there is growing concern that the news from the war is somehow being downplayed. In all these years there has been little gain, and some talk is going about that the Emperor may take a stand against the Warlord's policies. If so . . ." He let the thought go unfinished.

Milamber was silent for a time. "Hocho, I think it is time that I told you something, and if you feel it's sufficient to warrant my life, then you may return to the Assembly and bring charges."

Hochopepa was raptly attentive, all quips and tart remarks put aside.

"You who trained me did your work well, for I am filled with a need to do what is best for the Empire. I hold only a little feeling for the land of my birth anymore, and you will never know what that signifies. But in the process of making me what I am, you could never create the love of home within my being that I once felt for my own Crydee. What you have created is a man with a strong sense of duty, untempered by any love for that thing he feels duty toward." Hochopepa remained silent as the impact of what Milamber had said penetrated, then he nodded as Milamber continued.

"I may be the greatest threat to the Empire since the Stranger invaded your skies, for if I become involved with its politics I will be justice without mercy.

"I have known of the factions within the parties, the crossover of families from one party to another, and the consequences of those acts. Do you think because I sit atop my hill in the eastlands, I am unaware of the shifts and stirrings of the political animals in the capital? Of course not. If the Blue Wheel Party collapses and its members realign with the War Party or the Imperials, every street merchant in Ontoset is speculating on the news the next day in the marketplace. I know what is taking place as well as any other who is not directly involved. And in the months since I came to live here I have come to one conclusion: the Empire is slowly killing itself."

The older magician said nothing for a moment, then asked, "Have you wondered at all why our system is such that we are killing ourselves?"

Milamber stood and paced a little. "Of course. I am studying it, and have chosen to wait before I act. I need more time to understand the history you taught me so well. But I do have some speculation of sorts." He inclined his head, asking if he should go on. Hochopepa nodded that he should. "It seems to me there are several major problems here, problems I can only guess at in terms of impact upon the Empire.

"First"—he held up his index finger—"those in power

are more concerned with their own grandeur than with the well-being of the Empire. And as they are those who appear to the casual eye to be the Empire, it is an easy thing not to notice."

"What do you mean?" the older magician asked.

"When you think of the Empire, what comes to mind? A history of armies warring across the lands? Or the rise of the Assembly? Perhaps you think of a chronicle of rulers? Whatever it is, most likely the single most obvious truth is overlooked. The Empire is all those who live within its borders, from the nobles to the lowest servant, even the slaves who work the fields. It must be seen as a whole, not as being embodied by some small but visible part, such as the Warlord or the High Council. Do you understand that?"

Hochopepa looked troubled. "I'm not sure, but I think . . . Go on."

"If that is true, then consider the rest. Second, there must never be a time when the need for stability overrules the need for growth."

"But we have always grown!" objected Hochopepa.

"Not true," countered Milamber. "You have always expanded, and that seems like growth if you don't investigate closely. But while your armies have been bringing new lands into your borders, what has happened to your art, your music, your literature, your research? Even the vaunted Assembly does little more than refine that which is already known. You implied earlier that I was wasting my time finding new ways to 'toss energy around.' Well, what is wrong with that? Nothing. But there is something wrong with the type of society that looks upon the new as suspect.

"Look around you, Hocho. Your artists are in shock because I described what I had seen in paintings in my youth, and a few young artists became excited. Your musicians spend all their time learning the old songs, perfectly, to the note, and no one composes new ones, just clever variations on melodies that are centuries old. No one creates new epics, they only retell old ones. Hocho, you are a people stagnating. This war is but one example. It is unjustified, fought from habit, to keep certain groups in power, to reap wealth for those already wealthy, and to

play the Game of the Council. And the cost! Thousands of
lives are wasted each year, the lives of those who *are* the
Empire, its own citizens. The Empire is a cannibal, devour-
ing its own people."

The older magician was disturbed by what he heard,
in total contradiction with what he believed he saw: a
vibrant, energetic, alive culture.

"Third," said Milamber, "if my duty is to serve the
Empire, and the social order of the Empire is responsible
for its own stagnation, then it is my duty to change that
social order, even if I must destroy it."

Now Hochopepa was shocked. Milamber's logic was
without fault, but the suggested solution was potentially
fraught with danger to everything Hochopepa knew and
revered. "I understand what you say, Milamber, but what
you speak of is too difficult to contemplate all at once."

Milamber's voice took on reassuring tones. "I do not
mean to imply that the destruction of the present social
order is the only solution, Hocho. I used that to shock and
to drive home a point. That is what much of my research is
about, not only the visible mastery of energy, but also
investigations into the nature of the Tsurani people and the
Empire. Believe me, I am more than willing to spend as
much time on the question as I need. But when I reach a
judgment as to what must be done, I shall act."

Hochopepa stood, an expression of concern on his
face. "It is not that I disagree with you, my friend, it is
simply that I must have time to assimilate what you have
said."

"I could only speak the truth to you, Hocho, no matter
how disturbing."

Hochopepa smiled. "A fact I appreciate, Milamber. I
must spend some time considering the proposition." Some
of his usual humor crept back into his voice. "Perhaps you
will accompany me to the Assembly? You have been absent
much of the time with this house building and all, you
would do well to put in an appearance now and again."

Milamber smiled at his friend. "Of course." He indicated that Hochopepa should lead the way to the pattern.
As they walked, Hochopepa said, "If you wish to study our
culture, Milamber, I still suggest you come to the Imperial
Festival. There will be more political activity in the seats of

the arena in that one day than could be observed in a month in the High Council."

Milamber turned his head toward Hochopepa. "Perhaps you're right. I shall think about it."

When they appeared on the pattern of the Assembly, Shimone was standing close by. He bowed slightly in greeting and said, "Welcome. I was about to go looking for you two."

Hochopepa said with mild amusement, "Are we so vital to the business of the Assembly that you must be sent to fetch us back?"

Shimone inclined his head a little. "Perhaps, but not today. I merely thought you would find the business at hand interesting."

Milamber said, "What is happening?"

"The Warlord has sent messages to the Assembly, and Hodiku raises questions about them. We best hurry, for they are nearly ready to begin."

They walked quickly to the central hall of the Assembly and entered. Arrayed about a large open area was an amphitheater of open benches; they took seats in a lower row. Already several hundred black-robed Great Ones were in place. In the center of the floor they could see Fumita, the one-time brother of the Shinzawai Lord, standing alone; he would be presiding over the business of the day. The presidency was allotted by chance to one of those in attendance. It was only the second occasion Milamber had seen Fumita in the Assembly since the time he had brought Milamber here.

Shimone said, "It has been nearly three weeks since I saw you in the Assembly, Milamber."

"I must apologize, but I have been busy getting my home in order."

"So I hear. You're something of a source of gossip in the imperial court. I hear the Warlord himself is anxious to meet you."

"Perhaps someday."

Hochopepa said to Shimone, "Who can understand such a man? Taking to building such a strange home." He turned to Milamber. "Next you'll be telling me that you're taking a wife."

Milamber laughed. "Why, Hocho, how did you guess?"

Hochopepa's eyes grew wide. "You're not!"

"And why shouldn't I?"

"Milamber, it is not a wise course, believe me. To this day I have regretted my own marriage."

"Hocho, I didn't know you were a married man."

"I choose not to speak of it much. My wife is a fine woman, though given to an overly sharp tongue and scathing wit. In my own home I'm not much more than another servant to be ordered about. That is why I see her only on prescribed holidays; it would be bad for my nerves to see her more often."

Shimone said, "Who is your intended, Milamber? A noble daughter?"

"No. She was a slave with me at the Shinzawai estate."

Hochopepa mused, "A slave girl . . . hmm. That might work out."

Milamber laughed, and Shimone chuckled. Several other magicians regarded them with curiosity, for the Assembly was not a regular forum for mirth.

Fumita held up his hand and the Assembly became quiet. "Today there is a matter being brought before the Assembly by Hodiku."

A thin Great One, with shaved head and hooked nose, walked from his seat in front of Milamber and Hochopepa to the center of the floor.

He surveyed the magicians in the hall, then spoke. "I come today so that I may speak about the Empire." It was the formal opening of any business brought before the Assembly. "I speak for the good of the Empire," he added, completing the ritual. "I am concerned about the demand made today by the Warlord for aid so he may broaden the war against the Midkemian world."

A chorus of jeers and cries of "Politics" and "Sit down!" erupted from around the room. Soon Shimone and Hochopepa were on their feet with others crying, "Let him speak!"

Fumita held up a hand for silence, and soon the room quieted. Hodiku continued. "We are precedented. Fifteen years ago the Assembly sent an order to the Warlord to end the war against the Thuril Confederation."

Another magician jumped to his feet. "If the Thuril conquest had continued there would have been too few in the north to repulse the Thün migration that year. It was a clear case of the salvation of Szetac Province and the Holy City. Now our borders in the north are secure. The situation is not the same."

Arguments erupted over the entire hall, and it took several minutes for Fumita to restore order. Hochopepa rose and said, "I would like to hear Hodiku's reasons for considering this request vital to the security of the Empire. Any magician who is willing is free to work on behalf of the conquest."

"That is the point," responded Hodiku. "There is no reason for any magician who feels this war into another space-time is right and proper for the Empire not to work in support of the conquest. Without the Black Robes who already serve the Warlord, the rift would never have been prepared for such an undertaking. It is that he now makes demands of the Assembly itself I find objectionable. If five or six magicians choose to serve in the field, even to traveling to this other world to risk their lives in the battle, then it is their own concern. But if one magician responds to this *demand*, without considering the issues, it will appear the Assembly is now subject to the will of the Warlord."

Several magicians applauded this sentiment, and others seemed to weigh its merits. Only a few booed and jeered. Hochopepa stood again. "I would like to offer a proposal. I will undertake on behalf of the Assembly to send a message to the Warlord expressing our regret that the Assembly *as a body* may not order any magician to perform as *requested*, but that he is free to seek the services of any magician willing to work on his behalf."

A general murmur of approval ran through the room, and Fumita asked, "Hochopepa offers a proposition to send a statement of policy to the Warlord on behalf of the Assembly. Does anyone find this objectionable?" When no objections were forthcoming, he said, "The Assembly thanks Hochopepa for his wisdom."

After the meeting broke up, Shimone said, "You should make a point of coming more often, Milamber. We hardly see you anymore. And you spend too much time alone."

Milamber smiled. "That is true, but I plan to remedy the situation tomorrow."

The chime sounded throughout the house, and servants jumped to make ready for the Great One's visit. Kamatsu, Lord of the Shinzawai, knew that a Great One had struck a chime in the halls of the Assembly, willing the sound to come here, to announce his imminent appearance.

In Kasumi's room, Laurie and the elder son of the house sat engrossed in a game of pashawa, played with painted pieces of stiff paper. It was common to alehouses and inns in Midkemia and was one more detail in the young Tsurani's drive to master every facet of Midkemian life.

Kasumi stood. "It is most likely he who once was my uncle; I had best go."

Laurie smiled. "Or could it be that you wish to stem your losses?"

The Tsurani shook his head. "I fear I have created a problem in my own house. You were never a good slave, Laurie, and if anything you have grown more intractable. It is a good thing I like you."

They both laughed and the elder son of the house left. A few minutes later, a house slave came running to Laurie and informed him that the lord of the house commanded him to come at once. Laurie jumped up, more from the slave's obvious agitation than from any inbred obedience. He hurried to the lord's room and knocked on the doorjamb. The door slid to one side and Kasumi held it. Laurie stepped through and saw the Shinzawai lord and his guest, and then confusion overtook him.

The guest was wearing the black robe of the Tsurani Great Ones, but the face was Pug's. He started to speak, stopped, and started again. "Pug?"

The lord of the house looked outraged at this forward behavior by the slave, but his nearly voiced command was stopped by the Great One. "May I have the use of this room for a few minutes, Lord? I wish to speak to this slave in private."

Kamatsu, Lord of the Shinzawai, bowed stiffly. "Your will, Great One." He left the room with his son behind; he was still in shock over the appearance of the former slave and confused at the conflicts within himself. The Great One he was, there could be no thought of fraud: his manner of arrival proved it. But Kamatsu couldn't help feeling that his arrival heralded disaster for the plan he and his son had so carefully nurtured for the last nine years.

Milamber spoke. "Shut the door, Laurie."

Laurie shut it, then studied his former friend. He looked fit, but vastly changed. His bearing was nearly regal, as if the mantle of power he now wore reflected some inner strength he had lacked before.

"I . . ." Laurie began, then lapsed into silence, confused about what to say. Finally he said, "Are you well?"

Milamber nodded. "I am well, old friend."

Laurie smiled and crossed the room and embraced his friend, then pushed himself away. "Let me look at you."

Milamber smiled. "I am called Milamber, Laurie. The boy you knew as Pug is as dead as last year's flowers. Come, sit and we will talk."

They sat at the table and poured two cups of chocha. Laurie sipped at the bitter brew and said, "We heard nothing about you. After the first year I gave you up for lost. I'm sorry."

Milamber nodded. "It is the way of the Assembly. As a magician I am expected to forgo all my former ties, except for those that can be maintained in a socially acceptable manner. Being without clan or family, I had nothing to forgo. And you were always a poor slave who never knew his place. What better friend for a renegade, barbarian magician?"

Laurie nodded. "I am glad you have returned. Will you stay?"

Milamber shook his head no. "I have no place here. Besides, there is work I must be about. I now have an estate of my own, near the city of Ontoset. I have come for you. And Katala, if . . ." His voice trailed off, as if he were fearful of asking about her.

Sensing his distress, Laurie said, "She is still here and has not taken a husband. She would not forget you." He broke into a grin. "Gods of Midkemia! It completely slipped my mind. You would have no way of knowing."

"What?"

"You have a son!"

Milamber sat dumbstruck. "A son?"

Laurie laughed. "He was born eight months after you were taken. He is a fine boy, and Katala is a fine mother."

Milamber felt overwhelmed at the news and said, "Please. Would you bring her here?"

Laurie jumped to his feet. "At once."

He rushed from the room. Milamber sat fighting down the upsurge of emotion. He composed himself, using his magician's skills to relax his mind.

The door slid open and Katala was revealed, uncertainty on her face. Laurie stood behind, a boy of about four in his arms.

Milamber rose and spread his arms to her. Katala rushed to him and he nearly cried in his joy. They clung quietly for a moment, then she murmured, "I thought you gone. I hoped . . . but I thought you gone."

They stood for several minutes, each lost in the pure pleasure of the other's presence, until she pushed herself away. "You must meet your son, Pug."

Laurie brought the boy forward. He regarded Milamber with large brown eyes. He was a well-formed boy, with a stronger likeness to his mother, but something in the way he tilted his head made him resemble the boy from Crydee keep. Katala took him from Laurie and passed him to Milamber. "William, this is your father."

The boy seemed to take this in with some skepticism. He ventured a shy smile, but leaned back, keeping his distance. "I want down," he said abruptly. Milamber laughed and put the boy down. He looked at his father, then immediately lost interest in the stranger in black. "Ooh!" he cried, and rushed over to play with the Lord of the Shinzawai's shâh pieces.

Milamber watched him for a moment, then said, "William?"

Katala stood next to him with her arm around his waist, hugging him as if afraid he would disappear again. Laurie said, "She wanted a Midkemian name for him, Milamber."

Katala started. "Milamber?"

"It is my new name, love. You must get used to calling me that." She frowned, not entirely pleased with the thought. "Milamber," she repeated, testing the sound. She then shrugged. "It is a good name."

"How did he become William?"

Laurie went over to the boy, who was trying to stand the pieces one atop the other, and gently took them away. The boy threw him a black look. "I want to play," he said indignantly.

Laurie picked him up and said, "I gave her a bunch of names and she picked that one."

"I liked its sound," she said; "William."

At the sound of his name the boy looked at his mother. "I'm hungry."

"I favored James or Owen, but she insisted," Laurie said, while the boy tried to wriggle out of his arms.

Katala took him. "I must feed him. I'll take him to the kitchen." She kissed Milamber and left the room.

The magician stood quietly for a moment. "It is all more than I had hoped for. I was afraid she'd have found another."

"Not that one, P—Milamber. She would have nothing to do with any of the men who paid court to her, and there were a few. She's a good woman. You need never doubt her."

"I never will, Laurie."

They seated themselves; a discreet cough at the door made them turn. Kamatsu stood at the door. "May I enter, Great One?"

Milamber and Laurie started to rise, and the lord of the house waved them back into place. "Please, stay seated." Kasumi entered behind his father and closed the door. Milamber noticed for the first time that the son of the house was wearing garments that were Midkemian in fashion. He raised an eyebrow, but said nothing.

The head of the Shinzawai family looked deeply troubled and tried to collect his thoughts. After a few moments he said, "Great One, may I be frank with you? Your arrival today is something unexpected and the source of some possible difficulty."

"Please," said Milamber. "I do not intend to cause disruption in your household, Lord. I want only my wife and son. And I will require this slave also." He indicated Laurie.

"Your will, Great One. The woman and the boy should, of course, go with you. But if I may beg of you, please allow the slave to remain."

Milamber looked from face to face. The two Shinzawai maintained control, but by the way they glanced from one to the other and at Laurie, their distress was poorly hidden. Something had changed here in the last five years. The relationship between the men in the room was not what it should have been between masters and slave.

"Laurie?" Milamber looked at his friend. "What is this?"

Laurie looked at the other two men, then at Milamber. "I will have to ask you to promise me something."

Kamatsu's shock was signaled by a sharp intake of breath. "Laurie! You dare too much. One does not bargain with a Great One. His words are as law."

Milamber held up a hand. "No. Let him speak."

In imploring tones Laurie said to his friend, "I know little of these matters, Milamber. You know I have no sense about protocol. I may be violating custom, but I ask you for the sake of our former friendship, will you keep a trust and vow to keep what you hear in this room to yourself?"

The magician pondered the matter. He could command the Shinzawai lord to tell all, and the man would, as automatically as a soldier following orders, but his friendship for the troubadour was important to him. "I give you my word that I will not repeat what you tell me."

Laurie gave a sigh and smile, and the Shinzawai seemed to lose some of their tension. Laurie said, "I have struck a bargain with my lord here. When we have completed certain tasks, I am to be given my freedom."

Milamber shook his head. "That is not possible. The law does not permit a slave to be freed. Even the Warlord cannot free a slave."

Laurie smiled. "And yourself?"

Milamber looked stern. "I am outside the law. None can command me. Are you claiming to be a magician?"

"No, Milamber, nothing like that. It is true that I can only be a slave here. But I won't be here. I will return to Midkemia."

Milamber looked puzzled. "How is that possible? There is only one rift into Midkemia, and that is controlled by the Warlord's pet magicians. There are no others, or I would know of them."

"We have a plan. It is involved and will take much explaining, but simply put, it is this: I will accompany Kasumi, disguised as a priest of Turakamu the Red. He will be leading soldiers replacing troops at the front. No one is likely to notice my height, for the Red One's priests are given wide berth. The troops are all loyal to the Shinzawai. Once in Midkemia, we will slip through the lines and find our way to the Kingdom forces."

Milamber nodded. "Now I understand the language lessons and the clothes. But tell me, Laurie. Are you willing to spy for the Tsurani in exchange for your freedom?" There was no disapproval in his voice, it was a simple question.

Laurie flushed. "I am not going as a spy. I am going as a guide. I am to take Kasumi to Rillanon, for an audience with the King."

"Why?" Milamber was surprised.

Kasumi interrupted. "I go to meet the King and bring him an offer of peace."

Milamber raised an argument. "How can you possibly expect to end the war with the War Party still in control of the High Council?"

"There is one thing in our favor," responded Kamatsu. "This war has lasted for nine years, and the end is nowhere in sight. Great One, I don't presume to instruct you, but if I may explain some things?"

Milamber nodded that he should continue. Kamatsu sipped his drink and went on. "Since the end of the war with the Thuril Confederation, the War Party has been pressed to maintain its dominance over the High Council. Each border clash with Thuril brought the call for a renewal of the conflict. Between the fighting on the border, and the constant attempts by the Thün to break through the passes in the north and regain their former southern range, the War Party managed barely to maintain a majority. A coalition led by the Blue Wheel Party was on the verge of dislodging them ten years ago, when the Assembly discovered the rift into your former homeland. The call for war rang out in the council as soon as the rich metals of your homeland were known to exist. All the progress we had made over the years was lost in that instant.

"So we began at once to counter this madness. The metals being mined on your former world are, from what Laurie has told us, the leavings of abandoned mines, not considered worth the bother by those you call dwarves. There is nothing in this for Tsuranuanni but an excuse to raise the War Banner again and shed blood.

"You know our history. You know how difficult it is for us to settle our differences in a peaceful manner. I have been a soldier and know the glories of war. I also know its waste. Laurie has convinced me that my suspicions about those who live in the Kingdom were correct. You are not a very warlike people, in spite of your nobles and their armies. You would have been willing to trade."

Milamber interrupted. "This is all true. But I am not sure that it has any bearing on things as they stand now. My former nation had not fought a major war in nearly fifty years, except for skirmishes with the goblins of the north and along the Keshian border. But now the battle drums sound in the West. The Armies of the Kingdom have been blooded. The nation has been invaded without cause. They would not, I think, be willing simply to stop and forgive. There would be demands for retribution, or at least reparation. Would the High Council be willing to surrender both the honor of Tsuranuanni and make restitution for the wrong done at the hands of its soldiers?"

The Shinzawai lord looked troubled. "The council would not, I am sure. But the Emperor would."

"The Emperor?" Milamber said, surprised. "What has he to do with this?"

"Ichindar, may heaven bless him, feels the war is bleeding the Empire of its resources. When he campaigned against the Thuril, we learned that some frontiers are simply too vast and far from the Empire to control, save at costs far greater than the victories are worth. The Light of Heaven understands that nowhere could there be a frontier as vast or far as that we have found on Midkemia. He is taking a hand in the Game of the Council. It is perhaps the greatest game ever played in the history of Tsuranuanni. The Light of Heaven is willing to command the Warlord to peace, to have him removed from office if need be. But he will not take the risk of so great a break with tradition unless he is guaranteed the willingness of King Rodric to come to terms. He must go before the High Council with peace a fait accompli; otherwise he risks too much.

"Regicide has been committed only once in the history of the Empire, Great One. The High Council hailed the killer and named him Emperor. He was the son of the man he slew. His father had tried to order taxes imposed upon the temples, the last time an Emperor played in the Game of the Council. We can be a hard people, Great One, even with ourselves, and never has an Emperor sought to do what Ichindar seeks, what others, many others, will see as laying down the honor of the Empire, an unthinkable act.

"But if he can deliver peace to the council, then it will clearly show the gods give their blessing to such an undertaking, and none will dare challenge him."

"You risk much, Lord of the Shinzawai."

"I love my nation and the Empire, Great One. I would willingly die in the field for her, and I risked that often when I was younger, during the field for her, and I risked that often when I was younger, during the Thuril campaigns. I would also risk my life, my sons, the honor of my house, family, and clan to bring the Empire to sanity. As would the Emperor. We are a patient people. This plan is years in preparation. The Blue Wheel Party has long been secretly allied with the Party for Peace. We withdrew in the third year of the war to embarrass the Warlord and set the stage for Kasumi's training for the coming journey. Over a year was spent in traveling to various lords within the Blue Wheel and Peace parties, ensuring cooperation, that every member would play his part in the Game of the Council, before you and Laurie were brought here to be his tutors.

"We are Tsurani, and the Light of Heaven would not allow an overture to be made until he had a ready messenger. We have made Kasumi that messenger, seeking to give him the best possible chance of reaching your former King safely. It must be this way, for should any outside our faction learn of the attempt if it fails, many heads, including my own, would fall, the price of losing the game. If you take Laurie away, Kasumi has little chance of reaching your former King, and the peace effort will be postponed until we can find another trustworthy guide, a

delay almost certain to last one or two more years. The
situation is now critical. The Blue Wheel Party is again part
of the Alliance for War, after years of negotiation with the
War Party, and thousands of men are being sent to fight so
that Kasumi may slip through Kingdom lines into your
former homeland. The time will soon be ripe. You must
consider what even another year of war would mean. With
the conquest of your former homeland, the Warlord could
become invulnerable to any move we may make."

Milamber considered, then to Kasumi said, "How
soon?"

Kasumi said, "Soon, Great One, a matter of weeks.
The Warlord has spies everywhere and has some hint of
our plans. He has little trust of the Blue Wheel's sudden
shift in the council, but he cannot refuse the aid. He feels
the need to strike a great victory. He plans the major spring
offensive against the forces of Lords Borric and Brucal, the
Kingdom's main strength. It will be timed to occur just
before the Imperial Festival, orchestrated so he can announce the victory at the Imperial Games, for his own
personal glory."

Kamatsu said, "It is much like an end-game gambit in
shāh, Great One. A smashing victory will gain the Warlord
all he needs to take control of the High Council, but we risk
this to play for our final move. The front will be in
confusion as preparations are being made for the offensive.
Kasumi and Laurie will have their best opportunity to slip
through the lines. Should King Rodric agree, then the
Light of Heaven can appear in the High Council with an
announcement of peace, and all that the Warlord's power
and influence is based upon will crumble. In terms of shāh,
we expose our last piece to capture so that our Emperor
may checkmate a Warlord."

Milamber was thoughtful for a time. "I think you have
embarked on a bold plan, Lord of the Shinzawai. I will
honor my pledge to say nothing. Laurie may continue
here." He looked at Laurie. "May the gods of our fore-
fathers protect you and bring you success. I pray this war
may end soon." He stood up. "If you don't mind, I will
take my leave. I would have my wife and child home now."

Kasumi rose and bowed. "I should like to say one
thing more, Great One."

Milamber indicated he should proceed. "Years ago, when you asked for Katala for your wife, and I told you the request would be refused, I also told you there was a reason. It was our plan you would also return to your homeworld. I trust you understand that now. We are a hard people, Great One, but not cruel."

"It was apparent as soon as the plan was revealed." He looked at Laurie. "For what I am now, this is my homeland, but there is still a part of me unchanged within, and for that reason I envy you your homecoming. You will be well remembered, old friend."

So saying, Milamber left the room. Outside the great house he found Katala waiting in a garden, watching their son at play. She came to him and they embraced, savoring sweet reunion. After a long moment he said, "Come, beloved, let us take our son home."

NINE

FUSION

Longbow wept in silence.

Alone in a glade near the edge of the elven forests, the Huntmaster of Crydee stood over three fallen elves. Their lifeless bodies lay sprawled upon the ground with arms and legs bent at impossible angles, their fair faces covered in blood. Martin knew what death meant to the elves, where one or two children to a family in a century was the norm. One face he knew well, Algavins, Galain's companion since boyhood, less than thirty years of age, still a child by the elven folk's measure.

Footsteps from behind caused Martin to wipe away the tears and resume his usually impassive expression. From behind he heard Garret say, "There's another bunch down the trail, Huntmaster. The Tsurani went through this part of the forest like a bad wind.

Martin nodded, then set out without comment, Garret following. For all his youth, Garret was Longbow's best tracker, and they both moved lightly along the trail toward Elvandar.

After traveling for hours, they crossed the river west of a Tsurani enclave, and when they were safely into the elven forests, a voice hailed them from the trees. "Well met, Martin Longbow."

Martin and Garret halted and waited as three elves appeared from among the trees, seemingly forming out of the air. Galain and his two companions approached the Huntmaster and Garret. Martin inclined his head slightly back toward the river and Galain nodded. It was all the communication they needed to exchange the fact both knew of Algavins' death, along with the others. Garret noticed the exchange, though he was far from conversant with the subtleties of elvish ways.

"Tomas? Calin?" asked Martin.

"In council with the Queen. Do you bring news?"

"Messages from Prince Arutha. Are you bound for council?"

Galain smiled the elvish half-smile that indicated ironic humor. "It has fallen to us to guard the way. We must remain for a time. We will come as soon as the dwarves cross the river. They are due anytime now."

The comment was not lost on Martin as he bade them good-bye and continued toward Elvandar. Approaching the clearing surrounding the elvish tree-city, he wondered at the exclusion of Galain and the other young elves from council. They were all the constant companions of Tomas since he came to take up permanent residency in Elvandar. Martin had not been there since just before the siege of Crydee, but in those years he had spoken to some of the Natalese Rangers who ran messages from the Duke to Elvandar to Crydee. On several occasions he had spent hours talking with Long Leon and Grimsworth of Natal. While close-mouthed when not among their own kind, they were less guarded with Longbow, for in the Huntmaster of Crydee they sensed a kindred spirit. He was the only man not a Ranger of Natal who could enter Elvandar unbidden. The two Natalese Rangers had indicated great changes in the Elf Queen's court, and Martin felt a strange sort of silent disquiet.

As they approached Elvandar in an easy, loping run, Garret said, "Huntmaster, will they not send someone to fetch the fallen?"

"It is not their way. They will let the forest reclaim them, for they believe their true spirits are now abiding in the Blessed Isles."

They soon came to the edge of Elvandar. Martin stopped when Garret stood enraptured by the sight of the great trees. The late afternoon sun cast long shadows through the forest, but the high boughs were already glimmering with their own fairy light.

Martin took Garret by the elbow and gently guided the gawking tracker along, then left him with some elves and continued on alone to the Queen's court. He reached the council ring and entered, saluting the Queen.

Aglaranna smiled at sight of him. "Welcome, Martin Longbow. It has been too long since you last came to us."

Martin had grown alongside elven children and was as able as any man in hiding his emotions when need be, but the sight of Tomas rocked him to the point of nearly exclaiming. Biting back a comment, he forced himself not to stare. He had heard of the changes in Tomas, but nothing had prepared him for the sight of the towering man before him. Alien eyes regarded him. There was little remaining of the happy, grinning boy who had once followed him through the woods begging for tales of the elves. Without cordiality Tomas stepped forward and said, "What word from Crydee?"

Martin leaned upon his bow. "Prince Arutha sends his greetings," he said to the Queen, "and his affections, as well as his hope for your good health." Turning to Tomas, who had obviously usurped some position of command within the Queen's council, he said, "Arutha sends the following news: Black Guy, Duke of Bas-Tyra, now rules in Krondor, so no help will be forthcoming to the Far Coast. Also, the Prince has good cause to believe the outworlders plan to mount a major offensive soon, whether against Crydee, Elvandar, or the Duke's army he cannot tell. However, the southern enclaves are not being reinforced through the dwarven mines, though they are strongly dug in. My trackers have had some signs of northward movement, but nothing upon a large scale. It is Arutha's guess the most likely offensive will be against his father and Brucal's army." Then he said, "And I bring word that Arutha's Squire has been slain." He observed the elven avoidance of naming the dead.

Tomas's eyes betrayed a glint of emotion at the news of Roland's death, but all he said was, "In war men die."

Calin realized the exchange was something of a personal matter between Longbow and Tomas. No one else in the court had known Roland well, though Calin remembered him from the dinner that night so many years ago in Crydee. Returning to the business of the war, he said, "It is a logical thing. Should the Kingdom army in the West be broken, the outworlders could then turn their full attention on the other fronts, gaining the Free Cities and Crydee quickly. Within a year, two at the most, all of what once was Keshian Bosania would be under their banners. Then they could march easily upon Yabon. In time they could march to the gates of Krondor."

Tomas faced Calin, as if to speak, his eyes narrow. A flash of communication passed between the Queen and Tomas, and he stepped back into his place in the council circle. Calin continued, "If the outworlders are not staging to the west of the mountains, then we should be joined by the dwarves soon. We've had sorties across the river from the outworlders, but no sign of major attacks to come. I think Arutha is correct in his surmise, and should the Dukes call, we should try to aid them."

Tomas turned upon the Elf Prince. "Leave Elvandar unprotected!" His face showed outrage. Martin was startled by the ferocity of Tomas's barely checked anger. "Without stripping the elven forests of defenders, we could not mount enough numbers to matter in such a battle."

Calin's face remained impassive, but his eyes mirrored Tomas's anger. His words came forth quietly. "I am Warleader of Elvandar. I would not leave our forests unprotected. But should the outworlders mount a major offensive against the Dukes they will not leave sufficient soldiers along the river to menace our forests. They have not come against us since we defeated them with the sorcerer's aid and their Black Robes were killed. But should they battle Lords Borric and Brucal, and should the battle be a close thing, our numbers might tip the balance."

Tomas maintained his self-control, standing rigidly for a moment, then in icy tones he said, "The dwarves follow Dolgan, and Dolgan follows my lead. They will not come unless I call them to battle." Without another word he left the council circle.

Martin watched Tomas leave. His skin crawled as he felt for the first time the power contained within this strange blend of man and whatever else lived inside the boy from Crydee. He had only caught a glimpse of what was within Tomas, but it had been enough. Tomas was a being to be feared.

Martin then saw a flicker of expression on Aglaranna's face. She rose and said, "I had better have words with Tomas. He has been overwrought of late."

As she left, Martin was struck by a certainty. Whatever else he had seen, he had witnessed a conflict between the Elf Queen's son and her lover, and a deep conflict within herself, as well. Aglaranna had worn the expression of one caught in a hopeless fate.

The throbbing had become worse, not quite a pain, but a discomfort that grew unnervingly more persistent. Tomas sat in the cool glade, near the quiet pool, struggling within himself. Since coming to live in Elvandar, he had found his dreams little more than vague shadowy images, with half-remembered phrases and names to grasp. They were less troublesome, less fearful, less a presence in his daily life, but the pressure within his head, the dull near-ache had grown. When he was in battle, he became lost in red rage and there was no sense of the ache, but when the battle lust subsided, especially when he was slow to return to Elvandar, the throbbing returned.

Footsteps sounded lightly behind, and without turning, he said, "I wish to be alone."

Aglaranna said, "The pain, Tomas?"

A faint stirring of some strange feeling rose briefly within and he cocked his head as if listening for something. Then he answered curtly, "Yes. I will return to our rooms soon. Leave now and prepare for me to join you later."

Aglaranna stepped back, her proud features showing pain at being addressed in such a tone. She turned quickly and left.

As she walked through the woods, her emotions churned within. Since surrendering to Tomas's desire, and her own, she had lost the ability to command him, or to resist his commands. He was now lord over her, and she felt shame. It was a joyless union, not the return of lost happiness she had hoped for. But there was a will-sapping compulsion, a need to be with him, to belong to him, that stripped away her defenses. Tomas was dynamic, powerful, and sometimes cruel. She corrected herself: not cruel, just so removed from any other being, no comparison could be made. He was not indifferent to her needs; he simply was unaware she had any. As she approached Elvandar, the soft fairy lights reflected in the shimmering tears that touched her cheeks.

Tomas was only partially aware of her departure. Under the dull ache within his head, a voice faintly called to him. He strained to listen, knowing its timbre, its color, knowing who called. . . .

"Tomas?"

Yes.

Ashen-Shugar looked across the desolation of the plains, dry cracked lands devoid of moisture save for bubbling alkali pots that spewed foul odors into the air. Aloud, to his unseen companion, he said, "It has been some time since we last spoke."

Tathar and the others seek to keep us apart. You are often forgotten.

The fetid winds blew from the north, cold but cloying. The smell of decay was everywhere, and in the residue of the mighty madness that had gripped the universe around, only faint stirrings of life reasserting itself were felt.

"No matter. We are together again."

What is this place?

"The Desolation of the Chaos Wars. Draken-Korin's monument, the lifeless tundra that was once great grasslands. Few living things abide here. Most creatures flee to the south, and more hospitable climes."

Who are you?

Ashen-Shugar laughed. "I am what you are becoming. We are one. So you have said many times."

I had forgotten.

Ashen-Shugar called and Shuruga sped toward him over a grey landscape, while black clouds thundered overhead. The mighty dragon landed and his master climbed upon his back. Casting a glance at the spot marked by ash, the only reminder of Draken-Korin's existence, the Valheru said, "Come, let us see what fate has wrought."

Shuruga leaped into the heavens and above the desolation they flew. Ashen-Shugar was silent as he rode upon Shuruga's broad back, feeling the wind blowing across his face. They flew and time passed them by, as they shared the death of one age and the birth of another. High in the blue sky they soared, free of the horror of the Chaos Wars.

It is worthy of sorrow.

"I think not. There is a lesson, though I cannot bring myself to know it. Yet I sense you do." Ashen-Shugar closed his eyes as the throbbing returned.

Yes, I remember.

"Tomas?"

Tomas's eyes snapped open. He found Galain standing a short way off, near the edge of the clearing. "Shall I return later?"

Tomas rose slowly from where he had sat dreaming. His voice was rough and tired. "No, what is it?"

"Dolgan's dwarven band has reached the outer forest and waits for you near the winding brook. The dwarves struck an outworld enclave as they crossed the river." There was a merry smile upon the young elf's face. "They have finally captured prisoners."

A strange look of mixed delight and fury passed over Tomas's face. Galain felt strange emotions as he regarded the reaction of the warrior in white and gold to this news. As if listening to a distant call, Tomas spoke distractedly. "Go to the dwarven camp. I will join you there presently."

Galain withdrew, and Tomas listened. A distant voice grew louder.

"Have I erred?"

The hall echoed with words, for now it was vacant, the servants having slipped away. Ashen-Shugar brooded upon his throne. He spoke to shadows. "Have I erred?"

Now you know doubt, answered the ever-present voice.
"This strange quietness within, what is it?"
It is death approaching.
Ashen-Shugar closed his eyes. "I thought as much. So
few of my kind lived beyond battle. It was a rare thing. I
am the last. Still, I would like to fly Shuruga once more."
He is gone. Dead, ages past.
"But I flew him this morning."
It was a dream. As is this.
"Am I then also mad?"
You are but a memory. This is but a dream.
"Then I will do what is planned. I accept the inevi-
table. Another will come to take my place."
*So it has happened already, for I am the one who came, and I
have taken up your sword and put upon your mantle; your cause
is now mine. I stand against those who would plunder this world.*
"Then am I content to die."
Opening his eyes, he took one last look at his hall now
cloaked in ancient dust. Closing them for the last time, the
Ruler of the Eagles' Reaches cast his final spell. His waning
powers, still unmatched upon this world by any save the
new gods, flowed from his tired body, infusing his armor.
Smoky wisps wafted upward from where his body had
rested, and soon only the golden armor, white tabard,
shield, and sword of white and gold remained.
I am Ashen-Shugar; I am Tomas.

Tomas's eyes opened and for a moment he was
confused to find himself in the glade. A strange passion
grew within as he felt a new strength flowing throughout
his being. In his mind rang a clarion call: I am Ashen-
Shugar, the Valheru. I will destroy all who seek to plunder
my world.
With a terrible resolve he left the glade, to find the
place the dwarves had brought his enemies.

"It is good to see you again, friend Longbow," said
Dolgan, puffing away on his pipe. They had not seen each
other since a chance meeting several years before when the
dwarves passed through the forest east of Crydee on their
way to Elvandar.
Martin, Calin, and a few elves had come to see the

dwarves' prisoners, who were still bound. They waited in a group in a corner of the clearing, glaring at their captors. Galain entered the clearing and said, "Tomas is coming soon."

Martin said, "How is it, Dolgan, after all these years, you managed to capture prisoners, and an entire enclave at that?"

Behind the eight bound warriors stood a fearful group of Tsurani slaves, unbound but huddled together, uncertain of their fate. Dolgan gave an offhanded wave. "Usually we're raiding across the river, and prisoners tend to slow things down during a withdrawal, being either unconscious or uncooperative. This time we had little choice in the matter, as we needed to cross the river Crydee. In past years we'd wait to sneak across in darkness, but this year they're as close as nettles in a thicket everywhere along the river.

"We found this band in a relatively isolated spot, with only these eight to guard the slaves. They were repairing an earthwork, one which I judge was overrun a short while ago during an elven sortie. We slipped around them, then a few of the lads climbed into the trees—though they liked it little. We dropped down upon the three outer guards, silencing them before they could shout the alert. The other five were napping, the lazy louts. We slipped into camp, and after a few well-placed strokes with our hammers, we bound them. These others"—he indicated the slaves— "were too timid to make a sound. When it was clear we had not alarmed the nearby enclaves, we thought to bring them along. Seemed a waste to leave them behind. Thought we might learn something useful." Dolgan tried to keep an impassive expression, but pride over his company's work shone through like a beacon in the night.

Martin smiled his approval, and said to Calin, "I hope we may learn what is coming, if the feared offensive is really to be mounted and where. I've learned a few phrases of their tongue, but not enough to make any sense of what they might tell us. Only Father Tully and Charles, my Tsurani tracker, can speak to them fluently. Perhaps we should attempt to move them to Crydee?"

Calin said, "We have the means to learn their tongue, given time. I doubt they would lend much cooperation in their transport. Most likely they would try to raise the alarm every step of the way."

Martin conceded the point. Then a disturbance caused him to turn.

Tomas came striding into the clearing. Dolgan began to greet him, but something in the young warrior's manner and expression silenced him. There was madness in Tomas's eyes, something the dwarf had glimpsed before as a glimmer, but which now shone forth brightly.

Tomas regarded the bound prisoners, then pulled his sword slowly and pointed at them. The words he spoke were alien to both Martin and the dwarves, but the elves were rocked by what they heard. Several of the older elves dropped to their knees in supplication and the younger ones drew away in reflexive fear. Only Calin stood his ground, though he appeared shaken. Then slowly the Elf Prince turned to Martin, his face drained of color. In terrified tones he said, "At last the Valheru is truly among us."

Ignoring all others in the clearing, Tomas walked up to the first Tsurani prisoner. The bound soldier looked up with a mixture of fear and defiance. Suddenly the golden sword was raised high and arced down, severing the man's head from his shoulders. Blood splattered the white tabard, then flowed off, leaving it spotless. A low moan of fear came from the huddled slaves, and the remaining soldiers' eyes were wide in terror. Slowly Tomas turned to face the next prisoner, and again his sword took a life.

Martin freed himself from shocked paralysis, forcing his eyes away from the butchery. He felt terrible dread, but it appeared as nothing to what the elves revealed in their abasement before Tomas. Calin's face showed a struggle within as he tried to overcome a nearly instinctive obedience to the words spoken in the ancient language of the Valheru, masters of all, ages past. The younger elves, less studied in the old wisdom, simply had no understanding of the overwhelming need to obey this man in white and gold. The language of the Valheru was still the language of power.

Tomas turned away from his slaughter and Martin felt struck by the strength of his gaze. Gone was any vestige of the boy from Crydee. Now an alien presence suffused this being. Tomas's arm drew back, and Martin tensed to dodge the blow. Any human was a potential victim, and even the dwarves drew back at the awesome menace Tomas projected. Then a faint spark of recognition entered Tomas's eyes and he said, in a distant voice, "Martin, by the love I once bore you, be gone or your life is forfeit."

Mustering courage against the most consuming fear he had ever felt, Martin shouted, "I'll not stand and watch you slaughter helpless men!"

Again a distant voice answered, steeped in ancient majesty and lost grandeur regained. "These come into my world, Martin. None may seek that which is my domain, my preserve, mine alone! Shall you, too, come into my world, Martin?" With a nearly unseen quickness, Tomas wheeled and two Tsurani died.

Martin charged, crossing the gap between in a bound, and knocked Tomas away from the prisoners. They went down in a heap, and Martin grabbed at the wrist that held the golden sword.

A strong man capable of carrying a freshly killed buck for miles, Martin was no match for Tomas. As easily as picking up a bothersome infant, Tomas pushed Martin aside and came lightly to his feet. Martin sprang at Tomas again, but this time Tomas stood ready. He simply seized Martin by the tunic and said, "None may interfere with my will." He tossed Martin across the clearing as if he weighed less than a tenth his weight. Martin's arms flailed the air as he arced high over the ground, striving to control his fall. He landed hard, and all around could hear the breath explode from his lungs as he struck.

Dolgan rushed to his side, for the elves were still held in thrall by what they had witnessed. The dwarven chief poured water from a skin at his side upon Martin's face and shook him awake. The strangled cries of terror from the Tsurani slaves watching soldiers being butchered greeted Martin as he regained his wits.

Martin struggled to focus his vision, the scene before him swimming and shifting. When he could see, he drew a hissing breath in horror.

Tomas struck down the last Tsurani soldier and began to advance upon the cringing slaves. They appeared unable to move, watching with wide eyes the bringer of their destruction, looking like nothing so much to Martin than a band of deer startled by a sudden light in the night.

A ragged cry came from Martin's lips as Tomas killed the first Tsurani slave, a pitiful-looking willow of a man. Longbow struggled to rise, senses reeling, and Dolgan helped him to his feet.

Tomas raised his sword and another died. Again the golden blade was raised and he looked into the face of his victim. Eyes round with fear, a young boy, no more than twelve years old, stood waiting for the blow that would end his life.

Suddenly time expanded for Tomas, the moment frozen in his mind. He studied the shock of dark hair and the large brown eyes of the boy. The child crouched awaiting the death he saw over him, his head shaking no, as his lips formed a single phrase over and over.

In the faint light of the clearing, Tomas saw an old ghost, the specter of a friend long forgotten. A remembered bond, from his earliest memories as a child, reassociated itself with his consciousness. Images blurred, past and present confused, and he said, "Pug?"

Within his mind, pain exploded and another will sought to overwhelm him.

Pug! it shrieked.

Kill him! came a raging answer, and within him two wills battled.

No! screamed the other.

To all in the glade, Tomas stood frozen, shaking with some inner struggle, his sword still held high, waiting for release.

These are the enemy! Slay them!

He is a boy! Only a boy!

He is the enemy!

A boy!

Tomas's face became a mask of pain; his teeth clenched and every muscle drew taut, stretching skin tightly over skull. His eyes grew round and perspiration began to flow from under his helm, down his brows and cheeks.

Martin stumbled to his feet. He moved slowly, every gesture bringing pain from the battering he had taken.

Tomas's hand slowly moved downward, each inch a shaking, trembling passage as he warred within. The boy was transfixed, unable to move, his eyes following the movement of the blade.

I am Ashen-Shugar! I am Valheru! sang a voice within, in a torrent of anger, battle madness, and bloodlust.

Against this sea of rage stood a single rock, a calm, small voice within that said, simply, *I am Tomas.*

Again and again the sea of hate crashed over the rock of calm, each time engulfing it, then sliding back, to come again. But each time the tide diminished and the rock stood clear, rising above the mad surf. A shattering of something, the thundering of ages lost and passing, rocked Tomas's mind. He reeled, then swam within an alien landscape, seeking a pinpoint of light he knew was his way to freedom. Tides swept him along, and he battled, struggling to keep his head above the strangling black sea. A shrieking, evil wind blew overhead, and to his ears it sang a song of woeful meter. He struck out, and again he saw a pinpoint of light. Again the tide engulfed him, forcing him away from his goal, but this time it was weaker. Once more he struggled toward the light. Then came a surge, a last, terrifying assault culminating in a total attack upon him. *I am Ashen-Shugar!* There came a breaking of the will, something snapping like the dead branch of a tree under the weight of newly fallen snow, like the sound of old winter ice breaking at spring's touch, as if the last assault took too great a toll.

The black sea lost its fury and subsided, and he was again standing upon firm ground, a single rock. *I am Tomas.* In the distance the pinpoint of light began to expand before his eyes, racing forward to engulf him.

I am Tomas.

"Tomas!"

He blinked, and saw he was again in the glade. Before him crouched the boy, waiting to die. He turned his head and saw Martin, sighting along a cloth-yard arrow, drawn hard against his cheek. The Huntmaster of Crydee said, "Put down your sword, or by the gods, I'll kill you where you stand."

Tomas's gaze wandered about the glade, and he saw the dwarves with weapons drawn, as had some of the older elves. Calin, still shaking, had his sword out and was slowly advancing upon him.

Martin watched Tomas closely, not fearing him, but respectful of his awesome strength and speed. He waited, and saw the flicker of madness still in Tomas's eyes, then, as if a veil were lifted, saw them clear. Abruptly the golden sword fell from his hand and the pale, nearly colorless eyes filled with tears. Tomas dropped to his knees and a moan of terrible anguish was torn from his lips, and Tomas cried out, "Oh, Martin, what have I become?"

Martin lowered his bow, watching as Tomas gathered his arms about himself. Into the glade came Tathar and the other Spellweavers. They approached Tomas and then surveyed the others in the glade. So terrible were Tomas's sobs of anguish, so filled with sorrow and remorse, that many of the elves discovered they also wept.

Tathar said to Martin Longbow, "We felt the fabric of our spells torn asunder a short while ago, and came at once. We feared the Valheru had come, rightly it seems."

Martin said, "Now?"

"The other side of the balance. That the Valheru is at last displaced by the boy there can be no doubt, but the boy now must feel the weight of ages of slaughter, and the guilt over joy felt when taking other lives. The burdens felt by mortals are again his, and we shall now see if he can withstand them. This agony may prove his end."

Martin left the ancient elf and crossed to Tomas. In the dim light he was the first to perceive the change. Gone were the alien cast to his features, the gleaming eyes, the haughty brow. Again he was Tomas, a man, though there were still legacies of his experience that would forever proclaim him something more than a man: the elven ears, the pale eyes. Gone was the Lord of Power, the Old One, the Valheru. Where before a Dragon Lord had stood now crouched a troubled, sick man in torment over what he had done.

Tomas raised his head as Martin touched him upon the shoulder. Red-rimmed eyes, nearly mad from grief, regarded Martin for a brief moment, then closed as if seeking oblivion to all around. For some time the elves and dwarves watched, and the Tsurani slaves were silent, aware that some miracle had occurred, not understanding, but suddenly sure they were spared. For some time they watched, as Martin Longbow cradled the sobbing man in white and gold, who cried in anguish so terrible to hear.

Aglaranna sat upon her sleeping pallet, brushing her long red-gold hair. As before, she waited for Tomas, half hoping, half fearing he would come.

A shout from without caused her to rise. She gathered her robes around her and left her quarters. Standing upon a platform, she watched as a group of elves and dwarves came toward Elvandar's heart. With them came Martin Longbow and some humans, clearly outworlders from their dress.

Her hands went to her mouth as she gasped. In the center of the group walked Tomas, at his side a young boy with eyes wide at the splendor of Elvandar.

Aglaranna was unable to move, fearful that what she witnessed was the product of delusion born of hope. Time sped past as she waited, then Tomas stood before her. Leaving the boy, he stepped forward. Martin took the boy by the hand and led him away, the others following, giving the Elf Queen and Tomas the solitude they needed.

Tomas reached out slowly and touched her face, and he drank in the sight of her, as if seeing her as he had when she had first appeared at Crydee. Then, without words, he slowly, gently enfolded her in his arms. He held her in silence, letting her feel the warmth of the love that filled him at sight of her.

After a time he whispered in her ear, "For each moment of sorrow I have visited upon you, O my lady, I pray the gods grant me a year to gift you with joy. I am again your adoring subject."

Too filled with happiness to speak, the Elf Queen simply clung to him, her sorrow only a dim memory.

TEN

EMISSARY

The troops stood quietly.

Long columns of men awaited their turn at passing through the rift into Midkemia. Officers walked by, their presence ensuring discipline in the lines. Laurie, in the mask and robe of a Red Priest, was impressed at the level of control these officers had over their men. He judged the Tsurani code of honor, where orders were followed without question, a very alien thing.

He and Kasumi moved quickly down the line, heading for the first detachment behind the one now entering the rift. Laurie bent his knees and stooped, to detract from his noticeable height. As they had hoped, more soldiers than not looked away as the bogus Red Priest passed.

When they reached the head of the column, Kasumi fell in. His younger brother, who had been promoted to Strike Leader for this offensive, seemed to pay no attention to his commander's late arrival, or to the priest of Turakamu who arrived with him.

After a seemingly interminable delay, the command came and they stepped forward into the shimmering glow of "nothingness" that marked the rift between the two worlds. There was a brief flash of lights, a momentary dizziness, and they found themselves walking forward into a light Midkemian rain. Sheets of wetness, little more than a heavy mist, fell around them. The Tsurani soldiers, hot-weather-bred, wrapped cloaks about themselves.

A staging officer briefly conferred with Kasumi, and the troops were ordered to move off to the northeast a specified distance and erect a camp. Kasumi and Hokanu were then to report to the Warlord's tent for briefings. The Warlord himself was back in Kentosani, the Holy City, preparing for the Imperial Games, but his subcommander was to instruct them in their duties and areas of responsibility until his return.

They quickly moved up toward the front and set up camp. Once the commander's tent was up, Laurie and the Shinzawai brothers ducked inside. While bundles containing Midkemian clothing and weapons were unpacked, Kasumi said, "As soon as we return from our meeting with the subcommander, we will eat. Tonight we will lead a patrol of our area, and try to slip through the lines." Kasumi looked at his brother. "After we have gone, brother, it will be your responsibility to hide our departure for as long as possible. Once there has been fighting reported, you may claim we have been lost to the enemy."

Hokanu agreed. "We had best report now."

Kasumi looked at Laurie. "Stay inside. We want no risk. You are the tallest damned priest I have ever seen."

Laurie nodded. He sat upon some cushions, and waited.

The patrol moved silently through the trees. The rain had stopped, but the weather had turned colder, and Laurie suppressed a shiver. Years in the hot climes of Kelewan had driven away his former ability to ignore the chill. He wondered about the new troops from Tsuranu-anni and how they would react when the first snowfalls came. Most likely with studied indifference, regardless of what they felt inside. A Tsurani soldier would never let himself appear upset by something as trivial as solid water falling from the sky.

They elected the North Pass, for it led to the largest front and they were less likely to be noticed passing through the lines. They reached the head of the pass and a station guard passed them along. Once outside the valley they struck slightly more eastward than their patrol called for.

Beyond the rolling hills and light woods was the road from LaMut to Zūn. Once the two travelers had left their patrol and reached it, they would head for Zūn, buy horses, and ride south. With luck they would reach Krondor in two weeks. There they would change mounts and head for Salador, where they would find passage on a ship for Rillanon.

They moved at a dogtrot that ate up miles. Laurie ran beside Kasumi, marveling at the soldiers' stamina. They might not be showing fatigue, but he was feeling it. Hokanu signaled for the patrol to stop at the head of a large, flat area near the woods. "Here we will start our swing back to our patrol area. We should not see any Tsurani soldiers from here. Let us hope, for your sake, we don't meet with Kingdom troops either."

He gave a signal, and they moved out. Laurie and Kasumi were handed backpacks and clothing. They quickly changed, then followed the route taken by the patrol. They would follow for a short distance, using the patrol for cover should any Kingdom troops be nearby.

They moved into a small vale, and found the patrol held up by something ahead. The last man in line motioned them for quiet. They moved to the head of the line and Laurie looked around for a quick exit route should there be any trouble. Hokanu said softly, "I thought I heard something, but there has been no sound for several minutes."

Kasumi nodded. "Then move forward. We will wait until you have crossed that open area ahead, then follow." He indicated a broad flat area between the mouth of the vale where they stood, and a stand of trees at the opposite end.

When the patrol had reached the center of the open area, the clouds parted and shafts of moonlight lit up the area. "Damn!" Kasumi swore under his breath. "They might as well light torches now."

Suddenly the trees erupted with motion and sound. The ground trembled as riders came charging forward, out from the trees that hid them. Each wore heavy chain mail and a full helm. Long lances were leveled at the surprised Tsurani soldiers.

The Tsurani had barely enough time to ready a rude line for defense before the riders were upon them. Cries of horses and men filled the air and the Tsurani fell before the charge. The riders rode over the Tsurani and re-formed at the end of the vale where the two fugitives hid. They wheeled about and charged again. The Tsurani survivors of the last charge, less than half the men, moved quickly up the west side of the vale, where the trees and incline of the hillside would counter the horsemen's ability to charge.

Laurie touched Kasumi's arm and motioned to the right. It was evident the Tsurani officer was barely holding himself in check from joining his men. Suddenly Kasumi was off, hugging the edge of the trees as he ran low. Laurie followed and spotted what appeared to be a rough path heading eastward. He grabbed Kasumi's sleeve and pointed. They turned their backs to the fighting and moved off.

The next day found two travelers moving down the road to Zūn. Both wore woolen shirts, trousers, and cloaks. Closer examination by a trained eye would have revealed that the material was not really wool, but something like it. Their belts and boots were made from needra hide dyed to resemble leather. The fashion was Midkemian, as were the swords they wore on their belts.

One was obviously a minstrel, for he wore a lute slung over his backpack. The other looked to be a freebooter mercenary. Any casual observer would have been unlikely to guess their origins, or the riches carried in those backpacks, for each had a small fortune in gems tucked away in the bottom of his pack.

A northbound troop of light cavalry passed them on the road, and Laurie said, "Things have changed since I was last here. Those men in the forest were Royal Krondorian Lancers and those who just passed wore the colors of Shamata. All the forces of the Armies of the West must be marshaling here. Something seems to be in the air. Perhaps they have somehow gleaned your Warlord's plan for a major offensive?"

"I don't know. Whatever is happening does not seem to indicate that things are as stable as we have been led to believe back home. The concentration of troops here makes me think the Warlord's victory may not be easily won." Kasumi was quiet for a moment as they walked along the road. "I hope that Hokanu was among those who reached the trees." It was the first time he had mentioned his brother, and Laurie could think of nothing to say.

* * *

Two days later, Laurie, a minstrel late of Tyr-Sog, and Kenneth, a mercenary from the Vale of Dreams, sat in the Green Cat Inn in the city of Zūn. Both ate with hearty appetite, for they had lived on soldiers' rations—dried cakes of grain and fruit—for two days.

Laurie had spent over an hour negotiating with a less than reputable gem broker for several smaller stones' value. He had settled for one third their actual worth, stating, "If he thinks they are stolen, he will not be too quick to ask questions."

Kasumi asked, "Why didn't you sell him all the stones?"

"Your father has given us enough to retire on for the rest of our days. I doubt if all the brokers in Zūn could raise the gold to pay for them. We will sell a few as we travel; besides, they weigh less than gold."

Finishing their meal, the two men paid and left. Kasumi could only just refrain from staring at all the metal he could see everywhere, a lifetime's riches on Kelewan. Just the cost of the meal in silver could support a Tsurani family for a year.

They hurried along one of the city's business streets, heading to the south gate. Near there, they had been informed, a reputable trader in horses would sell them mounts and tack for a fair price. They found the man, a thin, hawk-beaked fellow by the name of Brin. Laurie spent the better part of an hour haggling with the horse trader for two of his better mounts. They left him expressing concern over their ability to sleep nights after cheating an honest businessman out of the money he needed to feed his starving children.

As they rode through the gate that put them on the road to Ylith, Kasumi said, "Much of this land of yours seems odd, but as you haggled with that merchant, I was reminded of home. Our traders are much more polite and would never think of raising their voices in such a manner, but it is still the same thing. They all have starving children."

Laurie laughed and spurred his mount forward. Soon they were out of sight of the city.

Fourteen days later, they reached the northern gate of Krondor. As they rode through, they were regarded suspiciously by several guards dressed in black and gold. Once beyond earshot of the gate guards, Laurie said, "Those are not the Prince's tabards. The banner of Bas-Tyra flies over Krondor."

They rode slowly for a minute, then Kasumi said, "What does it mean?"

"I don't know. But I think I know a place we can find out." He spurred his horse on, and Kasumi followed. They rode through a series of streets bounded on each side by warehouses and commercial enterprises. Sounds from the docks, several streets away, could be heard. Otherwise the district was quiet. "Strange," remarked Laurie, as they rode on. "This part of the city is usually busiest at this time of day."

Kasumi looked around, not sure of what he expected to see. The Midkemian cities, compared to those of the Empire, seemed small and dirty. Still, there was something strange about the lack of activity here. Both Zūn and Ylith had been teeming with soldiers, traders, and citizens at midday, even though they were smaller cities than Krondor. As they rode, a feeling of disquiet visited Kasumi.

They entered a section of the city even more run-down than the warehouse district. Here the streets were narrow, with four- with five-story buildings hugging closely on either side. Dark shadows abounded, even at noon. Those in the street, a few traders and women going to market, moved quietly and with speed. Everywhere the riders looked, they could see expressions of caution and distrust.

Laurie led Kasumi to a gate, behind which the upper part of a three-story building could be seen. Laurie leaned over in the saddle and pulled on a bell rope. When there was no answer after a few minutes, he pulled again.

A moment later, a peek window in the door slid aside, two eyes could be seen, and a voice said, "What's your business?"

Laurie's tone was sharp. "Lucas, is that you? What is happening when travelers can't gain entrance?"

The eyes widened and the peek window slid shut. The gate swung open with a creaking protest, and a man stepped out to push it wide. "Laurie, you scoundrel!" he said as he admitted the riders. "It's been five—no, six years."

They rode in and Laurie was shocked by the condition
of the inn. Off to one side was a dilapidated stable.
Opposite the gate a sign hung over the main entrance,
depicting in faded hues a parrot of many colors with wings
spread. They could hear the gate close behind them.

The man called Lucas, tall and gaunt, with grey hair,
said, "You'll have to stable the animals yourself. I am alone
here and must return to the common room before my
guests steal everything there. I'll see you and your friend
inside and we can talk." He turned away, and the two
riders were left to tend to their mounts.

As they removed the saddles from the horses, Laurie
said, "There is a lot happening here that I don't understand. The Rainbow Parrot was never a showplace, but it
was always one of the better taverns in the Poor Quarter."
He quietly rubbed down his animal. "If there is any place
we can find out what is truly going on in Krondor, this is it.
And one thing I have learned over my years of traveling
through the Kingdom is when gate guards are watching
travelers closely, it is time to stay somewhere they are not
likely to visit. You can get your throat cut quickly in the
Poor Quarter, but you'll rarely see a guardsman about. And
if they do come, the man who was trying to cut your throat
will more than likely hide you until they are gone."

"And *then* try to cut your throat."

Laurie laughed. "You understand quickly."

When the horses were cared for, the two travelers
carried their saddles and packs into the inn. Inside they
were greeted with the sight of a dimly lit common room,
with a long bar along the rear wall. On the left stood a large
fireplace, and on the right a stairway leading upward.
There were a number of empty tables in the room, and two
with customers. The newcomers were given a quick look
by the guests, who then returned to their drinks and quiet
conversation.

Laurie and Kasumi crossed over to the bar, where
Lucas stood cleaning some wine cups with a less than clean
rag. They dropped their packs at their feet, and Laurie
said, "Any Keshian wine?"

Lucas said, "A little, but it is expensive. There has
been little trade with Kesh since the trouble started."

Laurie looked at Lucas, as if weighing the cost. "Then
two ales."

Large tankards of ale appeared a moment later, and Lucas said, "It is good to see you, Laurie. I've missed that tender voice of yours."

Laurie said, "That's not what you said the last time. As I recall, you likened it to the screeching of a cat looking for a fight."

They chuckled over that, and Lucas said, "With things so bleak, I have mellowed toward those who were true friends. There are few of us left." He threw a pointed look at Kasumi.

Laurie said, "This is Kenneth, a true friend of mine, Lucas."

Lucas continued to regard the Tsurani for a moment, then smiled. "Laurie's recommendation counts heavily. Welcome." He extended his hand, and Kasumi shook with him, Kingdom fashion.

"I am pleased at your welcome."

Lucas frowned at the sound of his accent. "An outlander?"

"From the Vale of Dreams," said Kasumi.

"The Kingdom side," added Laurie.

Lucas studied the fighter. After a moment he shrugged. "Whatever. It matters not a whit to me, but be wary. These are suspicious times and there is little love wasted on strangers. Take care who you speak with, for there are rumors that Kesh's dog soldiers are ready to move north again, and you are not far from being Keshian."

Before Kasumi could say anything, Laurie said, "Is there to be trouble with Kesh, then?"

Lucas shook his head. "I can't say. The market has more rumors than a beggar has boils." His voice lowered. "Two weeks back, traders arrived with word the Empire of Great Kesh was again fighting far to the south, seeking to subdue their former vassals in the Confederacy once more. So things should stay quiet for a while. They learned the folly of a two-front war over a hundred years back when they managed to lose all of Bosania and still not beat the Confederacy."

Laurie said, "We have been traveling for a very long time and have heard little news. Why is Bas-Tyra's banner over Krondor?"

Lucas quickly looked around the room. The drinkers

seemed oblivious to the conversation at the bar, but Lucas motioned for silence. "I will show you a room," he said loudly. Both Laurie and Kasumi were a little surprised, but picked up their belongings and followed Lucas upstairs without comment.

He led them to a small room, with two beds and a nightstand. When the door was closed behind, he said, "I trust you, Laurie, so I'll ask no questions, but know things have changed greatly since last you were here. Even in the Poor Quarter there are ears that belong to the Viceroy. Bas-Tyra has the city under his bootheel, and it is a foolish man who speaks without seeing who is listening."

Lucas sat down on one of the beds, and Laurie and Kasumi sat across from him. Lucas continued, "When Bas-Tyra came to Krondor he carried the King's warrant naming him ruler of Krondor, with full viceregal powers. Prince Erland and his family were locked up in the palace, though Guy calls it 'protective custody.' Then Guy came down hard on the city. Press-gangs roamed the waterfront and many a man now sails in Lord Jessup's fleet without his wife or children knowing what became of their old pa. Since then, any who speaks against the Viceroy or King simply vanishes, 'cause Guy's got a secret police listening at every door in the city.

"Taxes increase each year to pay for the war, and trade's drying up, except for those selling to the army for the war, and they're getting paid in worthless vouchers. These are hard times, and the Viceroy's doing nothing to make them easier. Food is scarce, and there is little money to pay for what there is. Many farmers have lost their farms for taxes, and now the land lies fallow for want of someone to till it. So the farmers wander into the city, swelling the population. Most of the young men have been drafted into the army or the fleet. Be careful you aren't picked up by the guards, for whatever reason, and be wary of the press-gangs.

"Still," Lucas said with a chuckle, "things got lively around here for a time when Prince Arutha came to Krondor."

"Borric's son? He's in the city?" asked Laurie.

A twinkle of pleasure showed in Lucas's eyes. "No longer." He chuckled again. "Last winter, as bold as bright brass, the Prince comes sailing into Krondor. He must have taken the Straits of Darkness during the winter, or he never would have reached the city when he did." He quickly told them of Arutha's and Anita's escape.

Laurie said, "Did they return to Crydee?"

Lucas nodded. "A trader from Carse a week ago was full of news of this and that. One thing he heard was some Tsurani were acting up around Jonril and the Prince of Crydee was ready to come down to help if needed. So Arutha must have made it back."

Laurie said, "Guy must have been fit to burst at the news."

Lucas's smile vanished. "Well, he was, Laurie. He'd tossed Prince Erland into the dungeon to get his permission to marry Anita. He kept him there after he heard of Anita's escape. I guess he thought the girl would come back rather than let her father stay in a damp cell, but he was wrong. Now the word's on the street the Prince is near death from the chill. That's why the city's in such a state. No one knows what will happen if Erland dies. He's well liked, and there might be trouble." Laurie looked at Lucas with an unspoken question. "Nothing like rebellion," Lucas answered. "We're too dispirited. But a few of Guy's guards may turn up missing at muster, and there'll be many inconveniencies getting supplies to the garrison and palace and the like. And I wouldn't wish to be the Viceroy's taxman when he's next sent into the Poor Quarter."

Laurie considered what he had heard. "We are headed east. What about conditions on the road?"

Lucas slowly shook his head. "There is still some traveling done. Once past Darkmoor, you should have scant trouble, I'm thinking. We hear that things in the East are more as they used to be. Still, I'd move carefully."

Kasumi asked, "Will we be troubled leaving the city?"

"The north gate is still the best way. It is under-manned, as usual. For a small fee, the Mockers can see you safely through."

"Mockers?" asked the fighter.

Lucas raised his brows in surprise. "You are from a long way off. The Guild of Thieves. They remain in control of the Poor Quarter, and the Upright Man still has influence with the merchants and traders, especially along the docks.

The warehouse district is their second home, after the Poor Quarter. They can get you out, if you have any trouble at the gate."

Laurie said, "We will keep that in mind, Lucas. What of your family? I have not seen them around."

Lucas seemed to shrink into himself. "My wife is dead, Laurie, of the fever, a year ago. My sons are both in the army. I have heard little of them in a year. Last time I received a message they were in the north with Lords Borric and Brucal.

"The city is full of veterans of the war. You can see them everywhere. They are the ones with missing limbs, or blind eyes. But they always wear their old tabards. And a pathetic sight they are, too." He got a faraway look in his eyes. "I just hope my boys don't end up like that."

Laurie and Kasumi said nothing. Lucas came out of his reverie. "I must return downstairs. Supper will be ready in four hours, though nothing like I used to serve." As the innkeeper turned to go, he said, "If you need to contact the Mockers, let me know."

After he had left, Kasumi said, "It is a hard thing to know your country, Laurie, and still look upon the war as glorious."

Laurie nodded.

The warehouse was dark and musty. Except for Laurie and Kasumi and two fresh horses it was empty. They had stayed at the Rainbow Parrot the night before and had purchased new mounts at great expense, then had tried to leave the city. When they had reached the city gates, they had been stopped by a detachment of Bas-Tyra's guards. When it was obvious that the guards were not likely to let them leave without trouble, Laurie and Kasumi had broken away from them, and a mad dash through the city had followed. They had lost their pursuers in the Poor Quarter and had returned to the Rainbow Parrot. Lucas had sent word to the Upright Man, and now they waited for a thief to guide them out of the city.

A single whistle broke the silence, and Laurie and Kasumi had their swords in hand in an instant. A high-pitched chuckle greeted them, and a small figure dropped from above. In the dark it was difficult to see where the figure sprang from, but Laurie suspected their visitor had been hiding in the rafters for some time.

The figure stepped forward, and in the dim light they could see it was a boy, no older than thirteen. "There's a party at Mother's," the newcomer said.

"And a good time will be had by all," Laurie answered.

"You're the travelers, then."

"You're the guide?" asked Kasumi, taking no effort to hide the surprise in his voice.

The boy's voice was filled with bravado. "Aye. Jimmy the Hand is your guide. And a better one in all Krondor you'll not find."

Laurie said, "What's to be done?"

"First there's the matter of payment. It's a hundred sovereigns each."

Without comment, Laurie dug out several small gems and handed them over. "Will these do?"

The boy turned to the warehouse door and cracked it slightly, admitting a shaft of moonlight. He inspected the gems with an expert's eye and returned to stand before the two fugitives. "These'll do. For another hundred, you can have this." He offered a piece of parchment.

Laurie took it, but couldn't make out what was written on it in the dim light. "What is it?"

Jimmy chuckled. "A royal warrant, allowing the bearer to travel the King's Highway."

"Is it genuine?" asked the minstrel.

"My word. I nicked it myself from a trader from Ludland this morning. It's valid for another month."

"Done," said Laurie, and the minstrel gave the boy another gem.

When the gems were safely in the thief's pouch, he said, "Soon we'll be hearing a brouhaha at the gate. A few of the boys will put on some mummery for the guards. When everything's up in the wind, we'll slip through."

He returned to the door and looked out without further comment. While they waited, Kasumi whispered, "Can he be trusted?"

"No, but we have no choice. If the Upright Man could show a larger profit by turning us in, he might. But the Mockers have little love for the guards, and now less than usual, according to Lucas, so it is unlikely. Still, keep your wits about you."

Time stretched on interminably, then suddenly shouts could be heard. Jimmy signaled with a sharp whistle, which was answered by another from outside. "It's time," he said and was out the door.

Laurie and Kasumi led their horses out after him. "Follow closely and quickly," their small guide said as he set off.

They rounded the corner of a building and could see the north gate. A group of men were involved in a brawl, many appearing to be sailors from the docks. The guards were doing their best to restore order, but each time one pushed a combatant away from the fray, another would appear from the shadows around the gate and join in. In a few minutes every guard was involved in breaking up the fight, and Jimmy said, "Now!"

He broke from the building, with the travelers close behind, and dashed to the wall next to the gatehouse. They edged their way along in the shadows, the horses' clatter covered by the noise of the brawl. When they were near the gate, a single guard could be seen, on the other side, whom they hadn't been able to see from their previous location.

Laurie gripped Jimmy's shoulder. "We'll have to take him quickly."

Jimmy said, "No. If weapons are drawn, the guards will leave that little bit of fun like a burning whorehouse. Leave him to me."

Jimmy sprang forward and ran to the guard. As the guard brought his spear forward across his chest and shouted, "Halt!" Jimmy kicked him hard in the leg, above the boot. The man let out a howl, then looked at his small assailant with fury on his face. "Why you little—"

Jimmy stuck out his tongue and started to run toward the docks. The guard set out in hot pursuit, and the two travelers slipped through the gate. Once outside the city, they mounted quickly and rode off. As they rode away from Krondor, they could hear the sounds of the brawl.

The ship beat against the waves, while the crew reefed the sails. Laurie and Kasumi stood on deck watching the spires and towers of Rillanon as the ship put into harbor. "A fabulous city," said the former Tsurani officer. "Not as large as the cities of home, but so different. All those tiny fingers of stone and the colors of the banners make it look like a city of legend."

"Strange," said Laurie, "Pug and I felt the same when we first saw Jamar. I suppose it is simply that they're so different from each other."

They stood on the open deck, cool in the breezes, but still able to feel the warmth of the sun. Both were dressed in the finest clothing they could buy in Salador, for they wished to be presentable at court and knew they had little chance of being admitted to see the King should they look like simple vagabonds.

The ship's captain ordered the last sails taken in, and the ship slid into place alongside the docks a few moments later. Ropes were thrown to men waiting on the quay and the vessel was quickly made fast.

As soon as they were able, the two travelers were down the gangway and making their way through the city. Rillanon, the fabled and ancient capital of the Kingdom of the Isles, stood bedecked in colors, flashing brightly in the sunlight, but there was an undercurrent of tension in the atmosphere of the streets and markets. Everywhere they passed, people spoke in hushed tones, as if they feared someone might overhear them, and even the hawkers in the street stalls seemed to offer their wares halfheartedly.

It was nearly the noon hour, and without seeking rooms they headed straight for the palace. When they reached the main gate, an officer in the purple and gold of the Royal Household Guard inquired their business.

Laurie said, "We bring messages of the greatest importance to the King, regarding the war."

The officer considered. They were dressed well enough and didn't appear to be the usual madmen with predictions of doom, or prophets of some nameless truth, but they were not officials of the court or army either. He decided on the course of action followed most often in the armies of all nations in all times: passing them along to a higher authority.

A guard escorted them to the office of an assistant to the Royal Chancellor. Here they were made to wait for a

half hour before the assistant would see them. They
entered the man's office and were confronted by the
Steward of the Royal Household, a self-important little
man with a potbelly and a chronic wheeze when he spoke.
"What business do you gentlemen have?" he inquired,
making it clear that his estimation of them was provisional.

"We carry word to the King regarding the war," Laurie
answered.

"Oh?" he sniffed, "and why aren't these documents or
messages or whatever they are being delivered by the
proper military pouch?"

Kasumi, obviously frustrated with the wait now that
they were in the palace, said, "Let us speak with someone
who can take us to the King."

The Steward of the Royal Household looked outraged.
"I am Baron Gray. I am the one to whom you will speak,
man! And I have a good mind to have the guards toss you
into the street. His Majesty cannot be bothered with every
charlatan who tries to seek an audience. I am the one you
must satisfy, and you have not."

Kasumi stepped forward and gripped the man by the
front of his tunic. "And I am Kasumi of the Shinzawai. My
father is Kamatsu, Lord of the Shinzawai, and Warchief of
the Kanazawai Clan. I will see your King!"

Lord Gray paled visibly. He frantically pulled at
Kasumi's hand and tried to speak. His shock at what he
had just heard and what he felt at being handled this way
raced within him. It all proved to be too much for him to
speak. He nodded frantically until Kasumi released him.

Brushing at his tunic front, the man said, "The Royal
Chancellor will be informed—at once."

He walked to a door and Laurie watched him in case
he called for guards, thinking them madmen. Whatever
else the man thought, Kasumi's manner convinced him he
was something quite different from anything heretofore
seen. A messenger was sent, and in a few minutes an
elderly man entered the room.

He simply said, "What is it?"

"Your Grace," said the Steward, "I think you had best
talk to these men and consider if His Majesty should see
them."

The man turned to study the two other men in the

office. "I am Duke Caldric, the Royal Chancellor. What reason do you have to see His Majesty?"

Kasumi said, "I bring a message from the Emperor of Tsuranuanni."

The King sat in a pavilion on a balcony overlooking the harbor. Below, a mountain river passed directly before the palace, part of the original defense design though no longer needed as a moat. Graceful bridges could be seen arching above it, carrying people from one side of the river to the other.

King Rodric sat, seemingly attentive to what Kasumi was saying. He toyed absently with a golden ball in his right hand, while Kasumi outlined in detail the Emperor's message of peace.

Rodric was silent for a while after Kasumi finished, as if weighing what he had heard. Kasumi handed a sheaf of documents to Duke Caldric, then waited for the King's answer. After another moment of silence Kasumi added, "The Emperor's proposals are outlined in these parchments in detail, Your Majesty, should you wish to study them at your leisure. I will wait upon your convenience to carry your reply."

Still Rodric was silent, and the courtiers gathered nearby looked at one another nervously. Kasumi was about to speak again when the King said, "I am always amused when watching my little subjects hurrying about the city, like so many ants. I often wonder what they think, living out their simple little lives." He turned to look at the two emissaries. "You know, I could order any one of them put to death. Just pick one out, from this very balcony, should I choose. I could just say to my guards, 'See that fellow in the blue cap? Go hack his head off,' and they would, you know. That's because I'm King."

Laurie felt a chill run up his back. This was worse than anything he had imagined. The King seemed not to have heard a single word spoken. Kasumi said very quietly in the Tsurani language, "If we should fail, one of us must carry word back to my father."

At this, the King's head snapped up. His eyes grew wide and he spoke with a tremble in his voice. "What is this?" His voice rose in pitch. "I will have no one whispering!" His face took on a feral appearance. "You know they are always whispering about me, the disloyal ones. But I know who they are and I will see them on their knees before me; yes I will. That traitor Kerus was on his knees before I had him hanged. I would have hanged his family had they not fled to Kesh." He then studied Kasumi. "You think to trick me with your strange story and these so-called documents. Any fool could see through your guise. You are spies!"

Duke Caldric looked pained and tried to calm the King. Several guards stood nearby, slightly shifting their weight from foot to foot, uncomfortable at what they were hearing.

The King pushed the solicitous Duke away. His voice took on a near-hysterical tone. "You are agents of that traitor Borric. He and my uncle were plotting to take my throne. But I stopped that. My uncle Erland is dead. . . ." He paused for a moment, as if confused. "No, I mean he is ill. That is why my loyal Duke Guy was sent from Bas-Tyra to rule Krondor until my beloved uncle was well. . . ." His eyes seemed to clear for a moment, then he said, "I am not feeling well. Please excuse me. I will speak to you again tomorrow." He rose from his chair. After he had taken a step, he turned back to look at Laurie and Kasumi. "What was it you wanted to see me about? Oh yes, peace. Yes, that is good. This war is a terrible thing. We must end it so that I can go back to my building. We must begin the building again."

A page took the King's arm and led him away. The Royal Chancellor said, "Follow me, and say nothing."

He hurried them through the palace and led them to a room with two guards before the door. One guard opened the door for them and they entered. Inside they found a bedroom with two large beds and a table with chairs in the corner. The Chancellor said, "Your arrival is poorly timed. Our King is, as you no doubt are aware, a sick man, and I fear that he will not recover. I hope he will be better able to understand your message tomorrow. Please stay here until you are sent for. A meal will be brought to you."

He crossed over to the door, and before he left said, "Until tomorrow."

* * *

A shout awoke them in the night. Laurie rose quickly and went to the window. Peering through the curtains, he could see a figure on the balcony below. In his nightshirt, King Rodric stood sword in hand, poking into the bushes. Laurie opened the window as Kasumi joined him. From below they could hear the King's cries: "Assassins! They have come!" Guards ran out and searched the bushes, while court pages led the shrieking monarch back to his room.

Kasumi said, "In truth, the gods have touched him. They must truly hate your nation."

Laurie said, "I am afraid, friend Kasumi, that the gods have little to do with this. Right now, I think we had best see to finding a way out of here. I have a feeling that His Royal Majesty is ill suited for the finer points of negotiating a peace. I think we had best make our way west and speak with Duke Borric."

"Will he be able to stop the war, this Duke?"

Laurie crossed over to the chair upon which his clothing was draped. Picking up his tunic, he said, "I hope so. If the lords here can watch the King behave in such a manner and do nothing, then we will have civil war soon. Better to settle one war before beginning another."

They dressed quickly. Laurie said, "Let us hope we can find a ship putting out on the morning tide. If the King orders the port closed we are trapped. It is a long swim."

As they gathered up their belongings, the door opened and the Royal Chancellor entered. He stopped and saw them standing there, fully dressed. "Good," he said, quickly closing the door. "You have as much sense as I had hoped you would. The King has ordered the spies put to death."

Laurie was incredulous. "He thinks us spies?"

Duke Caldric sat in one of the chairs by the table, fatigue clearly showing on his face. "Who knows what His Majesty is thinking, these days? There are a few of us who try to stay his more terrible impulses, but it becomes more and more difficult each day. There is a sickness in him that is terrible to watch. Years ago he was an impetuous man, it is true, but there was also a vision to his plans, a certain mad brilliance that could have made this the greatest nation in Midkemia.

"There are many in the court now who take advantage of him, using his fears to further their own designs. I am afraid that soon I will be branded traitor and join the others in death."

Kasumi buckled on his sword. "Why stay, Your Grace? If this is true, why not come with us to Duke Borric?"

The Duke looked at the older son of the Shinzawai. "I am a noble of the Kingdom, and he is my King. I must do whatever I can to keep him from harming the Kingdom, even if the price is my life, but I cannot raise arms against him, nor aid those who do. I don't know how things are with your world, Tsurani, but here I must stay. He is my King."

Kasumi nodded. "I understand. In your place, I would do the same. You are a brave man, Duke Caldric."

The Duke stood. "I am a tired man. The King has taken strong drink, from my hand. He will drink from no other, for he fears poison. I had the chirurgeon give him something for sleep. You should be out to sea when he awakens. I don't know if he will remember your visit, but rest assured that someone will remind him, within a day, or two at the outside. So do not linger. Make straight for Lord Borric and tell him what has happened."

Laurie said, "Is Prince Erland truly dead?"

"Yes. Word reached us a week ago. His failing health could not withstand the cold dungeon. Borric is now heir to the throne. Rodric has never wed: his fear of others is too deep. The fate of the Kingdom rests with Borric. Tell him so."

They crossed to the door. Before the Duke opened it, he said, "Also tell him that it is likely I will be dead should he come to Rillanon. It will be a good thing, for I would have to stand against any who raised arms against the Royal Standard."

Before Laurie or Kasumi could say anything, he opened the door. Two guards stood outside, and the Duke ordered them to escort Laurie and Kasumi to the docks. "The *Royal Swallow* is anchored in the harbor. Give this to the captain." He held out a piece of paper to Laurie. "It is a royal warrant, commanding him to carry you to Salador." He held out a second paper. "This is another, commanding any of the Armies of the Kingdom to aid your travel."

They grasped each other by the hand, then the two emissaries followed the guards down the corridor. Laurie looked over his shoulder at Caldric as they left. The old Duke waited, stoop-shouldered and tired, his face lined by worry and sorrow, as well as fear. As they turned a corner, losing sight of the Duke, Laurie thought no price in the world would make him exchange places with that old man.

The horses were covered with froth as the riders whipped them up the hill. They were on the last leg of their journey to Lord Borric, begun over a month before, and the end was in sight. The *Royal Swallow* had sped them to Salador, where they had left at once for the West. They had slept little along the way, trading for fresh mounts or commandeering them, whenever possible, from horse patrols with the royal warrant given them by Caldric. Laurie wasn't sure, but he suspected they had covered the distance faster than it had ever been traveled before.

Several times since leaving Zūn, they had been challenged by soldiers. Each time they had presented the Chancellor's warrant and were passed through. Now they approached the Duke's camp.

The Tsurani Warlord had unleashed his major offensive. The Kingdom forces had held for a week, then collapsed, as ten thousand fresh Tsurani soldiers had come pouring through their lines. The fighting had been bitter then, a raging, running battle lasting three days, with the Kingdom army finally routed. When it was over, a large portion of the front had fallen and the Tsurani had thrown up a salient out of the North Pass. Now the elves and dwarves, as well as the castles of the Far Coast, were cut off from the main force of the Kingdom army. There was no communication of any sort, for the pigeons used to carry messages had been destroyed when the old camp had been overrun. The fate of the other fronts was unknown.

The Armies of the West were regrouping, and it took Laurie and Kasumi some time to find the headquarters camp. As they rode up to the command pavilion, they saw signs of bitter defeat on every side. It was the worst setback of the war for the Kingdom. Everywhere they looked they saw wounded or sick men, and those who showed no wounds had the look of despair.

A guard sergeant inspected their warrant and sent a guard with them to show them where the Duke's tent lay. They reached the large command tent, and a lackey took their mounts from them as the guard went inside. A moment later a tall young man, blond-bearded and wearing the tabard of Crydee, came out. Behind him appeared a stout man with a grey beard—a magician by his garb—and another man, large, with a ragged scar down his face. Laurie wondered if they might be old friends Pug had spoken of, but quickly focused his attention on the young officer, who stopped before him. "I bring a message to Lord Borric."

The young man smiled a bitter smile, then said, "You may give me the message, sir. I am Lyam, his son."

Laurie said, "I mean no disrespect, Highness, but I must speak with the Duke in person. So I was instructed by Duke Caldric."

At mention of the Royal Chancellor's name, Lyam exchanged glances with his companions, then held aside the tent flap. Laurie and Kasumi entered, the others following. Inside, there was a small brazier burning and a large table with maps upon it. Lyam led them to another section of the huge tent, curtained off from the rest. He pulled back the hanging and they saw a man lying upon a sleeping pallet.

He was a tall man, with dark hair streaked with grey. His face was drawn, drained of blood, his lips nearly blue. His breathing was ragged, each breath rattling loudly as he slept. He wore clean bed clothing, but heavy bandages could be seen beneath his loose collar.

Lyam put back the hanging as another man entered the tent. Old, with a near-white mane of hair, he was still erect and broad-shouldered. Softly he said, "What is this?"

Lyam answered, "These men bring messages for Father from Caldric."

The old warrior stuck out his hand. "Give them to me."

When Laurie hesitated, the man nearly barked, "Damn it, fellow, I'm Brucal. With Borric wounded, I'm commander of the Armies of the West."

Laurie said, "I've no written message, Your Grace. Duke Caldric says to introduce my companion. This is

Kasumi of the Shinzawai, emissary of the Emperor of Tsuranuanni, who carries an offering of peace to the King."

Lyam said, "Is there to be peace at last?"

Laurie shook his head. "Sadly, no. The Duke also said to say this: the King is mad, and the Duke of Bas-Tyra has slain Prince Erland. He fears only Lord Borric can save the Kingdom."

Brucal was visibly shaken by the news. To Lyam he quietly said, "Now we know the rumors to be true. Erland *was* Guy's prisoner. Erland dead. I can scarcely believe it." Shaking off his shock, he said, "Lyam, I know your mind is upon your father now, but you must bend thought to this: your father is near death; you will soon be Duke of Crydee. And with Erland dead, you will also be heir to the throne by right of birth."

Brucal sat heavily upon a stool near the map table. "This is a heavy burden thrust upon you, Lyam, but others in the West will look to you for leadership as they once looked to your father. If there was ever any love between the two realms, it is now strained to the breaking point, with Guy upon the throne in Krondor. It is now clear for all to see, Bas-Tyra means to be King, for a mad Rodric cannot be allowed his throne much longer." He fixed Lyam with a steady gaze. "You will soon have to decide what we in the West shall do. Upon your word, we have civil war."

ELEVEN

DECISION

The Holy City was festive.

Banners flew from every tall building. People lined the streets, throwing flowers before the nobles who were carried on their litters to the stadium. It was a day of high celebration, and who could feel troubled on such a day?

One who did feel troubled arrived in the pattern room

of the stadium, the final reverberations of a chime signaling
the appearance of a Great One of Tsuranuanni. Milamber
shrugged off his preoccupation for a moment as he left the
pattern room, near the central gallery of the Grand
Imperial Stadium. The crowd of Tsurani nobles, idling
away the time before the games began, parted to allow
Milamber to pass through the archway leading to the
magicians' seats. Glancing around the small sea of black
robes, he noticed Shimone and Hochopepa, who were
keeping a place for him.

They signaled greetings as he left the aisle between the
magicians' section and the imperial party's and joined
them. Below, on the arena floor, some of the dwarflike folk
from Tsubar—the so-called Lost Land across the Sea of
Blood—were fighting large insect creatures, like cho-ja but
without intelligence. Soft wooden swords and essentially
harmless bites from mandibles provided a conflict more
comic than dangerous. The commoners and lesser nobles
already in their seats laughed in appreciation. These
contests kept them amused while the great and near-great
were waiting to enter the stadium. Tardiness in Tsuranuanni became a virtue when one reached a certain social level.

Shimone said, "It is a shame you took so long getting
here, Milamber. There was a singularly fine match a short
while ago."

"I was under the impression the killing wasn't to begin
just yet."

Hochopepa, munching nuts cooked in sweet oils, said,
"True, but our friend Shimone is something of an aficio-
nado of the games."

Shimone said, "Earlier, young officers of noble family
fought with training weapons to first blood, to better
display their skills and win honors for their clans—"

"Not to mention the fruits of some rather heavy
wagering," interjected Hochopepa.

Ignoring the remark, Shimone continued, "There was
a spirited match between sons of the Oronalmar and the
Keda. I've not seen a better display in years."

While Shimone described the match, Milamber let his
gaze wander. He could see the small standards of the Keda,
Minwanabi, Oaxatucan, Xacatecas, and other great families
of the Empire. He noticed that the banner of the Shinzawai

was absent, and wondered at it. Hochopepa said, "You seem much preoccupied, Milamber."

Milamber nodded agreement. "Before leaving for to-day's festival, I received word that a motion to reform land taxes and abolish debt slavery had been introduced in the High Council yesterday. The message came from the Lord of the Tuclamekla, and I couldn't for the life of me understand why he sent it until, near the end, he thanked me for providing the concepts of social reform the motion was intended to enact. I was appalled at such an action."

Shimone laughed. "Had you been so thick-witted a student, you'd still be wearing the white robe."

Milamber looked back blankly, and Hochopepa said, "You go about causing all sorts of rumblings with your speeches before the Assembly, constantly harping on all manner of social ills, and then sit dumbfounded because someone out there listened?"

"What I said to our brother magicians was not intended for discussion outside the Assembly halls."

"How unreasonable," said Hochopepa. "Someone in the Assembly spoke to a friend who wasn't a magician!"

"What I'd like to know," said Shimone, "is how this potful of reforms placed before the High Council by the Hunzan Clan has your name appended to it?"

Milamber looked uncomfortable, to the delight of his friends. "One of the young artists who worked on the murals at my estate is a son of the Tuclamekla. We did discuss differences between Tsurani and Kingdom cultures and social values, but only as an outgrowth of our discussions of the differences in styles of art."

Hochopepa looked skyward, as if seeking divine guidance. "When I heard the Party for Progress—which is dominated by the Hunzan Clan, which is dominated by the Tuclamekla Family—cited you as inspiration, I could scarcely believe my hearing, but now I can see your hand is in every problem plaguing the Empire." He looked at his friend with a mock-serious expression. "Tell me, is it true the Party for Progress is going to change its name to the Party of Milamber?"

Shimone laughed while Milamber fixed Hochopepa with a baleful look. "Katala thinks it amusing when I get upset by this sort of thing, Hocho. And you might think it

funny as well, but I want it publicly known I did not intend
for this to happen. I simply offered some observations and
opinions, and what the Hunzan Clan and the Party for
Progress does with them is not my doing."

Hochopepa said in chiding tones, "I fear that if so
famous a personage as yourself wishes not to have such
things occur, then such a personage should have his mouth
sewn shut."

Shimone laughed and Milamber felt his own mirth
rise. "Very well, Hocho," answered Milamber. "I will take
the blame. Still, I don't know if the Empire is yet ready for
the changes I think needed."

Shimone said, "We have heard your arguments before, Milamber, but today is not the time, nor is this the
place for social debate. Let us attend to the matters at hand.
Remember, many of the Assembly are offended by your
concerns over matters they judge political. And while I
tend to support your notions as refreshing and progres-
sive, keep in mind you are making enemies."

Trumpets and drums sounded, signaling the approach
of the imperial party and cutting off further conversation.
The Tsubar folk and the insectoids were chased from the
arena, handlers herding them away. When the field was
cleared, grounds keepers hurried out with rakes and drags
to smooth the sand. The sound of the trumpets could be
heard again and the first members of the imperial procession, heralds in the imperial white, entered. They carried
long, curved trumpets, fashioned from the horns of some
large beast, that curled around their shoulders to end
above their heads. They were followed by drummers who
beat a steady tattoo.

When they were in position in the front of the imperial
box, the Warlord's honor guard entered. Each wore armor
and helm finished in needra hide bleached free of all color.
Around the breastplate and helm of each, precious gold
trim gleamed in the sun. Milamber heard Hochopepa
mutter at the waste of this rare metal.

When they were stationed, a senior herald shouted,
"Almecho, Warlord!" and the crowd rose, cheering. He
was accompanied by his retinue, including several in black
robes—the Warlord's pet magicians, as the others of the
Assembly referred to them.

Then the herald cried, "Ichindar! Ninety-one times Emperor!" The crowd roared its approval as the young Light of Heaven made his entrance. He was attended by priests of each of the twenty orders. The crowd stood thundering. On and on it went, and Milamber wondered if the love of the Tsurani people would sustain the Light of Heaven should a confrontation between Warlord and Emperor take place. In spite of the Tsurani reverence for tradition, he did not think the Warlord a man to step down meekly from his office—a thing unheard of in history— should the Emperor so order.

As the noise died down, Shimone said, "It seems, friend Milamber, that the contemplative life doesn't suit the Light of Heaven. Can't say that I blame him, sitting around all day with no one for company but a lot of priests and silly girls chosen for their beauty instead of conversational ability. Must become frightfully boring."

Milamber laughed. "I doubt most men would agree."

Shimone shrugged. "I constantly forget you were quite old when you were trained, and you have a wife also."

At mention of wives, Hochopepa looked pained. He interrupted. "The Warlord is going to make an announcement."

Almecho rose and held his hands aloft for silence. When the stadium fell quiet his voice rang out. "The gods smile upon Tsuranuanni! I bring news of a great victory over the otherworld barbarians! We have crushed their greatest army, and our warriors celebrate! Soon all the lands called the Kingdom will be laid at the Light of Heaven's feet." He turned and bowed deferentially to the Emperor.

Milamber felt a stab at the news. Without being aware, he began to stand, only to have Hochopepa grip his arm and hiss, "You are Tsurani!"

Milamber shook himself free of the unexpected shock and composed himself. "Thank you, Hocho. I nearly forgot myself."

"Hush!" said Hochopepa.

They returned thier attention to the Warlord. ". . . and as a sign of our devotion to the Light of Heaven, we dedicate these games to his honor." A cheer rang through the arena, and the Warlord sat down.

Milamber spoke quietly to his friends. "It seems the Emperor is less than ecstatic at the news." Hochopepa and Shimone turned to watch the Emperor, who was sitting with a stoic expression upon his face.

Hochopepa said, "He hides it well, but I think you are right, Milamber. Something in all this disturbs him."

Shimone tapped Milamber upon the shoulder. "The games begin."

As the doors on the arena floor opened to admit the combatants, Milamber studied the Emperor. He was young, in his early twenties, and possessed a look of intelligence. His brow was high, and his reddish-brown hair was allowed to grow to his shoulders. He turned in Milamber's direction, to speak with a priest at his side, and Milamber could see his clear green eyes glint in the sun. Their eyes made contact for a moment, and there was a brief flicker of recognition, and Milamber thought: So you have been told of my part in your plan. The Emperor continued his conversation, without missing a beat, and no one else saw the exchange.

Hochopepa said, "This is a clemency spectacle. They will all fight until only one stands. He will be pardoned for his crimes."

"What are their crimes?" Milamber asked.

Shimone answered. "The usual. Petty theft, begging without temple authority, bearing false witness, avoiding taxes, disobeying lawful orders, and the like."

"What about capital crimes?"

"Murder, treason, blasphemy, striking one's master, all are unpardonable crimes." His voice rose to carry over the crowd noises. "They are put in with war prisoners who will not serve as slaves. They are sentenced to fight over and over until they are killed."

A guard of soldiers left the floor, abandoning the sand to the prisoners. Hochopepa said, "Common criminals. There will be little sport."

There seemed to be accuracy in the remark, for the prisoners were a sad-looking lot. Naked but for loincloths, they stood with weapons and shields that were foreign to them. Many were old and sick, seemingly lost and confused, holding their axes, swords, and spears loosely at their sides.

The trumpet sounded the start of combat, and the old and sick ones were quickly killed. Several had never even raised their weapons in defense, being too confused to try to stay alive. Within minutes nearly half the prisoners lay dead or dying on the sand. Shortly the action slackened, as combatants came to face opponents of more equal skill and cunning. Slowly the numbers diminished, and the free-flowing riotous nature of the contest changed. Occasionally when an opponent fell, a combatant was left standing next to another fighting pair. Often this resulted in three-way combat, which the mob approved with loud cheering, as the awkward combat would result in an excess of bloodshed and pain.

At the end, three fighters remained. Two of them had not managed to resolve their conflict. Both were on the verge of exhaustion. The third man approached cautiously, keeping equal distance between himself and both men, looking for an advantage.

He had it a few seconds later. Using knife and sword, he jumped forward and dealt one of the combatants a blow to the side of the head that felled him. Shimone said, "The idiot! Couldn't he see the other man is the stronger fighter? He should have waited until one man was clearly at an advantage, then struck at him, leaving the weaker opponent to fight."

Milamber felt shaky. Shimone, his former teacher, was his closest friend after Hochopepa. Yet for all his education, all his wisdom, he was howling after the blood of others as if he were the most ignorant commoner in the least-expensive seat. No matter how he tried, Milamber could not master the Tsurani enthusiasm for the death of others. He turned to Shimone and said, "I'm sure he was a little too busy to trouble himself over the finer points of tactics." His sarcasm was lost on Shimone, closely watching the combat.

Milamber noticed Hochopepa was ignoring the contest. The wily magician was taking note of every conversation in the stands: to him, the games were only another opportunity to study the subtle aspects of the Game of the Council. Milamber found this blindness to the death and suffering below as disturbing as Shimone's enthusiasm.

The fight was quickly over, the man with the knife winning. The crowd greeted the victory with enthusiasm. Coins were thrown on the sand, so that the victor would return to society with a small amount of capital.

While the arena was being cleared, Shimone called over a herald and inquired about the balance of the day's activities. He turned to the others, obviously pleased at the news. "There are only a few matched pairs, then two special matches, a team of prisoners against a starving harulth, and a match between some soldiers from Mid-kemia and captured Thuril warriors. That should prove most interesting."

Milamber's expression indicated that he didn't agree. Judging the time right for the question, he said, "Hocho, have you noticed any of the Shinzawai Family in attendance?"

"No, Milamber. I can't say if any of your former, ah, benefactors are to be seen about. Not that I would expect them to be."

"Why?"

"They find themselves in the Warlord's bad graces of late. Something to do with failing some task or another he gave them. And I have heard that they are considered suspect, despite their clan's suddenly rejoining the war effort. The Kanazawai Clan is lost in its past glories, and the Shinzawai are the most old-fashioned of the lot."

Through the afternoon the matches wore on, each more artful than the previous as the skill level of the opponents increased. Soon the last pairs were done. Now the crowd waited in hushed anticipation, even the nobles quieted, for the next event was unusual. A team of twenty fighters, Midkemian from their size, marched out into the center of the arena. They carried ropes, weighted nets, spears, and long curved knives. They wore only loincloths, their bodies oiled and gleaming in the late afternoon light. They stood around looking relaxed, but the soldiers in the crowd recognized the subtle signs of tension common to fighters before a battle. After a minute the large double doors at the opposite end of the stadium opened and a six-legged horror came shambling into the arena.

The harulth was all long teeth and sharp claws, complete with a belligerent attitude and a hide like armor, and close to the size of a Midkemian elephant. It hesitated only long enough to blink at the light, then charged straight at the party of men before it.

They scattered before the creature, seeking to confuse it. The harulth, through simple- or single-mindedness, pursued one hapless fellow. In three enormous strides he ground the man underfoot, then gobbled him down in two bites. The others regrouped behind the animal and quickly deployed the nets. The hexapod spun about, faster than looked possible for a creature of such bulk, and charged again. This time the men waited until the last moment, tossed the nets, then dove away. The nets were edged with hooks to catch in the thick hide of the beast. It stepped into them and soon was busily tearing apart the mesh. While it was momentarily occupied, the spearmen ran in to strike. The harulth reacted in confusion, not being sure from which quarter its torment originated. The spears were proving ineffectual, for they could not penetrate the hide of the beast. Quickly realizing the futility of this approach, one fighter grabbed another and pointed to the rear of the creature. They dashed back along the tail, which was sweeping back and forth along the ground with the force of a battering ram.

They conferred momentarily, then dropped their spears as the creature decided upon a target. It lashed forward and had another man in its maw. For a moment it was still as it swallowed its prey. The two men at the rear ran forward, leaping high up onto the tail of the animal. It seemed not to notice for a moment, then reacted by swinging around violently, throwing the second man off. Having come completely about, it stopped to devour the stunned man. The other somehow contrived to hang on and employed the few moments the harulth used to eat his comrade to pull himself higher on the creature's tail, where it joined the animal's haunches. With an overhand stroke he plunged his long-bladed knife between two vertebrae where they were outlined by loose-hanging skin. It was a desperate gamble, and the stadium crowd screamed approval. The knife penetrated the tough cartilage between the bone segments and pierced the spinal column. The creature bellowed with rage and started to spin, threatening to toss the unwelcome rider, but in a moment the

rearmost pair of legs collapsed. The harulth stood baffled
for a moment, its two forward pair of legs pulling against
the dead weight of its hind quarters. Twice it tried vainly to
snap at its small tormentor, but its thick neck was insufficient for the task. The man pulled the blade loose and
crawled forward along the spine while the surviving
spearmen darted in and out, distracting the creature. Three
times he was nearly tossed off the animal's back, but
somehow he managed to retain his position. When he
found himself slightly forward of the middle pair of legs,
he drove his blade between vertebrae. The central legs
collapsed an instant later and the man was thrown clear of
the animal's back. The harulth screamed in rage and pain,
but was effectively immobilized. The fighters backed away
and waited. Two spinal cuts proved to be enough, for
minutes later the harulth fell over in shock, thrashed its
forelegs for a time, and lay still.

The crowd shouted its enthusiastic approval of the
contest, for never had a group of fighters bested a harulth
without losing at least five times as many men. In this
contest only three had died. The fighters stood around,
exhaustion causing weapons to fall from limp fingers. The
battle had lasted less than ten minutes, but the expenditure
in energy, concentration, sweat, and fear had worn each
man to near-prostration. Numbly, oblivious to the crowds
cheering, they stumbled toward the exit. Only the man
who had actually driven in the knife showed any expression, and he was openly weeping as he moved across the
sand.

"Why do you think that man is so distraught?" asked
Shimone. "It was a grand triumph."

Milamber said in a voice forced to calmness, "Because
he is exhausted and afraid, and sick from it." He then
added softly, "And he is very far from home." He swallowed hard, struggling against outrage, then said, "He
knows it is for nothing. Again and again he will march into
this area, to fight other creatures, other men, even friends
from his homeland, and sooner or later he will die."
Hochopepa stared at Milamber and Shimone looked confused. "But for chance, I might have been one with those
below," added Milamber. "Those who fought are men.
They had families and homes, they loved and laughed.
Now they wait to die."

Hochopepa waved a hand absently. "Milamber, you have a disturbing habit of taking things personally."

Milamber felt sickened and angry by the bloody spectacle, but forced those emotions down within himself. He was determined to stay. He would be Tsurani.

The sand was cleared and trumpets blew again, signaling the final match of the afternoon. A dozen proud-looking warriors dressed in leather battle harnesses, wristbands set with studs, and headdresses plumed in many colors came striding out of one end of the arena. Milamber had never seen their like in person, but recognized their dress from his vision on the tower. These were the descendants of the proud Serpent Riders, the Thuril. Each wore a hard-eyed expression of grim determination.

From the other end, twelve warriors in color-splashed imitations of Midkemian armor marched out. Their own metal armor had been deemed both too valuable and too dull for the contest and Tsurani artisans had provided stylized imitations.

The Thuril stood watching the newcomers with implacable contempt. Of all the races of humanity, only the Thuril had been able to withstand the Empire. The Thuril were uncontestedly the finest mountain fighters in Kelewan, and their mountain holds and high farm pastures were impossible to conquer. They had held the Empire at bay for years until peace had been declared. They were a tall people, the result of their lack of interbreeding with the shorter races of Kelewan, whom they considered inferior.

The trumpets blew again, and a hush fell over the crowd. A herald shouted in a clear voice, "As these soldiers of the Thuril Confederacy have violated the treaty between their own nations and the Empire, by making war upon the soldiers of the Emperor, they have been cast out by their own people, who have named them outlaws and bound them over for punishment. They will fight the captives from the world of Midkemia. All will strive until one is left standing." The crowd cheered.

The trumpet sounded, and the fighters squared off. The Midkemians crouched, weapons at the ready, but the Thuril stood tall, defiant looks upon their faces. One of the Thuril strode forward, halting before the nearest Midkemian. With contemptuous tones he spoke rapidly, and made a sweeping motion around the arena.

Milamber felt a hot flush of anger begin to grow inside, coupled with shame at what he was seeing. There were games in Midkemia—he had heard of them—but they were nothing like this. The men who fought in Krondor and other places throughout the Kingdom were professionals who made a living by fighting to first blood. Occasionally a duel to the death would be fought, but it was always a personal matter, after all other means of settling the dispute had been exhausted. This was a mindless waste of human life for the titillation of the bored and idle, the satiated in search of more and more vivid reminders that their own lives were worth something. Milamber looked around and felt disgust at the expressions on the faces of those nearby.

The Thuril warrior continued his ranting, while the Midkemians watched, with something in their manner suggesting a shift of mood. Before, they were tensed, battle-ready; now they seemed almost relaxed, as the Thuril continued pointing up at the assembled throng.

Then a Midkemian, tall and broad-shouldered, stepped forward as if to speak. The Thuril came on guard, his sword high, ready to strike. A voice rang out from behind, as another warrior said something that carried a note of reassurance. The first Thuril visibly relaxed.

The Midkemian slowly removed his helm, revealing a tired, haggard face, framed by damp, stringy black hair. He looked about the arena, while the crowd began to whisper and grumble at the unexpected behavior of the warriors, and then gave a curt nod. He dropped his sword and shield and said something to his companions. Quickly the other fighters in the arena followed suit, and soon all weapons were lying upon the ground.

Milamber wondered at this strange behavior, and Shimone said, "This will end a shambles. The Thuril will not fight their own kind, and it seems they won't fight the barbarians either. I once saw six Thuril kill everyone sent against them, then refuse to fight one another. When the guards came to kill them, they fought, driving them back. Finally bowmen on the walls had to shoot them down. It was a disgrace. The crowd rioted, and the games director was torn to bits. Over a hundred citizens died."

Milamber felt relief: at least he would be spared the

spectacle of Katala's people and his own killing one another. Then the crowd began to shout their disapproval, jeering the reluctant combatants.

Hochopepa nudged Milamber and said, "The Warlord appears less than amused by this."

Milamber saw the Warlord's livid expression as he watched his presentation to the Emperor turned into a farce. Almecho slowly rose from his place near the Light of Heaven and bellowed, "Let the fighting begin!"

Burly handlers, guards who worked on behalf of the games director, ran into the arena, wielding whips. They circled the motionless fighters and began lashing out at them. Milamber felt his gorge rise as the handlers laid about, tearing the exposed skin from the arms and legs of the Thuril and Midkemian soldiers. No stranger to the whip when in the swamp, he knew its terrible touch. He felt each stroke as it fell upon those on the sand below.

The crowd began to grow restive, for watching motionless men being whipped was not what they had come to see. Jeers and catcalls rang down upon those in the imperial box, and a few bolder souls threw litter and small coins into the arena, showing what they thought of such sport. Finally one of the handlers grew impatient, stepped up to a Thuril warrior, and struck him across the face with a whip handle. Before the handler could react, the Thuril sprang forward and tore the whip from the startled man's hands. In an instant he had it firmly wrapped about the man's throat, choking him.

The other handlers turned their attention to the warrior attacking their companion and began to flail wildly at him. After a dozen or so blows the Thuril began to wobble, and fell to his knees. But he held tightly to the whip, strangling the gasping handler. Again and again blows rained down upon the Thuril, until all his armor ran red with blood from the lashing. Still he held on to his victim.

When the handler died, eyes protruding from a blue face, whatever strength left to the Thuril seemed to die as well. As the handler's limp body came to rest on the sand, the Thuril warrior fell beside him.

It was a Midkemian soldier who reacted first. With cold detachment, he simply picked up a sword and ran one of the handlers through. Then, as one, the Thuril and Midkemian soldiers had weapons in hand and within a minute all the handlers were dead. Then, again as one, the prisoners threw their weapons to the ground.

Milamber battled to stay calm in the face of such display. He felt nothing but admiration for those men. They accepted death rather than slay one another. Possibly some of those men had ridden through the valley with him on the raid to discover the rift machine so many years before. Outwardly he appeared calm, a Tsurani, but inwardly he seethed.

Hochopepa whispered, "I have a bad feeling here. Whatever gain Almecho sought from this day to bolster his position with the Emperor is badly shaken. I fear he is not taking well your former countrymen's reluctance to die for the entertainment of the Light of Heaven."

Milamber nearly spit when he said, "Damn such entertainment." He looked at Hochopepa with a burning expression, one never seen by the fat magician before. Milamber half stood as he added, "And damn all those who find pleasure in such bloody sport."

Hochopepa seized him by the arm and tried to pull him firmly into his seat, saying, "Milamber, remember yourself!"

Milamber pulled himself free, ignoring the command.

Milamber and his companions looked to the imperial box, where a guard captain conferred with the Warlord. Milamber felt a strange hot flush inside and for a moment battled a sudden impulse to use his powers to put the Warlord amid those below, to see how he fared against those who refused to die gracefully at his command.

Then Almecho's voice rang out, silencing all those nearby. "No, no bowmen. Those animals will not die a warrior's death." He turned to one of his pet magicians and issued instructions. The black-robed man nodded and began to incant. Milamber felt his neck hairs rise as the presence of magic made itself known.

A hushed sound of awe swept about the stadium as those on the sand below fell senseless, to roll about in a daze.

The Warlord shouted, "Now go bind them, build a platform, and hang them for all to see."

Stunned silence greeted his words, then shouts of "No!"—"They are warriors!"—and "This is without honor!" rang throughout the crowd.

Hochopepa closed his eyes and sighed audibly. He spoke to himself as much as his companions. "The Warlord lets his famous temper get the best of him once more, and now we have a debacle before us. This will not help his position in the High Council or the stability of the Empire."

Like an enraged beast at bay, the Warlord turned, and all nearby fell silent, but those at greater distances picked up the cries. By Tsurani standards this was too much of an indignity to be visited on any save those without honor. While balking the mob's sport, the prisoners had shown they were still fighting men, and as such deserved an honorable death.

Hochopepa turned to speak to Milamber, then stopped himself as he saw the expression on his friend's face. Milamber's anger was now fully revealed, his rage a match for the Warlord's. Sensing something terrible was about to occur, Hochopepa sought Shimone's attention, only to find he was also silently watching Milamber's fearsome countenance. All Hochopepa could manage to say was a quiet "Milamber, no!" Then the slave become magician was moving.

He swept past the shocked Hochopepa, saying only, "See to the Emperor's safety." Milamber was now reeling with the impact of sudden emotions, bottled up for years, now surging free. A strange and powerful certainty struck him. *I am not Tsurani!* he acknowledged to himself. *I could never be a party to this.* For the first time since donning the black robe, his two natures were in harmony. This was a dishonor by the standards of both cultures, something that filled him with a dread purpose free of any doubt.

Save those near the imperial box, the entire crowd was chanting, "The sword, the sword, the sword," demanding a warrior's death for each man below. The rhythm became a pounding pulsebeat for Milamber, heightening his nearly unchecked fury.

Reaching a point between the magicians and the imperial box, Milamber regarded the soldiers and carpenters rushing onto the arena floor. The stunned Midkemians and Thuril were being bound like animals for slaughter,

and the crowd's anger was reaching a dangerous level.
Some of the younger officers of noble families in the lower
levels of the stadium seemed ready to take swords and
jump onto the sand, to contest personally for the prisoners'
right to die as warriors. These had been valiant foemen,
and many of those watching had fought against both
Thuril and Kingdom soldiers. They would willingly kill
these men on the field of battle, but would not bear to
watch this humiliation visited on brave enemies.

A black flood of anger, loathing, and sorrow poured
through Milamber. His mind screamed in outrage, despite
his attempts to control it. His head tilted back and his eyes
rolled up into his head, and as had happened twice before
in his life, letters of fire appeared in his mind's eye. But
never before had he had the strength to seize the moment,
and with a nearly animal joy he dove into the newly
opening well of power within. His right arm shot forward
and energy exploded from his hand. A bolt of blue flame,
scintillating even in the sunlight, hurled downward, to
strike the sand amid the Warlord's guards. Living men
were swept in all directions, like leaves before the wind.
Those just entering with the materials for the scaffolding
were knocked to their knees by the blast, and those in the
lower seats were stunned by its fury. All noise in the arena
stopped as the crowd fell into mute shock.

All eyes turned to the source of that bolt, while those
near him reflexively drew back. He was red-faced with
anger, the whites of his eyes showed around dark irises.
With a short chopping motion of one hand, the magician
said, "No more!"

No one moved save Hochopepa and Shimone. They
had no idea what Milamber's intentions were, but in the
face of this act they took his command seriously. They
hurried to where a half-stunned, half-fascinated young
Emperor sat watching with everyone else in the stadium.
They quickly conferred with Ichindar, and a moment later
the Emperor's seat was empty.

Milamber looked to his left as a bellow of outrage
sounded. "Who dares this!"

Milamber was confronted by the sight of the Warlord,
standing like an enraged demigod in his white armor. The
Warlord's expression matched Milamber's.

"I dare this!" Milamber shouted back. "This cannot be, will not be! No more will men die for the sport of others!"

Barely holding himself in check, Almecho, Warlord of the Nations of Tsuranuanni, screamed, "By what right do you do this thing!" The cords on his neck stood out clearly and every muscle of his body quivered as sweat beaded his brow.

Milamber's voice lowered, and his words came carefully measured with controlled, defiant rage. "By my right to do as I see fit." He then spoke to a nearby guard. "Those on the arena floor are to be released. They are free!"

The guard hesitated for a moment, then his Tsurani training came to the fore. "Your will, Great One."

The Warlord shouted, "You will stay!"

The crowd hissed with intaken breath. In the history of the Empire such a confrontation between Great One and Warlord had never occurred. The guard stopped, and Milamber spoke through a snarl. "My words are as law. Go!"

Suddenly the guard was moving and the Warlord screamed his rage. "You break the law! No one may free a slave!"

His anger boiling back up again, Milamber shouted back, "I can! I am outside the law!"

The Warlord fell back, as if struck an invisible blow. In his life no one had dared to thwart his will in this manner. No Warlord in history had ever been forced to endure such public shame. He seemed dazed.

Near the Warlord, another magician leaped to his feet. "I call you traitor and false Great One. You seek to undermine the Warlord's rule and bring chaos to the order of the Empire. You will recant this effrontery!"

Instantly there was frantic activity as all within earshot scrambled to get clear of the two magicians. Milamber regarded the Warlord's pet. "Do you think to match your powers against mine?"

The Warlord looked at Milamber with naked hatred on his face. He never took his eyes from the young magician's face as he said to his pet, "Destroy him!"

Milamber's arms shot upward, crossing at the wrists. Instantly a soft golden nimbus of light surrounded him. The other magician hurled a bolt of energy, and the blue ball of fire struck harmlessly against the golden shield.

Milamber tensed, suffused with anger. Twice before in his life, when attacked by the trolls and when fighting with Roland, he had reached into a hidden reservoir of power and drawn upon it. Now he tore aside the last barriers between his conscious mind and those hidden reserves. They were no longer a mystery to him but the wellspring from which all his powers stemmed. For the first time in his experience, Milamber came to understand fully what he was, who he was: not a Black Robe, limited by the ancient teachings of one world, but an adept of the Greater Art, a master in full possession of all the energy provided by two worlds.

The Warlord's magician regarded him in fear. Here was more than a curiosity of a barbarian magician. Here stood a figure of awe, arms stretched upward, body trembling with rage, eyes seemingly aglow with strength.

Milamber clapped his hands above his head, and thunder pealed, rocking those around him. Energy exploded upward from his hands, held high above his head. A vortex of coruscating forces spun above him, rising like a bowshot. The fountain continued until it was high overhead. It began to flatten, covering the stadium like some great canopy. The dazzling display continued briefly, then the skies seemed to explode, blinding many who were looking upward. The sky turned dark, and the sun faded as if grey veils were slowly being drawn before it.

Milamber's voice carried to all in the stadium as he said, "That you have lived as you have lived for centuries is no license for this cruelty. All here are now judged, and all are found wanting."

More magicians departed, disappearing from their seats, but many yet remained. More judicious commoners fled by nearby exits, but still many waited, thinking this but another contest for their amusement. Many were too drunk or excited by the spectacle for the magician's warning to reach them.

Milamber's arm swept an arc around him. "You who would take pleasure from the death and dishonor of others, see then how well you face destruction!" A gasp from the crowd answered his pronouncement.

Milamber raised one hand high overhead, and all became silent. Even the light summer breezed ceased.

Then with a terrible strength his voice carried to all in the arena. They paled at his words, for it was as if death had become incarnate and had spoken. Echoing throughout the stadium were the words of Milamber: "Tremble and despair, for I am Power!"

A shrill keening sound began, with Milamber at its source. The very air shuddered as mighty magic was forged. "Wind!" Milamber cried.

A bitter breeze reeking of carrion, foul and loathsome in its touch, blew through the stadium. A low moan of sorrow and fear was carried away by the wind. It blew stronger and, each moment it grew, carried more menace, more despair. It turned colder, until it was stinging to those who had rarely known cold. Men wept at its biting caress, and high above the stadium clouds formed in the murk.

The winds howled, drowning out the cries of the multitude in the arena. Nobles tried to flee, now too terrified to do anything but claw past their own families, trampling the old and slow underfoot. Many were buffeted to their knees, or knocked from the seats to the sands of the arena floor.

Great thunderheads, black and grey, raced overhead, seeming to swirl around a point directly over Milamber's head. The magician was engulfed in an eerie light, pulsating with energy. He stood at the center of the storm, a terrible figure in the dark. The wind shrieked its fury, but Milamber's voice cut through the sound like a knife.

"Rain!"

A cold spray of rain fell, blown hard before the gale. Quickly it grew in tempo, becoming a pounding torrent. The cascade pelted those below, painfully driving them down, beating them senseless with a frightening strength clearly unnatural. A few managed to flee to the tunnels, while others clutched at one another in terror.

Other magicians tried to counter the spells but could not, and fainted from the exertion. Never had there been such a display of raw power. Here was a true master of magic, one who could control the very elements, come into his own. The magician who had challenged Milamber lay back across his seat, stunned, his eyes blinking as he struggled to sort some semblance of order out of the chaos around. The Warlord tried to withstand the storm, struggling to remain upright and refusing to submit to the terror of those around him.

Milamber dropped his arm, then raised one hand before him, stretching outward. "Fire!" he shouted, and again all could hear him.

The clouds seemed to burn. The heavens erupted as sheets of terrible colors, flames of every hue, ran riot through the darkness. Jagged bolts of lightning flashed across the sky, as if the gods were announcing the final judgment of mankind. People screamed in primitive terror at the elements gone mad.

Then the rain of fire began. Drops struck arms and clothing, faces and cloaks, and began to burn. Shrieks of pain came from all sides and people tried vainly to swat out the fires that burned their flesh. More magicians disappeared from the arena, taking their unconscious comrades, until Milamber stood alone in the magicians' section. The stink of burned flesh filled the air, mixed with the acrid odor of fear.

Milamber crossed his arms before him. He turned his gaze downward.

"Earth!"

From below a deep rumbling commenced. The ground under the stadium began to tremble slightly. The vibrations grew in intensity, and the air was filled with an angry buzzing, as if a swarm of giant insects had surrounded the arena. Then a low rumbling added its harmony to the buzzing, and the ground began to move.

The vibrations became a shaking, then a violent rolling, surging motion. Milamber stood calmly, as if on an island. It was as if the soil, the very earth, had become fluid. People were thrown down onto the arena floor. The huge stadium throbbed from forces primeval. Statues tumbled from their pedestals, and the huge gates were ripped from their hinges, in a crackling splintering of ancient wood. They moved from before the tunnels in a staggering, drunken walk, then fell to the sand, crushing those who lay before them. Many of the beasts below the arena were driven mad by the earthquake and thrashed in their cages, smashing locks and opening doors. They fled the tunnels and raced over the fallen gates, then bellowed, howled, and roared at the fire rain. Enraged by terror, they fell upon the stunned spectators lying on the sand, killing at random. A man would sit dazed, absently slapping at the burning drops from the skies, while another a few feet away was being gutted by some horror from the distant forests.

Now the arena itself began to wail as the ancient stones moved, slipping across one another. Mortar a millennium old turned to dust in an instant as the very stadium crumbled. Cries for mercy were swept away by the winds or drowned in the cacophony of destruction. The fury mounted and the world seemed ready to be torn asunder. Milamber raised his hands above his head again. He brought his palms together and the mightiest thunder peal of all sounded. Then, abruptly, the chaos ceased.

Above, the sky was clear and sunny, a light breeze once more blowing from the east. The ground stood as it should, motionless and solid, and the rain of fire was a memory.

The silence that followed was deafening. Then the groans of the injured and the sobs of the terrified could be heard. The Warlord remained standing, his face drained of all color, small burns scarring his features and arms. In place of the mighty leader of the Empire stood a man bereft of any emotion save terror. His eyes were wide enough to show whites. His mouth moved, as if he were trying to speak, but no words were forthcoming.

Milamber raised his hands overhead again, and the Warlord fell back with a sob of fear. The magician clapped his hands and was gone.

The afternoon breeze carried the scent of summer flowers. In the garden, Katala was playing a word game with William; she had insisted they should both learn the language of her husband's homeland.

It was almost evening, for they were farther east than the Holy City. The sun was low in the west, and the shadows in the garden were long. Without the gong announcing Milamber's arrival, Katala was startled when her husband appeared in the doorway of their home. She rose slowly from her seat, for she sensed at once something was wrong. "Husband, what is it?"

William ran up to his father, while Milamber said, "I

will tell you everything later. We must take William and flee."

William tugged on his father's black robe. "Papa!" he cried, demanding attention. Milamber picked up his son and hugged him tightly, then said, "William, we are going on a journey to my homeland. You must be a brave boy and not cry."

William stuck out his lower lip, for if his father was asking him not to cry, then there must be a very good reason to do so, but he nodded and held back the tears.

"Netoha! Almorella!" Milamber called, and in a moment the two servants entered the garden. Netoha bowed, but Almorella rushed to Katala's side. Katala had insisted she accompany them to Milamber's new home when he brought his family from the Shinzawai estate. She was more a sister to Katala and aunt to William than a slave. She could see at once that something was wrong and tears came unbidden to her eyes.

"You're leaving," she said, a statement more than a question.

Netoha looked at his master. "Your will, Great One?"

Milamber said, "We are leaving. We must. I am sorry." Netoha took the news stoically, in the proper Tsurani fashion, but Almorella embraced Katala, openly weeping.

Milamber said, "I wish to ensure that you are both provided for. I have prepared documents against this day. When we have gone, you will find all my work cataloged in my study. Above my study table, on the top shelf, you will find a parchment with a black seal upon it. I am giving the estate to you, Netoha." He said to Almorella, "I know you two care for each other. The document giving Netoha the estate also contains a provision granting you your freedom, Almorella. He will make you a good husband, girl. Even the Emperor cannot set aside that document, bearing a Great One's seal, so do not worry."

Almorella's expression was a mixture of complete disbelief, happiness, and sorrow. She nodded slowly that she understood, thanks clearly showing in her eyes.

Milamber returned his attention to Netoha. "In my study you will also find several parchments sealed with red wax. These must be burned at once. Whatever you do, do not break the seals before you burn them. All other works are to be sent to Hochopepa of the Assembly, with my deepest affection and the wish that he find them useful. He will know what to do with them."

Almorella again embraced Katala, then kissed William. Netoha said, "Quickly, girl. You're not mistress of this estate yet, and there is important work to do." The hadonra started to bow, then said, haltingly, "Great One, I . . . I wish you well." He quickly bowed and started for the study. Milamber could see a hint of moisture in his eyes.

Almorella, tears running down her cheeks, followed Netoha into the house. Katala turned to Milamber. "Now?"

"Now." As he took them to the pattern room, he said, "There is one thing I must find out before we attempt the rift." He held his wife, with their son between them, and willed himself to another pattern.

They were shrouded in a white haze for an instant, then were in a different room. They hurried through the door, and Katala saw they were in the home of the Shinzawai lord.

They hurried to Kamatsu's study and opened the door without ceremony. Kamatsu looked up, annoyed at the interruption. His expression changed immediately when he saw who was at his door. "Great One, what is it?" he asked, as he arose.

Milamber quickly conveyed the events of the day, and Katala paled at the recounting. The Lord of the Shinzawai shook his head. "You may have set processes in motion that will forever change the internal order of the Empire, Great One. I hope it is not a death blow. In any event, it will take years to gauge their effects. Already the Party for Progress is making overtures to the Party for Peace for alliance. In a short time you have had great effect upon my homeland."

Kamatsu continued, preventing Milamber from speaking. "That is not a thing of the moment, though. You who were once my slave have learned greatly, but you are still not Tsurani. You must understand the Warlord cannot allow such a setback and save face. He most likely will take his life in shame, but those who follow his lead—his family, his clan, his subordinates—will all mark you for death. Already there may be assassins hired, or magicians who

are ready to act against you. You have no choice but to flee
to your homeland with your family."

William decided it was appropriate now to cry, for in
spite of his attempts at bravery his mother was frightened
and the boy felt it. Milamber turned away from Kamatsu
and incanted a spell and William was soon asleep. "He will
sleep until we are safe." Katala nodded and knew it was for
the best, but still she disliked the necessity.

"I have no fear of any magician, Kamatsu," Milamber
said, "but I fear for the Empire. I know now that, no matter
how hard my teachers in the Assembly tried, I can never be
Tsurani. But I do serve the Empire. In my disgust over
what I witnessed in the arena, I became sure of what I've
suspected for some time now. The Empire must change its
course, or it is doomed to fall. The rotten, weak heart of
this culture cannot support its own weight much longer,
and like a ngaggi tree with a rotten core, it will collapse
under its own weight.

"I must leave, for should I stay, the Assembly, the
High Council, all the Empire will be divided. I would have
difficulty leaving the Empire were it not in the best interest
of Tsuranuanni for me to depart. That is my training. But
before I leave, I must know, has there been word from
Laurie and your son of the Emperor's overture of peace?"

"No. We know they disappeared during a skirmish the
first night. Hokanu's men searched the area after the fight
and found no signs of them, so it is assumed they were
safely away. My younger son is certain they reached a road
behind Kingdom lines. Since then we have had no further
word. Other members of our faction wait with as much
trepidation as I."

Milamber considered. "Then the Emperor is still not
ready to act. I had hoped it might be soon, so we could
safely leave under the truce, before opposition to me
becomes organized. Now, with the Warlord's announcement of victory over Duke Borric's army, we may never see
peace."

Kamatsu said, "It is clear you are not Tsurani, Great
One. With the Warlord in disgrace from your destruction of
games he dedicated to the Light of Heaven, the War Party
will be in disorder. Now the Kanazawai Clan will once
more remove itself from the Alliance for War. Our allies in

the Blue Wheel will work doubly hard to press for a truce in the High Council. The War Party is without an effective leader. Even should the Warlord prove shameless and not kill himself, he will be quickly removed, for the War Party needs a strong leader. They will be in disarray, and we shall gain time to strengthen our position, as the Game of the Council continues."

Kamatsu looked long at Milamber. "As I have said, there are those who are already plotting to take your life. Make for your homeworld now. Do not delay, and you should likely win safely through. It might not occur to any but a few you will strike for the rift at once. Any other Great One would take a week putting his house in order." He smiled at Milamber. "Great One, you were a fresh breeze in a stale room while you were with us. I am sorry to see you leave our land, but you must go at once."

"I hope the day will come when we may meet again as friends, Lord of the Shinzawai, for there is much that our two people could learn from one another."

The Shinzawai lord placed his hand upon Milamber's shoulder. "I hope also for that day, Great One. I will send prayers with you. One thing more. If you should perchance see Kasumi in your homeworld, tell him his father thinks of him. Now go, and good-bye."

"Good-bye," said Milamber. He took his wife by the arm and hurried back toward the pattern room. When they reached it a chime sounded, and Milamber pushed his wife and son behind himself. A brief haze of white appeared over the pattern in the floor and Fumita stood there, startled.

"Milamber!" he said, stepping forward.

"Stop, Fumita!"

The older magician stood still. "I mean you no harm. Word of what occurred has reached those of the Assembly not attending the games. The Assembly is in turmoil. The Warlord's pets demand your life. Hochopepa and Shimone argue on your behalf. Never has such discord been seen. In the High Council, the War Party demands an end to the independence of the Assembly during times of war, and the Party for Progress and the Party for Peace are in open alliance with the Blue Wheel Party. The Empire is upside down."

The older magician seemed to droop visibly as he related this. He looked years older than Milamber had ever remembered seeing him. "I think you may have been right in many of your beliefs, Milamber. We must have changes in our nation if we are not to decay, but so many changes so quickly? I don't know."

There was a moment of silence between them; Milamber said, "What I did was for the Empire, Fumita. You must believe that."

The older magician nodded slowly. "I believe you, Milamber, or at least I wish to." He seemed to come more erect. "Whatever the outcome, there will be much for the Assembly to do when things have settled. Perhaps we can steer the Empire to a healthier course.

"But you must go quickly. No soldier will try to stop you, for only a few outside the Holy City know of your actions, but the Warlord's pets may already be seeking you out. You caught our brothers by surprise at the games, and none singly could stand against you, but if they coordinate against you, even your vaunted powers will avail you little. You would have to kill another magician, or be killed in turn."

"Yes, Fumita, I know. I must go. I have no desire to kill another magician, but I shall if I must."

Fumita looked pained at hearing this. "How are you to reach the rift? You haven't been to the staging area, have you?"

"No, but I go to the City of the Plains and from there I can command a litter."

"It is too slow. The litter will take over an hour to reach the staging area." He reached into his robe and pulled out a transfer device. He held it out to Milamber. "The third setting will take you directly to the rift machine."

Milamber took it. "Fumita, I mean to try and close the rift."

Fumita shook his head. "Milamber, even with your powers I don't think you can. Scores of magicians worked to create the great rift, and the controlling spells were established only on the Kelewan side. The Midkemian machine is only to stabilize the rift's location."

"I know, Fumita. You'll soon know, for I've sent my works to Hocho. My 'mysterious' research has been an intensive study of rift energies. I may now know more about them than any other magician in the Assembly. I know it would be a desperate, possibly destructive, action from the Midkemian side, but this war must end."

"Then get free to your homeworld and wait. The Emperor will act soon, I am sure. The Warlord could not have been handed a bigger blow by losing the war than the one you handed him in the arena. If the Light of Heaven orders peace, then perhaps we can deal with the question of the rift. Stay your hand until you've learned what the King's reaction to the peace offer is."

"Then you also play the Great Game?"

Fumita smiled. "I am not the only magician to descend into playing politics, Milamber. Hochopepa and I have been a part of this from the onset. Go now, and may the gods be with you. I wish you a safe journey and a long, prosperous life on your homeworld."

He then walked past Milamber and his family. Once he was out of sight, Milamber activated the device.

The soldier jumped. One moment he had been sitting under a tree, shaded from the setting sun's heat, then the next moment a magician with a woman and child suddenly appeared before him. By the time he was on his feet, they were moving toward the rift machine, several hundred yards away. When they reached the machine, a platform with tall poles rising up on either side of it, between which a glimmering "nothingness" could be seen, an officer who was in charge of the troops moving through snapped to attention.

"Get these men back from the platform."

"Your will, Great One." He barked orders and the men fell back. Milamber took Katala by the hand and led her through the rift.

One step, a moment of disorientation, and they were standing in the middle of the Tsurani camp in the valley in the Grey Towers. It was night, and campfires burned brightly. Several officers were startled at the unusual arrival, but stepped out of their way.

Milamber said, "Have you captured horses?"

One of the officers nodded dumbly.

"Bring two, at once. Saddled."

"Your will, Great One," said the man, and rushed off.

Soon a soldier brought two horses toward him. When the soldier came close, Milamber could see it was Hokanu. The younger Shinzawai son looked quickly about as he handed the reins to Milamber. "Great One, we have just received word something terrible has occurred at the Imperial Games, though the reports are vague. I suspect your sudden appearance here has something to do with those reports. You must be away quickly, for these are the Warlord's men in camp, and should they arrive at the same conclusion, there is no telling what they might risk."

Milamber held William while Katala mounted with Hokanu's aid. He handed their son up to her and mounted his own steed. "Hokanu, I have just seen your father. Go to him; he has need of you."

"I will return to my father's estate, Great One." The young Tsurani hesitated, then added, "Should you see my brother, tell him I live, for he does not know."

Milamber said he would, then turned to Katala and took the reins of her horse. "Hold to the saddle horn, beloved, and tightly to William."

Without another word they rode out of camp. Several times guards started to challenge them, but the sight of the black robe stopped them. They rode for hours in the moonlight. Milamber could hear the shouts of soldiers as he led his family to safety.

Katala bore up under it all like the warriors she was descended from, and Milamber marveled at her. She had never sat a horse before and was being bruised unmercifully, but she made no complaint. To be taken from her home and whisked away to a strange, dark world, where she knew no one, must be a frightening experience. She revealed a tough fiber to her character he had only guessed at before.

After the seemingly endless ride, a voice sounded from out of the darkness. Dim shadowy figures could be seen moving among the trees. "Halt! Who rides this night?" The voice was speaking the King's Tongue. The three riders halted, and the man in front, with relief in his voice, shouted, "Pug of Crydee!"

TWELVE

UPHEAVAL

Kulgan sat quietly.

It was a reunion tempered with sadness. Pug stood near Lord Borric's bed, openly showing his grief as the dying Duke smiled wanly up at him. Lyam, Brucal, and Meecham waited a short way off, speaking softly, and Katala distracted William while the Duke and Pug spoke.

Borric's voice came softly, weak from his illness, and his face contorted with pain as he struggled for breath. "I am glad to see you . . . returned to us, Pug. And doubly glad to see your wife and child." He coughed, and a foam appeared at the corner of his mouth, flecked with blood.

Katala's eyes were tearing, for the open affection her husband held for this man touched her. Borric motioned toward Kulgan, and the stout magician came to stand next to his former pupil. "Yes, Your Grace."

Borric whispered and Kulgan turned to Meecham. "Will you see Katala and the boy to our tent? Laurie and Kasumi are waiting there."

Katala threw Pug a questioning look, and he nodded. Meecham had already picked up the boy, who regarded him with some skepticism. When they had left, Borric struggled to sit higher, and Kulgan helped him, placing pillows behind his back. The Duke coughed loudly and long, his eyes clenched tightly shut from pain.

When at last he could breathe again, he sighed, then spoke slowly.

"Pug, do you remember when I rewarded you for saving Carline from the trolls?"

Pug nodded, afraid to speak for the emotions he felt. Borric continued, "Do you remember my promise of another gift?" Again Pug nodded. "Would that Tully were

259

here to give it to you now, but I will tell you in brief. I have
long thought the Kingdom wastes one of its greatest
resources by regarding magicians as outcasts and beggars.
Kulgan's faithful service over the years has shown me I was
right. Now you return, and though I understand only a
little of what you've told, I can see you have become a
master of your arts. It was my hope you would, for I have
had a vision.

"I had left a sum of gold in trust for you, against the
day you became a master magician. With it, I would like
you and Kulgan, and other magicians, to establish a center
for learning, where all may come and share. Tully will give
you the documents with my instructions, explaining in
detail my design. But for now I can only ask: Will you
accept this charge? Will you build an academy for the study
of magic and other knowledge?"

Pug nodded, tears in his eyes. Kulgan stood agape,
not trusting what he had heard. His fondest wish, his life's
ambition, shared with the Duke in the idle hours of
speaking of dreams over cups of wine, was now granted.

Borric began to cough again, then when the fit passed,
said, "I hold title to an island, in the heart of the Great Star
Lake, near Shamata. When this war is at last done, go there
and build your academy. Perhaps someday it will be the
greatest center for learning in the Kingdom."

Again the Duke was racked by coughing, the sound
more terrible than before. He gasped after the attack,
barely able to talk. He motioned for Lyam to come close,
pointed to Pug, and said, "Tell him," then fell back upon
his pillows."

Lyam swallowed hard, fighting back the tears, and
spoke to Pug. "When you were taken by the Tsurani,
Father wished for some memorial in remembrance. He
considered what would be proper, for you had shown
bravery on three occasions, twice saving Kulgan's life in
addition to my sister's. He judged the only thing you
lacked was a name, for none knew your parentage. So he
ordered a document drawn up and sent to the Royal
Archives, inscribing your name on the rolls of the family
conDoin, adopting you into our house." Lyam forced a
smile. "I only wish times were gladder to share such news
with you."

Overcome with emotion, Pug sank to his knees at the Duke's side. He took the Duke's hand and kissed his signet, unable to speak. Softly Borric said, "I could be no more proud of you than were you my own son." He gasped for breath. "Bear our name with honor."

Pug squeezed the once powerful hand, now weak and limp. Borric's eyes began to close and he struggled for breath. Pug released his hand and the Duke motioned for all to come closer. Even old Brucal was red-eyed as they waited for the Duke's life to slip away.

To Brucal he whispered, "You are witness, old companion."

The Duke of Yabon raised an eyebrow and looked questioningly toward Kulgan. "What does he mean?"

Kulgan said, "He wishes you to witness his dying declaration. It is his right."

Borric looked at Kulgan and said, "Care for all my sons, old friend. Let the truth be known."

Lyam said to Kulgan, "Why does he say 'all my sons'? What truth?"

Kulgan stared at Borric, who nodded weakly. The magician's words came quietly. "Your father acknowledges his eldest son, Martin."

Lyam's eyes grew wide. "Martin?"

Borric's arm shot out in a sudden surge of strength, catching at Lyam's sleeve. He pulled Lyam to him and whispered, "Martin is your brother. I have wronged him, Lyam. He is a good man and well do I love him." To Brucal he croaked a single word, "Witness!"

Brucal nodded. With tears streaming down into his white moustache he swore, "So do I, Brucal, Duke of Yabon, bear witness."

Suddenly Borric's eyes went blank and rolled up into his head. His death rattle sounded deep in his chest, and he lay still.

Lyam fell to his knees and wept, and the others also let their grief come unrestrained. Never to Pug had a moment been so bittersweet.

That night it was a quiet group in the tent that Meecham had commandeered for Pug and his family. The news of Borric's death had cast a pall over the camp, and much of Kulgan's joy at seeing his apprentice returned safely had been blunted. The day slowly passed, with all becoming reacquainted, though they spoke softly and felt little joy. Occasionally one would leave the tent, wandering off to be alone with his thoughts for a while. Nine years of history had been exchanged slowly, and now Pug spoke of his flight from the Empire.

Katala kept one eye on William, who lay curled up on a bed with one arm thrown over Fantus. The firedrake and the boy had taken one look at each other and decided they were friends. Meecham sat by the cook fire, watching the others carefully. Laurie and Kasumi sat on the floor, Tsurani fashion, while Pug finished his narrative.

Kasumi was the first to speak. "Great One, how is it that you could leave the Empire now, and not before?"

Kulgan raised one eyebrow. He was still absorbing the changes in his former apprentice. This talk of Greater Path and Lesser Path was still difficult to understand, and he couldn't believe the Tsurani attitude toward the boy. He amended that, the young man.

"After my confrontation with the Warlord, it became clear to me that I would serve the Empire by leaving, for my continued presence could only bring divisiveness at a time the Empire needs to heal itself. The war must be ended, and peace established, for the Empire is being drained."

"Aye," added Meecham, "as is the Kingdom. Nine years of war are bleeding us dry."

Kasumi was equally discomforted by the casual tone these people took toward Pug. "Great One, what if the Emperor cannot stop the new Warlord? The council will surely be quick to elect one."

"I don't know, Kasumi. I will then have to try to close the rift."

Kulgan pulled long on his pipe, then blew a thick cloud. "I am still not clear on everything you have said, Pug. From what you have told, I can see nothing that will prevent them from opening another rift."

"There is nothing, except that rifts are unstable things. There is no way to control where a rift will go; it was mere chance that caused the one between this world and Kelewan. Once that one was established, others could follow, as if the path between the two worlds acted to other rifts like a lodestone to metal.

"The Tsurani could attempt to reestablish the rift, but each attempt would probably take them to other, new worlds. If they returned here, it would be by the merest chance, one in thousands. If the rift is closed, it would be years before they returned, if ever."

"From what you said about the Warlord's taking his own life," said Kulgan, "can we expect a respite in the fighting?"

It was Kasumi who answered. "I fear not, friend Kulgan, for I know this Warlord's Subcommander. He is Minwanabi, a proud family from a powerful clan, and it would serve his cause well when the High Council meets for his clan to bring word of a great victory. Most likely he will attack in force within days."

Kulgan shook his head. "Meecham, you had best ask Lord Lyam to join us; he must hear this." The tall franklin rose and left the tent.

Kasumi frowned. "I have come to know this world a little, and I agree with the Great One. Peace would surely profit us both, but I do not see it coming."

The young Duke followed Meecham into the tent a few minutes later, and Kasumi repeated his warning. "We had best be ready, then, for the attack," said Lyam.

Kasumi looked uncomfortable. "Lord, I must beg your pardon, but should fighting come, I cannot stand against my own people. May I have your permission to return to my own lines?"

The Duke considered this, and Pug noticed that his face was becoming lined with the strain of command. Gone were the laughing eyes and ever-present smile. Now he resembled his father more than ever. "I understand. I will order you passed through the lines, if I have your parole that you will repeat nothing you have heard here."

Kasumi agreed and rose to leave. Pug stood also and said, "I will issue one last order to you, Kasumi, as a magician of Tsuranuanni. Return to your father, for he has need of you. One more soldier dying will aid your nation little."

Kasumi bowed his head. "Your will, Great One."

Kasumi embraced Laurie and left with Lyam.

Kulgan said, "You have told me so much that is difficult to absorb. I think for now we had best retire, for I feel the need of resting."

As the old magician rose, Pug said to him, "There is one thing I have been waiting to ask. What of Tomas?"

"Your childhood friend is well and with the elves of Elvandar. He is a warrior of great renown, as he had wished to be."

Pug smiled. "I am glad to hear that. Thank you."

Kulgan, Laurie, and Meecham bade them good night, and left. Katala said, "Husband, you are tired. Come rest."

Pug crossed over to the bed she sat upon. "You amaze me. You have been through so much tonight and yet you fret about me."

She took his hand. "When I am with you, everything is as it should be. But you look as if the weight of the world sits upon you."

"The weight of two worlds, I fear, love."

They were awakened by the sound of trumpets. As they rose from the bed, Pug and Katala were startled by Laurie rushing into the tent. From the light behind him as he tossed aside the tent flap, it was evident that they had slept late. "The King comes!" He held out some clothing to Pug. "Put these on."

Seeing the wisdom of not walking the camp in the black robe, Pug complied. Katala pulled her robe on over her head, while Laurie turned his back. She went over to William, who was sitting up in his bed, looking frightened. He quickly calmed down and started to pull on Fantus's tail, causing the drake to snort a protest over such indignities.

Pug and Laurie left the tent and walked to the commander's pavilion, overlooking the camp of the Kingdom armies. Away to the southeastern end of the camp they could see the royal party quickly approaching, and could hear the cheers of the soldiers as they saw the royal banner pass. Thousands of soldiers took up the cheer, for they had never seen the King before, and his presence served to lift their spirits, badly sagging since the rout by the Tsurani.

Laurie and Pug stood off to one side of the command

tent, but close enough to ensure they could hear what transpired. Duke Brucal kept his eyes on the King, but Lyam noticed the two and nodded his approval of their presence.

The two lines of Royal Household Guard rode up to the front of the tent, then parted so the King might ride to the fore. Rodric, King of the Realm, rode on a huge black war-horse, who pawed at the ground as he came to a halt before the two Dukes. Rodric was dressed in a gaudy array of gold-trimmed battle armor, with many flutings and reliefs fashioned into the breastplate. His helm was golden, with a circlet crown. A royal purple plume flew from the crest, blown by the morning wind.

When he had been sitting for a moment, he removed his helm and handed it to a page. He stayed atop his horse and studied the two commanders, looking down at them with a crooked smile. "What, have you no greeting for your liege lord?"

The Dukes bowed. Brucal said, "Your Majesty. We were just surprised. We had no word."

Rodric laughed, and the sound was tinged with madness. "That is because I sent no word. I wanted to surprise you." He looked at Lyam. "Who is this in the tabard of Crydee?"

"Lyam, Your Majesty," answered Brucal. "The Duke of Crydee."

The King shouted, "He is Duke only if I say he is Duke." With a sudden change of mood, he said, in solicitous tones, "I am sorry to hear of your father's death." He then giggled. "But he was a traitor, you know. I was going to hang him." Lyam tensed at Rodric's words, and Brucal gripped his arm.

The King saw and screamed, "You would attack your King? Traitor! You are one with your father and the others. Guards, seize him!" He pointed at the young man.

Royal guards dismounted and the soldiers of the West who stood nearby moved to stop them. "Stop!" commanded Brucal, and the western soldiers stopped. He turned to Lyam. "On your word, we have civil war," he hissed.

Lyam said, "I submit, Your Majesty." The western soldiers grumbled.

The King said coldly, "I shall have to hang you, you know. Take him to his tent and keep him there." The guards complied. The King turned his attention to Brucal. "Are you loyal to me, my lord Brucal, or shall there be a new Duke in Yabon as well as Crydee?"

"I am ever loyal to the crown, Your Majesty," came the answer.

The King dismounted. "Yes, I believe that." He giggled again. "You knew my father thought highly of you, didn't you?" He took the Duke's arm and they entered the command tent.

Laurie touched Pug's shoulder and said, "We had best stay in our tents. If one of those courtiers recognizes me, I may join the Duke on the gibbet."

Pug nodded. "Get Kulgan and Meecham, and have them meet us in my tent."

Laurie hurried off and Pug returned to his tent. Katala was feeding William from a bowl of stew from the night before. "I fear we have found another pot of trouble, love," Pug said. "The King is in camp and he is madder than I dreamed possible. We must leave soon, for he has ordered Lyam imprisoned."

Katala looked shocked. "Where will we go?"

"I can manage to take us to Crydee, to Prince Arutha. I know the court of Castle Crydee as well as if there were a pattern there. I should have no trouble transporting us."

Laurie, Meecham, and Kulgan joined them a few minutes later, and Pug outlined his plan for escape. Kulgan shook his head. "You take the boy and Katala, Pug, but I must stay."

Meecham added, "And I."

Pug looked incredulous. "Why?"

"I served Lyam's father, and now I serve him. If the King tries to execute Lyam, there will be fighting. The Armies of the West will not stand idly by and watch Lyam hanged. The King has only the Royal Guard, and they will be easily defeated. Once that happens, it is civil war. Bas-Tyra will lead the Armies of the East. Lyam will need my aid."

Meecham said, "The issue won't be quickly decided. The Armies of the West are veteran, but they're tired. There's little spirit left in them. The Armies of the East are fresh, and Black Guy is the best general in the Kingdom. Lyam's unproved. It'll be a long struggle."

Pug understood what they were saying. "It may not reach that point, though. Brucal seems ready to follow Lyam's lead, but if he changes his mind? Who knows if Ylith, Tyr-Sog, and the others will follow Lyam without Yabon's lead?"

Kulgan sighed. "Brucal will not waver. He hates Bas-Tyra as much as Borric did, though for less personal reasons. He sees Guy's hand in every move to break the West. I think the Duke of Yabon would happily take Rodric's head, but even so, Lyam may submit rather than risk a civil war and losing the West to the Tsurani. We shall have to see what passes.

"Which is all the more reason you must go to Crydee, Pug. If Lyam dies, then Arutha is heir to the crown. Once begun, the King cannot stop the killing until Arutha is dead. Even Martin, whose claim would be blemished by his illegitimacy, and Carline would be hunted down and killed. Perhaps Anita as well. Rodric would not risk a western heir to the throne. Once begun, it will not end until either Rodric or Arutha sits the throne of the Kingdom uncontested. You are the most powerful magician in the Kingdom." Pug started to protest. "I know enough of the arts to know your skills from the events you related to us. And I remember your promise as a boy. You are capable of feats unmatched by any in our world. Arutha will have grave need of your aid, for he would not let his brother's death go unpunished. Crydee, Carse, and Tulan will march once the Tsurani have been dealt with. Others, especially Brucal, would join them. Then we would have civil war."

Meecham spat out of the tent. He froze, holding aside the tent flap for a moment, then said, "I think the argument is over. Look."

They joined him at the opening. None had the franklin's sharp eyesight, and at first they couldn't see what he was pointing out. Then slowly they recognized the cloud of dust hanging in the air, far to the southeast. It spread across the horizon for miles, a dirty brown ribbon that ran below the blue of the sky.

The franklin turned to look at the others. "The Armies of the East."

* * *

They stood near the command pavilion, among a group of LaMutian soldiers. With Laurie, Kulgan, Pug, and Meecham was Earl Vandros of LaMut, the former cavalry officer who had commanded the raid through the valley years ago, when they had first seen the rift. He had gained the title upon his father's death, less than a year after Pug's capture, and had proven to be one of the Kingdom's most able field commanders.

A company of nobles was riding up the hill toward the pavilion. The King and Brucal stood waiting for them. Next to each Lord rode a standard-bearer, who held the banner of that noble. Vandros announced the name of each army represented. "Rodez, Timons, Sadara, Ran, Cibon, they're all here." He turned to Kulgan. "I doubt there are a thousand soldiers left between here and Rillanon."

Laurie said, "There is one whose banner I don't see. Bas-Tyra."

Vandros looked. "Salador, Deep Taunton, Pointer's Head . . . no, you are right. The golden eagle on black is not among the standards."

Meecham said, "Black Guy is no fool. He is already upon the throne of Krondor. Should Lyam be hanged, and Rodric fall in battle, it would be only a short step to the throne in Rillanon."

Vandros looked back at the gathering nobles. "Nearly the entire Congress of Lords is present. Should they return to Krondor without the King, then Guy would be King in short order. Many of these are his men."

Pug said, "Who is that under the banner of Salador? It is not Lord Kerus."

Vandros spat upon the ground. "It is Richard, formerly Baron of Dolth, now Duke of Salador. The King hung Kerus, and his family fled to Kesh. Now Richard rules the third most powerful duchy in the East. He is one of Guy's favorites."

When the nobles were assembled before the King, Richard of Salador, a red-faced bear of a man, said, "My liege, we are assembled. Where are we to camp?"

"Camp? We make no camp, my lord Duke. We ride!" He turned to Lord Brucal. "Marshal the Armies of the West, Brucal." The Duke gave the signal and heralds ran through the camp, shouting the order to muster. The battle drums and war trumpets were shortly sounding throughout the western camp.

Vandros left to join his soldiers, and soon, there were few observers nearby. Kulgan, Pug, and the others moved off to one side, keeping clear of the King's gaze.

The King said to the assembled nobles, "We have had nine years of the western commander's tender ways. I shall lead the attack that will drive the foe from out of our lands." He turned to Brucal. "In deference to your advancing years, my lord Duke, I am giving command of the infantry to Duke Richard. You will stay here."

The old Duke of Yabon, who was in the process of donning his armor, looked stung. He said nothing save "Your Majesty," his tone cold and strained. He stiffly turned and entered the command tent.

The King's horse was brought, and Rodric mounted. A page handed up his crowned helm, and the King placed it upon his own head. "The infantry shall follow as quickly as possible. Now we ride!"

The King spurred his horse down the hill, followed by the Royal Guard and the assembled nobles. When he was out of sight, Kulgan turned to the others and said, "Now we wait."

The day grew long. Every hour that passed was like a slowly unfolding day. They sat in Pug's tent, wondering what was occurring to the west. The army had marched forward, under the King's banner, with drums and trumpets sounding. Over ten thousand horsemen and twenty thousand foot soldiers had advanced upon the Tsurani. There were only a few soldiers left in camp, the wounded and an orderly company. The quiet outside was unnerving after the almost constant camp noise of the previous day.

William had grown restless, and Katala had taken him outside to play. Fantus welcomed the opportunity to rest untroubled by his tireless playmate.

Kulgan sat quietly, puffing on his pipe. He and Pug passed the time by occasionally speaking of matters magical, but mostly were silent.

Laurie was the first to break the tension. He stood and said, "I can't take this waiting anymore. I think we should go to Lord Lyam and help decide what is to be done once the King returns."

Kulgan waved him back into his seat. "Lyam will do nothing, for he is his father's son and would not start a civil war, not here."

Pug sat absently toying with a dagger. "With the Armies of the East in camp, Lyam knows that an outbreak of fighting would hand the West to the Tsurani and crown to Bas-Tyra. He'll walk to the gibbet and put the rope around his own neck rather than see that."

"It's the worst kind of foolishness," countered Laurie.

"No," answered Kulgan, "not foolishness, minstrel, but a matter of honor. Lyam, like his father before him, believes that the nobility have a responsibility to give their lives' work, and their lives if need be, for the Kingdom. With Borric and Erland dead, Lyam is next in line for the throne. But the succession is unclear, for Rodric has not named an heir. Lyam could not bear to wear the crown if he would be thought a usurper. Arutha is another matter, for he would simply do what was expedient, take the throne— though he would not wish to—and worry about what was said of him when it was said."

Pug nodded. "I think that Kulgan has the right of things. I do not know the brothers as well as he, but I think it might have been a better thing had the order of their birthing been reversed. Lyam would make a good King, but Arutha would make a great one. Men would follow Lyam to their deaths, but the younger brother would use his shrewdness to keep them alive."

"A fair assessment," conceded Kulgan. "If there is anyone who could find a way out of this mess, it is Arutha. He had his father's courage, but he also has a mind as quick as Bas-Tyra's. He could weather the intrigues of court, though he hates them." Kulgan smiled. "When they were boys, we called Arutha the 'little storm cloud,' for when he got angry, he would turn to black looks and rumbles, while Lyam would be quick to anger, quick to fight, and quick to forget."

Kulgan's reminiscences were interrupted by the sound of shouting from outside. They jumped up and rushed out of the tent.

A blood-covered rider, in the tabard of LaMut, sped

past them, and they ran to follow. They reached the command tent as Lord Brucal came out. The old Duke of Yabon said, "What news?"

"The Earl Vandros sends word. Victory!" Other riders could be heard approaching the camp. "We rode through them like the wind. The line on their east is breached and the salient is rent. We broke them, isolating those in the salient, then wheeled to the west and rolled back those who sought to aid them. The infantry now holds fast, and the cavalry drives the Tsurani back into the North Pass. They flee in confusion! The day is ours!"

A wineskin was handed to the rider, who sounded as if his voice would fail. He tilted it over his face and let the wine pour into his mouth. It ran down his chin, joining the deeper red splattered over his tabard. He threw aside the wineskin. "There is more. Richard of Salador has fallen, as has the Earl of Silden. And the King has been wounded."

Concern showed on Brucal's face. "How does he fare?"

"Badly, I fear," said the rider, holding his nervous horse as it pranced around. "It is a grievous wound. His helm was cleaved by a broadsword after his horse was killed beneath him. A hundred died to protect him, for his royal tabard was a beacon to the Tsurani. He comes now." The rider pointed back the way he had come.

Pug and the others turned to see a troop of riders approaching. In the van rode a royal guardsman with the King held before him. The monarch's face was covered in blood, and he held to the saddle horn with his right hand, his other arm dangling limply at his side. They stopped before the tent, and soldiers helped the King from the horse. They started to carry him inside, but he said, in a weak and slurred voice, "No. Do not take me from the sun. Bring a chair so I may sit."

Nobles were riding up even as a chair was placed for the King. He was lowered into it and leaned back, his head lolling to the left. His face was covered with blood, and white bone could be seen showing through his wound.

Kulgan moved to Rodric's side. "My King, may I attend?"

The King struggled to see who was speaking. His eyes seemed to lose focus for a moment, then became clear.

"Who is speaking? The magician? Yes, Borric's magician. Please, I am in pain."

Kulgan closed his eyes, willing his powers to ease the King's suffering. He placed his hand upon Rodric's shoulder, and those nearby could see the ruler of the Kingdom visibly relax. "Thank you, magician. I feel more at ease." Rodric struggled to turn his head slightly. "My lord Brucal, please bring Lyam to me."

Lyam was in his tent, under guard, and a soldier was sent to bring him out. A moment later the young man was kneeling before his cousin. "My liege, your wound?"

Kulgan was joined by a priest of Dala, who agreed with his assessment of the wound. He looked at Brucal and shook his head slowly. Herbs and bandages were brought, and the King was cared for. Kulgan left the priest to his ministrations and returned to stand where the others looked on. Katala had joined them, holding William in her arms. Kulgan said, "I fear it is a mortal wound. The skull is broken, and fluids seep through the crack."

In silence they watched. The priest stood to one side and began praying for Rodric. All the nobles, save those commanding the infantry, were now arrayed before the King. More horsemen could be heard riding into camp. They joined the others who stood watching, and were told what had happened. A hush fell over the assembly as the King spoke.

"Lyam," he said in a faint voice. "I have been ill, haven't I?" Lyam said nothing, his face betraying conflicting emotions. He had little love for his cousin but he was still the King.

Rodric ventured a weak smile. One side of his face moved only slightly, as if he could not control the muscles well. Rodric reached out with his good right hand, and Lyam took it. "I do not know what I have been thinking of late. So much of what has happened seems like a dream, dark and frightening. I have been trapped within that dream, but now I am free of it." Sweat appeared upon his brow, and his face was nearly white. "A demon has been driven from me, Lyam, and I can see much of what I have done was wrong, even evil."

Lyam kneeled before his King. "No, my King, not evil."

The King coughed violently, then gasped as the attack subsided. "Lyam, my time grows short." His voice rose a little and he said, "Brucal, bear witness." The old Duke looked on, his face an implacable mask. He stepped over next to Lyam and said, "I am here, Your Majesty."

The King gripped Lyam's hand, pulling himself a little more upright. His voice rose as he said, "We, Rodric, fourth of that name, hereditary ruler of the Kingdom of the Isles, do hereby proclaim that Lyam conDoin, our blood cousin, is of the royal blood. As oldest conDoin male, he is named Heir to the throne of our Kingdom."

Lyam shot Brucal an alarmed look, but the old Duke gave him a curt shake of his head, commanding silence. Lyam bowed his head, and his sorrow was heartfelt. He tightly gripped the King's hand. Brucal said, "So do I, Brucal, Duke of Yabon, bear witness."

Rodric's voice sounded faint. "Lyam, one boon do I ask. Your cousin Guy has done what he has done at my command. I grieve for the madness that drove me to have Erland deposed. I knew his going to the dungeon was his death warrant, and I did nothing to halt it. Have mercy on Guy. He is an ambitious man, but not an evil one."

The King then spoke of his plans for the Kingdom, asking that they be continued, though with more regard for the populace. He spoke of many other things: of his boyhood, and his sorrow that he had never married. After a time his speech became too slurred to understand, and his head fell forward upon his chest.

Brucal ordered guards to attend the King. They gently raised him and carried him inside. Brucal and Lyam entered the tent, while the other nobles waited outside. More new arrivals were gathering, and they were told the news. Nearly a third of the Armies of the Kingdom stood before the commander's pavilion, a sea of upturned faces extending down the hill. Each stood without speaking, waiting out the death watch.

Brucal closed the tent flap behind and shut out the red glow of the sunset. The priest of Dala examined the King, then looked at the two Dukes. "He will not regain consciousness, my lords. It is only a matter of time."

Brucal took Lyam by the arm and led him to one side. In a hushed whisper he said, "You must say nothing when I proclaim you Heir, Lyam."

Lyam pulled his arm from Brucal's grasp, fixing his gaze upon the old warrior. "You bore witness, Brucal," he whispered back. "You heard my father acknowledge Martin as my brother, legitimizing him. He is the oldest conDoin male. Rodric's proclamation of succession is invalid. He presumed I was the oldest!"

Brucal spoke quietly, but his words were ungentle. "You have a war to end, Lyam. Then, if you should accomplish that small feat, you have to take your father and Rodric back to Rillanon, to bury them in the tomb of your ancestors. From the day Rodric is interred, there will be twelve days of mourning, then on noon of the thirteenth, all the claimants for the crown will present themselves before the Priests of Ishap, and the entire, bloody damn Congress of Lords. Between now and then you'll have plenty of time to decide what to do. But for now, you needs must be Heir. There is no other way.

"Have you forgotten Bas-Tyra? Should you dither, he'll be in Rillanon with his army a month before you. Then you'll have bitter civil war, boy. As soon as you agree to keep your mouth shut, I'm ordering my own trusted troops to Krondor, under royal seal, to arrest Black Guy. They'll toss Bas-Tyra into the dungeon before his own men can stop them—there'll be enough loyal Krondorians around to ensure that. You can have him held until you reach Krondor, then cart him off to Rillanon for the coronation, either your own or Martin's. But you must act, or by the gods, we'll have Guy's lackeys brewing civil war within a day of your naming Martin the true Heir. Do you understand?"

Lyam nodded silently. With a sigh he said, "But will Guy's men let him be taken?"

"Even the captain of his own guard will not stand against a royal warrant, especially countersigned by the representatives of the Congress of Lords. I shall guarantee signatures on the warrant," he said, clenching his gloved fist before his face.

Lyam was quiet for some time, then said, "You are right. I have no wish to visit trouble upon the Kingdom. I will do as you say."

The two men returned to the King's side and waited. Nearly another two hours passed before the priest listened at the King's chest and said, "The King is dead."

Brucal and Lyam joined the priest in a silent prayer for Rodric. Then the Duke of Yabon took a ring from Rodric's hand and turned to Lyam.

"Come, it is time."

He held aside the tent flap and Lyam looked out. The sun had set and the night sky glittered with stars. Fires had been lit and torches brought, so that now the multitude appeared to be an ocean of firelight. Not one man in twenty had left, though they were all tired and hungry after the victory.

Brucal and Lyam appeared before the tent, and the old Duke said, "The King is dead." His face was stony, but his eyes were red-rimmed. Lyam looked pale but stood erect, his head high.

Brucal held something above his head. A glint of deep red fire reflected off the small object as it caught the torchlight. The nobles who stood close nodded in understanding, for it was the royal signet, worn by all the conDoin Kings since Delong the Great had crossed the water from Rillanon to plant the banner of the Kingdom of the Isles upon the mainland shore.

Brucal took Lyam's hand and placed the ring upon his finger. Lyam studied the old and worn ring, with its device cut into a ruby, still undimmed by age. As he raised his eyes to behold the crowd, a noble stepped forward. It was the Duke of Rodez, and he knelt before Lyam. "Your Highness," he said. One by one the others before the tent, nobles of both East and West, knelt in homage, and like a wave rippling, all those assembled knelt, until Lyam alone was standing.

Lyam looked at those before him, overcome with emotion and unable to speak. He placed his hand upon Brucal's shoulder and motioned for them all to stand.

Suddenly the multitude was upon its feet, and the cheer went up, "Hail, Lyam! Long live the Heir!" The soldiers of the Kingdom roared their approval, doubly so, for many knew that hours ago the threat of civil war had hung over their heads. Men of both East and West embraced and celebrated, for a terrible future had been avoided.

Lyam raised his hands and soon all were silent. His voice rang over their heads and all could hear him say, "Let no man rejoice this night. Let the drums be muffled and the trumpets blown low, for tonight we mourn a King."

Brucal pointed at the map. "The salient is surrounded, and each attempt to break through to the main body has been turned back. We have isolated nearly four thousand of their soldiers there." It was late night. Rodric had been buried with what honor could be afforded in the camp. There had been none of the trappings common to a royal funeral, but the business of war made it necessary. He had been buried in his armor next to Borric, on a hillside overlooking the camp. When the war was over, they would be returned to the tombs of their ancestors in Rillanon.

Now the young Heir looked over the map, gauging the situation in light of the latest communiqué from the front. The Tsurani held in the North Pass, at the entrance to the valley. The infantry had dug in before them, bottling up those in the valley, and isolating both the forces along the river Crydee and what was left of the salient.

"We have broken their offensive," said Lyam, "but it is a two-edged sword. We cannot attempt to fight on two fronts. We must also be ready should the Tsurani try to move against us from the south. I see no quick ending yet, in spite of our gains."

Brucal said, "But surely those in the salient will surrender soon. They are cut off, with little food or water, and cannot expect to be resupplied. In a matter of days they will be starving."

Pug interrupted. "Forgive me, Lord Brucal, but they will not."

"What can they gain by resisting? Their position is hopeless."

"They tie up your forces that would otherwise be attacking the main camp. Soon the situation in Tsuranuanni will be resolved enough for magicians to return from the Assembly. Then food and water can be transported in without interference. And each day they hold strengthens the Tsurani as reinforcements arrive from Kelewan. They are Tsurani and will gladly die rather than be taken captive."

Lyam asked, "Are they so honor bound to die, then?"

"Yes. On Kelewan they know only that captives

become slaves. The idea of a prisoner exchange is un-known to them."

"Then we must bring all our weight to bear upon the salient at once," said Brucal. "We must crush them, and free our soldiers to deal with other threats."

"It will prove costly," Lyam observed. "This time there will be no element of surprise, and they are dug in like moles. We could lose two men for each of theirs."

Kulgan had been sitting off to one side with Laurie and Meecham. "It is a tragedy that we have gained only a broadening of the fighting. And so soon after the Em-peror's offer of peace."

Pug said, "Perhaps it is still not too late."

Lyam looked at Pug. "What do you mean? Kasumi must have already sent word that the peace was refused."

"Yes, but there may still be time to send word that there will be a new King who is willing to talk peace."

"Who will carry the message?" asked Kulgan. "Your life might be forfeit if you return to the Empire."

"We may be able to solve two problems at once. Your Highness, may I have your leave to promise the Tsurani in the salient safe passage to their lines?"

Lyam considered this. "I will, if I have their parole not to return for a year's time."

"I will go to them, then," said Pug. "Perhaps we can still end this war in spite of the calamities that have befallen us."

The Tsurani guards, nervous and alert, tensed at the sound of an approaching rider. "They come!" one shouted, and men seized weapons and hurried to the barricades. The southern earthworks were still intact, but here at the western edge of the former salient the pickets had thrown up a hasty barrier of felled trees and shallow trenches.

Bowmen stood ready, arrows notched, but the ex-pected charge did not come. A single figure on horseback came into view. His hands were raised overhead, palms together in the sign for parley. And more, he wore the black robe.

The rider walked his horse to the edge of the barricade and said, in perfect Tsurani, "Who commands here?"

A startled officer said, "Commander Wataun."

The rider snapped, "You forget your manners, Strike Leader." He took note of the devices on the man's breastplate and helm. "Are the Chilapaningo so lacking in civility?"

The officer came to attention. "Your pardon, Great One," the man stammered. "It is only that you were unexpected."

"Bring Commander Wataun here."

"Your will, Great One."

The commander of the Tsurani salient came a short time later. He was a bandy-legged, barrel-chested old fighter, and Great One or not, his first concern was for the welfare of his troops. He looked at the magician suspiciously. "I am here, Great One."

"I have come to order you and your soldiers back to the valley."

Commander Wataun smiled ruefully and shook his head. "I regret, Great One, that I may not. Word of your exploits has been carried to us here, and that the Assembly has called your status into question. You may be no longer outside the law by now. If you had not come under a sign of parley, I would have you taken, though it would cost us dearly."

"Then I will make you an offer, Commander. You must decide if it is a trick or not. Kasumi of the Shinzawai carried an offer from the Light of Heaven to the Midkemian King. It was an offer of peace. The King rejected it, but now there is to be a new King who is willing to make peace. I would ask you to carry word to the Holy City, to the Emperor, that Prince Lyam will accept peace. Will you do so?"

The commander considered. "If what you say is true, then I would be a fool to waste my men. What guarantees are you willing to make?"

"I give you my word, as a Great One—if that means anything still—that what I say is true. I also promise that your men will be given safe conduct back to the valley, on promise they return to the Empire for a year's time. And I will ride to the valley entrance, to your lines, as hostage. Is that enough?"

The commander thought it over for a moment as he surveyed his tired, thirsty troops. "I will agree, Great One.

If it is the Light of Heaven's will that the war end, who am I to prolong it?"

"The Oaxatucan have long been known for their bravery. Let it be said they are also worthy of honor for their wisdom."

The commander bowed, then turned to his soldiers. "Pass the word. We march . . . home."

Word that the Emperor would agree to peace reached the camp four days later. Pug had given a message to Wataun to be carried through the rift. It bore the black seal of the Assembly and no one would impede its swift delivery. It had been addressed to Fumita, asking him to carry word to the Holy City that the new King of the Realm would not require retribution but would accept peace.

Lyam had shown visible emotion when Pug had read the message. The Emperor himself would come through the rift in a month's time and would sign formal treaties with the Kingdom. Pug had felt close to tears when he read the news, which soon spread through the camp that the war was over. A great cheering could be heard.

Pug and Kulgan sat in the older magician's tent. For the first time in years they had been feeling something like their old relationship. Pug was finishing up a long explanation of the Tsurani system of instructing novices.

"Pug," said Kulgan around a long pull on his pipe. "It seems that now the war is over, we can return to the business of magicians. Only now it is you who are master and I who would be student."

"There is much we may learn from each other, Kulgan. But I fear old habits die hard. I don't think I could ever get used to the idea of your being a student. And there are many things you are capable of that I still cannot do."

Kulgan seemed surprised. "Really? I would have thought my simple arts beneath your greatness."

Pug felt the old embarrassment from when he had been Kulgan's student. "You make sport of me yet."

Kulgan laughed. "Only a little, boy. And you are still a boy to one of my advancing years. It is not easy for me to see an indifferent apprentice become the most powerful magician of another world."

"Indifferent was the proper word for it. At first I only

wanted to be a soldier. I think you knew that. Then when I had finally decided to devote myself to study, the invasion began." Pug smiled. "I think you felt sorry for me that day when I stood alone before the Duke's court, the only boy not called."

"That is partly true, though I was the first to sense the power in you. And the judgment was borne out, no matter the amazing events required to bring your ability to fruition."

Pug sighed. "Well, the Assembly is nothing if not complete in its training. Once the power is detected there are but two options, success or death. With all other thoughts banished, there is little to concern the student but the study of magic. Without that, I doubt I would ever have amounted to much."

Kulgan said, "I think not. Had the Tsurani never come, there would still have been a path to greatness for you to follow."

They sat and talked and were comforted by each other's presence. After a while they lit fires, for darkness was falling. Katala came to the tent to see if her husband was to join her and the boy at the celebration feast being given by King Lyam. She looked inside and saw the two of them lost in conversation.

She backed out and, with a faint smile on her lips, returned to her son.

THIRTEEN

DECEPTIONS

Lyam sat quietly in his tent.

He was composing the message he would send to Crydee when a guard entered and announced the arrival of Pug and Kulgan. Lyam rose and greeted them, and when the guards had left them, indicated they should sit. "I am sorely in need of your wisdom." He sat back and waved at the parchments before him. "If Arutha is to reach us in time for the peace conference, these must leave today. But I have never been much for letters, and I also confess to great difficulty in sharing the events of the last week."

Kulgan said, "May I?" pointing to the letter.

Lyam waved approval, and the magician picked up the parchment and began to read. "'To my beloved brother and sister: It is with the deepest sorrow I must tell you of our father's death. He was injured mortally in the great Tsurani offensive, leading a counterattack to rescue surrounded soldiers, mainly Hadati hillmen, auxiliaries to the garrison of Yabon. The Hadati sing his name and make sagas in his honor, such was his bravery. He passed thinking of his children, and his love for us all was undiminished.

"'The King has also passed, and it has fallen to me to lead our armies. Arutha, I would have you here, for we now are at the war's end. The Emperor is willing to make peace. We shall meet in the north valley of the Grey Towers in twenty-nine days' time, at noon. Carline, I would have you take ship to Krondor with Anita, for there is much to be done there, and Princess Alicia will have need of her daughter. I will join you with Arutha once peace has been made. With love, and sharing in your sorrow, I am, your most loving brother, Lyam.'"

Kulgan was quiet for a moment, and Lyam said, "I thought you might be able to add something or other, to lend elegance to it."

Kulgan said, "I think you announced your father's passing with simplicity and gentleness. It is a fine message."

Lyam shifted uncomfortably in his chair. "There is so much yet to write. I have said nothing about Martin."

Kulgan took up a quill. "I will copy this again, for your pen is a bit strangled, Lyam." With a warm smile he added, "You were always one to prefer the sword to the quill. I'll add some instructions to the end, asking that Martin go to Krondor with your sister. Gardan and Fannon should also make the journey. And an honor company of the castle garrison. It will make it seem you mean to honor those who served so well in Crydee. Then you will have ample time to decide how to tell Martin what you must."

Pug shook his head sadly. "I only wish you could add Roland's name to that list." Since coming to the camp, he had learned of the Squire of Tulan's death. Kulgan had told him of what he knew of events in Crydee and elsewhere concerning his old friends over the last few years.

Lyam said, "Curse me for a fool! Carline has no idea you are back, Pug. You must add that, Kulgan."

Pug said, "I hope it will not come as too much of a shock."

Kulgan chuckled. "Not so much of a shock as discovering you've a wife and child."

Memories of his boyhood and his tempestuous relationship with the Princess returned, and Pug said, "I hope also she has outgrown some of the notions she held nine years ago."

Lyam laughed for the first time since his father's death, genuinely entertained by Pug's discomfort. "Rest assured, Pug. I've had many long communications with my brother and sister over the years, and I judge Carline a greatly changed young woman from the girl you once knew. She was fifteen years old when last you saw her. Think of your own changes in the last nine years."

Pug could only nod.

Kulgan finished his copy work and handed the document to Lyam. He read it and said, "Thank you, Kulgan. You've added just the right note of gentleness."

The tent flap opened and Brucal entered, his old lined face animated with glee. "Bas-Tyra's fled!"

"How?" asked Lyam. "Our soldiers must still be a week from Krondor, maybe more."

The old Duke sat heavily in a chair. "We found a hidden cage of messenger pigeons, belonging to the late Richard of Salador. One of his men sent word to Guy of Rodric's death, and your being named Heir. We've questioned the fellow, a valet of Richard's. Guy's fled the city, knowing one of your first acts as King will be to have him hung. My guess is he will make straight for Rillanon."

"I would have thought that would be the last place on Midkemia he would wish to be," remarked Kulgan.

"Black Guy is no man's fool, whatever else may be said

of him. He'll be underground, no doubt, but you'll see his handiwork again before we are through. Until the crown is resting upon Lyam's head, Guy is still a power in the Kingdom."

Lyam looked troubled at the last remark, thinking of his father's dying declaration. Since Brucal's admonition to say nothing of Martin, everyone had spoken only of Lyam's coronation, nothing of Martin's possible claim to the crown.

Lyam let these disturbing thoughts pass by as Brucal continued speaking: "Still, with Bas-Tyra on the sly, most of our troubles are now behind. And with the war near an end, we can get back to the business of rebuilding the Kingdom. And I for one am glad. I am getting too old for much more of this nonsense of war and politics. I only regret I am without a son, so I could announce in his favor and retire."

Lyam studied Brucal with affectionate disbelief. "You'll never bow down gracefully, old war dog. You'll go to your deathbed scratching and clawing every inch of the way, and that day is years off."

"Who's talking of dying?" snorted Brucal. "I mean to hunt my hounds and fly my falcons, and do some fishing as well. Who knows? I may find some comely wench hearty enough to keep up with me, say about seventeen or eighteen years of age, and remarry and father a son yet. If that young fool Vandros ever gathers his wits about him and marries my Felinah, you just see how fast he'll become Duke of Yabon when I retire. Why she still waits for him is anybody's guess." He heaved himself up from his chair. "I am for a hot bath and some sleep before supper. By your leave?"

Lyam motioned he might leave and, when he was gone, said, "I will never get used to this business of people needing my permission to come and go."

Pug and Kulgan rose from their chairs. Kulgan said, "You had better, for all will ask it of you from now on. With your permission . . . ?"

Feigning disgust, Lyam motioned they might go.

The council sat in assembly as Aglaranna took her place upon the throne. Besides the normal council, Martin

Longbow was present, standing beside Tomas. When all were in place, Aglaranna said, "You have asked for council, Tathar. Now tell us what cause you bring before us."

Tathar bowed slightly to the Queen. "We of the council felt it time for an understanding."

"Of what, Tathar?" asked the Elf Queen.

Tathar said, "We have labored long to bring a peaceful, secure ending to this business of Tomas. It is known by all here that our arts were turned to calming the rage within, softening the might of the Valheru, so the young man who was transformed would not be overwhelmed in the course of time."

He paused, and Martin leaned close to Tomas. "Trouble."

Tomas startled him with a slight smile and a wink. Once more Martin was reassured that the mirthful boy he had known in Crydee was as much present in this young man as the Dragon Lord. "Everything will be fine," said Tomas in a whisper.

"We have," said Tathar, "come to judge this business done, for Tomas is no longer to be feared as an Old One."

Aglaranna said, "That is happy news indeed. But is this then cause for a council?"

"No, lady. Something else must also be laid to rest. For while we no longer fear Tomas, still we will not place ourselves under his rule."

Aglaranna stood, outrage clear upon her face. "Who dares to presume this? Has there been a single word from any to suggest that Tomas seeks to rule?"

Tathar stood firm before his Queen's displeasure. "My lady, you see with a lover's eyes." Before she could answer, he held up his hand. "Speak not sharp words with me, daughter of my oldest friend; I make no accusations. That he shares your bed is no one's concern save yourself. We begrudge you nothing. But he now has the means of a claim, and we would have the matter settled now."

Aglaranna paled, and Tomas stepped forward. "What means?" he said, his voice commanding.

Tathar looked slightly surprised. "She carries your child. Did you not know?"

Tomas was bereft of words. Conflicting feelings ran

through him. A child! Yet he had not been told. He looked at Tathar. "How do you know?"

Tathar smiled, and there was no mockery in it. "I am old, Tomas. I can see the signs."

Tomas looked to Aglaranna. "It is true?"

She nodded. "I would not tell you until it was no longer possible to hide the truth."

He felt a stab of uncertainty. "Why?"

"To spare you any worry. Until the war is through, you must put your mind to nothing else. I would not burden you with other thoughts."

Tomas stood quietly for a moment, then threw back his head and laughed, a clear, joyous sound. "A child. Praise the gods!"

Tathar looked thoughtfully at Tomas. "Do you claim the throne?"

"Aye, I do, Tathar," Tomas said, a smile upon his face.

Calin spoke for the first time. "It is my inheritance, Tomas. You will have to contest with me for it."

Tomas smiled at Calin. "I will not cross swords with you, son of my beloved."

"If you seek to be King among us, then you must."

Tomas walked over to Calin. There had never been any affection between them, for more than the others, Calin had feared Tomas's potential threat to his people and now stood ready to fight if need be.

Tomas placed his hand upon Calin's shoulder and looked deeply into his eyes. "You are heir. I speak not of being your King." He stepped away and addressed the council. "I am what you see before you, a being of two heritages. I possess the power to the Valheru, though I was not born to it, and my mind remembers ages long gone to dust. But I can remember a boy's memories and can again feel the joy in laughter and a lover's touch." He looked at the Elf Queen. "I claim only the right to sit beside my Queen, with your blessings, as her consort. I will take only what rule she and you give, nothing more. Should you give none, still I will remain at her side." Then, with firmness, he added, "But I will not stand down from this: our child shall have a heritage unblemished by a sinister birth."

There was a general murmur of approval, and Tomas

faced Aglaranna. "If you will take me as husband?" he said in the ancient elven language.

Aglaranna sat with eyes gleaming. She looked to Tathar. "I will. Is there any who denies me the right?"

Tathar looked around at the other counselors. Seeing no dissension, Tathar said, "It is permitted, my lady."

Abruptly there was a shout of approval from the gathered elves, and soon others were coming to investigate the unusual display of activity in the council. They in turn joined in the celebration, for all knew of the Queen's love for the warrior in white and gold, and they judged him a fit consort.

Calin said, "You are wise in our ways, Tomas. Had you done otherwise, there would have been strife, or lingering doubt. I thank you for your prudence."

Tomas took his hand in a firm grip. "It is only just, Calin. Your claim is without question. When your Queen and I have journeyed to the Blessed Isles, then our child will be your loyal subject."

Aglaranna came to Tomas's side, and Martin joined them, to say, "Joy in all things." Tomas embraced his friend, as did the Queen.

Calin shouted for silence. When the noise had died, he said, "It is time for clear speaking. Let all know that what has been fact for years is now openly acknowledged. Tomas is Warleader of Elvandar, and Prince Consort to the Queen. His words are to be obeyed by all save the Queen. I, Calin, have spoken."

"And I, too, say this is true," echoed Tathar. Then all in the council bowed before the Queen and her husband-to-be.

Martin said, "It is well I shall leave Elvandar as happiness returns."

Aglaranna said, "You are leaving?"

"I fear I must. There is still a war and I am still Huntmaster of Crydee. Besides," he said with a grin, "I fear young Garret is growing overly content to rest and partake of your largess. I must harry him along the trail before he gets fat."

"You'll stay for the wedding?" asked Tomas.

As Martin began to apologize, Aglaranna said, "The ceremony can be tomorrow."

Martin conceded. "One more day? I will be pleased."

Another shout went up, and Tomas could see Dolgan pushing through the crowd. When the dwarf chief stood before them, he said, "We were not invited to the council, but when we heard the shouts, we came." Behind him, Tomas and Aglaranna could see the other dwarves approaching.

Tomas placed his hand upon Dolgan's shoulder. "Old companion, you are welcome. You have come to a celebration. There is to be a wedding."

Dolgan fixed them both with a knowing smile. "Aye, and high time."

The rider spurred his horse past the lines of Tsurani soldiers. He was still discomforted by the sight of so many of them passing to the east, and the recent enemy watched him ride by with guarded expressions as he headed toward Elvandar.

Laurie pulled in his horse near a large outcropping of rock where a Tsurani officer supervised the passing soldiers. From his insignia he was a Force Leader, surrounded by his cadre of Strike Leaders, Patrol Leaders, and junior officers. To the Force Leader he said, "Where lies the closest ford across the river?"

The other officers regarded Laurie with suspicion, but if the Force Leader felt any surprise at the barbarian's nearly perfect Tsurani, he did not show it. He inclined his head back the way his men marched from and said, "A short way from here. Less than an hour's march. Faster on your beast, I'm sure. It is marked by two large trees on either side of a clearing, above a place where the river falls a short way."

Laurie noticed the man's clan and family markings, and said, "Thank you, Force Leader. Honor to your house, son of the Minwanabi."

The Force Leader stood erect. He did not know who this rider was, but he was courteous, and that courtesy must be returned. "Honor to your house, stranger."

Laurie spurred his horse forward past the dispirited Tsurani soldiers plodding along the banks of the river. He found the clearing above the small falls and rode into the water. The river ran swiftly here, but the horse managed to cross without incident. Laurie could feel the spray from the falls as the wind blew it back in his direction. It felt cool and refreshing after the hot ride. He had been in the saddle since before daybreak and would not finish his ride until after night had fallen. By then he would be close enough to Elvandar to be intercepted by elven sentries. They would certainly be watching the Tsurani withdrawal with interest, and one could guide him to their Queen.

Laurie had volunteered to carry the message, for it was felt that the messenger would be less likely to encounter trouble if he could speak Tsurani. He had been challenged three times during his ride, and each time he had explained his way past suspicious Tsurani officers. There might be a truce, but there was little trust yet.

When he was clear of the river, Laurie dismounted, for his horse was tired. He walked the animal to cool it off. He pulled the saddle from the mount's back and was rubbing him down with a comb carried in his saddle bags when a figure stepped out from among the trees. Laurie was startled, for the figure was not an elf. He was a dark-haired man with grey at the temples, dressed in a brown robe, and holding a staff. He approached the minstrel, without hurry and seemingly at ease. He stopped a few feet away and leaned on his staff. "Well met, Laurie of Tyr-Sog."

The man possessed a strange manner, and Laurie did not remember having met him before. "Do I know you?"

"No, but I have knowledge of you, troubadour."

Laurie edged closer to his saddle, where his sword lay. The man smiled and waved his hand in the air. Abruptly Laurie was filled with calm, and he stopped moving for his sword. Whoever this man was, he was obviously harmless, he thought.

"What brings you to the elven forest, Laurie?"

Without knowing why, Laurie answered. "I bring messages to the Elf Queen."

"What are you to say?"

"That Lyam is now Heir, and peace has been restored. He invites the elves and the dwarves to the valley in three weeks' time, for there will they seal the peace."

The man nodded. "I see. I am on my way to see the Elf Queen. I will carry word. You must have better things you can do with your time."

Laurie started to protest, but stopped. Why should he travel to Elvandar when this man was bound there anyway? It was a waste of time.

Laurie nodded. The man chuckled. "Why don't you rest here for the night? The sound of water is soothing, and there is little chance of rain. Tomorrow, return to the Prince and tell him that you carried the message to Elvandar. The dwarves of Stone Mountain will hear also. Then tell Lyam that the elves and the dwarves come. He may rest assured, they will come."

Laurie nodded. What the man was saying made a great deal of sense. The stranger turned to leave, then said, "By the way, I think you'd best not mention our meeting."

Laurie said nothing, but accepted what the stranger said without question. After the man had gone, he felt a great sense of relief that he was on his way back from Elvandar and that his message had been received.

The ceremony took place in a quiet glade, with Aglaranna and Tomas exchanging vows before Tathar. No one else was there, as was the elven way, while they pledged their love. Tathar invoked the blessings of the gods and instructed them on their duty, one to the other.

When the ceremony was complete, Tathar said, "Now return to Elvandar, for it is time for feasting and celebration. You have brought joy to your people, my lady and my prince."

They rose from their kneeling positions and embraced. Tomas stepped back and said, "I would have this day remembered, beloved." He turned and cupped his hands around his mouth. In the ancient language of the elves he cried, "Belegroch! Belegroch! Attend us."

The sound of hooves pounding the earth could be heard. Then a small band of white horses raced into the glade, ran toward them, and reared in salute to the Elf Queen and her consort. Tomas leaped upon the back of one. The elf steed stood quietly, and Tathar said, "By no other way could you have shown so well that you are now one with us."

Aglaranna and Tathar mounted, and they rode back to Elvandar. When they came into sight of the tree-city, a great shout went up from the assembled elves. The sight of

the Queen and her Prince Consort riding the elf steeds
was, as Tathar said, a confirmation of Tomas's place in
Elvandar.

The feasting went on for hours, and Tomas observed
that the joy he felt was shared by all around. Aglaranna sat
next to him, for a second throne had been placed in the
council hall, acknowledging Tomas's rank. Every elf who
was not keeping watch over the outworlders came to stand
before them, pledging loyalty, and offering blessings on the
union. The dwarves also offered their congratulations and
joined in the festivities wholeheartedly, filling the glades of
Elvandar with their boisterous singing.

Long into the night the celebration wore on. Suddenly
Tomas stiffened. A chilled wind seemed to pass through
him. Aglaranna gripped his arm, sensing something amiss.
"Husband, what is it?"

Tomas stared into space. "Something . . . strange
. . . hopeful, but sad."

Abruptly there was a shout from the edge of the
clearing below Elvandar. It cut through the sound of the
celebration, but what was being said was unclear. Tomas
rose, with Aglaranna at his side, and crossed to the edge of
the huge platform. Looking down, he could see an elven
scout below, clearly out of breath. "What is afoot?" Tomas
shouted.

"My lord," came the reply, "the outworlders—they
withdraw."

Tomas was rooted in place. Those simple words struck
him like a blow. His mind couldn't comprehend the
Tsurani's leaving after all these years of fighting. He shook
off the feeling. "To what ends? Do they marshal?"

The scout shook his head. "No, my lord, they are not
staging. They move slowly, without alarm. Their soldiers
look dispirited. They break camp along every mile of the
Crydee and turn east." The guard's upturned face showed
an expression of stunned but joyful understanding. He
looked at those nearby, then with a smile said simply,
"They are leaving."

A shout of incredible joy went up, and many openly
wept, for it seemed that at last the war was ended. Tomas
turned and saw tears on the face of his wife. She embraced
him, and they stood quietly for a moment. After a time the

new Prince Consort of Elvandar said to Calin, who stood nearby, "Send runners to follow, for it may be a trick."

Aglaranna said, "Do you truly think so, Tomas?"

He shook his head. "I only wish to make sure, but something inside tells me this is truly the end. It was the hope of peace with the sadness of defeat mingled together."

She touched his cheek and he said, "I will send runners to the Kingdom camp and inquire of Lord Borric what is happening."

She said, "If it is peace, he will send word."

Tomas looked at her. "True. We shall wait, then." He studied her face, centuries old, but still filled with the beauty of a women in her first bloom. "This day will doubly be remembered as a day to celebrate."

Neither Tomas nor Aglaranna was surprised when Macros arrived in Elvandar, for they had ceased being amazed at the sorcerer after his first visit. Without ceremony he stepped forward from the trees surrounding the clearing and crossed toward the tree-city.

The entire court was assembled, including Longbow, when Macros came to stand before the Queen and Tomas. He bowed and said, "Greetings, lady, and to your consort."

"Welcome, Macros the Black," said the Queen. "Have you come to unravel the mystery of the outworlders' withdrawal?"

Macros leaned upon his staff and nodded. "I bring news." He seemed to consider his words carefully. "You should know that both the King and the Lord of Crydee are dead. Lyam is now Heir."

Tomas noticed Martin. The Huntmaster's face was drained of blood. His features remained impassive, but it was clear to Tomas that Martin was rocked by the news. Tomas turned toward Macros. "I knew not the King, but the Duke was a fine man. I am sorry for such news."

Macros went over to Martin. Martin watched the sorcerer, for while he had never met him, he knew him by reputation, having been told by Arutha of the meeting upon his island and by Tomas of his intervention during the Tsurani invasion of Elvandar. "You, Martin Longbow,

are to go at once to Crydee. There you will sail with the
Princesses Carline and Anita for Krondor." Martin was
about to speak when Macros raised his hand; all in the
court paused as if taking a breath. In a near-whisper,
Macros said, "At the last, your father spoke your name in
love." This his hand dropped and all was as it had been.

Martin felt no alarm, but rather a sense of comfort
from the sorcerer's words; he knew no one else had been
aware of the brief remark.

Macros said, "Now hear more glad tidings. The war is
over. Lyam and Ichindar meet in twenty days' time to sign
a peace."

A cheer went up in the court, and those above shouted
the news to those below. Soon all of the elven forests
echoed with the sound of rejoicing. Dolgan again entered
the council, wiping his eyes. "What's this? Another celebration without us while I nap? You'll make me think we're
no longer welcome."

Tomas laughed. "Nothing of the kind, Dolgan. Fetch
your brethren and have them join our celebration. The war
is over."

Dolgan took out his pipe and knocked the dottle from
it, kicking the burned-out tabac over the edge of the
platform. "Finally," he said as he opened his pouch. He
turned away, as if intent upon filling his pipe, and Tomas
pretended not to notice the wetness upon the dwarven
chief's face.

Arutha sat upon his father's throne, alone in the great
hall. He held the message from his brother, which he had
read several times, trying to understand that their father
was truly gone. Grief sat heavy upon him.

Carline had taken the news well. She had gone to the
quiet garden beside the keep, to be alone with her
thoughts, as he had come to the great hall.

Thoughts ran riot through his mind. He remembered
the first time his father had taken him hunting, then
another time when he had come back from hunting with
Martin Longbow and how proudly he had listened to his
father exclaim over the large buck he had taken. He
vaguely recalled the ache when he had learned of his
mother's death, but it was a distant thing, dulled by time.

The image of his father enraged in the King's palace suddenly came to him, and Arutha let out a slow sigh. "At least," he said to himself, "most of what you had wished has come to pass, Father. Rodric is gone and Guy is in disgrace."

"Arutha?" said a voice from the other side of the hall.

Arutha looked up: stepping from the shadows of the doorway came Anita, her satin-slippered feet making no sound as she crossed the stone floor of the hall.

Lost in his thoughts, he hadn't noticed her enter. She carried a small lamp, for evening had cast the hall into deep gloom. "The pages were reluctant to disturb you, but I couldn't see you sitting alone in the darkness," she said. Arutha felt pleasure at sight of her and relief she had come. A young woman of uncommon sense and tender ways, Anita was the first person Arutha had known to see beneath his surface calm and dry humor. More than those who had known him since boyhood, she understood his moods and could lighten them, knowing the right words to comfort him.

Without waiting for him to answer she said, "I have heard the news, Arutha. I am so terribly sorry."

Arutha smiled at her. "Not yet over your own grief at your father's passing, and you share mine. You are kind."

Word of Erland's death had come a week before on a ship from Krondor. Anita shook her head, her soft red hair moving in a rippling wave around her face. "Father was very ill for many years. He prepared us well for his death. It was a near-certainty when he was put into the dungeon. I knew that when we left Krondor."

"Still, you show strength. I hope I am able to bear up as well. There is so much to be done."

She spoke quietly. "I think you will rule wisely, Lyam in Rillanon, you in Krondor."

"I? In Krondor? I've avoided thinking about that."

She sat at his side, taking the throne Carline sat in when at her father's side in court. She reached over and placed her hand upon Arutha's, resting on the arm of the throne. "You must. After Lyam, you are heir to the crown. The Prince of Krondor is the Heir's office. There is no one to rule there but you."

Arutha looked uncomfortable. "Anita, I have always

assumed I would someday become Earl of some minor
keep, or perhaps seek a career as an officer in one of the
Border Barons' armies. But I had never thought to rule. I
am not sure I welcome being Duke of Crydee, let alone
Prince of Krondor. Besides, Lyam will marry, I am sure—he
always caught the girls' eyes, and as King he'll certainly
have his pick. When he has a son, the boy can be Prince of
Krondor."

Anita shook her head firmly. "No, Arutha. There is too
much work to be done now. The Western Realm needs a
strong hand, your hand. Another Viceroy is not likely to
win trust, for each lord will suspect any other who is
named. It must be you."

Arutha studied the young woman. In the five months
she had been at Crydee, he had come to care dearly for her,
though he had been unable to express his feelings, finding
words lacking when they were together. She was each day
more a beautiful woman, less a girl. She was still young,
which made him uncomfortable. With the war in progress,
he had kept his thoughts away from their respective
fathers' plans for a possible marriage, revealed to him that
night aboard the *Sea Swift*. Now, with peace at hand,
Arutha was suddenly confronted with that question.

"Anita, what you say is possibly true, but you also
have a claim to the throne. Didn't you say your father's
plan for our marriage was designed to bolster your claim to
Krondor?"

She looked at him with large green eyes. "That was a
plan to foil Guy's ambitions. It was to strengthen your
father's or brother's claim to the crown should Rodric die
heirless. Now you need not feel bound to those plans."

"Should I take Krondor, what will you do?"

"Mother and I have other estates. We can live quite
well upon the revenues, I am sure."

Struggling with emotions within himself, Arutha
spoke slowly, "I have not had time to weigh this in my
mind. When I was last in Krondor, I learned how little I
know of cities, and I know less than that of governing. You
were raised for such undertakings. I . . . I was only a
second son. My education is lacking."

"There are many able men, here and in Krondor, who
will advise. You have a good head for things, Arutha, the

ability to see what must be done, and the courage to act. You will do well as Prince of Krondor."

She rose and leaned over to kiss his cheek. "There is time for you to decide how best to serve your brother, Arutha. Try not to let this new responsibility weigh too heavily upon you."

"I will try. Still, I would feel better knowing you were close by—you and your mother," he added with a rush.

She smiled warmly. "We will be close at hand should you have need of our advice, Arutha. We will likely stay upon our estate in the hills near Krondor, just a few hours' ride from the palace. Krondor is the only home I've known, and Mother has lived nowhere else since she was a girl. Should you wish to see us, you have but to command and we will happily come to court. And should you wish to find respite from the burdens of office, you will be a welcome guest."

Arutha smiled at the girl. "I suspect I will be visiting with regularity, and I hope I do not wear out my welcome."

"Never, Arutha."

Tomas stood alone on the platform, watching the stars through the branches above. His elven senses informed him someone had come up behind. With a nod he greeted the sorcerer. "I am but twenty-five years in this life, Macros, though I bear memories of ages. All my adult life I have been waging war. It seems a dream."

"Let us not turn this dream into a nightmare."

Tomas studied the sorcerer. "What do you mean?"

Macros said nothing for a time, and Tomas awaited his words with patience. At last the sorcerer spoke. "There is this thing which must be done, Tomas, and it has fallen to you to finish this war."

"I like little the tone of your words. I thought you said the war was finished."

"On the day of the meeting between Lyam and the Emperor, you must marshal the elves and dwarves to the west of the field. When the monarchs meet in the center of the field, then will there be treachery."

"What treachery?" Tomas's face showed his anger.

"I may say little more, save that when Ichindar and Lyam are seated, you must attack the Tsurani with all your forces. Only this way can Midkemia be saved from utter destruction."

A look of suspicion crossed Tomas's face. "You ask much for one unwilling to give more."

Macros stood tall, holding his staff to one side, like a ruler his scepter. His dark eyes narrowed, and his brows met over his hooked nose. His voice stayed soft, but his words were hot with anger. Even Tomas felt something akin to awe in his presence.

"More!" he said, biting off the word. "I gave you all, Valheru! You are here by dint of my actions over the years. More of my life than you will know has been given to preparing for your coming. Had I not bested, then befriended Rhuagh, you would never have survived in the mines of Mac Mordain Cadal. It was I who prepared the armor and sword of Ashen-Shugar, leaving them with the hammer of Tholin and my gift to the dragon, so that centuries later you would discover them. It was I who set your feet upon the path, Tomas. Had I not come to aid you, years past, Elvandar would now be ashes. Do you think Tathar and the other Spellweavers of Elvandar were the only ones to work on your behalf? Without my aid over these last nine years, you would have been destroyed utterly by the dragon's gifts. No mere human could have withstood such ancient and powerful magic without the intervention only I could make. When you were swept along upon your dream quests to the past, it was I who guided you back to the present, I who returned you to sanity." The sorcerer's voice rose. "It was I who gave you the power to influence Ashen-Shugar! You were my tool!" Tomas stepped back before the controlled fury of the sorcerer's words. "No, Tomas, I have not given you much. I have given you everything!"

Tomas felt fear for the first time since donning the armor in Mac Mordain Cadal. In the most basic fiber of his being he suddenly was aware of how much power the sorcerer possessed, and that should Macros choose he could brush him aside like a nettlesome insect. "Who are you?" he asked quietly, controlled fear in his voice.

Macros's anger vanished. He leaned once again upon his staff, and Tomas's fears fled and with them all memory of his fears. With a chuckle, Macros said, "I tend to forget myself upon occasion. My apologies." Then he grew serious once again. "I do not ask this thing from any demand of gratitude. What I have done is done and you owe me nothing. But know this: both the creature called Ashen-Shugar and the boy called Tomas shared an abiding love of this world, each in his own way, incomprehensible to each other as that love was. You possess both aspects of the love of land: the desire to protect and control of the Valheru and the desire to nurture and nourish of the keep boy. But should you fail in this task I set before you, should you stint in resolve when the moment is nigh, then know with dread certainty, this world upon which we stand shall be lost, lost beyond recalling. This on my most holy oath is the truth."

"Then I shall do as you instruct."

Macros smiled. "Go then to your wife, Prince Consort of Elvandar, but when it is time, marshal your army. I go to Stone Mountain, for Harthorn and his soldiers will join you. Every sword and war hammer is needed."

"Will they know you?"

Macros gazed at Tomas. "Indeed they will know me, Tomas of Elvandar, never doubt."

"I shall gather all the might of Elvandar, Macros." A grim note entered his voice. "And for all time, we will put an end to this war."

Macros waved his staff and vanished. Tomas waited alone for a time, struggling with a newfound fear, that this war would last forever.

FOURTEEN

BETRAYAL

The armies stood facing one another.

Seasoned veterans eyed each other across the open valley floor, not quite ready to feel at ease in the presence of an enemy they had fought for nine years and longer. Each

side was composed of honor companies, representing the
nobles of the Kingdom and clans of the Empire. Each
numbered in excess of a thousand men. The last of the
Tsurani invasion army was now entering the rift, returning
home to Kelewan, leaving only the Emperor's honor
detachment behind. The Kingdom army was still camped
at the mouths of the two passes into the valley and would
not leave the area until the treaty was finalized. There was
still a cautious aspect to the newfound trust.

On the Kingdom side of the valley, Lyam sat astride a
white war-horse, awaiting the Emperor's arrival. Nearby
the nobles of the Kingdom, their armor cleaned and
polished, sat their horses. With them were the leaders of
the Free Cities militia and a detachment of Natalese
Rangers.

Trumpets sounded from across the field and the
Emperor's party could be seen emerging from the rift.
Imperial banners fluttered in the breeze as the procession
moved to the head of the Tsurani contingent.

Awaiting the Tsurani herald, who was walking across
the several hundred yards that separated the opposing
monarchs, Prince Lyam turned to regard those who sat on
horseback nearby. Pug, Kulgan, Meecham, and Laurie
were accorded their position of honor by dint of their
service to the Kingdom. Earl Vandros and several other
officers who had distinguished themselves were also close
by. Next to Lyam sat Arutha, astride a chestnut war-horse,
who pranced in place out of high spirits.

Pug looked around, feeling a giddy sensation at the
sight of all the symbols of two mighty nations with whose
fates he had been so closely tied. Across the open field
he could see the banners of the powerful families of the
Empire, all familiar to him: the Keda, the Oaxatucan, the
Minwanabi, and the rest. Behind him were the fluttering
banners of the Kingdom, all the duchies from Crydee in the
west to Ran in the east.

Kulgan noticed his former student's far-off gaze and
tapped him on the shoulder with the long staff he was
holding. "Are you all right?"

Pug turned. "I'm fine. I was just a little overwhelmed
for a moment, engulfed in memories. It seems strange to
see this day, in a way. Both sides of the war were bitter

enemies, and yet I have ties with both lands. I find I have feelings I have yet to explore."

Kulgan smiled. "There will be much time for introspection later. Perhaps Tully and I can offer some aid." The old cleric had accompanied Arutha on his brutal ride, not wishing to miss the peace meeting. The fourteen days in the saddle had taken a toll, however, and now he lay ill in Lyam's tent. It had taken a command from Lyam to keep him there, for he had been determined to accompany the royal party.

The Tsurani herald reached a place before Lyam. He bowed low, then said something in Tsurani. Pug rode forward to translate. "He says, 'His most Imperial Majesty, Ichindar, ninety-one times Emperor, Light of Heaven, and ruler of all the nations of Tsuranuanni, sends greetings to his brother monarch, His most Royal Highness, Prince Lyam, rule of the lands known as the Kingdom. Will the Prince accept his invitation to join with him at the center of the valley?'"

Lyam said, "Tell him that I return his greetings, and will be pleased to meet with him at the appointed place." Pug translated, with the appropriate Tsurani formality, and the herald bowed low and returned to his own lines.

They could see the imperial litter being carried forward. Lyam signaled that his escort should accompany him, and they rode out to meet the Emperor in the center of the valley floor. Pug, Kulgan, and Laurie rode with the honor escort; Meecham waited with the soldiers.

The Kingdom horsemen reached the designated place first and waited while the imperial retinue approached. The litter was borne on the backs of twenty slaves, chosen for their uniformity in height and appearance. Their thick muscles bunched under the strain of carrying the heavy, gold-encrusted litter. Gauzy white curtains hung from gold-inlaid wooden supports, decorated with gems of great value and beauty. The rare metal and gems caught the sun's rays and glittered brightly.

Behind the litter marched representatives of the most powerful families in the Empire, clan Warchiefs. There were five of them, one for each family eligible to elect a new Warlord.

The litter was lowered, and Ichindar, Emperor of the

nations of Tsuranuanni, stepped out. He was dressed in golden armor, its value immeasurable by Tsurani standards. Upon his head was a crested helm covered in the same metal. He walked over to Lyam, who had dismounted to meet him. Pug, who was to translate, dismounted and walked to stand to one side of the two rulers. The Emperor nodded curtly to him.

Lyam and Ichindar studied one another, and both seemed surprised at the other's youthfulness. Ichindar was only three years older than the new Heir.

Lyam began by welcoming the Emperor with friendship and the hope of peace. Ichindar responded in kind. Then the Light of Heaven stepped forward and extended his right hand. "I understand this is your custom?"

Lyam took the hand of the Emperor of Tsuranuanni. Suddenly the tension broke and cheers went up from both sides of the valley. The two young monarchs were smiling, and the handshake was vigorous and firm.

Lyam said, "May this be the beginning of a lasting peace for our two nations."

Ichindar answered, "Peace is a new thing to Tsuranuanni, but I trust we will learn quickly. My High Council is divided over my actions. I hope the fruits of trade and the prosperity gained by learning from one another will unify attitudes."

"That is my wish also," said Lyam. "To mark the truce, I have ordered a gift prepared for you." He signaled, and a soldier trotted out from the Kingdom lines, leading a beautiful black war-horse behind. A black saddle set with gold was upon its back, and from the saddle horn hung a broadsword, with a jeweled scabbard and hilt.

Ichindar regarded the horse with a little skepticism, but was awed by the workmanship of the sword. He hefted the great blade and said, "You honor me, Prince Lyam."

Ichindar turned to one of his escorts, who ordered a chest carried forward. Two slaves set it before the Emperor. It was carved ngaggi wood, finished to a deep and beautiful shine. Scrollwork surrounded bas-relief carvings of Tsurani animals and plants. Each had been cleverly stained in lighter and darker tones, in nearly lifelike detail. In itself it was a fine gift, but when the lid was thrown back, a pile of the finest cut stones, all larger than a man's thumb, glistened in the sun.

The Emperor said, "I would have difficulty justifying reparation to the High Council, and my position with them is not the best at present, but a gift to mark the occasion they cannot fault. I hope this will repair some of the destruction my nation has caused."

Lyam bowed slightly. "You are generous and I thank you. Will you join me for refreshments?" The Emperor nodded, and Lyam gave a command for a pavilion to be erected. A dozen soldiers galloped forward and dismounted. Several carried poles and rolls of material. In short order a large, open-sided pavilion was erected. Chairs and a table were set up under the covering. Other soldiers brought wine and food and placed them upon the table.

Pug pulled out a large, cushioned chair for the Emperor, as Arutha did for his brother. The two rulers sat, and Ichindar said, "This is quite a bit more comfortable than my throne. I must have a cushion made."

Wine was poured and Lyam and the Emperor toasted each other. Then a toast to peace was offered, and all drank to it.

Ichindar turned to Pug. "Great One, it seems that this meeting will prove more salubrious to those around than our last."

Pug bowed. "I trust so, Your Imperial Majesty. I hope I am forgiven my disruption of the Imperial Games."

The Emperor frowned. "Disruption? It was closer to destruction."

Pug translated for the others while Ichindar smiled ruefully in appreciation. "This Great One has done many innovative things in my Empire. I fear we may not see the end of his handiwork long after his name is forgotten. Still, that is a thing of the past. Let us concern ourselves with the future."

The honored guests from both camps stood around the pavilion as the two monarchs began their discussion of the best way to establish relationships between the two worlds.

Tomas watched the pavilion. Calin and Dolgan waited on either side. Behind them more than two thousand elves and dwarves stood ready. They had entered the valley through the North Pass, moving by the Kingdom forces that were gathered. They had circled around the clearing, gathering in the woods to the west, where they were accorded a clear view of the proceeding.

Tomas said to both his comrades, "I see little to indicate trickery."

A second dwarf, Harthorn of Stone Mountain, walked over to them. "Aye, elfling. All looks peaceful enough, in spite of the sorcerer's warning."

Abruptly there was a heat shimmer across the field, as if their vision swam and flickered, then Tomas and the others could see Tsurani soldiers drawing weapons.

Tomas turned to those behind and said, "Be ready!"

A soldier rode up to the pavilion. The Tsurani lords looked at him with distrust, for so far the only soldiers who neared the pavilion were those serving refreshments.

"Your Highness!" he shouted. "Something strange is occurring."

"What?" said Lyam, disturbed at the man's excitement.

"From our position we can see figures moving through the woods to the west."

Lyam rose and saw figures near the edge of the trees. After a moment, while Pug translated the exchange for the Emperor, Lyam said, "That would be the dwarves and elves." He turned to Ichindar. "I sent word to the Elf Queen and the dwarven Warleaders of the peace. They must be now approaching."

The Emperor came over to Lyam and studied the woods. "Why are they remaining in the trees? Why do they stay hidden?"

Lyam turned to the horseman. "Ride and bid those in the trees to join us."

The guard obeyed. When he was halfway to the woods, a shout went up from the trees and green-clad elves and armored dwarves came running forward. Battle chants and cries filled the air. Ichindar looked at the onrushing figures in confusion. Several of his companions drew weapons. A soldier from the Tsurani lines dashed to the pavilion and cried, "Majesty, we are undone. It is a trap!"

Every Tsurani backed away, swords drawn. Ichindar shouted, "Is this how you treat for peace? Mouthing pledges while you plot treachery?"

Lyam didn't understand the words, but the tone made the meaning clear. He gripped Pug's arm and said, "Tell him I know nothing of this!"

Pug tried to raise his voice over the commotion in the pavilion, but the Tsurani nobles were backing away, surrounding the Light of Heaven, while soldiers were rushing forward from the Tsurani lines to join in protecting Ichindar.

Lyam shouted, "Back! Back to our own lines!" as the Tsurani soldiers approached. The Midkemians quickly mounted.

Pug heard Ichindar's voice carrying over the noise: "Treacherous one, you show your true nature. Never will Tsuranuanni deal with those without honor. We will grind your Kingdom into dust!"

Sounds of fighting erupted as the elves and dwarves clashed with the Tsurani soldiers. Lyam and the others raced back to their own soldiers, who sat waiting to join the fight. As Lyam reined up, Lord Brucal said, "Shall we advance, Highness?"

Lyam shook his head. "I will not be a party to treachery."

He regarded the scene before him. The elves and dwarves were pushing the Tsurani back toward the rift machine. The Emperor and his guards were circling, avoiding the fighting, keeping the thousand honor guards between the attackers and themselves. Runners could be seen disappearing into the rift.

A moment later, Tsurani soldiers erupted from the rift. They rushed forward to engage the attackers. The collapsing Tsurani line held, then started to push the elves and dwarves back.

Arutha moved his horse next to Lyam's. "Lyam! We must attack. Soon the elves will be overwhelmed. There are ten thousand more Tsurani on the other side of that rift, only a step away. If you ever hope to end this bloody war, we must capture and hold that machine."

Pug forced his own horse to the other side of Lyam's mount. "Lyam!" he shouted. "You must do as Arutha says."

Doubt still held the young Heir. Pug raised his voice even louder. "Understand this: for nine years you've faced only a part of the might within the Empire, only those soldiers belonging to the clans of the War Party. Until now you had many hidden allies, blocking a major effort against the Kingdom. But now this betrayal has inflamed the one man who can command unquestioned obedience from all the clans of the Empire. Ichindar can order every clan of Tsuranuanni to marshal!

"You've never faced more than thirty thousand warriors along all fronts. By tomorrow those thirty thousand can be back in this valley. In a week, double again that number. Lyam, you have no idea how vast his powers are. Within a year he can send a million men and a thousand magicians against us! You must act!"

Lyam sat stiffly, the bitterness of the moment clearly showing in his expression. "Can you aid us?"

"I may, should you open a path for me to reach the machine, but I don't know if I have the ability to shut off the rift. Other powers I have, but even if I overcame my conditioning and could oppose the Empire and I killed every man on this field, it would avail little, for a greater host would still be but a step away."

Lyam gave a curt nod. Slowly he faced Arutha. "Send gallopers to the North and South passes. Call all the Armies of the Kingdom to arms." Arutha wheeled and shouted the order, and riders sped away toward both passes.

Lyam looked back toward Pug. "If you can help, do so, but not until the way is safe. You are the only master of your arts upon this world." Indicating Laurie, Meecham, and Kulgan, he said, "Keep them from the fighting as well, for they have no part in it. Stay back, and should we fail, use your arts to go to Krondor. Carline and Anita must needs be taken to the east, to their grand-uncle Caldric, for the West will surely be Tsurani." He drew his sword and gave the order to advance.

The thousand horsemen lumbered forward, a moving wall of steel gaining momentum as officers shouted orders, keeping the columns orderly. Then Lyam signaled the charge and the lines became ragged as horsemen rushed across the clearing toward the Tsurani. The Tsurani heard the rumbling of cavalry, and many fell back from the elves and dwarves to form a shield wall. Pug, Laurie, Meecham, and Kulgan watched while the Kingdom horsemen collided with it. Horses and men screamed as long spears bent and broke. The shield wall wavered as men died, but others leaped forward to take their places and the Kingdom host was turned back. Lyam re-formed his troops and charged again, this time breaking through the shields.

Pug could see the right side of the Tsurani forces rolled back before the horsemen, but the Emperor himself rallied the balance of his soldiers and the center of the line held. Even at this distance, Pug could see the Tsurani nobles entreating the Emperor to flee.

The Emperor stood with sword drawn, shouting orders. He refused to leave the field. He was forming his men into a tight circle protecting the rift machine, so others could return to this valley from Kelewan. He looked and saw that soldiers were now rushing forth from the rift in greater numbers. Soon there would be enough of them to destroy the King's small force.

A faint trembling could be felt beneath his feet, then one of the Tsurani lords pointed behind the Emperor. Ichindar saw hundreds of horsemen erupting from the trees to the north. The northern cavalry units were the first to answer Lyam's call. The Emperor directed newly arriving soldiers to the north line to meet the new threat.

A shout from the left caused him to turn. A tall warrior, clad in white and gold, was cutting a swath through the Tsurani guards, heading straight for the Light of Heaven. All the Tsurani lords rushed to cut him off. A clan Force Leader stood nearby. He raced to the Emperor and shouted, "Your Majesty, you must leave. We can hold only a short while. If you are lost, the Empire is without a heart, and the gods will turn their faces from us."

The Emperor tried to push past him, as the gold and white giant cut down another Tsurani lord. The officer said, "May heaven understand," and struck Ichindar across the back of the head with the flat of his sword. The Emperor crumpled to the ground, and the Force Leader shouted for soldiers to carry him through the rift. "The Emperor is overcome! Take him to safety!" Without question the soldiers picked up the supreme ruler and conveyed him to the machine.

A Strike Leader rushed to the Force Leader's side, shouting, "Sir, all our lords have been killed!" The Force Leader saw that the tall warrior was being forced back by the sheer number of Tsurani soldiers intercepting him, but not until after he had butchered every senior Warchief who had accompanied the Emperor. A quick glance informed the Force Leader the Emperor was near safety, as the guards carrying Ichindar disappeared from view at the far side of the rift. More soldiers came streaming through from the near side of the rift. Seeing no more time to waste, the Force Leader said, "I will act as Force Commander! You are acting Subcommander. More men to the north!" The man rushed off to place more men along the north line as the cavalry from the North Pass bore down in a mad gallop.

The attackers from the north hit the Tsurani position with a thunderous crash. The hastily erected shield wall wavered, but finally held. The Force Commander looked about and prayed they could hold until sufficient reinforcements arrived.

Pug and his three companions could see the northern elements of the Kingdom army hit the shield wall. Spears shattered and horses fell, while men were trampled screaming underfoot. The wall still held and the Kingdom forces withdrew to re-form for another charge. Lyam's command was being pushed back and he ordered a withdrawal, so that he could coordinate his attack with the one from the north. The elves and dwarves under Tomas were among the Tsurani, to the west, and were causing them the most difficulty, though they also were being slowly repulsed.

As the horsemen pulled back, the Tsurani's attention was turned to the elves and dwarves. Those behind the north and south shield positions left their posts to lend support to their comrades on the west flank.

Seeing this, Meecham observed, "If the elves don't withdraw, the Tsurani will overwhelm them." As if he had been heard, the four observers could see the western confrontation broken off. Elves and dwarves retreated under cover of elven bowmen.

Kulgan said to Pug, "This respite serves to strengthen the Tsurani." They could see the flood of Tsurani soldiers coming through the rift. "If Lyam does not reach the machine after the next charge, the Tsurani will gain in strength as we weaken."

Pug said, "He can bottle them up only if he can station bowmen at the entrance to the rift. A steady stream of bowfire through it should keep them back long enough to erect some sort of barrier. Then we might be able to render it inoperative."

Laurie said, "Can't it be destroyed? The other way is fraught with risk."

Pug sat quietly for a moment. "I don't know if my powers are sufficient to destroy the rift. But I think it is time to try."

As he started to spur his horse, a voice behind rang out: "No!"

They all turned and saw a brown-clad figure standing, staff in hand, where no one had been a moment earlier. "Even your powers are not equal to the task, Great One."

"Macros!" Kulgan exclaimed.

Macros smiled a bitter smile. "As I foretold, I am here when the need is greatest, the hour most grave."

Pug said, "What is to be done?"

"I will close the rift, but I have need of your aid." He returned his attention to Kulgan. "I see you still have the staff I gave you. Good. Dismount."

Pug and Kulgan got down from their mounts. Pug had forgotten that Kulgan's ever-present staff had been the one Macros had given him.

Macros went over to stand before Kulgan. "Plant the end of the staff firmly in the ground." He turned and handed the staff he carried to Pug. "This staff is twin to that one. Hold it tightly and never for an instant release your hold, if you have any hope of surviving our task." He regarded the conflict a short distance away. "It is almost the appointed hour, but not quite. Listen carefully, for time grows short." He looked at Pug, then Kulgan. "When this is all over, if the rift is destroyed, then return to my island.

There you will find explanations for everything that has occurred, though perhaps not to your full satisfaction." Again there was a bitter smile. "Kulgan, if you have any hope of seeing your former pupil again, hold to that staff with all the strength you possess. Keep Pug in your mind, and never let the staff break contact with Midkemian soil. Is that understood?"

Kulgan said, "But what of yourself?"

Macros's tone was harsh. "My safety is my own concern. Trouble not yourself about me. My place in this drama was as foreordained as your own. Now watch."

They returned their attention to the battle. The northern elements of the Kingdom army charged and Lyam and Tomas gave orders for their own units to join in the attack. The horsemen hit the shield walls again, and the Tsurani lines broke. For a moment the Kingdom cavalry was in command of the field, and the Tsurani collapsed inward. Then, as the advantage of the charge was offset by the milling swarm of foot soldiers who cut horses out from under riders, or conspired to pull horsemen to the ground, the balance returned. A sea of battling figures could be seen around the rift machine. There was no organization, and little discipline. Men fought to survive, not for any gain in position. The sounds of metal clashing against hardened wood and hides rang through the valley. Everywhere the onlookers turned their attention, blood flowed and the sound of death was terrible.

Macros looked at Pug and said, "Now is the time. Walk with me."

Pug walked behind the brown-robed sorcerer. He held tightly to Macros's staff, for he believed the sorcerer's warning that it was his only hope of surviving what lay before them. They walked through the battle, as if some agent was protecting them. Several times a soldier turned to strike, only to be intercepted by one from the other side. Horses would be ready to trample them only to wheel away at the last instant. It was as if a path opened before them and closed behind.

They approached what was left of the Tsurani line. A shield holder fell to a horseman's lance. They stepped over the fallen body and entered the small, relatively calm circle around the rift. Soldiers were still pouring forth from the rift and the circle was widening. Macros and Pug mounted the platform to the far side of the rift, while soldiers rushed out of the near side. The soldiers seemed oblivious of the two workers of magic.

Macros stepped into the void of the rift. Pug entered behind. Instead of the expected emergence into Kelewan, they hung in a colorless place. There was little sensation of direction. The place was without light, but not dark. It was various shades of grey, blacks and whites absent. Pug found himself alone, with only the sound of his heart beating in his ear to reassure himself that existence had not ceased. Softly he said, "Macros?"

Macros's voice came to him: "Here, Pug."

"I cannot see you."

A chuckle was heard. "No, for there is no light. What you see is a faint illusion granted by my arts so you might have some point of reference here. Without ample preparation, even your vaunted powers would avail you little in keeping your sanity, Pug. Simply accept that the human mind is poorly equipped to deal with this place."

"What is this place?"

"This is the place between. Here the gods struggled during the Chaos Wars, and here we shall do our work."

"Men are dying, Macros. We should hurry."

"Here there is no time, Pug. Relative to those who battle, we are frozen in an instant. We could grow old and die and not a full second would pass upon the battlefield.

"But we must still be quickly about our task. Even I could not do this without spending a bit of energy to keep us alive, energy we'll need to finish this business. We dare not tarry long, but there are a few things I would say to you. I have waited a long while for you to fulfill your promise. I could not close the rift without your aid."

Pug spoke, though his senses rebelled at the grey landscape on all sides and the disembodied voice that seemed a short distance before him. "It was you who turned the rift aside, when the Stranger came and the Enemy sought to reclaim the nations of Tsuranuanni. Surely that took awesome power."

He could hear the sorcerer chuckle. "You remember that detail? Well, I was younger then." As if he knew it was an unsatisfactory answer, Macros added, "Then the rift was a wild thing, created by the wills of those who stood atop the towers of the Assembly. I but turned it to another place, balking the Enemy's design, and that at great risk. Now this rift is a controlled thing, firmly anchored in Kelewan, managed by a machine. That which controls it, many intricate spells, keeping it in harmony with Midkemia, keeps me from manipulating it. All I may do is end it, and for that I need help.

"But before we end this particular drama, I would say this to you: you will understand most things after you reach my island. But one thing above all I ask of you to bear in mind as you hear my message. Please remember I did what I did because it was my fate. I would have you think of me kindly."

While he could not see the sorcerer, Pug felt his presence close by. He started to speak, but was interrupted by Macros's voice. "When I am done, use whatever shred of energy you have left to will yourself to Kulgan. The staff will aid you, but you must bend all your efforts to that task. If you fail, you will perish."

It was Macros's second warning and Pug felt dread for the first time in years. "What of yourself?"

"Take care of yourself, Pug. I have other concerns."

There came a sensation of change, as if the fabric of nothingness around them was subtly altering. Macros said, "At my command, you must unleash the full fury of your power. All that you did at the Imperial Games was but a shadow of what you must do now."

"You know of that?"

Again there was a chuckle. "I was there, though my seat was poor compared to your own. I must admit it was quite impressive. Even I would have been hard pressed to provide as spectacular a show. Now, there is no more time. Await my command, and let your power flow toward me."

Pug said nothing. He could feel the sorcerer's presence before him, as if it were being defined for him by Macros. Again he felt the sensation of twisting change around him. Suddenly there was a blinding light, then darkness. An instant later, all around him erupted in mad displays of energy, much like those he witnessed in the rift of the Golden Bridge. On every side, blinding colors exploded, primal forces he did not recognize.

"Now, Pug!" came Macros's cry.

Pug bent his will to the task. He reached down into the deepest recesses of his being. From there he brought forth all he could of the magic power he had gained from two worlds. Forces sufficient to destroy mountains, move rivers from their courses, and level cities to rubble, all these he focused. Then, like casting away something painful to hold, he directed all this energy toward where he sensed the sorcerer to be. There came an unimaginable, insane explosion of those forces, and the primal matter of time and space screamed in protest at its presence. Pug could feel it writhe and twist around him, as if the fundamental universe were trying to cast the invaders out. Then there came a sudden release, and they were expelled.

Pug found himself floating in total blackness. He drifted, numb and without coherent thought. His mind was unable to accept what he had sensed and he was close to losing consciousness. He felt his fingers go lax, and the staff began to slip from his hand. He clutched spasmodically at it from blind instinct. He then felt a faint tugging. His mind resisted the cool blackness that was trying to overtake him, and he tried to remember something. It was growing cold around him, and he could feel his lungs burning for lack of air. He tried to remember something once more, but it would not come to him. Then he felt the tug again, and a faint but familiar voice seemed to sound close by.

"Kulgan?" he said, weakly, and let the darkness take him.

The Tsurani Force Commander was alive. He wondered at that miracle as he saw those around him who lay dead before the rift machine. The explosion a minute before had killed hundreds, and others lay dazed a little way beyond.

He rose and took stock of what was occurring. The terrible destruction of the rift had not served to aid the Kingdom forces, either. Riders frantically tried to control near-hysterical horses, and other mounts could be seen running madly away, their riders thrown from their backs. All about, confusion reigned. But those at the edge of the conflict were less dazed than the others, and the fighting was resuming.

There was little hope, now that Kelewan was cut off to them, either of aid or of a safe return. Still, they numbered only slightly less than the enemy, and there was a chance that the field could yet be theirs. There might be time to worry about the rift later.

Abruptly the sounds of fighting stopped as the Kingdom forces withdrew. The Force Commander looked about and, still seeing no officer of greater rank, started shouting orders to ready the shield wall for another assault.

The Kingdom forces were slowly regrouping. They did not attack, but took up a position opposite the Tsurani. The Force Commander waited, while his soldiers made ready the lines. On all sides, Kingdom horsemen stood ready, but still they did not come.

Slowly the tension grew. The Force Commander ordered a platform raised. Four Tsurani grabbed a shield, he stood upon it, and they lifted him up. His eyes widened. "They have reinforcements." Far to the south, he could see the advancing columns of the South Pass Kingdom forces. They had been farther removed from the parley site and were only now reaching the battlefield.

A shout from the opposite direction caused him to look to the north: lines of the Kingdom infantry were advancing from the trees. Again he turned his attention southward and strained his eyes. In the distant haze he could see the signs of a large force of infantry following behind the cavalry. The officer ordered the shield lowered and his Subcommander said, "What is it?"

"Their entire army is in the field." He swallowed hard, the usual Tsurani impassivity broken. "Mother of gods! There must be thirty thousand of them."

"Then we shall give a battle worthy of a ballad before we die," said the Subcommander.

The Force Commander looked about him. On all sides stood bleeding, wounded, and dazed soldiers. Of the Kingdom armies arrayed against them, only a third had fought. Fully twenty thousand rested soldiers approached four thousand Tsurani, half of them unable to fight at their normal efficiency.

The Force Commander shook his head. "There will be

no fighting. We are cut off from home, perhaps for all time. There is no purpose."

He stepped past his startled Subcommander and walked beyond the shield wall. Raising both hands above his head in the sign of parley, he walked toward Lyam, slowly, dreading the moment when he would be the first Tsurani officer in living memory to surrender his forces. It took only a matter of minutes to reach the Prince. He removed his helm and knelt.

He looked up at the tall, golden-haired Prince of the Kingdom and said, "Lord Lyam. Into your care I give my men. Will you accept surrender?"

Lyam nodded. "Yes, Kasumi. I will accept surrender."

Darkness. Then a gathering greyness. Pug forced his heavy eyelids open. Above him was the familiar face of Kulgan.

The face of his old teacher split into a wide smile. "It is good to see you are with us again. We did not know if you were really alive. Your body was so cold to the touch. Can you sit up?"

Pug took the offered arm, and found that Meecham knelt next to him, aiding him to sit up. He could feel the cold leave his limbs as the bright sunlight warmed his body. He sat still for a moment, then said, "I think I will live." As he said it, he could feel strength returning to him. After a moment he felt able to stand and did so.

Around him he could see the assembled armies of the Kingdom. "What has happened?"

Laurie said, "The rift is destroyed, and the Tsurani who remain have surrendered. The war is over."

Pug felt too weak for emotion. He looked at the faces of those around him and could see deep relief in their eyes. Suddenly Kulgan engulfed him in a hug. "You risked your life to end this madness. It is your victory as much as any man's."

Pug stood quietly, then stepped away from his former master. "It is Macros who ended the war. Did he return?"

"No. Only you, and as soon as you were here, both of the staffs disappeared. There is no sign of him."

Pug shook his head, clearing away the fogginess. "What now?"

Meecham looked over his shoulder. "It might be wise if you joined Lyam. There seems to be some commotion taking place."

Laurie and Kulgan assisted Pug along, for he was still weak from his ordeal within the rift. They walked to where Lyam, Arutha, Kasumi, and the assembled Kingdom nobles stood waiting. Across the field they could see the elves and dwarves approaching, with the northern Kingdom forces behind.

Pug was surprised to see the older son of the Shinzawai present, for he had thought him back on Kelewan. He looked a figure of dejection, standing without weapon or helm, and with head downcast, so he didn't see Pug and the others arrive.

Pug turned his attention to the elves and dwarves. Four figures walked at their head. Two he recognized, Dolgan and Calin. There was another dwarf with them who was unknown to the magician. As the four reached a place before the Prince, Pug realized that the tall warrior in white and gold was his boyhood friend. He stood speechless, amazed at the change in Tomas, for his old friend was now a towering figure who resembled an elf as much as a human.

Lyam was too exhausted for outrage. He looked at the Warleader of Elvandar and said, quietly, "What cause did you have to attack, Tomas?"

The Prince Consort of the elves said, "The Tsurani drew weapons, Lyam. They were ready to attack the pavilion. Could you not see?"

In spite of his fatigue, Lyam's voice rose. "I only saw your host attack a conference of peace. I saw nothing in the Tsurani camp that was untoward."

Kasumi raised his head. "Your Highness, on my word, we drew weapons only when we were set upon by those." He pointed at Tomas's forces.

Lyam turned his attention back to Tomas. "Did I not send word that there was to be a truce, and a peace?"

"Aye," answered Dolgan, "I was there when the sorcerer brought word."

"Sorcerer?" said Lyam. He turned and shouted, "Laurie! I would have words with you."

Laurie stepped forward and said, "Highness?"

"Did you carry word to the Elf Queen as I bid?"

"On my honor. I spoke with the Elf Queen herself."

Tomas looked Lyam in the eye, head tilted back, an expression of defiance upon his face. "And I swear that I have never seen that man before this moment. Word of the planned Tsurani treachery was carried to us by Macros."

Kulgan and Pug both came forward. "Your Highness," said Kulgan, "if the sorcerer's hand is in this—and it has been in everything else, it seems—then it may be best to unravel this mystery at leisure."

Lyam still fumed, but Arutha said, "Let it lie. We can sort out this mess back at the camp."

Lyam gave a curt nod. "We return to camp." The Heir turned to Brucal and said, "Form a proper escort for the prisoners and bring them along." He then looked at Tomas. "You I would also have in my tent when we return. There is much we must explain." Tomas agreed, though he did not look happy at the prospect. Lyam shouted, "We return to camp at once. Give the order."

Kingdom officers rode toward their companies and the order was given. Tomas turned away and found a stranger standing next to him. He looked at the smiling face, then Dolgan said, "Are you blind, boy? Can't you recognize your own boyhood companion?"

Tomas looked at Pug as the exhausted magician moved close. "Pug?" he said softly. Then he reached out and embraced his once lost foster brother. "Pug!"

They stood together quietly, amid the clamor of armies on the move, both with tears upon their faces. Kulgan placed his hands upon both men's shoulders. "Come, we must return. There is much to speak of, and thank the gods, there is now ample time to do so."

The camp was in full celebration. After more than nine years, the soldiers of the Kingdom knew that they would not have to risk death or injury tomorrow. Songs rang out from around campfires, and laughter came from all quarters. It mattered little to most that others lay wounded in tents, tended by the priests, and that some would not live to see the first day of peace, or taste the fruits of victory. All the celebrants knew was that they were among the living, and they reveled in the fact. Later there would be time for mourning lost comrades. Now they drank in life.

Within Lyam's tent, things were more subdued. Kulgan had given a great deal of thought to the day's occurrences as they had ridden back. By the time they had reached the tent, the magician from Crydee had pieced together a rough picture of what had occurred. He had presented his opinion to those assembled there, and was now finishing.

"It would seem, then," said Kulgan, "that Macros intended for the rift to be closed. Everything points to the terrible duplicity as having been used for that purpose."

Lyam sat with Arutha and Tully by his side. "I still can't understand what would possess him to undertake such grave measures. Today's conflict cost over two thousand lives."

Pug spoke up. "I suspect we may find the answer to that and other questions when we reach his island. Until then I don't think we can begin to guess."

Lyam sighed. He said to Tomas, "At least I am convinced that you acted in good faith. I am pleased. It would have been a hard thing to imagine you responsible for all the carnage today."

Tomas held a winecup, from which he sipped. "I also am pleased that we have no cause for contention. But I feel ill used in this matter."

"As were we all," echoed Harthorn and Dolgan.

Calin said, "It is likely that we have all played a part in some scheme of the Black One's. Perhaps it is as Pug has said, and we shall learn the truth at Sorcerer's Isle, but I for one resent this bloody business."

Lyam looked to where Kasumi sat stiffly, eyes forward, seemingly oblivious to what was being said around him. "Kasumi," Lyam said, "what am I to do with you and your men?"

Kasumi's eyes came into focus at mention of his name. He said, "Your Highness, I know something of your ways, for Laurie has taught me much. But I am still Tsurani. In our land the officers would be put to death, and the men enslaved. I may not advise you in this matter. I do not know what is the usual method of dealing with war prisoners in your world."

His tone was flat, without emotion. Lyam was about to say something, but a signal from Pug silenced him. There was something the magician wanted to say. "Kasumi?"

"Yes, Great One?" Tomas looked surprised at the honorific, but said nothing. There had been time only for the most superficial exchange of histories between the two boyhood friends as they had returned to the camp.

"What would you have done if you had not surrendered to the Prince's custody?"

"We would have fought to the death, Great One."

Pug nodded. "I understand. Then you are responsible for preserving the lives of nearly four thousand of your men? And thousands more Kingdom soldiers?"

Kasumi's expression softened, revealing his shame. "I have been among your people, Great One. I may have forgotten my Tsurani training. I have brought dishonor upon my house. When the Prince has disposed of my men, I will ask permission to take my own life, though it may be too much of an honor for him to grant."

Brucal and others looked shocked at this. Lyam showed no expression, but simply said, "You have earned no dishonor. You would have aided no cause in dying. There ceased to be one when the rift was destroyed."

Kasumi said, "It is our way."

Lyam said, "No longer. This is now your homeland, for you have no other. What Kulgan and Pug have said about rifts makes it unlikely you shall ever return to Tsuranuanni. Here you will remain, and it is my intention to see that prospect turned to good advantage for us all."

A faint flicker of hope entered Kasumi's eyes. The Heir turned toward Lord Brucal and said, "My lord Duke of Yabon. How do you judge the Tsurani soldiers?"

The old Duke smiled. "Among the finest I have ever beheld." Kasumi showed a little pride at the remark. "They match the Dark Brotherhood for ferocity, and are of a nobler nature; they are as disciplined as Keshian dog soldiers and have the stamina of Natalese Rangers. On the whole they are without question superior soldiers."

"Would an army of such provide additional security for our troubled northern borders?"

Brucal smiled. "The LaMutian garrison was among the

hardest hit during the war. They would be a valuable addition there."

The Earl of LaMut echoed his Duke's comment. Lyam turned to Kasumi. "Would you still take your life if your men could remain freemen and soldiers?"

The Shinzawai son said, "How is that possible, Your Highness?"

"If you and your men will swear loyalty to the crown, I will place you under the command of the Earl of LaMut. You will be both freemen and citizens and will be given the charge to defend our northern border against the enemies of humanity who abide in the Northlands."

Kasumi sat silently, unsure of what to say. Laurie stepped over to Kasumi and said, "There is no dishonor."

Kasumi's face broke into an expression of open relief. "I accept, as I am sure my men will." He paused, then added, "We came as an honor guard for the Emperor. From what I have heard said here, we have been used by this sorcerer as much as anyone. I would not have any more blood spilled on his account. I thank Your Highness."

Lord Vandros said, "I think a Knight-Captaincy would be proper for the leader of nearly four thousand. Do you agree, my lord Duke?" Brucal nodded in agreement, and Vandros said, "Come, Captain, we should speak with your new command."

Kasumi rose, bowed to Lyam, and left with the Earl of LaMut. Arutha touched his brother on the shoulder. Lyam turned his head, and the Prince said, "Enough of matters of state. It is time to celebrate the ending of the war."

Lyam smiled. "True." He turned to Pug. "Magician, run and fetch your lovely wife and fine son. I would have things that smack of home and family about."

Tomas looked at Pug. "Wife? Son? What is this?"

Pug laughed. "There is much to talk about. We can catch up with each other after I bring my family."

He made his way to his own tent, where Katala was telling William a story. They both jumped up and ran to him, for they had not seen him since his return. He had sent a soldier with the news that he was well but busy with the Prince.

"Katala, Lyam would like you to join us for dinner."

William tugged at his father's robe. "I want to come too, Papa."

Pug picked up his son. "You too, William."

The celebration within the tent was of a quieter sort than the one taking place outside. Still, they had been entertained by Laurie's ballads and had enjoyed the exhilaration of knowing that peace had finally come. The food was the same camp fare as before, but somehow it tasted better. A great deal of wine had also added to the festive mood.

Lyam sat with a cup of wine in his hand. Around the tent the others were engaged in quiet conversation. The Heir was a little drunk, and none grudged him that relief, for he had endured much in the last month. Kulgan, Tully, and Arutha, who knew him best, understood that Lyam was thinking of his father, who but for a Tsurani arrow would now be sitting here with them. With the responsibility of first the war, then the succession thrust upon him, Lyam had not found time for mourning as his brother had. Now he was fully feeling the loss.

Tully stood. In a loud voice he said, "I am tired, Your Highness. Have I your leave to withdraw?"

Lyam smiled at his old teacher. "Of course. Good night, Tully."

The others in the tent quickly followed suit and took leave of the Heir. Outside the pavilion guests bade each other good night. Laurie, Kulgan, Meecham, and the dwarves also left, leaving Pug and his family standing with Calin and Tomas.

The childhood friends had spent the evening exchanging histories of the last nine years. Each was equally amazed at the other's story. Pug had expressed interest in the Dragon Lords' magic, as had Kulgan. They expressed an interest in visiting the Dragon's Hall someday. Dolgan allowed he would be willing to guide them should they wish to make the journey.

Now the reawakened friendship glowed within the two young men, though they understood it was not what it had once been, for there had been many and great changes in both. As much as by the dragon armor and the black

robe, this point was dramatized by the presence of William
and Katala.

Katala had found the dwarves and elves fascinating—
William had found everything fascinating, especially the
dwarves, and now lay asleep in his mother's arms. Of
Tomas she didn't know what to make. He resembled Calin
in many ways, but still looked a great deal like the other
men in camp.

Tomas regarded the sleeping boy. "He has his mother's
looks, but there is enough devil in him to put me in mind of
another boy I knew."

Pug smiled at that. "His life will be far calmer, I hope."

Arutha left his brother's tent and came to join them.
He stood beside the two boys who had ridden with him to
the mines of Mac Mordain Cadal so many years ago. "I
should probably not say this, but years ago—when you
first came to visit my father, Calin—two boys were overheard in conversation while they tussled in a hay wagon."

Tomas and Pug both looked at the Prince uncom-
prehendingly. "You don't remember, do you?" Arutha
asked. "A blond, thin-ribbed lad was sitting atop a shorter
boy promising he would someday be a great warrior who
would be welcomed in Elvandar."

Pug and Tomas both laughed at that. "I remember,"
said Pug.

"And the other promised to become the greatest magician in the Kingdom."

Katala said, "Perhaps William will also grow up to
realize his dream."

Arutha smiled with a wicked light in his eyes. "Then
watch him closely. We had a long chat before he went to
sleep and he told me he wanted to grow up to be a dwarf."
All of them laughed, except Katala, who looked at her son
with open worry on her face, but then she, too, joined in
the merriment.

Arutha and Calin bade the others good night, and
Tomas said, "I, too, will be to bed."

Pug said, "Will you come to Rillanon with us?"

"No, I may not. I would be with my lady. But when the
child is born, you must guest with us, for there will be a
great celebration." They promised they would come.
Tomas said, "We are for home in the morning. The

dwarves will return to their villages, for there is much work to be done there. They have been overlong from their families. And with the return of Tholin's hammer, there is talk of a moot, to name Dolgan King in the West." Lowering his voice, he added, "Though my old friend will most likely use that hammer on the first dwarf to openly suggest it in his presence." Placing his hand upon Pug's shoulder, he said, "It is well we both came through this; even in the depths of my strange madness, I never forgot about you."

Pug said, "I never forgot you either, Tomas."

"When you unravel this mystery on Sorcerer's Isle, I trust you will send word?"

Pug said he would. They embraced, saying good-bye, and Tomas walked away, but stopped and looked back, a boyish glint in his eyes. "Still, I would love to be there when you meet Carline again with a wife and son in tow."

Pug flushed, for he viewed that coming reunion with mixed feelings. He waved to Tomas as he walked from sight, then found Katala regarding him with a determined look upon her face. In even, measured tones she said, "Who is Carline?"

Lyam looked up as Arutha entered the command tent. The younger brother said, "I thought you would have retired by now. You're exhausted."

"I wanted some time to think, Arutha. I have had little time alone and wanted to put things in order." His voice was tired and troubled.

Arutha sat next to his brother. "What sort of things?"

"This war, Father, you, I"—he thought of Martin—"other things. . . . Arutha, I don't know if I can be King."

Arutha raised his eyebrows a little. "It is not as if you had a choice, Lyam. You will be King, so make the best of it."

"I could refuse the crown in favor of my brother," said Lyam slowly, "as Erland renounced it in favor of Rodric."

"And what a fine kettle of soup that became. Should you want a civil war, that would be one way to get it. The Kingdom cannot afford a debate in the Congress of Lords. There are still too many wounds to be healed between East and West. And du Bas-Tyra is still at large."

Lyam sighed. "You would make a better King, Arutha."

Arutha laughed. "Me? I am little pleased at the prospect of being Prince of Krondor. Look, Lyam, when we were boys I envied you the affection you gained so quickly. People always preferred you to me. As I grew older, I understood that it wasn't that I was disliked; it was simply there was something about you that brings out trust and love in people. That is a good quality for a King to possess. I never envied the fact you would follow Father as Duke, nor do I now envy your crown. I once thought I might take some time after the war to travel, but now that will not be possible, for I must rule Krondor. So do not wish this additional burden of the entire Kingdom upon me. I would not take it."

"Still, you would make a better King." Lyam caught Arutha's gaze and held it.

Arutha paused, frowned, then fixed his brother with a skeptical look. "Perhaps, but you are to be King, and I expect you will remain King for quite some time." He stretched as he rose. "I am for bed. It has been a long and hard day." Nearing the entrance to the tent, he said, "Ease your doubts, Lyam. You will be a good ruler. With Caldric to advise you, and the others, Kulgan, Tully, and Pug, you will lead us through this time of rebuilding."

Lyam said, "Arutha, before you go . . ." Arutha waited, as Lyam made a decision. "I wish you to go with Kulgan and Pug to Sorcerer's Isle. You've been there once before, and . . . I'd like your judgment on what is found there." Arutha was displeased and started to object. Lyam cut him off. "I know you wish to go to Krondor, but it will only take a few days. There will be twelve days between the time we reach Rillanon and the coronation, ample time for you to join us."

Arutha again began to object, then with a wry smile, acceded. "Trust in yourself, Lyam. If I won't take the crown, you're left with it." As he departed the tent he added with a laugh, "There's no other brother to claim it."

Lyam sat alone, absently sipping at his wine. With another long sigh, he said to himself, "There is one other, Arutha, and may the gods help me decide what is right to do."

FIFTEEN

LEGACY

The ship dropped anchor.

The crew secured the sails aloft while the landing party made ready. Meecham watched the preparation of the longboat. The magicians were anxious to reach the castle of Macros, for they had more questions than the others. Arutha was also curious, after resigning himself to the voyage. He found he also had little desire to take part in the long funeral procession that had left from Ylith the day they sailed. He had buried his grief for his father deep inside and would deal with it in his own time. Laurie had stayed with Kasumi to aid the assimilation of the Tsurani soldiers into the LaMutian garrison, and would meet them later in Rillanon.

Lyam and his nobles had shipped for Krondor, escorting the bodies of Borric and Rodric. They would be joined by Anita and Carline, then all would convey the dead in a procession of state to Rillanon, where they would be laid to rest in the tomb of their ancestors. After the traditional period of twelve days' mourning, Lyam would be crowned King. By then all who would attend the coronation would have gathered in Rillanon. Pug and Kulgan's business should be completed in ample time for them to reach the capital.

The boat was readied and Arutha, Pug, and Kulgan joined Meecham. The longboat was lowered, and six guards bent their backs to the oars. The sailors had been greatly relieved that they were not required to accompany the landing party, for in spite of the magicians' reassurances, they had no desire to set foot upon Sorcerer's Isle.

The boat was beached and the passengers stepped out

upon the sand. Arutha looked about. "There seems to have
been no change since we last came."

Kulgan stretched, for the ship's quarters had been
cramped and he enjoyed the sensation of dry land under
his feet again. "I would have been surprised to find it
otherwise. Macros was one to keep his house in order, I
wager."

Arutha turned and said, "You six will stay here. If you
hear our call, come quickly." The Prince started toward the
path up the hill, and the others fell in without comment.
They reached the place where the path forked, and Arutha
said, "We come as guests. I thought it best not to appear
invaders."

Kulgan said nothing, being occupied with observing
the castle they were approaching. The strange blue light
that had been so visible when they had last visited the
island was absent from the window of the high tower. The
castle had the look of a place deserted, without movement
or sound. The drawbridge was down and the portcullis
raised. Meecham observed, "At least we won't have to
storm the place."

When they reached the edge of the drawbridge, they
halted. The castle rose above them, its high walls, and
taller towers, forbidding. It was built of some dark stone,
unfamiliar to them. Around the great arch over the bridge,
strange carvings of alien creatures regarded them with
fixed gazes. Horned and winged beasts sat perched atop
ledges, seemingly frozen in an instant, so cleverly were
they fashioned.

They stepped upon the bridge and crossed a deep
ravine that separated the castle from the rest of the island.
Meecham looked down, seeing the rock walls of the crevice
fall away to the level of the sea, where waves crashed
through the passage between. "It serves better than most
moats I've seen. You'd think twice before trying to cross
this while someone was shooting at you from the walls."

They entered the court and looked about, as if expecting to see someone appear at one of the many doors in the
walls at any moment. Nowhere in sight was there sign of
any living creature, yet the grounds about the central keep
were well tended and in order.

When no one was forthcoming, Pug said, "I imagine

we'll find what we're after in the keep." The others moved with him toward the broad stairs that led to the main doors. As they mounted the steps, the large doors began to swing open, until they could all see a figure standing in the darkness beyond. As the doors finished their movement with a loud thump against the keep walls, the figure stepped forward into the sunlight.

Meecham's sword was in his hand without thinking, for the creature before them bore a strong resemblance to a goblin. After a brief examination, Meecham put up his weapon; the creature had made no threatening gesture, but simply stood waiting for them at the top of the stairs.

It was taller than the average goblin, being nearly Meecham's height. Thick ridges dominated its forehead, and a large nose was the focus of its face, but it was nobler in features than a goblin. Two black, twinkling eyes regarded them as they resumed their climb. As they came up to it, the creature gave a toothy grin. Its head was covered with a thick mat of black hair, and its skin was tinged with the faint green of the goblin tribe, but it lacked the hunched-shouldered posture of a goblin, instead standing erect much like a man. It wore a finely fashioned tunic and trousers, both bright green. Upon its feet were a pair of polished black boots, reaching nearly to its knees.

The creature said, grinning, "Welcome, masters, welcome. I am Gathis, and I have the honor of acting as your host in my master's absence." There was a slight hiss to its speech.

Kulgan said, "Your master is Macros the Black?"

"Of course. It has been ever thus. Please enter."

The four men accompanied Gathis into the large entry hall and stopped to look about. Except for the absence of people and of the usual heraldic banners, this hall looked much like the one in Castle Crydee.

"My master has left explicit instructions for your visit, as much as was possible to anticipate, so I have prepared the castle for your arrival. Would you care for some refreshments? There are food and wine ready."

Kulgan shook his head. He was unsure of what this creature was, but he was not overly comfortable with anything that so resembled a servant of the Dark Brotherhood. "Macros said there would be a message. I would see it at once."

Gathis bowed slightly. "As you will. Please come with me."

He led them along a series of corridors to a flight of stairs that spiraled up into the large tower. They mounted the steps and soon came to a locked door. "My master said you would be able to open this door. Should you fail, you are impostors, and I am to deal with you harshly."

Meecham gripped his sword at hearing this, but Pug placed his hand on the big franklin's arm. "Since the rift is closed, half my power is lost, that which I gained from Kelewan, but this should prove no obstacle."

Pug concentrated upon opening the door. Instead of the usual response of the door swinging open, a change occurred in the door itself. The wood seemed to become fluid, flowing and ebbing as it fashioned its surface into a new form. In a few moments, a face could be seen, formed in the wood. It looked like a bas-relief, with a slight resemblance to Macros. It was very lifelike in detail and appeared to be asleep. Then its eyelids opened and they could see that the eyes were alive, black centers showing against white. Its mouth moved and a voice issued from it, the sound deep and resonant as it spoke in perfect Tsurani. "What is the first duty?"

Without thinking, Pug answered, "To serve the Empire."

The face flowed back into the door, and when there was no trace of it before them, the door swung aside. They entered and found themselves in the study of Macros the Black, a large room occupying the entire top of the tower.

Gathis said, "I take it I have the honor of hosting Masters Kulgan, Pug, and Meecham?" He then studied the fourth member of the party. "And you must be Prince Arutha?" When they nodded, he said, "My master was unsure if Your Highness would attend, though he thought it likely. He was certain the other three gentlemen would be here." He indicated the room with a sweep of his hand. "All that you see is at your disposal. If you will excuse me, I will return with your message and some refreshments."

Gathis left and all four looked at the contents of the room. Except for one bare wall where it was obvious that a bookcase or cupboard had recently been removed, the entire room was surrounded with tall shelves from floor to ceiling, all heavily laden with books and scrolls. Pug and Kulgan were paralyzed by indecision about where to begin their investigation.

Arutha solved the problem by crossing over to a shelf where lay a large parchment bound with a red ribbon. He took it down and laid it upon the round table in the center of the room. A shaft of sunlight from the room's single large window fell across the parchment as he unrolled it.

Kulgan came over to see what he had found. "It is a map of Midkemia!"

Pug and Meecham crossed over to stand behind Kulgan and Arutha. "Such a map!" Prince Arutha exclaimed. "I have never seen its like." His finger stabbed at a spot upon a large landmass in the center. "Look! Here is the Kingdom." Across a small portion of the map were inscribed the words *Kingdom of the Isles*. Below could be seen the larger borders of the Empire of Great Kesh. To the south of the Empire, the states of the Keshian Confederacy were clearly shown.

"To the best of my knowledge," said Kulgan, "no one from the Kingdom has ever ventured to the Confederacy. Our only knowledge of its members is through the Empire. We hardly know the names of these nations, and nothing about them."

Pug said, "We learn much about our world in an instant. Look at how small a part of this continent the Kingdom is." He pointed to the great sweep of the Northlands to the north of the Kingdom, and the far-reaching mass of land below the Confederacy. The entire continent bore the inscription *Triagia*.

Kulgan said, "It appears there is a great deal more to our Midkemia than we had dreamed." He indicated additional landmasses across the sea. These were labeled *Wiñet* and *Novindus*. Upon each, cities and states were delineated. Two large chains of islands were also shown, many with cities marked. Kulgan shook his head. "It would be a brave captain who set his ship upon a course for so far a port. It is small wonder we have never heard of these places."

They were brought out of their study by the sound of Gathis returning to the room. He carried a tray with a decanter and four winecups. "My master bade me say that you are to enjoy the hospitality of his home as long as you desire." He placed the tray on the table and poured wine into the cups. He then removed a scroll from within his tunic and handed it to Kulgan. "He bade me give you this. I will retire while you consider my master's message. Should you need me, simply speak my name and I will return quickly." He bowed slightly and left the room.

Kulgan regarded the scroll. It was sealed with black wax, impressed with the letter *M*. He broke the seal and unrolled the parchment. He started to read to himself, then said, "Let us sit."

Pug rolled up the large map and put it away, then returned to the table where the others were sitting. He pulled out a chair and waited with Meecham and Arutha while Kulgan read. Kulgan shook his head slowly. "Listen," he said, and read aloud:

" 'To the magicians Kulgan and Pug, greetings. I have anticipated some of your questions and have endeavored to answer them as best I can. I fear there are others that must go begging, as much about myself must remain known only to me. I am not what the Tsurani would call a Great One, though I have visited that world, as Pug knows, upon a number of occasions. My magic is peculiar to myself and defies description in your terms of Greater and Lesser Paths. Suffice it to say I am a walker of many paths.

" 'I see myself as a servant of the gods, though that may only be my vanity speaking. Whatever the truth is, I have traveled to many lands and worked for many causes.

" 'Of my early life I will say little. I am not of this world, having been born in a land distant both in space and time. It is not unlike this world, but there are ample reasons to count it strange by your standards.

" 'I am older than I care to remember, old even by the elves' reckoning. For reasons I do not understand, I have lived for ages, though my own people are as mortal as yours. It may be that when I entered into the magic arts, I unwittingly gave this near-immortality to myself, or it may be the gift—or curse—of the gods.

" 'Since becoming a sorcerer, I have been fated to know my own future, as others know their pasts. I have never retreated from what I knew to be before me, though often I wished to. I have served great Kings and simple peasants both. I have lived in the greatest cities and the rudest huts. Often I have understood the meaning of my participation, sometimes not, but always I have followed the foreordained path that was set for me.'"

Kulgan stopped for a moment. "This explains how he knew so much." He resumed his reading.

"'Of all my labors, my role in the rift war was the hardest. Never have I experienced such desire to turn from the path before me. Never have I been responsibile for the loss of so many lives, and I mourn for them more than you can know. But even as you consider my "treachery," consider my situation.

"'I was unable to close the rift without Pug's aid. It was fated for the war to continue while he learned his craft on Kelewan. For the terrible price paid, consider the gain. There now is one upon Midkemia who practices the Greater Art, which was lost in the coming of man during the Chaos Wars. The benefit will be judged only by history, but I think it a valuable one.

"'As to my closing the rift once peace was at hand, I can only say it was vital. The Tsurani Great Ones had forgotten that rifts are subject to the Enemy's detection.'" Kulgan looked up in surprise. "Enemy? Pug, this refers to something I think you need to explain."

Pug told them quickly of what he knew of the legendary Enemy. Arutha said, "Can such a terrible being really exist?" His expression betrayed disbelief.

Pug said, "That it once existed, there is no doubt, and for a being of such power still to endure is not beyond imagining. But of all conceivable reasons for Macros's actions, this is the last I would have thought possible. No one in the Assembly had dreamed of it. It's incredible."

Kulgan resumed reading. "'It is to him like a beacon, drawing that terrible entity across space and time. It might have been years more before he would have appeared, but once here, all the powers of your world would be hard pressed, perhaps even insufficient, to dislodge him from Midkemia. The rift had to be closed. The reasons I chose to ensure its closing at the cost of so many lives should be apparent to you.'"

Pug interrupted. "What does he mean, 'should be apparent'?"

Kulgan said, "Macros was nothing, it seems, if not a student of human nature. Could he alone have convinced the King and Emperor to close the rift, with so much to be gained by keeping it open? Perhaps, perhaps not, but in any event there would have been the all-too-human temptation to keep it open 'just a little longer.' I think he knew that and was ensuring there would be no choice." Kulgan returned to reading the scroll. "'As to what will happen now, I cannot say. My seeing of the future ends with the explosion of the rift. Whether it is, finally, my appointed hour, or simply the beginning of some new era of my existence, I do not know. In the event you have witnessed my death I have decided upon the following course. All my research, with some exceptions, is contained within this room. It is to be used to further the Greater and Lesser Arts. It is my wish that you take possession of the books, scrolls, and tomes contained here and use them to that end. A new epoch of magic is beginning in the Kingdom, and it is my wish for others to benefit from my works. In your hands I leave this new age.'

"It is signed 'Macros.'"

Kulgan placed the scroll upon the table. Pug said, "One of the last things he said to me was he wished to be remembered kindly."

They said nothing for a time, then Kulgan called, "Gathis!"

Within seconds the creature appeared at the doorway. "Yes, Master Kulgan?"

"Do you know what is contained within this scroll?"

"Yes, Master Kulgan. My master was most explicit in his instructions. He made sure that we were aware of his requirements."

"We?" said Arutha.

Gathis smiled his toothy grin. "I am but one of my master's servants. The others were instructed to keep from your sight, for it was feared their presence might cause you some discomfort. My master lacked most of the human prejudices and was content to judge each creature he met on its own merits."

"What exactly are you?" asked Pug.

"I am of a race akin to the goblins, as the dwarves are to the Dark Brotherhood. We were an old race and perished

but for a few, long before humans came to the Bitter Sea.
Those that were left were brought here by Macros, and I
am the last."

Kulgan regarded the creature. In spite of his appearance, there was something about him that was likable.
"What will you do now?"

"I will wait here for my master's return, keeping his
home in order."

"You expect him to return?" asked Pug.

"Most likely. In a day, or a year, or a century. It does
not matter. Things will be ready for him should he return."

"What if he has perished?" asked Arutha.

"In that event, I shall grow old and die waiting, but I
think not. I have served the Black One for a very long time.
Between us is . . . an understanding. If he were dead, I
think I would know. He is merely . . . absent. Even if he
is dead, he may return. Time is not to other men as it is to
my master. I am content to wait."

Pug thought about this. "He must truly have been the
master of all magic."

Gathis's smile broadened. "He would laugh to hear
that, master. He was always complaining of there being so
much to learn and so little time to learn it. And that from a
man who had lived years beyond numbering."

Kulgan said, as he rose from his chair, "We will have to
fetch men to carry all these things back to the ship."

Gathis said, "Worry not, master. Retire to your ship
when you are ready. Leave two boats on the beach at the
cove. At first light the next day you will find all has been
placed aboard, packed for shipment."

Kulgan nodded. "Very well; then we should start at
once to catalog all these works, before we move them."

Gathis went over to a shelf and returned with a rolled
parchment. "In anticipation of your needs, master, I have
prepared such a listing of all the works here."

Kulgan unrolled the parchment and began reading the
inventory of works. His eyes widened. "Listen," he said,
excitedly. "There's a copy of Vitalus's *Expectations of Matter
Transformation* here." His eyes grew bigger still. "And
Spandric's *Temporal Research*. That work was thought lost a
hundred years ago!" He looked at the others, wonder upon

his face. "And hundreds of volumes with Macros's name on them. This is a treasure beyond measure."

Gathis said, "I am pleased that you find it so, master."

Kulgan started to ask for those volumes to be brought to him, but Arutha said, "Wait, Kulgan. Once you begin, we'll have to tie you up to get you out of here. Let us return to the ship and wait for all this to be brought. We must be off soon."

Kulgan looked like a child whose sweets had been taken from him. Arutha, Pug, and Meecham all chuckled at the stout magician. Pug said, "There is no good reason to stay now. We shall have years to study these after the coronation. Look around, Kulgan. Do you mean to inhale all this in one breath?"

A look of resignation crossed Kulgan's face. "Very well."

Pug surveyed all in the room. "Think of it. An academy for the study of magic, with Macros's library at the heart."

Kulgan's eyes grew luminous. "I had all but forgotten the Duke's bequest. A place to learn. No longer will an apprentice learn from this master or that, but from many. With this legacy and your own teachings, Pug, we have a wonderful start."

Arutha said, "Let us be on our way if we're to have any sort of start. There's a new King to crown, and the longer you tarry, the more likely you'll lose yourself in here."

Kulgan looked as if his good name were impugned. "Well, I will take a few things to study while on the ship—if you have no objections?"

SIXTEEN

RENAISSANCE

Rillanon was in a festive mood.

Everywhere banners rippled in the breeze, and garlands of summer flowers replaced the black bunting that had marked the period of mourning for the late King and his cousin Borric. Now they would be crowning a new King, and the people rejoiced. The people of Rillanon knew little of Lyam, but he was fair to view, and generous with his smile in public. To the populace it was as if the sun had come out from behind the dark clouds that had been Rodric's reign.

Few among the people were aware of the many royal guards who circulated throughout the city, always alert for signs of Guy du Bas-Tyra's agents and possible assassins. And fewer still noticed the plainly dressed men who were always near when groups gathered to speak of the new King, listening to what was said.

Arutha spurred his horse toward the palace, leaving Pug, Meecham, and Kulgan behind. He cursed the fate that had delayed them nearly a week, becalmed less than three days from Krondor, then the slowness of their journey to Salador. It was midmorning, and already the Priests of Ishap were bearing the King's new crown through the city. In less than three hours they would appear before the throne and Lyam would take the crown.

Arutha reached the palace, and shouts from the guards echoed across the vast courtyard, "Prince Arutha arrives!"

Arutha gave his mount to a page and hurried up the steps to the palace. As he reached the entranceway, Anita came running in his direction, a radiant smile on her face. "Oh," she cried, "it is so good to see you!"

He smiled back at her and said, "It is good to see you, also. I must get ready for the ceremony. Where is Lyam?"

"He has secreted himself in the Royal Tomb. He left word you were to come straight away to him there." Her voice was troubled. "There is something strange taking place here, but no one seems to know what it is. Only Martin Longbow has seen Lyam since supper last night, and when I saw Martin, he had the strangest look upon his face."

Arutha laughed. "Martin is always full of strange looks. Come, let us go to Lyam."

She refused to let him ignore the warning. "No, you go alone; that is what Lyam ordered. Besides, I must dress for the ceremony. But, Arutha, there is something very queer in the wind."

Arutha's manner turned more reflective. Anita was a good judge of such things. "Very well. I'll have to wait for my things to be brought from the ship, anyway. I will see Lyam, then when this mystery is cleared up, join you at the ceremony."

"Good."

"Where is Carline?"

"Fussing over this and that. I'll tell her you've arrived."

She kissed his cheek and hurried off. Arutha hadn't been to the vault of his ancestors since he was a boy, the first time he had come to Rillanon, for Rodric's coronation. He asked a page to lead him there, and the boy guided him through a maze of corridors.

The palace had been through many transformations over the ages, new wings being added on, new constructions over those destroyed by fire, earthquake, or war, but in the center of the vast edifice the ancient first keep remained. The only clue they were entering the ancient halls was the sudden appearance of dark stone walls, worn smooth by time. Two guards stood watch by a single door over which was carved a bas-relief crest of the conDoin Kings, a crowned lion holding a sword in its claws. The page said, "Prince Arutha," and the guards opened the door. Arutha stepped through into a small anteroom, with a long flight of stairs leading down.

He followed the stairs past rows of brightly burning torches that stained the stones of the walls with black soot.

The stairs ended and Arutha was before a large, high-arched doorway. On both sides loomed heroic statues of ancient conDoin Kings. To the right, with features dulled with age, stood the statue of Dannis, first conDoin King of Rillanon, some seven hundred fifty years past. To the left stood the statue of Delong, the only King called "the Great," the King who first brought the banner of Rillanon to the mainland with the conquest of Bas-Tyra, two hundred fifty years after Dannis.

Arutha passed between his ancestors' likenesses and entered the burial vault. He walked between the ancient forebears of his line, entombed in the walls and upon great catafalques. Kings and Queens, Princes and Princesses, scoundrels and rogues, saints and scholars lined his way. At the far end of the huge chamber he found Lyam sitting next to the catafalque that supported his father's stone coffin. A likeness of Borric had been carved in the coffin's surface, and it looked as if the late Duke of Crydee lay sleeping.

Arutha approached slowly, for Lyam seemed deep in thought. Lyam looked up and said, "I feared you might come late."

"As did I. We had wretched weather and slow progress, but we are all here. Now, what is this strange business? Anita told me you've been here all night, and there is some mystery. What is it?"

"I have given great thought to this matter, Arutha. The whole of the Kingdom will know within a few hours' time, but I wanted you to see what I have done and hear what I must say before any others."

"Anita said Martin was here with you this morning. What is this, Lyam?"

Lyam stepped away from his father's catafalque and pointed. Inscribed upon the stones of the burial place were the words:

HERE LIES BORRIC, THIRD DUKE OF CRYDEE,
HUSBAND OF CATHERINE,
FATHER OF
MARTIN,
LYAM,
ARUTHA,
AND CARLINE

Arutha's lips moved, but no words came forth. He shook his head, then said, "What madness is this?"

Lyam came between Arutha and the likeness of their father. "No madness, Arutha. Father acknowledged Martin on his deathbed. He is our brother. He is the eldest."

Arutha's face became contorted with rage. "Why didn't you tell me?" His voice was tormented. "What right had you to hide this from me?"

Lyam raised his own voice. "All who knew were sworn to secrecy. I could not risk anyone knowing until the peace was made. There was too much to lose."

Arutha shoved past his brother, looking in disbelief at the inscription. "It all makes an evil sense. Martin's exclusion from the Choosing. The way Father always kept an eye on his whereabouts. His freedom to come and go as he pleased." Bitterness rang in Arutha's words. "But why now? Why did Father acknowledge Martin after so many years of denial?"

Lyam tried to comfort Arutha. "I've pieced together what I could from Kulgan and Tully. Besides them, no one knew, not even Fannon. Father was a guest of Brucal's when he was in his first year of office, after Grandfather's death. He tumbled a pretty serving girl and conceived Martin. It was five years before Father knew of him. Father had come to court, met Mother, and married. When he learned of Martin, he had already been abandoned by his mother to the monks of Silban's Abbey. Father chose to let Martin remain in their care.

"When I was born, Father began to feel remorse over having a son unknown to him, and when I was six, Martin was ready for Choosing. Father arranged to have him brought to Crydee. But he wouldn't acknowledge him, for fear of shaming Mother."

"Then why now?"

Lyam looked at the likeness of their father. "Who knows what passes through a man's mind in the moments before death? Perhaps more guilt, or some sense of honor. Whatever the reason, he acknowledged Martin, and Brucal bore witness."

Anger still sounded in Arutha's voice. "Now we must deal with this madness, regardless of Father's reasons for creating it." He fixed Lyam with a harsh stare. "What did he say when you brought him down to see this?"

Lyam looked away, as if pained by what he now said. "He stood silently, then I saw him weep. Finally he said, 'I am pleased he told you.' Arutha, he knew." Lyam gripped his brother's arm. "All those years Father thought him ignorant of his birthright, and he knew. And never once did he seek to turn that knowledge to his own gain."

Arutha's anger subsided. "Did he say anything more?"

"Only 'Thank you, Lyam,' and then he left."

Arutha paced away for a moment, then faced Lyam. "Martin is a good man, as good a man as I've ever known. I'll be the first to say so. But this acknowledgment! My gods, do you know what you've done?"

"I'm aware of my actions."

"You've placed all we've won over the last nine years in the balance, Lyam. Shall we fight ambitious eastern lords who might rally in Martin's name? Do we end one war to simply begin an even more bitter one?"

"There will be no contestation."

Arutha stopped his pacing. His eyes narrowed. "What do you mean? Has Martin promised to voice no claim?"

"No. I have decided not to oppose Martin should he choose the crown."

Arutha was speechless for a moment, in shock as he regarded Lyam. For the first time he understood the terrible doubts his brother had been voicing over being King. "You don't want to be King," he said, his tone accusatory.

Lyam laughed bitterly. "No sane man would. You have said as much yourself, brother. I don't know if I am a match for the burdens of kingship. But the matter is out of my hands now. If Martin speaks for himself as King, I will acknowledge his right."

"His right! The royal signet passed to your hand, before most of the Lords of the Kingdom. You are not sick Erland deferring to his brother's son because of ill health and by reason of no clear succession. You are the *named Heir!*"

Lyam lowered his head. "The announcement of succession is invalid, Arutha. Rodric named me Heir as 'eldest conDoin male,' which I am not. Martin is."

Arutha confronted his brother. "A pretty point of law, Lyam, but one that may prove the destruction of this Kingdom! Should Martin voice a claim before the congress

assembled, the Priests of Ishap will break the crown and
the matter passes to the Congress of Lords for resolution.
Even with Guy in hiding, there are dozens of Dukes, scores
of Earls, and a host of Barons who would willingly cut their
neighbors' throats to convene such a congress. Such
bargaining would end with half the estates in the Kingdom
switching hands in trade for votes. It would be a *carnival*!

"If you take the crown, Bas-Tyra cannot act. But if you
back Martin, many will refuse to follow. A deadlocked
congress is exactly what Guy wishes. I'll bet all I own he is
somewhere in the city at this very moment, plotting
against such an event. If the eastern lords bolt, Guy will
emerge, and many will flock to his banner."

Lyam appeared overwhelmed by his brother's words.
"I cannot say what will happen, Arutha. But I know I could
not do other than I have done."

Arutha looked on the verge of striking Lyam. "You
may have inherited the burden of Father's sense of family
honor, but it will fall to the rest of us to deal with the
killing! Heaven's mercy, Lyam, what do you think will
happen if some heretofore nameless huntsman sits the
conDoin throne simply because our father tumbled a pretty
maid nearly forty years ago! We shall have civil war!"

Lyam stood firm. "Should our positions have been
reversed, would you have robbed Martin of his birthright?"

Arutha's anger vanished. He looked at his brother
with open amazement on his face. "Gods! You feel guilt
because Father denied Martin all his life, don't you?" He
stepped away from Lyam, as if trying to gain perspective
on him. "Should our positions have been reversed, I most
assuredly would deny Martin his birthright. After thirty-
seven years, what matter a few more days? After I was
King, firm on my throne, then I would make him a Duke,
give him an army to command, name him First Adviser,
whatever need be to salve my conscience, but not until the
Kingdom was secure. I would not wish Martin to play
Borric the First to Guy's Jon the Pretender, and I would do
whatever must be done to see that would not come to
pass."

Lyam sighed with deep regret. "Then you and I are
two different sorts of men, Arutha. I told you back at camp

I thought you would make a better King than I. Perhaps you are right, but what's done is done."

"Does Brucal know of this?"

"Only we three." He looked directly at Arutha. "Only our father's sons."

Arutha flushed, irritated at the remark. "Don't misunderstand me, Lyam. I hold Martin in no little affection, but there are issues here much larger than any personal consideration." He thought quietly for a moment. "Then it is in Martin's hands. If you had to do this, at least you did right in not making it a public matter. There will be shock enough should Martin come forth at the coronation. At least with advance warning we can prepare."

Arutha moved toward the stairs, then stopped and faced his brother. "What you said cuts both ways, Lyam. Perhaps because you cannot deny Martin you'll make a better King than I. But as much as I love you, I'll not let the Kingdom be destroyed over the succession."

Lyam seemed unable to contest with his brother any longer. Fatigue, a weary resignation toward what fate would bring, sounded in his words. "What will you do?"

"What must be done. I will ensure that those who are loyal to us are forewarned. If there comes a need to fight, then let us have the advantage of surprise." He paused for a moment. "I have nothing but the greatest affection for Martin, Lyam, you must know that. I hunted with him as a boy, and he was in no small part responsible for my safely getting Anita away from Guy's watchdogs, a debt beyond repaying. In another time and place, I would gladly accept him as my brother. But should it come to bloodshed, Lyam, I'll willingly kill him."

Arutha left the vault of his ancestors. Lyam stood alone, feeling the chill of ages press in upon him.

Pug looked out the window, reminiscing. Katala came to his side, and he came out of his reverie. "You look lovely," he said. She was dressed in a brilliant gown of deep red, with golden trim at the bodice and sleeves. "The finest duchess of the court could not match your beauty."

She smiled at his flattery. "I thank my husband." She spun, showing off the gown. "Your Duke Caldric is the true magician, I am thinking. How his staff could manage

to find all these things and have them ready in two short
hours is true magic." She patted at the full skirt. "These
heavy gowns will take some practice getting around in. I
think I prefer the short robes of home." She stroked the
material. "Still, this is a lovely cloth. And in this cold world
of yours, I can see the need." The weather had turned
cooler, now that summer was waning. In less than two
months snow would begin falling.

"Wait until winter, Katala, if you think it's cold now."

William came running into the room, from the bedroom that adjoined their own. "Mama, Papa," he yelled in
boyish exuberance. He was dressed in a tunic and trousers
befitting a little noble, of fine material and workmanship.
He leaped into his father's outstretched arms. "Where are
you going?" he asked with a wide-eyed look.

Pug said, "We go to see Lyam made King, William.
While we are gone, you mind the nurse and don't tease
Fantus."

He said he would and wouldn't, respectively, but his
impish grin put his credibility in doubt. The maid who was
to act as William's nurse entered and took the boy in tow,
leading him back into his own room.

Pug and Katala left the suite Caldric had given them
and walked toward the throne room. As they turned a
corner, they saw Laurie leaving his room, with Kasumi
standing nervously to one side.

Laurie brightened upon seeing them and said, "Ah!
There you are. I was hoping we'd see you two before all the
ceremonies had begun."

Kasumi bowed to Pug, though the magician now wore
a fashionable russet-colored tunic and trousers in place of
his black robe. "Great One," he said.

"That is a thing of the past here, Kasumi. Please call
me Pug."

"You two look so handsome in your new clothes and
uniform," said Katala. Laurie wore bright clothing in the
latest fashion, a yellow tunic with a sleeveless overjacket of
green, and tight-fitting black trousers tucked into high
boots. Kasumi wore the uniform of a Knight-Captain of the
LaMutian garrison, deep green tunic and trousers, and the
grey wolf's-head tabard of LaMut.

The minstrel smiled at her. "In all the excitement of the

last few months, I had forgotten I had a small fortune in gems with me. Since I cannot conspire to return them to the Lord of the Shinzawai, and his son refuses to take them, I suppose they are mine by rights. I will no longer have to worry about finding a widow with an inn."

Pug said, "Kasumi, how goes it with your men?"

"Well enough, though there is still some discomfort between them and the LaMutian soldiers. It should pass in time. We had an encounter with the Brotherhood the week after we left. They can fight, but we routed them. There was much celebrating among all the men in the garrisons, both Tsurani and LaMutian. It was a good beginning."

It had been more than an encounter. Word had reached Rillanon of the battle. The Dark Brothers and their goblin allies had raided into Yabon, overrunning one of the border garrisons, weakened during the war. The Tsurani had turned from their march to Zūn, dashed northward, and relieved the garrison. The Tsurani had fought like madmen to save their former enemies from the larger goblin host, which they had driven back into the mountains north of Yabon.

Laurie winked at Pug. "Having made something of heroes of themselves, our Tsurani friends were given quite a welcome when they arrived here in Rillanon." Being distant from the center of the war, the city's citizens felt little fear or hatred toward their former enemies, giving them a welcome that would have been unimaginable in the Free Cities, in Yabon, or along the Far Coast. "I think Kasumi's men were a little overcome by it all."

"In truth they were," agreed Kasumi. "Such a reception on our homeworld would have been unlikely, but here . . ."

"Still," continued Laurie, "they seemed to take it in stride. The men have developed a rapid appreciation for Kingdom wines and ale, and they've even managed to overcome their distaste for tall women."

Kasumi looked away with an embarrassed smile on his face. Laurie said, "Our dashing Knight-Captain was guested a week ago by one of the richer merchant families—one seeking to develop broader trade with the West. He has since been seen often in the company of a certain merchant's daughter."

Katala laughed and Pug smiled at Kasumi's embarrassment. Pug said, "He was always a quick student."

Kasumi lowered his head, cheeks flushed, but grinning broadly. "Still, it is a hard thing learning that your countrywomen have such freedom. Now I see why you two were always so strong-willed. You must have learned from your mothers."

Laurie's attention was diverted by someone approaching. Pug noticed a look of open admiration upon the singer's face. The magician turned and was greeted by the sight of a beautiful young woman approaching with a guard escort. Pug's eyes widened as he recognized Carline. She was as lovely a woman as her girlhood had promised. She came up to them and with a wave of her hand dismissed the guard. She looked regal in a fine green gown, with a pearl-studded tiara crowning her dark hair.

"Master magician," she said, "have you no greeting for an old friend?"

Pug bowed before the Princess, and Kasumi and Laurie did also. Katala curtseyed as she had been shown by one of the maids. Pug said, "Princess, you flatter me by remembering a simple keep boy."

Carline smiled, with a gleam in her blue eyes. "Oh, Pug . . . you were never a simple anything." She looked past him to Katala. "Is this your wife?" When he nodded and introduced them, the Princess kissed Katala's cheek and said, "My dear, I had heard you were lovely, but the reports my brother gave did you little justice."

Katala said, "Your Highness is gracious."

Kasumi had returned to his nervous posture, but Laurie stood unable to take his eyes from the young woman in green. Katala had to grip his arm firmly to recapture his attention. "Laurie, will you show Kasumi and me about the palace a little, before the ceremonies begin?"

Laurie smiled broadly, bowed to the Princess, and accompanied Kasumi and Katala down the hallway. Pug and the Princess watched their retreating backs.

Carline said, "Your wife is a most perceptive woman."

Pug smiled. "She is indeed remarkable."

Carline looked genuinely glad to see him. "I understand you also have a son."

"William. He is a little devil, and a treasure."

There was a trace of envy in Carline's expression. "I would like to meet him." She paused, then added, "You've been most fortunate."

"Most fortunate, Highness."

She took his arm and they slowly started to walk. "So formal, Pug? Or should I call you Milamber, as I have heard you were known?"

He saw her smile and returned it. "I sometimes don't know, though here Pug seems more proper." He grinned. "You seem to have learned a great deal about me."

She feigned a small pout. "You were always my favorite magician."

They shared a laugh. Then, lowering his voice, Pug said, "I am so very sorry about your father's death, Carline."

She clouded a little. "Lyam told me you were there at the last. I am glad he saw you safely back before he died. Did you know how much he cared for you?"

Pug felt himself flush with emotion. "He gave me a name; there is little more he could have done to show me. Did you know that?"

She brightened. "Yes, Lyam also told me that. We're cousins of sorts," she said with a laugh. As they walked, she spoke softly. "You were my first love, Pug, but even more, you were always my friend. And I am pleased to see my friend once more home."

He stopped and kissed her lightly upon the cheek. "And your friend is most pleased to be home."

Blushing slightly, she led him to a small garden on a terrace. They walked out into bright sunlight and sat upon a stone bench. Carline let out a long sigh. "I only wish Father, and Roland, could be here."

Pug said, "I was also grieved to hear of Roland's death."

She shook her head. "That jester lived as much in his few years as most men do in their entire lives. He hid much behind his raffish ways, but do you know, I think he may have been one of the wisest men I'll ever know. He took every passing minute and squeezed all the life from it he could." Pug studied her face and saw her eyes were bright with memory. "Had he lived, I would have married him. I suspect we would have fought every day, Pug; oh, how he could make me angry. But he could make me laugh as well. He taught me so very much about living. I shall always treasure his memory."

"I am pleased you are at peace with your losses, Carline. So many years a slave, then a magician, in another land have changed me much. It seems you have greatly changed as well."

She tilted her head to look at him. "I don't think you've changed all that much, Pug. There's still some of the boy in you, the one who was so rattled by my attentions."

Pug laughed. "I guess you're right. And in some ways you are also unchanged, or at least you still have the knack of rattling men if friend Laurie's reaction is any measure."

She smiled at him, her face radiant, and Pug knew a faint tugging, an echo of what he had felt when he was a boy. But now there was no discomfort, for he knew he would always love Carline, though not in the way he had imagined as a boy. More than any tumultuous passion, or the deep bond he had with Katala, he knew what he felt was affection and friendship.

She pursued his last comment. "That beautiful blond man who was with you a few minutes ago? Who is he?"

Pug smiled knowingly. "Your most devoted subject, from all appearance. He is Laurie, a troubadour from Tyr-Sog, and a rascal of limitless wit and charm. He has a loving heart and a brave spirit, and is a true friend. I'll tell you sometime of how he saved my life at peril of his own."

Carline again cocked her head to one side. "He sounds a most intriguing fellow." Pug could see that while she was older and more self-possessed, and had known sorrow, much about her remained unchanged.

"I once, in jest, promised him an introduction to you. Now I am sure he would be most delighted to make Your Highness's acquaintance."

"Then we must arrange it." She rose. "I fear I must go make ready for the coronation. Any time now the bells will sound and the priests will arrive. We shall speak again, Pug."

Pug came to his feet as well. "I shall enjoy it, Carline."

He presented his arm. A voice from behind said, "Squire Pug, may I speak with you."

They turned around and found Martin Longbow

standing some distance away, farther back in the garden. He bowed to the Princess. Carline said, "Master Longbow! There you are. I've not seen you since yesterday."

Martin smiled slightly. "I've had a need to be alone. In Crydee when such a mood strikes, I return to the forest. Here"—he indicated the large terraced garden—"this was the best I could manage."

She looked quizzically at him, but shrugged off the remark. "Well, I expect you will manage to attend the coronation. Now, if you'll excuse me, I must be off." She accepted their polite good-byes and left.

Looking at Pug, Martin said, "It is good to see you once again, Pug."

"And you, Martin. Of all my old friends here, you are the last to greet me. Except for those still in Crydee I've yet to see, you've made my homecoming complete." Pug could see Martin was troubled. "Is something wrong?"

Martin looked out over the garden, toward the city and sea beyond. "Lyam told me, Pug. He told me you know as well."

Pug understood at once. "I was there when your father died, Martin," he said, his voice remaining calm.

In silence Martin began to walk, and when he came to the low stone wall around the garden he gripped it hard. "My father," he said, bitterly. "How many years I waited for him to say, 'Martin, I am your father.'" He swallowed hard. "I never cared for inheritance and such things. I was content to remain Huntmaster of Crydee. If only he had told me himself."

Pug thought over his next words. "Martin, many men do things they regret later. Only a few are granted the opportunity to make amends. Had a Tsurani arrow taken him quickly, had a hundred other things come to pass, he might not have had the chance to do what little he did."

"I know, but still that is cold comfort."

"Did Lyam tell you his last words? He said, 'Martin is your brother. I have wronged him, Lyam. He is a good man and well do I love him.'"

Martin's knuckles turned white gripping the stone wall. Quietly he replied, "No, he did not."

"Lord Borric was not a simple man, Martin, and I was only a boy when I knew him, but whatever else may be said of him, there was no meanness of spirit in the man. I don't pretend to understand why he acted as he did, but that he loved you is certain."

"It was all such folly. I knew he was my father, and he never knew I had been told by Mother. What difference in our lives had I gone to him and proclaimed myself?"

"Only the gods might know." He reached out and touched Martin's arm. "What matters now is what you will do. That Lyam told you means he will make public your birthright. If he's already told others, the court will be in an uproar. You are the eldest and have the right of first claim. Do you know what you will do?"

Studying Pug, Martin said, "You speak calmly enough of this. Doesn't my claim to the throne disturb you at all?"

Pug shook his head. "You would have no way of knowing, but I was counted among the most powerful men in Tsuranuanni. My word was in some ways more important than any King's command. I think I know what power can do, and what sort of men seek it. I doubt you have much personal ambition as such, unless you've changed a great deal since I lived in Crydee. If you take the crown, it will be for what you believe are good reasons. It may be the only way to prevent civil war, for should you choose the mantle of King, Lyam will be the first to swear fealty. Whatever the reason, you would do your best to act wisely. And if you take the purple, you will do your best to be a good ruler."

Martin looked impressed. "You have changed much, Squire Pug, more than I would have expected. I thank you for your kind judgment of me, but I think you are the only man in the Kingdom who would believe such."

"Whatever the truth may be, you are your father's son and would not bring dishonor upon his house."

Again Martin's words were tinged with bitterness. "There are those who will judge my birth itself a dishonor." He looked out over the city below, then turned to stare at Pug. "If only the choice were simple, but Lyam's seen that it is not. If I take the crown, many will balk. If I renounce in Lyam's favor, some may use me as an excuse to refuse Lyam their allegiance.

"Gods above, Pug. Were the issue between Arutha and myself, I would not hesitate for an instant to stand aside in his favor. But Lyam? I've not seen him for seven years, and those years have changed him. He seems a man beset with doubts. An able field commander, no question, but a King? I am faced with the fearful prospect I would prove a more able King."

Pug spoke softly. "As I have said, should you claim the throne, you will do so for what you judge good reasons, reasons of duty."

Martin's right hand closed into a fist, held before his face. "Where ends duty and begins personal ambition? Where ends justice and begins revenge? There is a part of me, an angry part of me, which says, 'Wring all you can from this moment, Martin.' Why not King Martin? And then another part of me wonders if Father may have placed this upon me knowing someday I must be King. Oh, Pug, what is my duty?"

"That is something each of us must judge for himself alone. I can offer you no counsel."

Martin leaned forward upon the rail, hands covering his face. "I think I would like to be alone for a time, if you do not mind."

Pug left, knowing a troubled man considered his fate. And the fate of the Kingdom.

Pug found Katala with Laurie and Kasumi, speaking with Duke Brucal and Earl Vandros. As he approached, he could hear the Duke saying, "So we'll finally have a wedding, now that this young slow-wit"—he indicated Vandros—"has asked for my daughter's hand. Maybe I'll have some grandchildren before I die, after all. See what comes of waiting so many years to marry. You're old before your children marry—" He inclined his head when he saw Pug. "Ah, magician, there you are."

Katala smiled when she saw her husband. "Did you and the Princess have a nice reunion?"

"Very nice."

Prodding him in the chest with her forefinger, she said, "And when we're alone, you'll repeat every single word."

The others laughed at Pug's embarrassment, though he could see she was only having some fun with him.

Brucal said, "Ah, magician, your wife is so lovely, I

wish I were sixty again." He winked at Pug. "Then I'd steal
her from you, and damn the scandal." He took Pug by the
arm and said to Katala, "If you'll forgive me, lady, instead
I'll have to steal a moment of your husband's time."

He steered Pug away from the surprised group and
when they were out of earshot said, "I have grave news."

"I know."

"Lyam is a fool, a noble fool." He looked away for a
moment, his eyes filming over with memory. "But he is his
father's son, and his grandfather's grandson as well, and
like both before him has a strong sense of honor." The old
eyes came into sharp focus again. "Still, I wish his sense of
duty were as clear." Lowering his voice even more, he said,
"Keep your wife close about. The guards in the hall wear
the purple and will die defending the King, whoever he
may be. But it may get messy. Many of the eastern lords are
impulsive men, overly used to having their petty demands
instantly gratified. A few might open their mouths and find
themselves chewing steel.

"My men and Vandros's are positioned throughout the
palace, while Kasumi's Tsurani are outside, at Lyam's
request. The eastern lords don't like it, but Lyam's Heir,
and they cannot say no. With those who will stand with us,
we can seize the palace and hold it.

"With du Bas-Tyra hiding, and Richard of Salador
dead, the eastern lords have lost their leadership. But there
are enough of them on the island, with enough of their
'honor guards' in and around the city, to turn this island
into a pretty battleground should they flee the palace
before a King is named. No, we'll hold the palace. No
traitorous easterner will leave to plot treason with Black
Guy. Each one will bend a knee before whichever brother
takes the crown."

Pug was surprised by this. "You'll support Martin,
then?"

Old Brucal's voice became harsh, though he kept it
low. "No one will plunge my Kingdom into civil war,
magician. Not while I have a breath left to spend. Arutha
and I have spoken. Neither of us likes the choices, but we
are clear on our course. Should Martin be King, all will bow
before him. Should Lyam take the crown, Martin will swear
fealty or not leave the palace alive. Should the crown be

broken, we hold this palace and no lord leaves until a congress has named one brother King, even if we're a year in that bloody damned hall. We've already picked up several of Guy's agents in the city. He's here in Rillanon, there's no doubt. If even a handful of nobles can win free of the palace before a congress is convened, we have civil war." He struck his fist into his open hand. "Damn these traditions. As we speak, the priests walk toward the palace, each step bringing them closer to the moment of choice. If only Lyam had acted sooner, given us more time, or not acted at all. Or if we could have caged Guy. If we could have spoken to Martin, but he's vanished. . . ."

"I've spoken to Martin."

Brucal's eyes narrowed. "What is his mood? What are his plans?"

"He's a troubled man, as well you might imagine. To have all this put upon him with scant time to adjust. He has always known who his father was, and was resigned to take the secret with him to the grave, I'll wager, but now he is suddenly thrust into the heart of the matter. I don't know what he will do. I don't think he'll know, until the priests put the crown before him."

Brucal stroked his chin. "That he knew and tried not to use that knowledge for his own gain speaks well of him. But there's still no time." He indicated the group by the main door to the hall. "You'd best be back to your wife. Keep your wits sharp, magician, for we may have need of your arts before this day is through."

They returned to the others, and Brucal led Vandros and Kasumi inside, speaking with them in low tones. Before Katala could speak, Laurie said, "What is afoot? When I took Katala and Kasumi outside to a balcony overlooking the courtyard, I saw Kasumi's men everywhere. For a moment I thought the Empire had won the war. I couldn't get a thing from him."

Pug said, "Brucal knows they can be trusted to follow Kasumi's orders without question."

Katala said, "What is this, husband? Trouble?"

"There is little time to explain. There may be more than one claimant to the crown. Stay near Kasumi, Laurie, and keep your sword loose. If there's trouble, follow Arutha's lead."

Laurie nodded, his face set in a grim expression of understanding. He entered the hall, and Katala said, "William?"

"He is safe. If there is trouble it will be in the great hall, not in the guest quarters. It will be afterward the true grief will begin." Her expression showed she didn't understand fully, but she quietly accepted what he said. "Come, we must take our places inside."

They hurried into the great hall, to a place of honor near the front. As they passed by the throng gathered to see the King crowned, they could hear the buzz of voices as rumor swept the room. They came up to Kulgan, and the stout magician nodded greeting. Meecham waited a few paces behind, his back to a wall. His eyes surveyed the room, marking the positions of all within a sword's length of Kulgan. Pug noticed the old, long-bladed hunter's knife was loose in its scabbard. He might not know what the problem was, but he would be instantly ready to protect his old companion.

Kulgan hissed, "What is going on? Everything was calm until a few minutes ago; now the room is abuzz."

Pug leaned his head closer to Kulgan's and said, "Martin may announce for the crown."

Kulgan's eyes widened. "Gods and fishes! That'll set this court on its ear." He looked around and saw most of the Kingdom's nobles had taken their places within the hall. With a sigh of regret he said, "It's too late to do anything now but wait."

Amos crashed through the garden, swearing furiously. "Why the hell does anyone want all these bloody posies about anyway?"

Martin looked up and barely caught the crystal goblet thrust at him by Amos Trask. "What—" he said, as Amos filled it with wine from a crystal decanter he held.

"Thought you might be in need of a bracer, and a shipmate to share it with."

Martin's eyes narrowed. "What do you mean?"

Amos filled his own goblet and took a long pull. "It's all over the palace now, fellow-me-lad. Lyam's a good enough sort, but he's got rocks for ballast if he thinks he can have a crew of stonecutters put your name on your father's tomb, then hush them up with something as petty as a royal command. Every servant in the palace knew you were the new first mate within an hour after those boys finished work. It's all up in the wind, you can believe me."

Martin drank the wine and said, "Thank you, Amos." He studied the deep red wine in the glass. "Shall I be King?"

Amos laughed, a good-natured, hearty sound. "I have two thoughts on that, Martin. First, it's always better to be captain than deckhand, which is why I'm a captain and not a deckhand. Second, there's some difference between a ship and a kingdom."

Martin laughed. "Pirate, you're no help at all."

Amos looked stung. "Blast me, I got you to laugh, didn't I?" He leaned over, resting an elbow on the garden wall while he poured more wine into his cup. "See here, there's this pretty little three-master in the royal harbor. I've not had much time, but with the King's pardon being declared, there's plenty of good lads fresh from the brig who'd jump to sail with Captain Trenchard. Why don't we cast off from here and go aroving?"

Martin shook his head. "That sounds fine. I've been on a ship three times in my life, and with you I nearly got killed all three times."

Amos looked injured. "The first two times were Arutha's fault, and the third time wasn't my fault. I didn't send those Ceresian pirates to chase us from Salador to Rillanon. Besides, if you sign aboard with me, we'll do the chasing. The Kingdom Sea's a whole new sea for Trenchard to sail. What do you say?"

Martin's voice turned somber. "No, Amos, though I'd almost as soon sail with you as return to the forest. But what I must decide cannot be run from. For good or ill, I am the eldest son, and I have the first claim to the crown." Martin looked hard at Amos. "Do you think Lyam can be King?"

Amos shook his head. "Of course, but that's not the question, is it? What you want to know is, can Lyam be a good King? I don't know, Martin. But I'll tell you one thing. I've seen many a sailor gone pale with fear in battle, yet fight without hesitation. Sometimes you can't know what a man's capable of until the time comes for him to act." Amos paused for a moment, considering his words. "Lyam's a good enough sort, as I said. He's scared silly of becoming King, and I don't blame him. But once upon the throne . . . I think he could be a good enough King."

"I wish I could know you were right."

A chime sounded, then great bells began to ring. "Well," said Amos, "you don't have much time left to decide. The Priests of Ishap are at the outer gates, and when they reach the throne room, there's no cutting grapples and sailing away. Your course will be set."

Martin turned away from the wall. "Thank you for your company, Amos, and the wine. Shall we go change the fate of the Kingdom?"

Amos drank the last of the wine from the crystal decanter. He tossed it aside and over the sound of shattering glass said, "You go decide the fate of the Kingdom, Martin. I'll come along later, perhaps, if I can't arrange for that little ship I spoke of. Maybe we'll sail together again. If you change your mind about being King, or decide you're in need of quick transportation from Rillanon, fetch yourself down to the docks before sundown. I'll be about somewhere, and you'll always be welcome in my crew."

Martin gripped his hand tightly. "Always fare well, Pirate."

Amos left and Martin stood alone, ordering his thoughts as best he could, then, making his decision, he began his journey to the throne room.

By craning his neck, Pug could see those entering the great hall. Duke Caldric escorted Erland's widow, Princess Alicia, down the long isle toward the throne. Anita and Carline followed. From Kulgan came the observation, "By those grim expressions and pale complexions, I wager Arutha has told them what may come."

Pug noticed how Anita held tightly to Carline's hand when they reached their appointed places. "What a thing, to discover you've an elder brother in these circumstances."

Kulgan whispered, "They all seem to be taking it well enough."

Gongs announced the Ishapian priests had entered the

anteroom, and Arutha and Lyam entered. Both wore the red mantles of Princes of the Realm and walked quickly to the front of the hall. Arutha's eyes darted around the room, as if trying to judge the temper of those on all sides. Lyam looked calm, as if somehow resigned to accept whatever fate brought.

Pug saw Arutha whisper a short word to Fannon, and the old Swordmaster in turn spoke to Sergeant Gardan. Both looked about tensely, hands near sword hilts, watching everyone in the room.

Pug could see no sign of Martin. He whispered to Kulgan, "Perhaps Martin has decided to avoid the issue."

Kulgan looked about. "No, there he is."

Pug saw where Kulgan indicated with a bob of his head. By the far wall, near a corner, a giant column rose. Standing deep within its shadow was Martin. His features were hidden, but his stance was unmistakable.

Bells began to chime, and Pug looked to see the first of the Ishapian priests entering the great hall. Behind, others followed, all walking in unison at the same measured pace. From the side doors came the sound of bolts being driven into place, for the hall traditionally was sealed from the start of the ceremony to its end.

When sixteen priests had entered the room, the great doors were closed behind. The last priest paused before the door, a heavy wooden staff in one hand and a large wax seal in the other. Quickly he affixed the seal to the doors. Pug could see that the seal bore the seven-sided device of Ishap inscribed upon it, and felt the presence of magic within it. He knew the doors could not be opened save by the one who affixed the seal, or by another of high arts and then at great risk.

When the doors were sealed, the priest with the staff walked forward between the lines of his brother priests, who waited, incanting soft prayers. One held the new crown, fashioned by the priests, resting upon a cushion of purple velvet. Rodric's crown had been destroyed by the blow that had ended his life, but had it survived, according to custom it would have been interred with him. Should no new King be crowned today, this new crown would be smashed upon the stones of the floor, and no new one made until the Congress of Lords informed the priests they

had elected a new King. Pug marveled how much importance could be attached to such a simple circlet of gold.

The priests moved forward, to stand before the
throne, where other priests of the lesser orders were
already waiting. As was the custom, Lyam had been asked
if he wished his family priest to officiate at the investiture,
and he had agreed. Father Tully stood at the head of the
delegation from the temple of Astalon. Pug knew the old
priest would be quick to take charge of things without
question, regardless of which of Borric's sons took the
crown, and counted it a wise choice.

The chief Ishapian priest struck his staff upon the floor,
sixteen even, measured blows. The sound rang through
the hall, and when he was done, the throne room was
silent.

"We come to crown the King!" exclaimed the head
priest.

"Ishap bless the King!" answered the other priests.

"In the name of Ishap, the one god over all, and in the
name of the four geater and twelve lesser gods, let all who
have claim to the crown come forth."

Pug found himself holding his breath as he saw Lyam
and Arutha come to stand before the priests. A moment
later, Martin stepped from the shadows and walked
forward.

As Martin came into view there was a hissing of
intaken breath, for many in the hall had either not heard
the rumor or not believed it.

When all three were before the priest, he struck the
floor with the heavy staff. "Now is the hour and here is the
place." He then touched Martin upon the shoulder with his
staff, resting it there as he said, "By what right do you
come before us?"

Martin spoke in a clear, strong voice. "By right of
birth." Pug could feel the presence of magic. The priests
were not leaving the claims to the throne subject to honor
and tradition alone. Touched by the staff, no one could bear
false witness.

The same procedure was repeated and the same
answer given by Lyam and Arutha.

Again the staff rested upon Martin's shoulder as the
priest asked, "State your name and your claim."

Martin's voice rang out. "I am Martin, eldest son of Borric, eldest of the royal blood."

A slight buzzing ran through the hall, silenced by the priest's staff striking the floor. The staff was placed upon Lyam's shoulder, and he answered, "I am Lyam, son of Borric, of the royal blood."

A few voices could be heard saying, "The Heir!"

The priest hesitated, then repeated the question to Arutha, who answered, "I am Arutha, son of Borric, of the royal blood."

The priest looked at the three young men, then to Lyam said, "Are you the acknowledged Heir?"

Lyam answered with the staff resting upon his shoulder. "The right of succession was given to me in ignorance of Martin. It is a false bequest, for Rodric thought me the eldest conDoin male."

The priest removed the staff and conferred with his fellow priests. The hall remained silent as the priests gathered together to discuss the unforeseen turn of events. Time passed torturously, until at last the chief priest turned once more to face them. He surrendered his staff and was handed the golden circle that was the crown of the Kingdom. He uttered a brief prayer: "Ishap, give all before us in this matter guidance and wisdom. Let the appointed one do right." In a strong voice he said, "That the succession is flawed is clear." He placed the crown before Martin. "Martin, as eldest son of the royal blood you have the right of first claim. Will you, Martin, take up this burden, and will you be our King?"

Martin looked at the crown. Silence hung heavy in the room as every eye was fixed upon the tall man in green. Breath was held as the throng in the hall waited upon his answer.

Then Martin slowly reached out and took the crown from the cushion upon which it rested. He raised it up, and every gaze in the room followed it, as it caught a ray of light entering through a high window, scattering glittering glory throughout the hall.

Holding it above his head, he said, "I, Martin, do hereby abdicate my claim to the crown of the Kingdom of the Isles, for now and forever, on my own behalf and on behalf of all my issue from now henceforth to the last generation." He moved suddenly and the crown rested upon Lyam's brow. Martin's voice rang out once more, his words a defiant challenge. "All hail Lyam! True and undoubted King!"

There was a pause, as those in the hall took in what they had seen. Then Arutha faced a stunned, silent crowd, and his voice filled the air. "Hail Lyam! True and undoubted King!"

Lyam stood flanked by his brothers, one to each side, and the hall erupted into shouts and cheers. "Hail Lyam! Hail the King!"

The chief priest let the shouting continue for a time, then recovered his staff and struck the floor, bringing silence. He looked at Lyam and said, "Will you, Lyam, take up this burden and be our King?"

Looking at the priest, Lyam answered, "I will be your King."

Again the room sounded with cheers and the chief priest let the din go unchecked. Pug looked and saw relief on the faces of many, Brucal, Caldric, Fannon, Vandros, and Gardan, all who had stood ready to face trouble.

Again the head priest silenced the room with the striking of his staff. "Tully of the order of Astalon," he called, and the old family priest stepped forward.

Other priests removed Lyam's red mantle, replacing it with the purple mantle of kingship. The priests stepped away and Tully came before Lyam. To Martin and Arutha he said, "All in the Kingdom thank you for your forbearance and wisdom." The brothers left Lyam's side and returned to stand with Anita and Carline.

Carline smiled warmly at Martin, took his hand, and whispered, "Thank you, Martin."

Tully faced the crowd and intoned, "Now is the hour and here is the place. We are here to witness the coronations of His Majesty, Lyam, first of that name, as our true King. Is there any here who challenge his right?"

Several eastern lords looked unhappy, but no objection was raised. Tully again faced Lyam, who went on his knees before the priest. Tully placed his hand upon Lyam's head. "Now is the hour and here is the place. It is to you this burden has fallen, Lyam, first of that name, son of Borric, of the conDoin line of Kings. Will you take up this burden and will you be our King?"

Lyam answered, "I will be your King."

Tully removed his hand from Lyam's head and reached down to take his hand, gripping the royal signet upon it. "Now is the hour and here is the place. Do you, Lyam conDoin, son of Borric, of the line of Kings, swear to defend and protect the Kingdom of the Isles, faithfully serving her people, to provide for their welfare, weal, and prosperity?"

"I, Lyam, do so swear and avow."

Tully began a long liturgy, then when the prayers were done, Lyam rose. Tully removed his ritual miter and handed it to the head priest of Ishap, who passed it along to another of Tully's order. Tully knelt before Lyam and kissed his signet. He then rose and escorted Lyam to the throne, while the Ishapian priest incanted, "Ishap bless the King!"

Lyam sat. An ancient sword, once carried by Dannis, the first conDoin King, was brought to him and rested across his knees, a sign he would defend the Kingdom with his life.

Tully turned and nodded to the chief priest of Ishap, who struck the floor with his staff. "Now it is past, the hour of our choosing. I hereby proclaim Lyam the First our right, true, and undisputed King."

The crowd responded with a roar. "Hail Lyam! Long live the King!"

The Priests of Ishap chanted low and the chief priest led them to the door. He struck the wax seal with his staff, and it split with a cracking sound. He struck the door three times more, and the guards outside opened it. Before stepping out, he intoned the last phrase of the ritual of coronation. To those outside the hall, not privileged to watch the ceremony, he announced, "Let the word go forth. Lyam is our King!"

Faster than a bird's flight, the word went out of the hall, through the palace, and into the city. Celebrants in the street toasted the new monarch, and not one in a thousand knew how close disaster had come to visiting the Kingdom this day.

The Ishapian priests left the hall and all eyes returned
to the new ruler of the Kingdom.

Tully motioned to the members of the royal family, and
Arutha, Martin, and Carline came before their brother.
Lyam extended his hand and Martin knelt and kissed his
brother's signet. Arutha followed, then Carline.

Alicia led Anita to the throne, the first of the long line
of nobles who followed, and the lengthy business of
accepting the fealty of the peers of the realm began. Lord
Caldric bent a trembling knee to his King, and there were
tears of relief upon his face as he rose. When Brucal swore
his loyalty, he briefly spoke to the King as he stood, and
Lyam nodded.

Then in turn came the other nobles of the Kingdom
until, hours later, the last of the Border Barons, those
guardians of the Northern Marches, vassal to no Lord but
the King, rose and returned to stand with the others in the
hall.

Handing the sword of Dannis to a waiting page, Lyam
stood and said, "It is our wish that a time of celebration be
at hand. But there are matters of state that must be
attended to at once. Most are of a happy nature, but first
there is one sad duty which must be discharged.

"There is one absent today, one who sought to gain the
throne upon which we are privileged to sit. That Guy du
Bas-Tyra did plot treason cannot be denied. That he did
commit foul murder is unquestioned. But it was the late
King's wish that mercy be shown in this matter. As it was
Rodric's dying request, I shall grant this boon, though it
would be our pleasure to see Guy du Bas-Tyra pay in full
for his deeds.

"Let the word go from this day that Guy du Bas-Tyra is
named outlaw and banished from our Kingdom, his titles
and lands forfeit to the crown. Let his name and arms be
stricken from the role of Lords of the Kingdom. Let no man
offer him shelter, fire, food, or water." To the assembled
lords he added, "Some here have been allied with the
former Duke, so we have little doubt he will hear our
judgment. Tell him to flee, to go to Kesh, Queg, or Roldem.
Tell him to hide in the Northlands if no other will take him,
but should he be found within our borders within a week's
time, his life is forfeit."

No one in the hall spoke for a moment, then Lyam said, "It has been a time of great sorrow and suffering in our realms; now let us embark upon a new era, one of peace and prosperity." He indicated that his two brothers should return to his side, and as they approached, Arutha looked at Martin. Suddenly he grinned and, in an unexpected display of emotion, hugged both Martin and Lyam. For a brief instant all in the hall were silent as the three brothers clung closely to one another, then again cheers filled the room.

While the clamor continued, Lyam spoke to his brothers. At first Martin smiled broadly, then suddenly his expression changed. Both Arutha and Lyam nodded vigorously, but Martin's face drained of color. He started to say something, his manner intense and remonstrative. Lyam cut him off and held up his hand for silence.

"There is a new ordering of things in our Kingdom. Let it be known that from this day forward, our beloved brother Arutha is Prince of Krondor, and until such time as there is a son in our house, heir to the throne." At the last, Arutha seemed less than pleased. Then Lyam said, "And it is our wish that the Duchy of Crydee, home of our father, stay within our family so long as his line remains. To this end I name Martin, our beloved brother, Duke of Crydee, with all lands, titles, and rights pertaining thereunto."

A cheer again rose from the crowd. Martin and Arutha left Lyam's side and the new King said, "Let the Earl of LaMut and Knight-Captain Kasumi of LaMut approach the throne."

Kasumi and Vandros started. Kasumi had been nervous all day, for Vandros had placed a great trust in him. His Tsurani impassivity asserted itself and he fell in beside Vandros as he reached the throne.

Both men knelt before Lyam, who said, "My lord Brucal has asked us to make this happy announcement. His vassal the Earl Vandros will wed his daughter, the Lady Felinah."

From the crowd, Brucal's voice could be heard clearly saying, "And it's about time." Several of the older courtiers from Rodric's court blanched, but Lyam joined in the general laughter.

"It is also the Duke's wish that he be allowed to retire

to his estates, where he may seek the rewards of a long and useful service to his Kingdom. We have given consent. And as he has no son, it is also his wish that his title pass to one able to continue in the service of the Kingdom, one who has shown uncommon ability in commanding the LaMutian garrison of the Armies of the West during the late conflict. For his many brave actions and his faithful service, we hereby approve his marriage, and are pleased to name Vandros Duke of Yabon, with all lands, titles, and rights pertaining thereunto. Rise, Lord Vandros."

Vandros rose, a little shaken, then returned to the side of his father-in-law-to-be. Brucal struck him a friendly blow on the back and gripped his hand. Lyam turned his attention to Kasumi and smiled. "There is one here before us who was recently counted our enemy. He is now counted as our loyal subject. Kasumi of the Shinzawai, for your efforts to bring peace to two warring worlds, and your wisdom and courage in the defense of our lands against the Brotherhood of the Dark Path, we give to you command of the garrison of LaMut, and name you Earl of LaMut, with all lands, titles, and rights pertaining thereunto. Rise, Earl Kasumi."

Kasumi was speechless. He slowly reached out and took the King's hand, as he had seen the other nobles do, and kissed the signet. To the King he said, "My lord King, my life and my honor do I pledge."

Lyam said, "My lord Vandros, do you accept Earl Kasumi as your vassal?"

Vandros grinned. "Happily, Sire."

Kasumi rejoined Vandros, his eyes illuminated by pride. Brucal administered another hearty slap on the back.

Several more offices were given, for there were vacancies from the intrigues of Rodric's court and from deaths in the war. When it seemed all business was over, Lyam said, "Let Squire Pug of Crydee approach the throne."

Pug looked at Katala and Kulgan, surprised at being called. "What . . . ?"

Kulgan pushed him forward. "Go and find out."

Pug came before Lyam and bowed. The King said, "What has been done was a private matter, between our father and this man. Now it is our wish all in our realm know that this man, once called Pug the orphan of Crydee,

has had his name inscribed upon the rolls of our family."
He held out his hand, and Pug knelt before him. Lyam
presented his signet and then took Pug by the shoulders
and bade him rise. "As it was our father's wish, so it is
ours. From this day let all in our Kingdom know this man is
Pug conDoin, member of the King's family."

Many in the hall were surprised by Pug's adoption and
elevation, but those who knew of his exploits cheered
lustily as Lyam said, "Behold our cousin Pug, Prince of the
Realm."

Katala ignored all propriety and ran forward to embrace her husband. Several of the eastern lords frowned,
but Lyam laughed and kissed her upon the cheek.

"Come!" Lyam cried. "It is now time for celebration.
Let the dancers, musicians, and tumblers come forth. Let
tables be brought and food and wine be placed upon them.
Let merriment reign!"

The festivities continued. Celebration had run unchecked throughout the afternoon. A herald next to the
King's table read messages to the King from those unable to
attend, many nobles and the King of Queg, as well as
monarchs of the small kingdoms of the eastern shores.
Important merchants and Guildmasters from the Free
Cities also sent congratulations. There were also messages
from Aglaranna and Tomas, and from the dwarves of the
West at Stone Mountain and the Grey Towers. Old King
Halfdan, ruler of the dwarves of the East in Dorgin, sent
his best wishes, and even Great Kesh had sent greetings,
with a request for more meetings to settle peacefully the
issue of the Vale of Dreams. The message was personally
signed by the Empress.

Hearing the last message, Lyam said to Arutha, "For
Kesh to have sent us a personal message in so short a time,
the Empress must boast the most gifted spies in Midkemia.
You'll have to keep your wits about you in Krondor."

Arutha sighed, not happy at that prospect. Pug,
Laurie, Meecham, Gardan, Kulgan, Fannon, and Kasumi
all sat at the royal table. Lyam had insisted they join the
royal family. The new Earl of LaMut still seemed in shock at
his office, but his happiness was clearly showing, and even
in this noisy hall the sound of his warriors outside singing

Tsurani songs of celebration could be faintly heard. Pug mused over the discomfort that must be causing the royal porters and pages.

Katala joined her husband, reporting their son napping, and Fantus as well, exhausted from play. Katala said to Kulgan, "I hope your pet will be able to withstand such constant aggravation."

Kulgan laughed. "Fantus thrives on the attention."

Pug said, "With all those rewards being passed out, Kulgan, I'm surprised there was no mention of you. You've given faithful service to the King's family as long as anyone save Tully and Fannon."

Kulgan snorted. "Tully, Fannon, and I all met with Lyam yesterday, before we knew he was going to acknowledge Martin and throw the court into turmoil. He began to mumble something or another about offices and rewards and such, but we all begged off. When he began to protest, I told him I didn't care what he did for Tully and Fannon, but if he tried to haul me up before all those people, I'd straightaway turn him into a toad."

Anita, overhearing the exchange, laughed. "So it is true!"

Pug, remembering the conversation in Krondor so many years ago, joined in the merriment. He looked back on all that had occurred to him in the years since he had first chanced to come to Kulgan's cottage in the forests, and reflected for a moment. After much risk and many conflicts he was safe with family and friends, with a great adventure, the building of the academy, yet to come. He wished that a few others—Hochopepa, Shimone, Kamatsu, Hokanu, as well as Almorella and Netoha—could share in his happiness. And he wished Ichindar and the Lords of the High Council could know the true reason for the betrayal on the day of peace. And most of all, he wished Tomas could have joined them.

"So thoughtful, husband?"

Pug snapped out of his mood and smiled. "Beloved, I was but thinking that in all things I am a most fortunate man."

His wife placed her hand upon his and returned his smile. Tully leaned across the table and inclined his head toward the other end, where Laurie sat enraptured by Carline, who was laughing at some witticism he had made. It was obvious she found him as charming as Pug had promised; in fact, she looked captivated. Pug said, "I think I recognize that expression on Carline's face. I think Laurie may be in for some trouble."

Kasumi said, "Knowing friend Laurie, it is a trouble he will welcome."

Tully looked thoughtful. "There is a duchy at Bas-Tyra now in need of a duke, and he does seem a competent enough young man. Hmmm."

Kulgan barked, "Enough! Haven't you had your fill of pomp? Must you go marrying the poor lad off to the King's sister so you can officiate in the palace again? Gods! They just met today!"

Tully and Kulgan seemed about to launch into another of their famous debates when Martin cut them both off. "Let us change the subject. My head is awhirl, and we don't need your bickering."

Tully and Kulgan exchanged startled looks, then both smiled. As one they said, "Yes, my lord."

Martin groaned while those close by joined in the laughter. Martin shook his head. "This seems so strange, after so much fear and worry such a short time back. Why, I nearly chose to go with Amos—" He looked up. "Where is Amos?"

Upon hearing the seaman's name, Arutha also looked up from his conversation with Anita. "Where is that old pirate?"

Martin answered. "He said something about arranging for a ship. I thought he was only making light, but I haven't seen him since the coronation."

Arutha said, "Arranging for a ship! The gods weep!" He stood and said, "With Your Majesty's permission."

Lyam said, "Go and fetch him back. From all you have told me, he warrants some reward."

Martin stood and said, "I'll ride with you."

Arutha smiled. "Gladly."

The two brothers hurried from the hall, making quick time to the courtyard. Porters and pages held horses for guests departing early. Arutha and Martin grabbed the first two in line, unceremoniously leaving two minor nobles without mounts. The two noblemen stood with mouths open, caught halfway between anger and amazement. "Your pardon, my lords," shouted Arutha as he spurred his horse toward the gate.

As they rode through the gates of the palace, across the arched bridge over the river Rillanon, Martin said, "He said he would sail at sundown!"

"That gives us scant time!" shouted Arutha. Down winding streets they flew to the harbor.

The city was thick with celebrants, and several times they had to slow to avoid harming those who crowded the streets. They reached the harborside and pulled up their mounts.

A single guard sat as if sleeping before the entrance to the royal docks. Arutha jumped down from his horse and jostled the man. The guard's helm fell from his head as he toppled over, slumping to the ground. Arutha checked him and said, "He's alive, but he'll have a head on him tomorrow."

Arutha regained his saddle and they hurried along Rillanon's long dockside to the last wharf. Shouts from men in the rigging of a ship greeted them as they turned their horses toward the end of a long pier.

A beautiful vessel was slowly moving away from the docks, and as they pulled up, Martin and Arutha could see Amos Trask standing upon the quarterdeck. He waved high above his head, still close enough so they could see his grinning face. "Ha! It seems all ends well!"

Arutha and Martin dismounted as the distance between ship and pier slowly lengthened. "Amos!" shouted Arutha.

Amos pointed at a distant building. "The boys who stood watch here are all in that warehouse. They're a little bruised, but they're alive."

"Amos! That's the King's ship!" yelled Arutha, waving for the ship to put back.

Amos Trask laughed. "I thought the *Royal Swallow* a grand name. Well, tell your brother I'll return it someday."

Martin began to laugh. Then Arutha joined in. "You

»irate!" shouted the youngest brother. "I'll have him give it
o you."

With a deep cry of despair, Amos said, "Ah, Arutha,
ou take all the fun out of life!"

'Is it time? Shall I do now that which was ordained?"

A bright green flame sprang from the coin and danced.
The witch followed its movement closely, her eyes seeing
something within the flame only she could divine. After a
vhile she said, "The Bloodstones form the Cross of Fire.
That which you are, you are born to do. . . . You stand
not unopposed, for there is one who is your bane. You
stand not alone, for behind you . . .

"I do not understand. Something . . . something
vast, something distant . . . something evil."

With this dire prophecy, a year of peace in the
Kingdom of the Isles is shattered. One night Jimmy the
Hand foils an assassin whose target is Prince Arutha. And
so begins the adventure of *Silverthorn*. . . .

Arutha soon learns that dark powers seek his death,
powers who bring promises of destruction beyond that
threatened by the Tsurani invasion. Arutha must move
against those behind the assassins, and he needs the help
of the Mockers to find them. But with each dark mystery
solved, an even blacker one is encountered, and Arutha
discovers that he faces an inhuman enemy, one able to
send agents into the Prince's own palace, able even to raise
and control the dead.

What awful plan links these attempts upon Arutha,
and what is the relationship between assassins in the night
and the Brotherhood of the Dark Path? What fate has inter-
twined the destinies of a boy thief and the Prince of
Krondor? What terrible secret does Pug discover in Macros's library? What forces Arutha to risk his life, the lives of
those dear to him, and perhaps his Kingdom, on a
desperate gamble? What is the mysterious Silverthorn?

Arutha, Martin, Jimmy, and Pug, with old friends a: well as new, embark on a perilous quest in search of the answers to these questions. Arutha and his companions must travel from Pug's new academy at Stardock into the heart of the Northlands, to the legendary Black Lake Moraelin, where an army of moredhel guard the secret of Silverthorn.

The groundbreaking novels of

GREGORY BENFORD

☐ **In the Ocean of Night** (26578-4 • $3.95/$4.95 in Canada) From far beyond the shores of space, a mystery emerges as vast as the limitless sea of stars. This is one man's encounter with that mystery. *The Magazine of Fantasy and Science Fiction* called this "A major novel."

☐ **Across the Sea of Suns** (28211-5 • $4.50/$5.50 in Canada) Technology has created a new age of enlightenment for humanity. As earth falls prey to attack, from the far reaches of space comes an alien message of astounding importance, revealing great wonders and terrifying danger.

☐ **Great Sky River** (27318-3 • $4.50/$5.50 in Canada) The story of the last surviving humans, their struggle to survive against a mechanical alien civilization, and the unexpected fate that awaits them.

☐ **Tides of Light** (hardcover • 05322-1 • $18.95/$24.95 in Canada) Killeen and his band gain an unexpected ally in their battle for survival, and make an unexpected contribution to the new order of life developing at the galactic center.

☐ **Heart of the Comet** (with David Brin) (25839-7 • $4.95/$5.95 in Canada) chronicles the daring mission to the heart of Halley's Comet by a team of brilliant—and very human—scientists. *The San Diego Union* called it "Better than *Dune*...a breathtaking effort from two of science fiction's brightest stars."

☐ **If the Stars Are Gods** (with Gordun Eklund) (27642-5 • $3.95/$4.95 in Canada) Scientist Bradley Reynolds must decode a mysterious signal hinting at intelligent life amid the gasses of Jupiter, and must ultimately make a challenging journey to find his answers.

Buy these titles wherever Bantam Spectra books are sold, or use this handy page to order:

— — — — — — — — — — — — — — — — — — — —

Bantam Books, Dept. SF33, 414 East Golf Road, Des Plaines, IL 60016

Please send me the items I have checked above. I am enclosing $_____ (please add $2.00 to cover postage and handling). Send check or money order, no cash or C.O.D.s please.

Mr/Ms _____

Address _____

City/State _____ Zip _____

Please allow four to six weeks for delivery.
Prices and availability subject to change without notice.

SF33-11/89